Urthred saw the face of a young girl in the primitive lamp she held in her hand. He could see the terror on the girl's face as she looked from one to the other of them as they spoke.

"We better find out exactly where we are," Urthred said. "Now, child, tell me what your name is."

The girl mumbled something, but Alanda had heard. "She's called Imuni."

"Why has she come here alone, in the dark?"

"She came to make an offering at the shrine," Alanda said. "But when she got here, she found that the three guardians had woken."

"She thinks we are guardians? Then, who is the shrine dedicated to?"

Alanda's eyes didn't leave their faces. "The Lightbringer."

They turned and stared at where Thalassa lay on the highest plinth, her face a ghastly white in the growing sunlight.

"Someone knew the Lightbringer would come, that her spirit would inhabit the statue, give it life?" Jayal asked incredulously.

Alanda nodded. "Marizian: he wrote the books of prophecy. He saw this day."

Urthred was still looking at Thalassa's face. "He may have seen this day, but did he see what has happened to Thalassa, that she has been bitten by the Dead in Life?"

"There may be a cure," Alanda said. . . .

Book Two of the
Lightbringer Trilogy

THE
NATIONS
OF THE
NIGHT

Oliver Johnson

A ROC BOOK

ROC
Published by New American Library, a division of
Penguin Putnam Inc., 375 Hudson Street,
New York, New York 10014, U.S.A.
Penguin Books Ltd, 27 Wrights Lane,
London W8 5TZ, England
Penguin Books Australia Ltd, Ringwood,
Victoria, Australia
Penguin Books Canada Ltd, 10 Alcorn Avenue,
Toronto, Ontario, Canada M4V 3B2
Penguin Books (N.Z.) Ltd, 182–190 Wairau Road,
Auckland 10, New Zealand

Penguin Books Ltd, Registered Offices:
Harmondsworth, Middlesex, England

Published by Roc, an imprint of New American Library,
a division of Penguin Putnam Inc.
Previously published in a Roc Trade Paperback edition.
Originally published in Great Britain by Legend Books.

First Roc Mass Market Printing, September 2000
10 9 8 7 6 5 4 3 2 1

Cover art by Paul Youll

 REGISTERED TRADEMARK—MARCA REGISTRADA

Printed in the United States of America

PUBLISHER'S NOTE
This is a work of fiction. Names, characters, places, and incidents either
are the product of the author's imagination or are used fictitiously,
and any resemblance to actual persons, living or dead, business
establishments, events, or locales is entirely coincidental.

BOOKS ARE AVAILABLE AT QUANTITY DISCOUNTS WHEN USED TO PROMOTE
PRODUCTS OR SERVICES. FOR INFORMATION PLEASE WRITE TO PREMIUM
MARKETING DIVISION, PENGUIN PUTNAM INC., 375 HUDSON STREET, NEW
YORK, NEW YORK 10014.

To Dave Morris—
Friend, advisor, inspiration

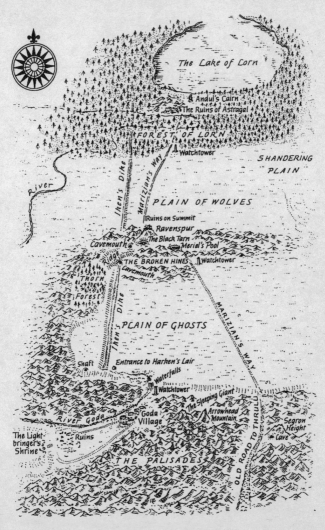

The Nations of the Night

CHAPTER ONE

A Light upon the Plains

It was night. The bloodshed was nearly at an end. The battle of Thrull was lost. Baron Illgill stood upon the mound on which his tent had been pitched that morning, the slopes on all sides carpeted two and three deep with the dead and the dying. Only a few of his men remained with him, hemmed in by the massed ranks of the enemy's crack troops, the Reapers of Sorrow. They stood on the lower slopes of the mound, their ivory horns sounding far and wide over the marshland. Each one wore a skull mask beneath his helmet. Each one stared bonily at the small circle of the baron's men. They were about to charge.

The baron prepared for the end. He threw down his shield. The lead casket in which the Rod of the Shadows was kept was at his feet. He opened it, and a dazzling white light stabbed into the air. He saw the enemy's ranks flinch back at the unexpected light. Reverently, he removed the glowing object and wrapped it in a legion standard. Though it was covered, the Rod glowed through the red-and-orange thread like a magic lantern, illuminating the corpses that lay like mown sheathes of corn on the slopes. He raised the Rod in his left hand, his sword in his right.

The taking of the Rod had started the war, and now, as it was raised before them, it acted as a goad to Faran's army. The Reapers of Sorrow threw themselves forward in a tide of copper armour, their cow horns blaring like the voice of death. They struggled up the slope, their feet slipping on the dead, the ranks behind pushing them forward. Swords clashed and

sparked. But the forward momentum of the Reapers
was inexorable. The baron was pushed backwards by
the mass of bodies until he lost his balance and fell
against the side of his tent.

He struggled back to his feet. The skull-masked
enemy were milling around him. He struck out to left
and right, saw his sword buckle the neck plate of a
Reaper of Sorrow. He parried a blow, then pushed
his assailant back with the brute muscles that years of
training had given him. But now more Reapers came
from the right; he fell back, parrying with the Rod. A
blow from a copper mace exploded in a coruscating
flash of light as it cut through the cloth and struck the
enchanted metal. For a moment all he could see was
the afterimage of the flash. Now the crush of bodies
was such he had no control over his movements. He
was being carried away to the left, down the slope. He
stumbled and fell, rolling over and over. Still he
clutched the Rod. He struggled back to his feet, but
another surge pushed him back again, towards the
depths of the marshes, away from the gates of Thrull.
He struggled against the tide of bodies, but it was
futile. His feet were lifted from the ground. The press
of men was so tight that he felt himself blacking out.

Then his vision cleared as the crush eased. He was
miraculously free. He looked towards the top of the
mound, but it was now a long way away—a faint eminence silhouetted by the lights of the corpse pyres.

His heartbeat began to slow and with it came rational thought. He was safe. And with that knowledge
came guilt. Why had the enemy swords not touched
him, when his men had fallen like butchered steers?
Was it because the light of the Rod had blinded them?
Or because they were afraid, seeing in its light a man
who, having lost everything, was not afraid to die, and
not afraid to kill a few of them while doing so? Or
was there a divinity in the face of a ruler that shone
out, paralyzing the hand that would kill him?

A ruler? No, he had lost everything: the city and
the kingdom he had once commanded. He was only

a mortal: carrion feed like his men. It was fate that had protected him, pushed him away from the slaughter, left him unscathed when the rest had died. A fate that had decreed he would live, live to see what he had set in motion fulfilled. Had he not sent his son Jayal on a quest that very night, a quest that would bring the Worm to its end, even if this battle hadn't?

However it had happened, he had been spared. Now he must make good his escape. He struggled on through the marshes, the dark peat sucking at his ankles. Men moved in the darkness all around him, but he couldn't tell whether they were friend or foe. To the east he saw the great walls of Thrull looming upward into the night beyond the bulk of Marizian's tomb.

Marizian's tomb: that was where it had all begun. Marizian, the author it seemed of all this woe, this bloodshed. The baron knew that what he had discovered there had set him upon a circle of pain; one that he would never escape until his death. He wondered whether his friend, the High Priest Manichee, had escaped; but he remembered the Elder's words—Manichee had known he was going to die. He, at least, would have found final peace in the battle.

The Rod was heavy, weighing down his left hand. Though it was swaddled in the legion colours, he felt its power, its heat beginning to burn his hand and the left side of his face even through the visor of his helmet. Its light now lit up the surrounding mist in a penumbra of blue-white. As he trudged on, other fugitives moved in and out of the area of illumination, shambling figures caught in harsh silhouette. He glimpsed their features: his own men, haggard, blood-soaked, their stares a thousand miles in front of them, not caring what they blundered into, or how many times they fell. The exhaustion of a defeated army.

His black-and-red armour was clearly illuminated in the light of the Rod. If his men recognized him, they didn't rally to their commander. He remembered an old saw passed on to him by his father: a victorious general has many friends, but a defeated one is always alone. He was left to himself in the circle of light, the roar of blood rage slowly dying from his ears and a deep despair taking its place. He walked alone through the night. He thought of the past and, more and more as the night wore on, of his son.

Eighteen years he had forged him in his mould; uttered harsh words; given him beatings; toughened him to the world. For the baron had seen the curse, seen what would happen to the city the Illgills had inherited, the city behind even now being pillaged, its inhabitants being put to the sword.

Others had seen it, too. The seeress, Alanda, had spoken to him months before, even before he had dug into Marizian's tomb, warned him what would come: this night of slaughter, the curse so heavy that his son had had to be returned by magic from the dead. But he had marched his army out in the morning light, sent thousands to their deaths. Why? Fate, the groove of destiny from which no man could escape but plough onwards down it, even into the teeth of destruction.

But, Reh willing, his son would be over the causeway by now, climbing up into the Fire Mountains, an open road before him to the south. And beyond? Surrenland, the Astardian Sea, the deserts of the south. He turned to look behind him, but the night hid the road and mountains. Somewhere out there was hope, a future. Hope in the sword his son would find in far-off Ormorica. Dragonstooth, a weapon that could change destiny, just as this Rod might have done if Manichee had used it earlier, resurrected the dead and sent them back out onto the field as blood-crazed revenants, as deadly as Faran's vampires. He must save the Rod. One day he would find a man who could wield it, another pyromancer as skilled as Manichee had been.

His feet had been carrying him in an arc around the northern curtain wall of the city. After hours of wading ankle deep through the sucking bog, he found himself miraculously on solid ground. The ancient roadway to the north—its broad flagstones sunk into the marsh, some huge stretches of it swallowed up in the black swamp. In his mind's eye he could see it running arrow straight to the north. Now there was a distinct route to follow, he set out with renewed strength. Somewhere up ahead, fifty miles or so, were the first foothills of the Palisades. He would carry the Rod over them, into the Northern Lands, past Shandering Plain and the Nations of the Night, all the way to Iskiard.

The records of those who had gone there in ancient times, the survivors of the Legions of Flame who had gone to war with the Nations, had written that the road to the north still survived, even in the mountains. Now he conjured a mental vision of those as-yet-invisible passes, glowing in the night. Winter was only just beginning; the snowdrifts wouldn't be too high yet. A man might pass over them still.

He set off again, wading on through the pools of swamp water, sometimes sinking to his waist. He felt the ooze sucking him down, his armour a deadweight. But the light of the Rod burned in his soul, a voice spoke to him, telling him that it must never be extinguished in the mud. He fought out of the bog's muddy grip time and time again, his limbs aching. He forced himself to concentrate, to look ahead for danger. He saw bubbling sink holes, deeper even than the swamps he had survived, sink holes which could swallow a man. He skirted around them, hacking his way through man-high bulrushes with his sword. In his other hand, the Rod burned, blistering his skin. He squinted against the relentless light.

Only dimly did he become aware that, beyond the blinding glare, the sky had taken on a grey hue and that it was nearly dawn. He looked back to the south. The rock of Thrull thrust up from the marshes some ten miles behind; a dark column of smoke reached up into the heavens. With that smoke went his home and his dreams: the Hall with his ancestor's paintings he saw in his mind's eye as an inferno, the study where he had left Jayal his instructions, the demon that guarded them, all consumed by the very fire he worshipped.

He tilted his head back and laughed at the irony of it all. Then he shook his head, trying to clear it. This was not the way. With such thoughts he would go giddy with madness; it would be too easy to slide down into that abyss from which there was no return. Instead, he turned his eyes to the west—now he could see the Fire Mountains clearly, just emerging from the darkness, strong black lines against the satin of the night—had Jayal made it to safety?

He knew the boy would: fate and prophecy could not be denied. Even his survival seemed ordained—somehow he had known he would get away—why else had he constructed this elaborate plan for Jayal to follow him to the north? Given him his own mount, Cloud? When he had written the letters that he'd placed in his horse's saddlebags on the eve of the battle he had wondered why he had done so, wondered why he had written them even. Now he knew.

And now there seemed providence of another order: in the stark light of dawn, he saw a riderless horse by one of the marsh pools, its reins thrown over its head, cropping at the grass. He waded towards it, sheathing his sword and stripping off one of his metal gauntlets. The horse whickered at the light of the Rod as the baron approached, and it flinched away slightly, but the baron made soothing noises and placed a hand on its withers, calming it. He placed his foot in one of the stirrups and hauled himself up, placing the Rod across the pommel of the bloodstained saddle. The gelding tossed its mane, feeling the unwonted heat on its back, but seemed biddable enough.

He looked across the expanse of grey water in front of him. The mere was some hundred yards across. For a moment he contemplated jilting his destiny, taking the Rod and throwing it into the waters. Already the hand that had held it all night long, despite the protection of his metal gauntlet, burned agonizingly. Surely this instrument was as much a curse as a blessing? Let the marsh decide the fate of humankind. Was he not only mortal? Was not the weight of this object, as Manichee had warned, too much for him alone to bear? He felt its power and its terror as he never had before. If he threw it into the waters, maybe another generation would take up the quest? He'd heard of long-lost corpses reappearing perfectly preserved in the peat of the swampland. Wouldn't the Rod resurface, too, be found by some wanderer in some indeterminate time from now?

But even as he thought these thoughts, he felt the magic of the Rod, magic that gave power, a drug that promised its wielder access to a hidden world locked from mortal eye, power that would make a man omnipotent. Its power was an addiction, an addiction he'd first experienced when he'd penetrated Marizian's maze and seen the Rod glowing in the tomb. An addiction he could no longer quit.

He must have remained thus for an hour or so as he contended with himself, for when he looked up again the red ball of the sun had risen fully over the Niasseh Range. Silently some fellow survivors had come up and now stood around him by the edge of the mere; they wore the differing colours of the legions which, that previous dawn, had been arrayed against Faran's army. Now their surcoats were ragged and torn. Many of them were wounded. Their faces were grey, exhausted, yet they all stared at him, and in their looks he saw an accusation.

Why did they haunt him like this, accusing him, blaming him for their defeat? Couldn't the fools see that it was ordained, just as the sun's rising was ordained? Even as he watched he saw more men coming, like grey wraiths through the mists. One or two were still mounted on battle-weary nags. They trailed the remnants of gay caparisons in the mud, like melancholy creatures who drag the failed dreams of youth behind them.

Not a word was uttered. They stared at him, as if

expecting him to speak. Enough of ghosts! Illgill set
his boots to the gelding's flanks, the horse tossed its
head, whickering—it was tired. But another kick set
it moving, its head low to the ground. Illgill's head
was bowed as well, low over the pommel. Horse and
rider skirted the mere, finding a way through the high
bulrushes. Through the haze of exhaustion, Illgill
heard the sound of sucking footsteps behind and the
rustle of reeds, and he knew some of his men had
chosen to follow. He didn't look back to count them:
the Rod filled his mind, its light telling him that if
needs be he alone would cross the mountains and go
into the Northern Lands.

He rode all the morning, his eyes never leaving the
ground in front of the horse's mane, knowing only that
he followed the line of the old road, for the horse's
hooves occasionally rang on the ancient, mossy stone.
The horse, at least, had a sense of self-preservation,
though he no longer did: he would not have cared if
it had carried him into the deepest part of the swamps.

Not once did he look behind until, towards the end
of the day, he saw, at the furthest rim of the marshes,
the ground begin to rise in a series of low folds. The
foothills; the mountains themselves were still nearly
invisible, grey outlines reaching up to the sky in the
misty air to the north.

It was then he stopped and wheeled the horse and
looked at those that followed. They came through the
shreds of fog like ghosts. Stumbling forward without
apparent volition, their heads bowed. But when they
saw the horse and rider had halted, each in turn came
to a stop and raised their weary heads to him. Now,
though his brain had been numb all this time, the
discipline of the parade ground returned, and he
began to methodically count them, as if he were at
roll call in the temple square. He lost his count once
as his head nodded and nearly dropped to his chest
in exhaustion, but he caught himself and forced himself to begin the count again.

One hundred and thirteen in all: all that remained

of the Hearth Knights and the Legion of Flame: men at arms, lancers, ballistae teams, archers. One hundred and thirteen of the twenty thousand. Yet suddenly the humming was gone from his head, and his vision cleared. One hundred and thirteen, he thought—enough perhaps for what he had in mind.

He turned his horse once more to the Palisades, knowing that he had an army of sorts. And if the men had come this far, would they not follow him to the land beyond the Palisades, a land where no one had gone in one thousand years?

CHAPTER TWO

✤

The Legion of Flame

The battle had taken place at that season where a few last mild autumn days contend with the icy finality of winter. But in the saw-toothed mountains of the Palisades it was always winter, whatever the time of year. Ice crevasses, glaciers, dragon-tailed ridges covered waist deep in snow. The baron's men had little climbing gear: a few short lengths of rope salvaged from backpacks, some improvised spikes hammered from daggers. It was suicide to make the attempt, but there was no choice: they had marched into the mountains knowing there was no looking back. And they died as they went, uncomplaining.

The avalanches took most of them. The snow had begun to fall in earnest as they passed through the foothills. Ahead the overhanging snow cornices on the ridges and peaks looked dangerous already, looming precariously over the ancient roadway as it began to switchback upwards.

The first avalanche came the second day in. There was a clear blue sky and the looming peaks were visible. They saw the snow break off from a cornice high above them. The column halted, looking at the fall as it snaked and curled down the slope coming towards them, a thing of strange beauty. Then the roaring came, the roaring that obliterated everything else.

The baron had heard climbers talk of the claws of an avalanche, the powder reaching forward in front of the snow following behind. After that day, how he came to hate the sight of the powder drifts outracing the thunderous mass of packed snow as it fell down from the snow-gabled peaks like surf upon a storm-swept beach! Then, swifter than the fastest horse, swifter than a jaguar, a white lava, opposite of fire, came roaring over them. A lava which set like cement around its victims.

That first day it took an hour to reach the first body. Many of the rescuers suffered frostbitten hands—they had no digging tools. Despite their efforts, the man was dead already, suffocated by the packed snow.

Only four others were lost that first time, but, on the next day, another avalanche and thirty were taken at a stroke. After that second avalanche the baron had told the survivors to stop digging: there was no conquering this white sea that reared all around them, a white sea in which all hope was lost, in which their antlike progress was an insignificance in the numbing chaos of snow and rock. Let the snow swallow them, he prayed, if Reh so willed.

They climbed upwards, the road giving way to a barely visible path. They dug snow holes at night to shelter from the bitter wind. As they neared the highest of the glassy blue peaks the blizzards swept in, lifting men bodily from their handholds and toppling them to their deaths, and in the blizzards came the banshees, screaming spirits placed here by the gods to prevent ingress to their hidden world north of the mountains. Their noise was like cloth ripping, but a hundred times louder, accompanied by a ghostly ululation that modulated high and low as they swooped and soared in the bitter winds. Some men went mad with the noise and threw themselves over the precipices.

Yet, it was not the avalanches or the banshees, but thirst that was their greatest enemy. A paradox: in that sea of frozen water, no amount of eaten snow could assuage it. The climb was arduous, and the men sweated more liquid than they could ever take in from handfuls of snow. Many of them became dehydrated, then delirious. They would disappear from their shelters in the night, no doubt led away by feverish mi-

rages of water. No one saw them go, or where they
fell. But every morning fewer and fewer men emerged
from the snow.

In the baron's mind, in that place untouched by the
howling of the wind and the thirst, he carried a map
of the mountains, imperfectly remembered from a
map he had studied in his youth: the legendary names
of its summits, once the subject of schoolboy fascina-
tion, now of fear. Ever upwards into the sky, peak
succeeded peak, but always he looked for one, the
one that stood on the very roof of the world. At last
it loomed out of the driving snow, white and brittle,
spear-shaped in a sudden break in the clouds: Segron
Height, the highest of the Palisades. Below it was the
only pass over the mountains.

It was then he dared count his men again, for the
first time since the marshes. He did it slowly, pedanti-
cally, passing a snowbitten finger over their ranks. But
this time the count would not have taken long, however deliberate he had been: only fifteen had survived.
Ninety-eight had perished.

Men had come to the pass below Segron before.
The last had been those in another Legion of Flame
a millennium before, in a crusade against the dark
creatures who lived in the north. But no comfort was
to be found in their expedition: no one in that legion
had ever returned to Thrull, and they had gone in the
summer. Now winter sat perched forever on the
ridges, in the shadows of the dying sun.

Only once after that legion had men attempted the
crossing. Furtal, the court singer, had once sung of it
on a cold winter's night in the palace on the Silver
Way. He had been the only man to return from the
mountains in that later, equally disastrous expedition.
He had never spoken of what had happened apart
from in the lines of that cryptic lay:

> In the halls of glass on Segron side
> An army stands in armoured pride.
> Ahead the summits of despair,

The Plain of Ghosts and ancient fear.
South—the hearth that never warms
The home of widows, the child who mourns.

As night fell on the day of the counting they approached the col beneath the peak. Another storm threatened. A shadow in the banked snow covering a rock buttress indicated there was a hidden cave in the lee of the mountain. They crossed a frozen tarn and broke down the curtain of ice covering the cave mouth.

Inside, in the blue depths of the cave, they found their predecessors. They seemed to be grey statues, row upon row, huddled at the back of the chamber. Corpses, frozen and perfectly preserved in the ice. Their ancestors dressed for war, a war a thousand years old: antique armour, embossed, sporting wave-shaped shoulder pieces and pointed helmets. The ancient battle standards stood frozen like sheet metal by their sides.

The cave was miraculously warm after the windchill outside. But the temperature was nevertheless well below freezing. Staying would lead to death in a short time; then they would join these dead ancestors.

Illgill didn't know where the voice came from, but it was a voice that belonged to another time: when his engineers had at his command dug in Marizian's tomb, over the protests of the priests of Reh; a time when he had commanded the gates of Thrull to be thrust open and all his armour had poured onto the marshes to face Faran Gaton; a time when his word was the law.

It was a voice that the men heard and obeyed, despite their exhaustion, for all but two followed him as he ordered them to leave the cave and the dead behind. As for the two who remained, they already had the look of dead men. The baron gave them one last glance and plunged into the blizzard that raged outside.

In the driving snow they found some cairns leading
down the other side of the col. Some of the earlier
legion had evidently survived and gone on to the
north.

There were so few of his men left that now, at least,
there was enough rope for them to tie themselves into
a line. They descended an ice slope in the roaring gale,
so wind-smoothed it seemed a linen sheet pulled tight
over the shoulder of the mountain. A world of peaks
and cloud lay right beneath their feet; each step
seemed a step into the chasms that called up to them.
Above them, the ice cornices hung precariously from
the lee of Segron's north face. They looked up at
them, waiting for them to fall. All that could be heard
was the howl of the wind, the crunch of their worn
boots and the swish of threadbare clothes as they
struggled through the knee-high snow. But the avalanche never came, the wind abated, as if the ancient
gods had at last conceded: they would live.

Illgill had been in a dream for days, hunger and
thirst barely assuaged by the pitiful rations that his
men had brought, and from the meat of the horses,
his included, slaughtered in the foothills. But thirteen
had survived. And he still had the Rod, the Rod that
cast a bright light as the clouds descended once more
and they struggled through the whiteout.

They inched down, tied together by the scrap of
rope: sometimes it was as if he pulled the others, other
times they pulled him. They were parts of one organ-
ism, consciousness obliterated, completely taken over
by the battle for survival. Men fell off the razorback
ridges: without a word the others hauled them back
up again and the men would without a murmur of
thanks begin their crawl downwards again.

Then finally they were off Segron's highest slopes.
They descended a glacier fractured by six-foot-wide
crevasses, crossing the blue chasms on fragile snow
bridges. Twice a bridge fell with a dull explosion of
powder. Both times the fallers were hauled back, the
men's eyes empty of fear, beyond exhaustion.

The end of the glacier. A hanging valley below. They descended through the black-and-white wasteland of a scree slope, the view hidden by the thick mists that rose around them, curled about as if inspecting them, then soared up to the heights.

As he descended and the danger seemed to lessen, Illgill began to snap out of his torpor; a certain madness which he acknowledged as a strength entered his spirit so that his heart beat quickly again, despite the ice in his soul. All thirteen had survived the descent from Segron Height. A legion of sorts. Providence or the Rod, or maybe both together, had preserved them: they had scaled the Palisades.

But then the blizzard descended again. They huddled in their snow shelters for two more days. Two more died of frostbite; another walked off into the blizzard while the others slept, never to be seen again. The ten who remained also suffered, but their minds were toughened, for the crossing of the Palisades would have tempered any man in steel.

These were the names of the nine who accompanied the baron: Endil Sparrowhawk, Gorven Whiteblaze, two Hearth Knights; Andul, Gorven's brother, a squire; Nyrax the Brave; Zar Surkut; Otin, the sergeant at arms of the Surkut family; Minivere, a Surren noble who'd joined Illgill's ranks just before the battle, and Argon and Krastil, the only two enlisted men to have survived. History has forgotten the other names: the frostbite cases; the madmen; the fallers; those that remained in the cave when safety was so near.

The two who died on the last descent were buried in cairns and their swords planted on top. Illgill and the nine others set off again, roped precariously together by the length of frayed hemp, none of them now with the strength to haul up another if they fell. Their food was down to the last few frozen pieces of horse biltong left in their pouches. Their thirst was desperate, despite the snow they incessantly crammed into their mouths.

At the close of that day the clouds lifted, and they

saw the sunset for the first time in a week. The blue
and white of the mountains was transformed to purple
and rose in its glow. And, through a gap between two
snow-covered peaks, they saw something else. A dull
triangle of green framed by the mountains, the Plain
of Ghosts. To the east they saw a blaze of ruby-red
light in the falling sunbeams: Shandering Plain, the
battleground of the gods, a wilderness of isinglass reflecting the sun's fiery plummet into the western
ranges. Beyond, like faint traceries on the powder blue
sky, they could see columns of white smoke reaching
up to the heavens: the smoke that still rose from the
final holocaust, when the gods had fought one another
ten thousand years before.

Illgill turned to face his men. He felt alive for the
first time in the whole deadly passage and his blistered
face shone with a messianic zeal. He told them what
they saw was the Land of Lorn, the home of the gods
written of in the epics and the *Book of Light*. The
nine looked at one another, daring not even to hope
that they would reach it, so far away did it seem from
their lonely perch. Then the wind got up again and
began to howl, and another storm hurtled in, as if
enraged that even so few had escaped the passage.
They swiftly dug shelters in the drifts. That night they
heard the voice of the ancient god of the mountains,
howling and raging over his domain, looking for the
survivors who had dared his vengeance, as they clung
tightly to each other, seeking a last heartbeat of
warmth.

They dug themselves out the next day when the
storm had abated: it was the last storm, as if the fair
land below them now stretched its influence up to the
forbidding peaks and made the winds less fierce. The
sky was cerulean blue, and for the first time in two
weeks they saw birds of prey riding the thermals
above them. None of the survivors once looked back
at the black buttresses of snow and ice behind them
that had claimed so many of their number. They followed a gorge between two eroding cliffs. It was steep,

but they inched their way down the side of a torrent
of black water, carefully negotiating the sides of the
waterfalls, which plunged downwards to the mythical
land below.

And thus the ten came to Lorn: they carried with
them few mementos of their previous glory: Zar had
with him the coat of arms of the Surkut family swaddled around his frozen body like a cloak; the Sparrowhawk war banner, shredded into threads by the
winds, still fluttered from the stump of Endil's lance,
the same he had broken against the copper armour of
one of the Reapers of Sorrow at the battle a month
before. Others clutched small mementos of their previous life, of their families and friends. But they still
bore their weapons proudly, as proudly as they had
that morning, a morning that seemed so long ago, in
Thrull.

And Illgill still held in his hand the Rod wrapped
in the charred remnants of the standard; the standard
of the Legion of Flame. The light had burned him,
the wound in turn suppurating and then cauterised by
the heat. His face was blistered and raw from being
so close to the shining light, day and night.

After the gorge the mountains relinquished their icy
grip with surprising ease. The torrents became gaily
rushing streams sparkling in the sunlight—the first
stand of conifers appeared, huddling around a gem-
blue tarn filled with water so clear that every rock and
pebble beneath its surface was as distinctive as if it
were seen in a mirror. Strangely, the air felt warmer
here than it had on the other side of the mountains,
though a month had passed and winter should have
set in long before. Here and there were patches of
rocky ground clear of snow. They were close to life
once more. They joked, forgetting the dead, as they
slaked their thirst in the waters, enjoying the beams
of the sun.

And when they had drunk their fill, Illgill held up
his maimed hand, silencing them. Below them they
could see a patchwork quilt of ancient fields and

roughstone walls cut through by the white rushing brooks. But the walls were merely lines in the hillside and seemed abandoned for generations. Evidently the people who had lived here had been a civilised race. But he knew from the books and the prophecies that here also dwelt mankind's greatest enemy: the Nations of the Night. Surely the signs of this extinct civilisation were proof enough that evil forces had driven mankind from this northern world? Across the dun plain below he could see another range of snaggle-toothed peaks. The Broken Hines: the home of the Nations of the Night.

Yet, as he looked upon those sinister mountains, wondering, there came a warm breeze blowing from the north. Was it a sign that better things lay beyond that accursed country?

Illgill set the Rod upon a rock and turned to the others. His face was peeling and burned. His lips so chapped that he struggled to speak, but the words came eventually. "Below our future lies—behind is death and dust. How many brothers did we leave in the mountains?" He raised his eyes to the peaks, now all innocence in the blue sky. "We won't forget them, though their graves will be never found. They are part of the mountains, their spirits will live with Reh's sacred birds—they will not taste corruption, but will wait, perfectly preserved, as they died, for the Second Dawn. Now there are only ten, but we are a fellowship, bound by the Rod and the standard of the Legion of Flame. This is our legion now—all of you are my hearth brethren. History will sing of us in years to come."

"Where will we go?" asked Gorven.

Illgill pointed to the north. "When I dug in Marizian's tomb, I saw his magical scrying device, the Orb. It showed me all the world, a world long lost to our fathers. Beyond the next range of mountains is a forest, the Forest of Lorn. It holds the second prize, the second artefact that Marizian brought from the north: Talos, the Man of Bronze." He picked up the Rod

again and lifted it reverentially to the sun, holding it
out in two hands, like an offering. "By the Rod's
power, we will find him."

"What is this Man of Bronze?" Gorven asked.

A smile broke the baron's ravaged lips: "He was
the champion of Reh: clad in bronze armour from top
to toe, he stood thirty cubits tall: his gaze was red fire
that melted his enemies before him."

"And he will obey you?"

The baron shook his head. "Not I: the *Book of
Light* says he will only obey one called the Lightbringer."

"But don't you carry the light, the light of the Rod?
Are you not the Lightbringer?"

Once more, Illgill smiled faintly, his frozen beard
crackling as the ice splintered off it. "Not I, but one
who comes after."

Zar spoke. "But from the *Book of Light* we know
Marizian brought three objects of power from the
north—what of the third?"

Now a shadow passed over the baron's face. "The
third? It is the sword Dragonstooth. It is in the Southern Lands."

All as one turned their heads back to the towering
peaks behind them.

"But, lord, how will we get it now?" Zar asked.

The baron's look was abstracted, as if he hadn't
heard him at first, then he shook himself from his
reverie. "Well asked, but more difficult to answer.
When I saw the battle was lost, I knew desperate measures were called for. Do you wonder what happened
to Jayal?" The others were silent, clearly thinking that
the baron's son had died in the battle. But there came
a sudden gleam into the baron's eyes. "I have sent
him to the Southern Lands to fetch the sword."

"One man?" Zar answered. "There were over a
hundred of us before the Palisades—now there are
only ten. What chance does he have of crossing the
mountains on his own?"

There would have been a time when the baron

would have choked off the questioning words in mid-
sentence, but the mountains had made all of them
equal, so he heard him out. "The Flame and Providence will deliver him," he said patiently. "Have
faith—Jayal is my son."

"Amen to that," Zar said, and the other men answered feebly with a cheer which was instantly
whipped away by a blast of warm wind from the north.

Without another word, Illgill stumbled down the
slope towards the north, the Rod held out in front of
him, bathing his face in a blue-white luminance. His
men trailed behind, fear of the terrible burns on his
face and arms, fear of the mad light in his eyes making
them keep each other's company rather than his.

They reached the plains and saw the line of an old
road, slightly raised over the flat prairie in front of
them, disappearing arrow straight towards the sinister
mountains ahead. Though darkness was falling fast,
they did not quibble when the baron set off down it,
the Rod blazing in the coming darkness.

And thus the Legion of Flame came to the Land
of Lorn.

CHAPTER THREE

Imuni

Seven years later.

The other civilisations that had, like Lorn, once existed north of the Palisades had been destroyed in the battle of the gods ten thousand years before. Their cities were razed to the ground and the kingdoms left desolate, inhabited only by dark creatures, spawned by the fires of destruction: the Nations of the Night.

Yet on the northern slopes of the mountains was another place that no southerner had ever laid eyes upon, though the baron and his legion had passed nearby seven years before. A tiny pocket of humanity had survived through the hardships and calamities of the intervening centuries since the battle of the gods. Their numbers had been whittled down over the generations, and the survivors now dwelt in a small village clinging to the mountain slopes. Its name was Goda.

It was a tight huddle of grey stone buildings, its roofs nearly invisible in the stony valley in which it nestled. Beyond the jigsaw of roofs, the steep, grey, barren slopes of the mountains suddenly flattened out and became as smooth as a tabletop. Here there was a small area covered with a patchwork of emerald fields, like green ponds nestling in the valley—green for the yak pastures, and burnt sienna where the corn had just been harvested, some black where the stubble had been burned.

The landscape that surrounded the village was dramatic. To the north the river gorge ended in a sharp V between two mountain slopes. There, the river Goda

seemed to pour over the edge of the world in a graceful arc falling three thousand feet in a white torrent
to the empty grassland the village folk called the Plain
of Ghosts.

The plain was shaped like an amphitheatre: the Palisades to the south, and, to the north, a series of jagged
peaks, the Broken Hines, the home of the Nations. A
line of lesser mountains to the west connected the two
ranges. In the east, the Broken Hines expired in a
broken series of gullies and dark ravines. Beyond,
where the sun rose, a desert spread away, flat and
empty, to where the edge of the world must be; for
there it seemed to vanish, just where it met the sky.
This was Shandering Plain, the final battle place of the
gods. Beyond the edge of the world, white columns of
smoke reached up, like chalk against the blue of the
heavens. Beyond the horizon there was just a vast
emptiness of air. The villagers spoke of travelling to
that fearful place and tumbling over its edge, falling
endlessly down.

The plain was bisected by the line of a great gorge
running north to south. It showed on the grey flatlands
like a giant crack, and was called Iken's Dike. The
river Goda, after its three-thousand-foot fall, was
sucked into its depths, flowing on, the villagers believed, to the centre of the earth, to Iss' Underworld.
To the south the Dike disappeared into the Palisades
in a huge cave known as Harken's Lair, named after
the charioteer of the gods. Some said that this chasm
was where the dragon steeds of the gods had been
stabled in the Elder Times.

To the north, the Dike travelled to the flank of the
Broken Hines and disappeared into another cave beneath the highest peak—the mountain called Ravenspur.

The Broken Hines: a place of evil. Even the appearance of its peaks was sinister, made more so by a dark
mist that for the last two years had cloaked its scarred
slopes, peaks and knife-edge ridges of red sandstone.
Ancient ruins clung to the summits, and occasionally
dark shapes could be seen swooping through the

cloud. It was from there every winter the wolf packs came, and, when the winter gales howled loudest, the Great Wolf itself, Fenris. And there, every two generations, the Black Cloud gathered, as it did now, presaging the dark time to come.

The cloud hung there in defiance of a wind, curiously warm, and balmy though winter was coming, which swept over the grasslands and the villagers' eyrie. Some said this beneficent wind came from the kingdom of Lorn, a place none of the villagers had ever seen. It blew all year long, its warmth only slightly dissipated in the winter months.

The villagers had no written records, and their knowledge was passed on orally from one generation to the next. Their headman performed the offices of priest. His name was Garadas. He lived in the largest house in the village. The villagers bowed their heads respectfully when he passed, for in him was carried the wisdom of their people, handed down from one headman to the next from the days of Marizian, the wizard who long ago had founded this place and built the shrine in the mountains.

Garadas knew what the appearance of the Black Cloud meant. It had last come a hundred years before in his grandfather's time. The warm wind would soon die out. In the months afterwards spring would be late, and there would be a long winter. It was then that the Nations of the Night came from the dark realm where they had brooded all the intervening years and marched northwards to the magical kingdom of Lorn, hoping to snuff out forever the fire that sent the warm wind to Goda.

Goda was surrounded by the highest mountains of the Palisades, each named by the villagers' forefathers' forefathers: Segron Height, the Sleeping Giant, the Anvil, the Arrowhead, and many more. The spirits of their ancestors were up there in the snow-cloaked peaks, where the eagles took their bones from the burying plot above the village. The ghosts lived in the clouds that stood straight out like sails from their summits in the clear blue sky, at one with its great stillness.

To the right of the village an ancient road came down from the mountains between Segron Height and the Sleeping Giant. This was the road that the great wizard Marizian had taken on his journey from Iskiard to the Southern Lands, a journey from which he had never returned. No one from the village went near it now, not since a day nearly seven years before.

Marizian had promised their ancestors that one day the southerners would come to this land. At dusk that day a villager tending his flock on the cliff tops had seen a group of antlike figures moving northwards on the road far below. No one had been seen on it for forty generations. They could only be men from the Southern Lands, the ancestors of the people of Goda. Perhaps, at last, they brought news of Marizian.

There was a ropeway that went down the mountainside by the falls of Goda, connecting it with the plain below. The ice had still not set in, and Garadas led some of the men down it. The climb had taken many hours, and complete darkness fell during that time. In the blackness the men had seen in the distance a blazing light on the road, moving slowly north towards the Broken Hines.

The first snow of the season had begun falling, slowing them even further, so it was only as dawn broke they reached the plains. On the road they found only barely distinguishable footprints in the snow on the roadway. Instead of waiting for them, the strangers had gone on towards the Nations of the Night, a place the villagers dared not follow.

They had debated long and hard. Were these the ones Marizian had told them to wait for? Why had they passed down the road, without turning towards Goda? But then a glint of something bright and metallic high up in the mountains behind them caught their attention. A flash as of metal glinting in the sun. Despite the dangers of the season Garadas had led them up the ancient road, higher than any of them had dared climb before.

For two days they climbed, high into the places where their ancestors dwelt beneath Segron Height. There they reached an ice slope and saw before them what they had seen from the plains below. The glinting sword planted atop a cairn of stones: a grave. They went higher up and found dead bodies frozen in a cave beneath Segron Height—clad in armour, carrying golden and silver standards, their frozen faces and limbs like marble. They had the physiques of giants. Footprints led out of the cave as if the dead had come to life.

The villagers had fled in terror, a blizzard claiming two of them as they descended. Whoever had come down from the mountains could not have been mortal. Only Marizian had crossed them before, and he had been half a god.

So they had returned, and on many an evening since they had gathered in Garadas's house and told the story of the frozen warriors under Segron Height.

Now the seventh winter after their discovery was coming. It was time for the people of Goda to make their annual sacrifice at the shrine. Two thousand feet above the village, at the head of the river valley, stood the ruins of the city which had been founded by Marizian. Here were the remains of what centuries of wind and weather had left, no piles of stone more than a few feet high, but the street plan was still visible in the ascending wilderness of rock. The ruins reached up until they ended in a mighty stone buttress under the summit of the mountain. There some lava spill at the birth of the mountains had frozen into a huge wave of rock. Their ancestors had carved a mighty, fifty-foot-wide staircase into it, leading up to a flat plateau on which grew a stand of oak trees. There were four trees, symbolic of the four deities who lived within the cave behind it.

Every year, a solitary nightingale made its nest in the grove. No one knew where it came from, or whether it was the same one that came through the generations: it seemed immortal. In the early summer its song rang out bravely over the ancient ruins, but now as winter drew in, its strain grew ever more plaintive until that day when it at last flew to the south.

Each autumn a sacrifice was made to the four spirits who lived in the cave. Lots were drawn to decide who among the young girls of the village would make it. This year the headman's daughter, whose name was Imuni, had drawn the short straw. She waited anxiously for the day to come as summer waned, for the offerings that the people of Goda sent with the young virgin had to be made before the day the nightingale flew. Not too early, when the bird still sang, for then the offerings, of wine, snow and a bouquet of corn and flowers, would lose their potency: the snow would melt, the wine sour and the plants wither. Then the village would be plagued by heavy rainfall that would spoil the crops, mildew the fruit on the trees and reduce the harvest. But even worse if the offering was made after the bird had left: that would bring a year's bad luck to the village: miscarriages to the womenfolk, famine and disease and blizzards that lasted well into the spring.

A yak was sacrificed every year and its entrails inspected by the headman to predict when the nightingale would fly away. So far, Garadas had always predicted right. Earlier generations had not been so lucky.

It was three hours before dawn on the day Garadas had prescribed for the offering. Imuni waited in the cold in the front room of the stone house. Once it had been a matter of pride to hear that she lived in the largest house of the village, and her father and mother kept servants. But, at this hour, the house resembled more a tomb than a dwelling place; she had never been up so early. There was no bustle as there was customarily in the place, no fire flamed in the grate, no smoke hung from the low rafters, and the packed-earth floor was cold from the mountain air.

Most evenings, the senior men of the village would come here and chew betel and talk of village affairs, drinking fermented yak's milk until late into the evening. But none had come last night, nor would they again until she returned—if she returned. If only she could have her past life back! She was only nine. Her duties up to that day had been simple: to fill the leather drinking beakers, to receive from the old men in return kind words and the presents of the scrimshaw they had whittled during the hours they spent tending their flocks. Only a short while ago, that had been her place, and all she had ever wished for.

But now the grate was cold, and the chill of the earth floor seeped through her thin sandals. All was silent. Only the presence of her mother, Idora, sitting on a stool by the door gave her any comfort. Outside the night was at its darkest: no animal stirred in the barns, and the cocks were silent in their roosts. The world seemed poised, suspended, waiting for that moment when her mother would give her the sign to leave the house and go up the mountainside to the lonely cave there.

The cold and the fear combined together; she couldn't stop her body trembling. She wondered, even if it had been allowed, whether she could have managed to speak.

A week ago the prospect of the journey had been so distant; now it seemed to have come rushing upon her like the swiftest horse. It was often dark when she got up, but this darkness was the blackest she had ever known—the silence absolute. There was only stillness, the silence of a mountain's heart.

She started as her mother rose abruptly. Some inner clock had told her the hour had come. Imuni's heart leapt into her throat as she stood, too. It was time for her to leave. Her mother pulled a thick wool coat from a peg by the front door and draped it over her shoulders. It was slightly too large for her, and its hem trailed on the floor, rasping when she moved. Next her mother handed her a tallow lamp flickering in a terra-cotta jar, and then the muslin bag that contained this year's wreath, the refermented yak's milk and lastly, taken by one of the menfolk from one of the slopes above the village the day before, the bag of snow. She could feel the frozen brittleness of its crystals through the sides of the bag.

All was ready. They went to the door of the hut, and her mother took her out into the street. No one waited there, for it was considered bad luck for the coming winter if anyone saw the virgin on her way up the mountain. The girl had to go alone and unobserved. Her mother whispered to her, her breath condensing on the chill autumn air.

"Remember: keep the lamp alight, Imuni," Idora said, a slight tremor to her voice giving away her anxiety. Imuni nodded silently. "Let the God of the Sun speed you so you are at the shrine before him." Then she caressed the child's face and nodded down the street.

Imuni now thought of a thousand questions she wanted to ask Idora: anything but walk up the dark road ahead, but before she knew it, her feet were moving over the broken paving of the street, the coat trailing behind on the frosty pavement. She looked back when she got to the last house, where the white stupa glowed in the feeble light of her lamp. Her mother was invisible in the darkness. There was no one there for her now.

She took a deep breath, then she was on her way, the night swallowing her up, the strange objects and clothes her mother had given her occupying her mind sufficiently for her to be out of the village before she realised again that she was alone and afraid. Through the orchard of crab apples. Her feet crunched on the windfalls, then the second stupa loomed out of the darkness ahead.

She glanced back at the sleeping village, tempted to hide the sacred objects and wait until daylight. She would tell the villagers she had gone up to the old city and made the offerings. But no, the next girl who went there would see nothing had been left the year before. If the winter was fierce and many died, or if more deformed or stillborn children came, they would blame it on her. She climbed past the stupa, and into the wilderness of rock, stumbling over the stones littering the rough track, her eyes straining for the next waymark.

After a little while, she looked back to the east, towards Shandering Plain, but no glimmer of light shone there yet: it was still at least two hours before dawn. Her mother, in her anxiety for Imuni to be at the shrine at the prescribed time, had sent her off early. She had thought herself grown-up for her age, serving the old men in her father's house while the other children slept, but now all the fears of childhood returned. Every gust of wind through the fir trees, every shadow cast by the stunted bushes by the wayside, held terror. She thought of the wolf packs that roamed the mountains. Three years before the child who had been sent to the mountain had disappeared; only later had they found a fragment of cloth that could have been her cloak. . . . That had been a bad winter, the stored grain becoming mildewed, the remainder running out well before the thaw. Many had died of hunger, their bodies carried up to the burying ground where the eagles came to take the bodies to heaven. . . .

She walked in the cold, the wick floating on its sea of fat, trembling and guttering with each gust. Alone in that fragile pool of light, as if she were a separate universe to the dark one that surrounded her, it was almost a surprise when she came to the first grey wall of the ruined city and saw the terraces mounting above her. She took the path upwards to the great cliff through the place where her ancestors had lived and died, feeling their ghosts close in the air around her. Pale avenues where feet had once trod, the empty spaces where the thresholds of houses had been. She could almost hear their voices, their laughter, their cries. . . . Then at last she reached the end of the ruins.

She looked up at the set of great steps carved into

the mountainside. They rose to the holy grove from
which she could just hear the plaintive notes of the
nightingale's song over the noise of the wind. The bird
was still there. She was not too late. Now she paused.
This was as far as she had ever come before: none of
the children would go up to the grove and the cave
beyond it, even for a dare. But other girls who in
previous years had made the sacrifice had told her
what waited beyond.

The cave lay beyond the holy grove. It had been
excavated from the cliff long ago in the time of Marizian. A dozen yards on in the dark shadows of the
cavern was the chamber of the statues. There were
four of them arranged on two ledges, three feet high,
one above the other.

Three human figures stood on the first and lower
ledge. The faces of the figures were said to be extremely weathered by the meltwater that dripped from
the ceiling, but enough could still be seen of what the
villagers had carved under Marizian's instructions
those centuries before.

First there was the figure that all the girls before
her had feared most: he who stood at the centre of
the Three: the demon. The face was a whirl of scars
and devastation, without a nose, without ears or lips,
deep holes gouged where its eyes should have been.
It held its hands before it, like the claws of a bird of
prey. Even though it was only a stone effigy, the figure
had filled each of her predecessors with terror.

Two more figures stood on each side of the demon.
To the right was the figure of an old lady, slightly
stooped and wrapped in a thick cloak, her features
aquiline and sharp. To the girls, there was something
familiar in the face. Even though the features were
water ravaged, the woman's kindly expression bore an
uncanny resemblance to any one of the many old la-
dies of the village. The contrast between the old lady
and the cruel demon that stood by her side was stark.
Surely this woman represented all that was good; the
scarred one, evil?

Next the warrior. The girls who had gone up to the shrine before her had told her, hiding their smiles behind their hands, of the handsome features of the youth, the power of his limbs, the nobility of his high forehead, the brave sword he carried in his hand. . . . There was no one in the village, they said, amongst the young men, who could compete with the man's beauty, though he was made only of weathered stone. They all prayed quietly, the girls who came to this place, that their future husbands would look like the warrior.

Finally, the highest plinth. This figure lay flat on the ledge. The virgin of the mountains, the Lightbringer, the object of the sacrifice and the guardian spirit of the village. She who was woken by the first beams of the light every day as they travelled over the eastern plains into this cave. If the warrior was said to be the epitome of male beauty, the Lightbringer surely was that of womanly grace, Imuni's predecessors told her. The Lightbringer's eyes were closed, her fine features framed by a luxuriant growth of hair. Her body was moulded by a flimsy dress, slightly dishevelled. The body was fair, tall and slim, taller than even the tallest man of her village. So the scene in the cave had been described to her a hundred times, and the description, through constant repetition, had become familiar, almost like an old friend. But now she was alone on the mountainside in the darkness, any comfort in its familiarity had long gone, replaced by stark fear. She would sooner have travelled into Harken's Lair on the Broken Hines as the cave mouth above her.

Once more she looked behind her to Shandering Plain. Was there now the barest hint of grey light in that direction? Hurriedly she felt in the satchel and drew out the offerings, hugging them in the crook of one arm, holding the lamp with the other. The steps beckoned her, but first she must rehearse the prayer. What were the words her mother had so painstakingly taught her? She sought for them, but she was too terrified: the words would not come:

"Spirit of Light . . ." then what?

All she could remember was a line begging the guardians of the shrine not to harm her. But of course they would if she came without the words! The demon would wake; she would die in its talons.

She began to cry, her shoulders heaving spasmodically. She must find courage, the light was growing every second. She blinked back her tears and saw a definite greyness in the sky to the east, marching over the ruins. The outlines of the mountains were suddenly visible in the dimness. But still the words would not come. She closed her eyes again, her mind a blank. How many precious minutes did she stand thus, rigid with terror?

When she looked again she saw that there were now orange-and-red flecks in the eastern sky, barring a grey cloud rolling in from the north. The snow had begun to melt through the bag into the crook of her arm. Soon it would be too late: the sun would strike the statues in the cavern, and there would be no offerings there to greet the Lightbringer.

She would have to enter the cave without the prayer. She swallowed hard and began climbing the steps hurriedly, arriving at the top breathless. In front stood the grove of four trees. Suddenly the nightingale's song seemed transformed, not the uninhibited gush of trilling notes that she had heard before, but a harsh and mocking caw. How? When its voice had seemed so beautiful before? But the sun was rising: time was running out. She ran through the shadows of the trees.

Then she was at the entrance to the great cave. One last look behind: the golden disc of the sun was rising over Shandering Plain, shadows raced across the flat expanse and over the flanks of the mountain, throwing their buttresses and crags into sudden relief. She turned and hurried into the darkness, one step, then two, then she tripped on the hem of the trailing cloak: the lamp slipped from her grasp and shattered. The spilt oil caught light, licking at her feet as she struggled back to a standing position. In the flames she could see the ledges at the back of the cave.

Empty. The lower course was empty: the statues of the demon, the warrior and the old lady were not there. Had her friends lied to her? Had they never existed? But something still lay on the top ledge—it must be the statue of the Lightbringer. But even as she craned her neck to get a better view of it she saw the chest of the statue rising and falling slowly in the growing light of the morning. . . . It was alive. She took a step back. Then a shadow fell over her: she turned. A silhouette stood outlined by the golden disc of the sun and the flames of the lamp: a figure that blocked out the light. She could not see its face, but she saw the clawlike arms hanging by its side as it came towards her.

The demon had woken. . . .

CHAPTER FOUR

✦

The Fiery Cross

Thrull.

As the first beams of the morning sun swept over the marshes, Urthred stood on the top of the pyramid of skulls. He held Dragonstooth above his head. The sun rose slowly over the rocky eminence of the city, throwing it into stark silhouette, burning through the mists, driving the undead into the lee of the pyramid, their bodies igniting, burning, reducing to tarry pools. . . . Once more Reh had defeated his brother Iss in the dark labyrinth of the night. The God had struggled back once more to light the world of humans.

The sun gave Urthred power, the seeds of fire that lay dormant in his veins were inspirited by its rays. He knew he and his companions must leave this place; the undead were dying, boiling away as the sun curved around the pyramid. Soon they would all be destroyed. But there was still danger in Thrull: Faran was there, and so was the demon that Faran's sorcerer had summoned. Nekron: Eater of Souls. Darkest of Iss' avatars. The ancient prophecies of Marizian were fulfilled: five thousand years before he had seen this day, seen this destruction, how no one would live in the city or on the surrounding marshes after nightfall.

Urthred shut his eyes, seeing the seeds of fire dancing there behind the closed lids, like fireflies, moving in erratic patterns. His power had returned, the power that he'd had in Forgeholm as a boy, when he had conjured the Flame Dragon from the air, when he had known that he was a pyromancer. He had lost that power ironically in the flames that had burned him, scarred him for life. Now they were back. Love had made it so: love gained and love lost. His whole body tingled with those sparks of power, now coalescing, coming together in a fiery mass so his inner mind was full of their flames. No longer would he need the magic of this mask. Now they would fly, fly with the rays of the sun spreading over the land, fly he knew not where, except that it would be the land promised him by Manichee, the place where the secrets of his past and his future would be revealed. . . .

His soul was as the eagle's before a flight: already imagining the blue sky and the sound of the wind beneath its wings though it still rested in its nest. So his whole spirit yearned upwards, towards the new-born sun. He opened his eyes one last time and looked down at his feet. A thousand skulls lay there, but he had eyes only for one. The one that stood proud of all the rest, lightning-blackened, its jaw agape as if laughing at the folly of the world: all that remained of his master, Manichee. He bade him a silent farewell, the thunder of the raging flames in his ears almost drowning his thought. The world began to spin upon its axis, and no longer could he control the power seething within him.

He didn't hear his words of power, words once learned from Manichee's book of pyromancy, but which came here unbidden from the molten lake of his heart. For his mind was beyond conscious thought: he only saw Dragonstooth, the sword a crucifix held up against the red ball of the rising sun. And his energies soared into the crosspiece of the hilt and through it, his mind following. Vatic, unconquerable, an eagle that would soar to the sun.

Then the world began to spin faster and faster; the rock of Thrull and the sun blurred. And as it spun he glanced desperately at Thalassa, lying at his feet; thinking, despite his faith, that this might be the last time he saw her, that Reh might choose to take them

into the heart of the sun, into the Hall of the White
Rose, where all was extinguished in ineluctable light.
He snatched the vision of her, her tangled, golden
brown hair, her features whiter than snow . . . then,
with a stab, he saw the twin puncture wounds oozing
blood, her ripped dress, exposing one rosy-tipped
breast, and a savage gash across the top of it. And
though half of him now flew upwards, half remained,
wanting to reach out to the soft down of her cheek
and stroke it. . . .

The thought nearly brought him back, to the earth,
to its desires, its damnations and soft lusts. He nearly
fell backwards from where his spirit now was, a distant
speck in the blue dome of the sky, a fall that would
have killed his soul like a winged bird falling to the
ground. But once more he shut his eyes and became
what he was predestined to be: a creature of the fire
and not of earth. Desire burned away as paper in a
flame, like white, weightless ash ascending to heaven.
He went with it and the others too: Thalassa, Jayal
and Alanda—he sensed them with him in the inferno.
And his flesh was left behind and he saw Thalassa as
she would be, had been in the Lightbringer's Shrine:
a purer vision, the glowing Naiad who had stood trans-
figured before him then, who had cracked open Marizian's tomb and showed the mysteries of the ages to
be no more than crumbled dust and bones.

Then, conscious thought was obliterated by the
speed of their flight, so now he only saw and sensed.

He felt the power of the sword ignite like a fiery
brand snatched from the heart of the sun. The sword,
several pounds of inert metal a moment before, now
seemed feathery light. He flew with it. The world spun
around him, the light of the sun became smaller and
smaller, until it became a tiny vortex of light towards
which the sword was pulled. Then even that light was
snuffed out, and he followed the fiery cross of the
sword through a maelstrom of howling blackness,
where the air shrieked and groaned, where the wind
went from cold to hot, to cold again. Like a pilot fish

at the side of a shark, so did Urthred follow the sword through that ocean of darkness until, ahead, the tiny vortex of light appeared again, and then his vision was filled with the gold-and-orange flames of the dying sun. He plunged into the flames, flames just like those of the Hearth Fire at Forgeholm, but flames that this time didn't burn.

Then there came a feeling of dislocation, as darkness returned and his flight rapidly ceased and he felt his spirit fall like a plunging hawk to the earth. But not the unconsciousness that overcomes some who fall to their deaths, nor a bone-crushing impact . . .

He found he stood on solid rock. His first sensations were of cold and, once more, an utter darkness. But then he realised that his eyes had been momentarily blinded by the dazzling light of the sun. As the blackness ebbed away, light did return, from the blade of Dragonstooth, which he still held over his head, glimmering whitely in the darkness, but with much-diminished power, as if its energy had been drained by the journey. He stood on a low stone dais in a dark cavern, its black rock sparkling with condensation in the coruscating light of the sword. A fresh breeze came from in front of him, carrying with it the melancholy call of a bird, a nightingale perhaps.

He turned. Jayal was to his right, shaking his head as if recovering from a blow. Alanda, her pale face even whiter than usual, stood on his left. All their breath condensed in the heavy, moisture-laden air. They had survived, but where was Thalassa? He swivelled and saw a stone ledge behind him. She lay upon it, laid out like a figure on a tomb. She was exactly as she had been before: unconscious, her breathing laboured, the wound at her neck trickling blood. But alive. Once more a prayer came to his lips. They had come through the heart of the sun. He had touched Reh and lived. Surely they had been blessed by the God's preserving spirit.

He stared at Thalassa for a moment more, drinking in the sight of her. Then he turned away, his head still spinning. How much time had passed? The journey through the heart of the sun had seemed to happen in a second and take an age at the same time. What time and place was this?

He lowered Dragonstooth and, reversing its blade, held it out to Jayal. "Here," he said. The young knight took it almost unconsciously, his head still swivelling to left and right, unable to comprehend their new surroundings. He stared at Urthred, then at the sword, seeking for words, but none came.

Though Urthred's head still spun, his sense of urgency had come back to him. He climbed the step up to the higher plinth and knelt next to Thalassa. He reached out his gloves, but then drew them back, seeing their steel-tipped claws, cursing. They would rip that fair skin. . . . How he longed to touch her, but he knew he could only look. Alanda had recovered her wits. She, too, climbed up to the ledge, and knelt on the opposite side to Urthred, shrugging off her travelling cloak and covering Thalassa with it. She touched the girl's brow.

Her eyes met the slits of Urthred's mask. "She is in a fever," she said.

He stared at her face, his mind racing. "The Ways of Light I know," he said slowly, "but those of Iss are a mystery. But I have read that the soul of one who is bitten is not forfeited to the Worm if he who has taken their blood is destroyed."

Jayal had now drawn close and stared at Thalassa in the half-light of the sword. "I saw the vampire who bit her burned away by the sun."

"I, too—burned by the fire. It is the only way to kill one of the Dead in Life forever," Urthred said.

"Then she's not infected?"

He turned to look at the young Illgill. "I can only pray, my friend."

"She needs warmth," Alanda said.

"There is none here," Urthred said, looking around the dank cave.

"What land is this?" Jayal asked.

Urthred got slowly to his feet, his eyes straying to where the breeze came freshly from the cave mouth. "It isn't even dawn here. We have travelled from the middle latitudes of the world where the nights are shorter. So, we are in the north or south."

"You don't know which?"

"Again," Urthred replied, "I can only guess—but I think we're in the north, beyond the Palisades, as Manichee promised."

"Then it should be winter here. Feel the air, it is warmer here than it was in Thrull."

And Urthred did feel it. The chill was only the cold of the predawn. It was swiftly being dissipated by a warm breeze funnelling down the corridor in front of them. What had been written of the lands north of the Palisades? Was it not a land of perpetual winter? What then was this breeze? For a moment his heart sank. Could he have been wrong? Were they no nearer the objects of their quest: the Man of Bronze and the Rod of the Shadows?

He stared at Dragonstooth. He knew enough of the hidden correspondence of magic: like attracted like. Thousands of years before all three artefacts had been brought together by Marizian; now they were scattered, would not a secret magnetism draw them back together again, as a lodestone attracts metal to it? Was that not what the prophecies had promised in the *Book of Light*? And when the three were reunited it was written that the shadows would be driven away from the sun, and the followers of Iss defeated. . . . then he remembered: he had been in Marizian's tomb. He had seen the *Book of Light*: it was dust. Nothing was certain, not even the prophecies with which later generations had perhaps glossed the scriptures. He stepped down from the plinth.

"You and I better go and see what world this is," he said to Jayal. The young knight nodded, trying to see what lay beyond the dim arc of light cast by the sword. The song of the bird came from in front of them again.

"What bird sings when it is dark?" Jayal asked.

"There is only one—the nightingale," Alanda answered from behind.

"We must take the light," he said to the old lady, nodding at the glimmering blade.

"I will watch Thalassa," she replied.

The two men walked cautiously down the corridor, the warm breeze getting stronger. Grey light came from a rectangular entrance in front of them. The branches of trees could be seen beyond it. The birdsong came to them again; though they strained their eyes, they couldn't locate its source in the dark boughs. Jayal sheathed the sword lest the light betray them to any enemy nearby, then they went forward, emerging on a ledge of rock. The land was dark, though they could see a wide flight of steps carved into the rock slope in front of them. In the distance they could hear a muffled roar. It took Urthred a moment to recognise it: a river roaring down a gorge. There was no light save the greyness in the sky in front of them. It was as if every star in the sky had been extinguished.

Gradually, the light increased in front of them. It was strange, watching a second dawn in such a short span of time. Was this not how it would be at the end of time when Iss' powers would conquer the sun as it rose? But the *Book of Light* told how even in that absolute darkness a Second Dawn would come in which the reborn sun would rise above the world, forever conquering the dominion of the night. That was the world's hope. Urthred felt a shiver of premonition, as if he had been blessed with a vision of the end of time.

Then he saw a flickering glowworm of light in the darkness below them. Both men instinctively drew back into the shadows of the trees. Below them, the glowworm hesitated, then began to zigzag upwards towards their position. They watched as whoever was coming hesitated again. To the east, the dawn's light grew in intensity so they could now see the shapes of mountains all around them and an expanse of grey ruins cloaking the mountainside below them. In the silence, they heard a reedy voice reciting fragments of a song, carried up to them by the blustering wind. Then the light came on, up the flight of steps. The melody of the nightingale suddenly ceased, as if sensing the newcomer.

Now the sky was flecked with red and orange. The first barred stripes of cloud emerged from the gloom like ripples on a grey sea.

"What shall we do?" Jayal asked.

"Go and warn Alanda. I'll see who this is," Urthred said. Jayal nodded and, keeping low, stepped back into the cave. Urthred crouched down in the shadow of one of the trees and waited. Presently, a slim figure dressed in an oversize wool coat hauled itself onto the platform and stood hesitantly, silhouetted by the light in the east. He saw the face of a young girl in the light of the primitive lamp she held in her hand. Even from this distance, he could see the terror on the girl's face, the trembling of her lips, the nervous glances she cast into the shadows.

Now he saw that it was only a girl, he would have left his hiding place, but he knew what effect the mask would have on anyone he approached too suddenly. He remained in the shadows of the trees. The sky behind was brightening all the time and he could see that she carried some objects in the crook of her arm. Then the edge of the sun appeared on the distant horizon and the shadows covering the mountains fled away. In a moment she would see him. But then the girl stirred herself and, with one last desperate look to the east, plunged into the cavern.

Urthred followed as quietly as he could. Sunlight poured down the shaft at his back. The child ran in front of him, then stumbled on the hem of her coat, so she tripped. The lamp fell from her hand and burst into flame on the floor. In an instant she was up again and ran on. Urthred skirted around the pool of burning oil. In front the girl had stopped. She stood in

front of the first empty plinth; Thalassa still lay on the
second. Alanda and Jayal were nowhere to be seen.
The girl began backing away, then turned and saw
Urthred—and screamed, a scream that sent a spike of
anguish through him as, reflected in the horror in her
face, he saw what she must see.

He held up his hands placatingly, but the child staggered backwards again. It was then Jayal and Alanda
emerged from where they had been hiding in the shadows at the end of the cavern. The girl ran right into
them. Jayal reached out a hand to steady her, but the
unexpected touch drew yet another fit of hysterical
cries from her. The items in her hands fell onto the
floor as she struggled. Then Alanda stepped in front
of her, and a strange transformation overcame her,
a sudden stillness, of recognition. Urthred saw what
it was: Alanda could have been a blood relation of
the girl's—her grandmother perhaps. They both had
the same aquiline features, high foreheads, blue eyes.
The girl stared at her for a moment, forgetting the
terror of a second before. Then, remembering where
she was, she glanced behind, and seeing Urthred
again, backed away, right into the furthest corner of
the cave. But Alanda was already speaking, trying to
soothe her.

"Tell her I mean her no harm," Urthred said.

"I have," Alanda replied, "but she keeps repeating
over and over the same word: the demon."

"She speaks our language?"

"A version of it, as it would have been spoken centuries ago."

"That is strange."

Alanda shook her head. "Not if we are in the
Northern Lands as you suppose: all our knowledge
was brought from the north by Marizian, including the
language we speak now. This girl's people must have
been here for centuries, ever since he passed through
the land."

"You look so like her."

"As well I might," Alanda said, never taking her

eyes off the child. "As I have told you, priest, my people came from this land as well, from a place called Astragal. My guess is it's not far."

"We better find out exactly where we are," he said.

"Then don't come near—she's terrified of you."

"Tell her this thing is only a mask."

"She's only a child. How could she not be afraid?" But nevertheless, the girl had calmed a bit hearing the human words coming from behind the mask. She now looked from one to the other of them as they spoke.

"Now, child, do you understand me?"

The girl nodded her head.

"Then tell me what your name is."

The girl mumbled something, but Alanda had heard. "She's called Imuni.

"Where do you live?" she asked coaxingly. The girl again said something inaudible to the two men, nodding fractionally towards the cave mouth as she did so.

Alanda turned to Urthred and Jayal. "A place called Goda: it's a little way down the mountain. She is the headman's daughter."

"Why has she come here alone, in the dark?"

Again, Alanda asked a question, and the girl mumbled a reply. "She came to make an offering at the shrine," Alanda said, pointing at the bag lying on the floor. "But when she got here she found that the three guardians had woken."

"She thinks we are guardians?"

Alanda nodded gravely. "She says three statues stood on that lower plinth: statues that resembled us." Now the two men turned to stare at the ledge. Light streamed down the cave onto it, and they could see three lighter, unweathered circles, on the lower plinth. They were unblemished by rainwater as if something had once stood on the stone. Each of them remembered how after they had arrived they had stood in those exact same spots on the ledge.

Urthred's hand went up to touch his cloak as if he expected it to be made of stone rather than wool. But the material was soft. The stone had become flesh.

"Then, if we are the guardians, who is the shrine dedicated to?"

Alanda's eyes didn't leave their faces. "The Light-bringer."

They turned and stared at where Thalassa lay on the highest plinth, her face a ghastly white in the sun.

"Someone knew the Lightbringer would come, that her spirit would inhabit the statue, give it life?" Jayal asked incredulously.

Alanda nodded. "Marizian: he wrote the books of prophecy. He saw this day."

Urthred was still looking at Thalassa's face. "He may have seen this day, but did he see what has happened to Thalassa, that she has been bitten by the Dead in Life?"

"There may be a cure," Alanda said.

"Let Reh make it so," Urthred replied, the weight on his heart telling him otherwise. Alanda knelt by the village girl and took her hand. Imuni returned the grip fiercely; she was still staring fearfully at Urthred. The old lady coaxed her to look round at her. "Imuni, we mean you no harm. We are travellers, from the south. Have you heard of the Southern Lands?"

The girl nodded slowly. "My father speaks of them. When I was very little, strangers came over the mountains from the south."

"Strangers?" Jayal asked in sudden excitement. "Did they come here?"

The girl shook her head. "They went north across the plains. But my people found their dead in the mountains."

"But some survived?"

"Yes: they carried a burning light with them that could be seen even from the village."

The girl's words came rapidly, encouraged by Jayal's rapt attention.

He turned away and stared at the cave mouth. "It must have been the Rod—its light was brighter than anything else I have ever seen. My father is alive," he said, his eyes alight with sudden hope.

Imuni by now had calmed enough to relax her grip on Alanda's hand.

Urthred delicately picked up the fallen bag in his steel talons and pulled open its drawstrings: inside he found a nosegay, a broken pot that gave off the scent of alcohol and a black bag from which moisture was seeping.

"What were you going to do with these offerings?" he asked Imuni.

"They are for the Lightbringer and her guardians," Imuni answered. "The poppies and the corn for the old lady; the wine for the young warrior; the snow for the Lightbringer . . ." Her voice trailed off. *And nothing for the one she called the demon,* Urthred thought wryly.

"Why snow?" he asked.

"The first snow of winter will wake the Lightbringer from her sleep. So that her light will not pass from the world in the dark season." Urthred looked at the bag. Marizian had no doubt been the one who had ordained that it should be so, foreseeing some future event where it might have significance. An event, perhaps, like Thalassa's wounding. Sometimes some long-forgotten truth lingered behind these old rituals.

"What were you to do with the snow?" he asked.

"I was to place it on the Lightbringer's lips."

Urthred looked questioningly at Alanda, who nodded slightly. "Then do as you would have done if we hadn't come."

"But she is alive," the girl said.

"No, she sleeps—she needs to be woken," Urthred replied.

The girl looked at Thalassa's unconscious body uncertainly. Alanda pulled her gently to her feet and led her from the shadows. Imuni glanced fearfully at Urthred, then down at the bag in the pincers of his glove. She reached forward with shaking fingers and took the black bag and pulled open the top, revealing a mess of half-melted snow within. She pulled out a handful of crystals which shone in the early-morning light.

"Go on," Urthred said, nodding towards Thalassa. Hesitantly the girl approached, glancing back frequently, but with the eyes of three strangers upon her, she was too scared to disobey. She mounted the step and, crushing the snow in her fist, trickled the ice water onto Thalassa's pale lips. The icy beads fell onto them then ran down her chin. Thalassa moaned slightly. But did not wake.

Alanda stepped up onto the plinth and crouched next to her. "Thalassa?" she whispered. Thalassa stirred slightly, then a faraway smile broke over her lips and she cracked open her eyes.

"Can you see me?" Alanda asked.

"The light," Thalassa whispered, shutting her eyes tight again. "It's so bright. . . ."

"We are all here, child: I, and Urthred, and Jayal."

"What happened?" she asked dreamily, as if she were about to slip back into unconsciousness again.

"You must stay awake, child," Alanda said urgently. "You were bitten by a vampire, you may sink into the second sleep. . . ."

A sudden expression of pain crossed Thalassa's face. "I remember now: I was on the marshes, on the pyramid of skulls, the undead. . . ." She moaned as the memory of the struggle came back to her. "I was bitten, it's true. Alanda, I am infected!" Her face cracked in despair.

"The vampire who bit you is dead."

Thalassa touched the livid puncture wounds on her neck and winced. "And yet, I feel it: its poison is in my veins. . . ."

"That may be the wound and not the venom," Urthred said. "Open your eyes again," he commanded, and she did so.

"It's so bright. . . ." she complained again.

"But you can still look into the light." He gestured behind him with his gloves. "How could you abide the sight of the sun if you were one of them?"

"You forget, priest, the change comes slowly, not in an hour." Nevertheless she did lift up her head, fighting her giddiness and clenching her eyes. She squinted at the sunlight streaming down the passage: her pale skin seemed to glow like alabaster. "Where is this place?"

"In the north; the magic of the sword brought us here in the blink of an eye. Faran is far away, we're safe."

"Can you stand?" Alanda asked. Thalassa hesitantly swung her feet from the slab and placed them carefully on the floor. She pushed herself up and stood, her legs trembling like a newborn foal's. Urthred and Alanda steadied her. All the time Imuni stared at her with saucer eyes. "Who is this?" Thalassa asked, noticing her for the first time.

"A girl from the local village. They have a ritual each autumn equinox: the child was carrying an offering to this shrine."

"What shrine?" Thalassa asked.

"This is a place of worship: four statues stood here, until this morning."

"Statues?"

"Aye; effigies of the four of us, placed here by Marizian at the beginning of time."

"But why?"

Alanda took her hand and stared into Thalassa's eyes. "He saw this day, millennia ago."

Thalassa's knees gave out, and she sat back heavily on the plinth.

The sun by now lent a golden glow to the rock all around them. Seeing Thalassa sitting on the slab, conscious, Urthred felt some of the anxiety lift from his shoulders. At least she was alive, perhaps even free from infection. Their enemies were far away, and there was Thalassa's smile, as she lifted her head again and looked at him: a tonic that lifted his spirits until they seemed to reach as high as the sword had lifted them—as high as the sun itself.

"Come," he said. "Let us go to the village."

He gently placed one of his taloned hands around Thalassa's shoulders, and, with a visible effort, she stood once more, with Jayal supporting her on the other side. They walked slowly towards the cavern mouth. Alanda followed with the village girl.

They emerged at the top of the monumental steps. Now it was light, the orange globe of the sun had already risen several degrees into the sky. The whole of the land was visible: the purple-and-coral gradations of light and shade on the snowcapped mountains to the south: the deep gorge to their left; and the sparkling plain of isinglass on the horizon to the east. Urthred took all this in, then his eyes moved up, across the plain. It was then he saw for the first time the broken, jagged peaks of the Broken Hines and the dark cloud sitting on them. He drew in his breath sharply.

Thalassa noticed the sudden catching of his breath. "What is it, priest?" she asked.

"I don't know. . . ." Urthred replied uncertainly. "Those mountains . . . it is as if I have been here before."

"How?" Jayal asked. "You have spent your whole life in a monastery, priest. No one but a handful of our people have ever seen this land."

Urthred shook his head. "It is true: I spent all my years at Forgeholm, yet I wasn't born there: my brother and I were brought to the monastery as infants."

"You think you were brought from here? How could an infant remember?"

"Nevertheless, there is something here, something familiar. . . ." Urthred replied. He turned to Imuni. "What are those mountains called?" he asked.

She looked at her feet, cowed by the mask. "The Broken Hines," she whispered. "They are haunted, with ghosts and inhuman creatures. The things that live there are called the Nations of the Night."

"The Nations!" Jayal breathed. "The Legions of Flame were sent centuries ago to destroy them."

"And never returned," Urthred replied grimly. "How can people live here, so near evil?" he asked.

"Normally we are left alone," Imuni answered.

"The dark cloud comes only every two generations. Then my people suffer," she said, a quiver in her voice as she looked at the Broken Hines and the sinister cloud. As they watched, it was shot through with lightning.

Urthred felt a strange pull towards the distant mountains. His heart was racing with excitement and dread. There was something there, he was sure of it—the place that Manichee had told him to discover, the place where his origins were hidden.

"Let's go on to the village," Alanda said. Urthred broke off staring at the mountains and, taking hold of Thalassa's arm again, began to help her down the broad flight of rock-cut steps.

Before they were halfway down, they saw a large group of men in the distance moving towards them through the ruins.

"My father!" Imuni shouted, breaking from them and running down the steps towards the men. The villagers looked up when they heard her shout. Then they noticed the four strangers further up the steps and halted abruptly. The two groups stared at one another, separated by the running girl.

"They look friendly enough," Alanda said eventually. Urthred didn't reply but waited to see what would happen when the girl met up with the villagers.

Imuni reached the group below. She gesticulated up the steps in an excited way. Urthred could see that the men were ordinary villagers, like the superstitious folk of the isolated hamlets under Forgeholm, the ones who had come to his tower hoping for cures. He remembered peeking down at them from his hidden eyrie: they had looked just like these. He knew with what horror the villagers of Forgeholm would have greeted him if he had actually descended the tower and presented himself at its doors. Then he would not have been their salvation, but the demon, just as he was to these people, if the young girl's reaction was anything to go by.

Whatever rejoicing the villagers might feel at the

Lightbringer's coming would be dispelled when they saw him. Might endanger the others. "Take Thalassa," he ordered Jayal.

"Why?" the young Illgill asked.

"You have got used to this mask, my friend; those villagers have not. I will wait here by the top of the steps. Explain to them that I mean them no harm."

"Very well," Jayal said, taking his place next to Thalassa.

Urthred watched as his friends continued down the steps, then climbed back to the platform and the trees. Their branches were silent now. The nightingale had flown. He sat on the packed earth under them, just as another warm gust of wind came over the mountains.

Below, the villagers had surged forward to the base of the steps. They murmured, as the southerners got closer, seeing the resemblance between Alanda and themselves. The mountain folk were short, bandy-legged men, dressed in brown cloaks and wool leggings and armed with cudgels, spears and bows. Imuni was easily the fairest of her people, for amongst the others there was a fair sprinkling of the misshapen, the walleyed, the lame.

Imuni was being led by her father, Garadas. He was no taller than she, wiry and tanned by the wind, with bushy dark hair and beard, his legs bowed. It was easy to see why he had been chosen headman: there was a hard, shrewd intelligence in his eyes. He halted a few paces away from the base of the steps and confronted the strangers. The two parties eyed each other warily. "Where have you come from?" he asked eventually. The southerners understood him, as they had understood Imuni, though he spoke their language in a guttural, archaic manner.

Alanda left Thalassa with Jayal and took a step down towards the villagers. "From the shrine," she answered.

"No one has passed through the village in the night,

though many eyes watched, since today is a holy day. How did you get to it?"

"We woke in it, just before dawn."

Garadas's eyes narrowed, but then Imuni spoke, her reedy voice cutting through the air. "Father, the statues are gone!" Now all the villagers turned and stared at her.

"Gone?"

"Yes, the ledges were empty: only these people were there."

Garadas looked back at the three, and his brown face creased even more. "Who is that under the trees?" he asked, gesturing up at the platform in front of the cave.

"The demon," Imuni answered. There was a gasp of horror from the assembled villagers.

"He knows that he is a pariah to you, that is why he has gone back," Alanda said quickly.

Garadas thought for a moment. "This is all very strange. I must go to the cave and see for myself. Keep the warrior and the girl," he said to his men. "I will go with the old woman." It wasn't clear whether the villagers had heard his words, for they were all talking volubly amongst themselves, gesticulating up at the shrine. Garadas gestured to Alanda, and together they climbed up the steps.

"We mean no harm," she said as she climbed with him.

"That I believe, since my daughter is safe," he said. "But my people are more superstitious than I. I must see what has happened to the statues."

As they approached, Urthred stood up from the shadows of the trees. The headman stared hard at Urthred's mask, before gesturing for Alanda to wait. Then he continued under the shadow of the trees into the cave. Urthred and Alanda exchanged a silent look, but said nothing, the silence broken only by the soughing of the wind over the shoulder of the mountain. After a few minutes Garadas reappeared, his face white under the tan and his beard. "My daughter spoke the truth. The statues have gone," he said. "Tell me again how you came here." So Alanda did so. When she had finished, Garadas lowered his head. "I am a humble man: the people of Goda call me a priest, but I have no learning. The last man who could read or write died hundreds of years ago. Forgive me. When the God Marizian left he expected a priest to be here on this day. Now it is only I, a herder of yaks."

"Then you believe our story?" Alanda asked.

The headman didn't answer straightaway but looked down the hill at Thalassa, who was sitting slumped on a rock at the bottom of the steps, shielded from the gawking villagers by Jayal. "I may not be a holy man except in name, but the legend of my people is that a divine being, this Lightbringer, will come and rekindle the dying sun. But she," he said, nodding at Thalassa again, "is sick. She looks like one of the race of men, not a goddess." Then he turned to Urthred. "We expected a demon, but this man wears a pantomime mask. And you," he said, looking into her blue eyes. "You look like one of our people." He shrugged, no further words possible.

"I understand your difficulties," Alanda replied. "You cannot believe we are the ones you have waited for. We are, I admit, all too human, and no one saw the statues disappear. Treat us no differently than you do other strangers."

"Strangers?" Garadas replied. "No strangers ever come to Goda."

"May we be your guests then? After the girl is recovered we will go on our way."

"On your way? Where? This is the world, there is nowhere else."

"What of the plains, the forest beyond?" Alanda said, gesturing in that direction.

"Winter has come. The Great Wolf will soon roam the plains. There is nowhere to go, old lady, except Goda."

"Then that is where we must go."

Garadas turned to Urthred. "Now I see that you

wear a mask; that you aren't the monster we feared. But you cannot come into our village in that guise— for generations my people have believed you to be a demon. The mask will terrify them. Remove it, and you, too, will be our welcome guest."

Urthred shook his head. "I have taken a vow never to remove it. Even my companions have not seen what lies beneath it."

Garadas's face set. "Then you cannot enter the village." Alanda was about to protest, but he stilled her with a gesture of his hand. "As I said, I am a herder of yaks, a practical man. But my people are superstitious. I must tell them the statues have gone, that the girl is the Lightbringer. Otherwise, they will think you have destroyed the statues—they will blame any disasters that follow on you. So your friend will be the demon, she, the Lightbringer. It must be this way."

"You'll let him die on the mountain?"

Garadas shook his head. "There is a watchtower beyond the village. No one will go there now it is winter. I will arrange for food and firewood to be brought there. He will have to remain there until spring comes, and you can leave."

Alanda was about to speak again, but Urthred silenced her. "It is just: this mask has kept me apart from my fellows since I was a child. So it will be again. I will go to this tower if you tell me where to find it."

Garadas pointed at a track leading around to the right of the amphitheatre in the mountains in which the ruins nestled. "Follow that path, but give us time to leave. The people must not see you." Then he turned to Alanda. "Come, we must rejoin the others." Alanda glanced at Urthred again, but he gestured for her to go, and she and the headman set off down the mountain.

The villagers stirred and muttered amongst themselves when they saw Garadas returning. When he reached the bottom of the steps, he held up his hand to quell their murmuring.

"The statues are gone," he said. There was intake

of breath from the villagers when they heard the words. "The miracle has come, the Lightbringer is here," he said, pointing at Thalassa. For a moment, each of the assembled men looked at one another, doubting the words he had spoken, but Garadas stood his ground, his dark eyes daring them to contradict him. A moment passed, then there was a rustle of clothing, and, as one, the villagers knelt in front of the rock on which she sat.

Alanda hurried to Thalassa's side. Her face was very pale, and she seemed unconscious of the attention being paid her. She shook her gently. Thalassa stirred and looked up, her eyes narrowed against the sun, and saw the villagers. "Why are they kneeling?" she whispered.

"You are the Lightbringer," Alanda murmured quietly.

Thalassa shook her head. "I'm no god: I am human like you." Indeed, it would have been difficult to imagine anyone more frail and mortal: her face was very pale, and the purple puncture wounds on her neck stood out harshly in the morning light. Though the air was quite warm, she was trembling uncontrollably.

Alanda looked at Garadas in mute appeal. The headman was suddenly all action. "Make a litter," he commanded. "The Lightbringer must be borne with ceremony." The villagers rose quickly and dispersed about the hillside.

Soon they had two good lengths of wood cut from two of the stunted trees that grew on the slopes. Having lashed them together into a crude frame and secured a cloak over the middle, they laid Thalassa gently upon it. Immediately four villagers took up the four ends of the poles.

When all was ready, Garadas nodded, and they set off through the ruins. They struck up a low humming song as they went, which echoed back off the stony slopes around them.

Urthred stood on the platform for a long time after the procession was gone, though their song still carried to him on the gusting winds that blew in from the north. He was alone again, torn from the companionship of the last twenty-four hours. Loneliness fell upon him like dusk: the promise of words and laughter was gone, the ties that made others human, severed. The sense of belonging went with his disappearing friends like the ebb tide, with that song which was now the merest susurration on the wind. As the procession passed over the crest of the ridge it died altogether.

Why had his master given him this mask, that forever set him aside from humanity? Why hadn't he given him a mask of a lively, smiling youth, the man he might have grown into had he not been burned? But Urthred knew the answer: what good would it be to flatter to deceive? The reality of what lay beneath the mask could not be denied. Those he got close to must one day discover the truth, inadvertently glimpse his real face when he removed it, however careful he was. He would forever remain scarred, an abomination. Manichee had ordained it thus: he would always be alone, never to have the fulfillment of what other men dreamed. Only in solitude could he have pride, could he find the inner strength to discover the secret flame that brought the magic, and the strength to fight the enemies of the Sun. Never would he have the joy of mixing and breathing with his fellows. For a brief few moments, when Thalassa had stared into the unpitying eyes of the mask, when she had touched him or held his gloved hands and he had felt the softness of her fingers, he had known what it was like to be another man. Now she was gone and, with her, his hope.

His role had been fulfilled: he had been the Herald, had played the first act of the prophecies in Thrull. Somewhere in the world below them was the Man of Bronze, waiting for the Lightbringer to come. He knew nothing of this creature, only that Manichee had copied his gloves from its hands: but surely it was mightier than he: a creature that could summon fire from its molten heart, who could crush mountainsides in its talons. His companions had no more need of him.

His work was over. He had done his brother's bidding and Manichee's. Now the mountains to the north beckoned, the mountains that Manichee had promised him contained the secrets of his past. He would go alone. It was easier that way. He accepted that his destiny was not the same as the others'. It was all as the prophecies dictated: Jayal to follow his father; Alanda to find the ancient land of her people; Thalassa to find the Man of Bronze. All of them had a purpose in this except him. Thalassa had seen what he had seen in the Orb, knew where to go.

As for Thalassa, she would find her destiny without him. She was free now, with her two friends. They would find the magic to cure her, then the three of them would go on and cast the shadows from the sun: great magic would be unleashed. One day in the future, as he wandered the empty places of the dying world, he would see the reborn sun rise over the horizon and know her work was done, knowing that it was her, the one woman he had ever touched, who had given birth to that miracle. That, and only that, would be his reward: knowing that once, for a brief few hours, he had been close to her.

He set off down the track that Garadas had pointed out. It circled high around the mountainside. Presently he saw the village of Goda nestling below. His eyes went over the village and the patchwork of fields surrounding it. There, in the distance, against the grey of the plain far below he saw a single spire of grey stone: a tower camouflaged by the background colour of the surrounding rocks. It lay a long way from the village bounds and seemed a desolate place.

The track continued around the semicircular ring of mountains, passing high over the top of the village, and dropped down towards it. He continued on his way, gradually descending. He passed small pastures, ringed by dry stone walls. They were empty. He could hear song coming from the village. They were celebrating the Lightbringer's arrival, he guessed. The thought sent a sharp pain through him: he wanted to be there now. But he had given up the promise of ever seeing her again.

The track led around the village in a huge arc, plunging precipitously towards the cliffs. The pastures gave way to the mountain edge: an expanse of huge flat rocks, which in turn led to the edge of the precipice. The tower rose in front of him, on the very edge of the world it seemed. The plains beyond were like a patchwork quilt of hurrying cloud shadows. A warm wind raced in from the north, in complete contradiction to the seasons. Surely it should be an arctic blast, coming from the frozen north?

He shook his head and followed a path that led away to the left around the base of the tower. Now he saw some wooden handrails set into the cliff face. The beginning of the steps leading down to the plains. He walked over to them and peered down: a wooden staircase, built on stilts out from the cliff. It zigzagged out into space, but apart from mighty buttresses of rock that stuck out from the cliff face below, it was as if he had grown wings and hovered above an infinity of emptiness. Thousands of feet below the plains loomed up at him. This, evidently, was the only way out of the mountain people's land.

He looked once more over at the Broken Hines. Manichee had promised him that he would find a destiny in this land, find the place in which the secrets of his past were written. The tortured red sandstone slopes, the summit spires and razorback ridges, and dark ruins stood under the purple cloud. As he watched, lightning shot through it again and, moments later, he heard the dull retort of thunder.

On a whim, he pulled from his backpack the leech gatherer's staff. He stared at it. When he had first been given it, in the underground chamber in Thrull, it had seemed but a dead branch of a tree. But the Elder of the leech gatherers had told him it had been hewn from a tree, here in the far north, in the Forest of Lorn. The longer it had been in his possession, the more it seemed that the dead branch was coming back to life: after the Lightbringer's Shrine in Thrull when he had first seen Thalassa transformed, a small shoot and a green leaf had burst from it, and still hung there. Even through the gloves, he felt a tingle of energy, and a slight pull, as he had heard diviners felt when searching with their hazel rods for hidden water. The pull was towards the north, further confirmation to him that that was where he had to go. Now it pulled towards home, somewhere in that distant invisible greenwood beyond the Broken Hines.

Only one thing held him back: Thalassa. Only a little time before he had steeled himself to leave her and go alone to the north. But could he go without seeing her one more time?

He stared at the scene for an hour or more, his mind a whirl of contradictory thoughts. His eyes followed the grey-etched lines on the snow covering the mountains: the ice-filled gullies and buttresses, the corniced ridges twisting upwards to the snowcapped peaks. And he asked himself again: why was it that he knew this place?

CHAPTER FIVE

✦

To the Oubliettes

Two hundred leagues to the south—Thrull.

Deep underground in the Temple of Iss, earth-trembling quakes sent cascades of dust and brick-work onto the small group of people assembled in Lord Faran Gaton Nekron's throne room. It was several hours into the day, but as always the room was in semidarkness. The only light came from skull lanterns positioned at the four corners of the room. The chamber was an ossuary; its ceiling, walls, and piers were faced with human bone. The ceiling itself was lost in the darkness, but the walls and arches of the room glowed whitely in the ghostly light.

The little group assembled there were waiting to die.

Faran Gaton himself sat on the throne, his head thrown back so that it rested on the symbol of Iss, a serpent eating its own tail, carved onto its back. He was still dressed in the black leather armour and cape he had worn the night before when he'd gone to Marizian's tomb chamber. Both were caked with white plaster dust. The cape was thrown back over his shoulders. His one remaining hand protruded from it to clutch an armrest. At the other shoulder there was a slack space where the other arm once had been.

The fingers of the remaining hand were white as bone, and jewelled rings flashed red and green in the flickering light. These were the only evidence of colour on his whole person. His face was matted with dust, the dust and the pain of his wound giving it an even greater pallor than usual. His eyes burned darkly from beneath his pale brow.

Unlike the others, he took no notice of the debris that fell from the ceiling as each vibration shook the chamber. He didn't flinch even when a chunk of masonry as large as a human torso fell only a few feet away, sending up yet more dust. The humans around began coughing as it ballooned out into the ill-lit chamber. But the dust was nothing to him. His lungs were already choked with more ancient dust than this newly fallen. His mouth gave a loud wheeze as his chest slowly moved, drawing in the fetid air.

The servants were jabbering away in panic: Faran would have silenced their noise with an angry gesture, but, in truth, he was barely aware of it. His mind was far away, detached even from the dead, gnawing chill that played over the area where his left arm had once been.

His mind, unusually, was full of self-recrimination. He had lived two hundred years, but no matter how many years a man lived, he ruminated, the lessons were never learned. Never learned, that was, until it was too late. Seize the day . . . who had told him this, when he had been a young man years before in Tiré Gand? Yet in these seven years in Thrull he had dabbled with time just as he had ever since he had been given the Life in Death—tinkered with it, knowing that the years stretched to eternity before him and pleasures taken too swiftly would quickly pall. He had spun the hours and days and months as an old lady spins out her yarn, stretching it for the loom, setting aside the things that might be done tomorrow, or the day after, or the day after that. He had flirted with pleasure rather than crushing its petals in his hands.

There were many examples of his dilatoriness: for one, he had let the spirit of rebellion fester too long in Thrull. He had been well informed by his network of spies, those that pretended to serve Reh, but secretly coveted the eternal life offered by his own god, Iss. But he had not acted as quickly as he should on their information. In his pride he had not expected any serious threat to his power. Next, he had laughed at the prophecies of older times which the abbots had brought to him, showing him where it was written that Thrull must fall within seven years of his conquest. Then, just as the mouldering pages had predicted, yesterday the masked priest had come, Jayal Illgill, too. In a matter of hours, Thrull had been destroyed.

But Thrull had been dying long before then. Dying because of his lack of activity. His power was based on the undead, but the blood that they needed to drink to remain awake had been running out for years. What had he done? Had he sent for slave caravans to come from Tiré Gand? Had he travelled to the capital to petition the Elders there? No, his pride had been too great to show such weakness. Had he not believed himself even greater than the Elders? How they would mock him now! Now a mere handful of the thousands he had once ruled were left alive, and they were in this throne room.

Above all this, it was one person's loss that rankled most. Thalassa. If he had been told the month before that it was she, whey-faced and trembling, the girl shackled naked here before his burning eyes, that it was she who was at the heart of all the coming ruin, would he not have laughed? She had been only his plaything then, the amusement for him had been, perversely, in restraint, in refraining from taking her life, in not making her his blood servant. What pleasure was there in possession? The Dominant quickly tired of its victim. Now she had escaped: strangely, he felt the vacancy, as if all along he had known what she was. The Lightbringer. The same that had been written about in the books of prophecy that he had waved away time and time again. Who would have believed it?

The image of her face came to his mind and with it a surprisingly sharp stab to his atrophied heart—the memory of her cold beauty, offset by the delicate shape of her mouth. She had possessed the vulnerability yet the hardness of a whore who had known a thousand men but had never let one touch her heart. He had cherished that coldness, recognising that here was a match to his own separateness, of a destiny set aside that could not be touched by mere circumstance. Perhaps he had recognised a power, hidden behind the lantern of the skin? Had treasured it, been beguiled by it, had not wished to reduce her to another blood slave like the others, for he had known she was greater than they?

So he had held back each month, hoping somehow he would conquer her spirit, hoping she would willingly give her soul to him. A hundred nights had passed thus, a hundred moments of potential satiation drained away like sand in an hourglass. If only he had seized the moment! At least then he would have been satisfied for a brief period, seeing her soul drain away. A moment when he would have finally destroyed that mute accusation, that otherness with which she had mocked him. Now nothing was left.

For had he not destroyed her—set the vampires out on the marshes—given them the blood that he had so many times denied himself? And for what? Why had he not gone out with the Brethren in the dawn, the sun rising and him in the open? So this empty life should not be dissolved by the sun's rays in a mist? The sun would only have done what the demon would surely achieve in a few minutes when it reached the throne chamber.

Nekron: the demon that carried his own last name— a name in the ancient language of the temple which meant, simply, "death." He had seen it with his own eyes, hours earlier. The thousand barbed teeth of its mouth, its throat an endless purple tunnel beyond. Its horned head . . . Nekron—half worm, half demon summoned from the abyss of Hel. For what? To save him, that was the irony! Freed from the wards that had controlled him on this plane, the demon now fed on every soul it could find in the city of Thrull. Few remained: after those taken by the vampires and the

thousands who had burned themselves alive in the
Temple of Reh, the only ones left were here in the
Temple of Iss—the Reapers of Sorrow who had protected him through the long march from Tiré Gand
seven years before, who had kept the temple secure
in the years since; the pale-faced acolytes who had not
yet achieved their desire of the Life in Death; these
slaves, trembling with fear. The demon could scent
fear like a cat could scent prey. If only the fools had
realised: their souls screamed out silently to the
demon—and it was coming.

It had burrowed into the temple catacombs hours
before, driven underground by the rising sun, seeking
its way like a huge snub-nosed worm through the underworld, scenting the souls of the living waiting to be
harvested. In the hours since, he had sat here unmoved, his destiny settled in his own mind.

Now there was only one thing that kept him alive,
a flicker of curiosity that only one man could satisfy
before he died. He waited for the sorcerer, Golon. He
had ordered him back onto the parapets, to see what
had happened to the fugitives on the marshes. He
cared not for the masked priest, nor for the young
Illgill, only for Thalassa. But Golon had been gone
since dawn, had become, no doubt, just another of the
thousands consumed by the demon's flashing teeth.
The demonologist who had created it in the first place.
There was an irony, a fitting symbol of Iss. The creator
consumed by his own creature, just as the worm devoured its own tail.

But if he was alive, and if any man in Thrull had a
chance of surviving, surely it was he, why didn't he
return, to tell him what he'd seen as dawn broke?

Another crash of falling masonry. Finally Faran
stirred and looked about him. He noticed for the first
time the pallor of the moon-eyed attendants who
stood staring at him, and nearly laughed. They, unlike
him, prized the half-life they still had, still wished to
live on and on as the sun died and the earth grew
dark. But he, why should he be afraid? The grave held

no terror if his desires could not be fulfilled. Let Golon come and tell him Thalassa was dead, and that would be the end of it; he would sit here until Nekron destroyed them all.

From far away, over the crash of falling walls, they now heard the dying screams of those in the higher reaches of the temple. Heard the mournful groans as first one then another of the massive copper gates leading to the catacombs, gates which siege engines could not have damaged in a month of battering, were bent and wrenched from their hinges in seconds. And after the clangour of the falling doors, there suddenly came a vacuum: the air was sucked from the room; papers lifted up from the tables on which they rested and candles snuffed. The demon had entered the temple precincts, drawing everything and everyone in its path into its all-consuming vortex.

Faran traced its progress through the temple: the sudden stilling of the drumbeat that played forever in the temple's sanctuary, the screams as it reached the library. Then the fluttering blizzard of torn paper striking the door to the throne room. Now they heard the demon's scaly sides rasping on the walls near them. It was coming, deeper and deeper underground, driven away from the sun, attracted to this chamber, where the last humans breathed in Thrull. Now it must be too late for Golon to come.

Faran glared at the few survivors of his once-mighty empire. The slaves huddled around the throne: bloodstock, no more. Then there were the surviving guards, a hundred strong, most crowded into the antechamber, but ten or so were in here with him standing guard over the two captives. Their stoic silence behind their skull masks, so unlike the mewling of the slaves, proclaimed them the elite, the men who would protect their lord with their lives.

But even their presence was unnecessary: there was nowhere for their captives to flee to. The first of them, Malliana, the High Priestess of the Temple of Sutis, knelt before Faran, her white face bowed to the floor, spewing

inarticulate words into the dust that coated it. Many
people over the years had begged for their lives in
front of him; he'd always watched them with amusement: why did they value something so pitiful as life?
What could one really guarantee if you were one of
the living? Only death, extinction—only that was inev-
itable: the rest was a dream. Faran had only ever been
at one with his victims as they drew their final breaths,
those from whom he'd taken the fatal bite, or whom
he had had executed in front of his eyes. Then they
had what he would never have: the surety of death.
What a prize that was! No threat of waking again, like
he had woken in Marizian's tomb, no better than a
broken cockroach lacking an arm or a limb. No, they
had the second sleep, as would he when the demon
had consumed him.

There was no pleasure now in the High Priestess's
entreaties—her blood was too wasted, smelt stale, her
life force was sapped. Her pleas were merely the whining noise of an insect in his ear, her moans the lowing
of cattle. He would have had the guards toss her out
to the demon had it not been too dangerous to open
the door to the antechamber. There came another
bone-shaking shudder as another foundation pillar collapsed nearby.

But one person in the chamber did stand unmoved;
the second captive, the Doppelgänger. The near double of Jayal Illgill. He stood in front of him, slightly
hunchbacked, flanked by two of the Reapers. The
right side of his face was scarred out of recognition,
but the other was a perfect hemisphere of what Jayal's
face would look like now, seven years after the battle
of Thrull. He had given a strange tale of his existence
since his capture: a tale of Jayal possessed by evil as
a child, then an exorcism that drove away the darker
half, the Doppelgänger, into the place of the damned,
Shades. And how the Doppelgänger had been plucked
back into this world by the power of the Rod at the
battle of Thrull when the young Illgill was dying, so
Jayal's soul once more inhabited its body and the

Doppelgänger was left with Jayal's maimed and broken one.

Faran believed the story: had he not seen the Shadow World shimmering before him in his two hundred years? And had not Baron Illgill staked everything on the Rod of Power that opened the gate to that world? His whole kingdom in fact. Yet he had only saved one man with its powers: his own son.

Like the baron, Faran had lost his once-proud army: only those assembled around the throne were left. But if he had had the Rod, he would not have had Illgill's scruples. He would have inhabited the world with creatures such as this: this Doppelgänger. Immune to pain, soulless, dedicated to darkness and the extinction of Reh. Then there would have been a final victory! The creature that had inherited Jayal's broken body was the only living person that Faran had known who did not give out the butcher's scent of blood. Not this man. He had no scent, remained unaffected by Faran's mesmerism, as if he still dwelt in the Shadow World.

And he held knowledge that Faran had once desperately wanted. Perhaps that was why, as their eyes met, a sly smile played over the Doppelgänger's puckered mouth. He had managed what Faran had failed to do, had penetrated Marizian's tomb chamber. He knew its secrets, secrets that by rights should have been Faran's; but he had remained silent on this point ever since he had been captured. Now he stared back evenly, his face creased in a mirthless joy, his glacial single eye far distant from this place. He didn't even show pain though his bandaged hands were tied behind his back in leather thongs. One of the Reapers, seeing his insolent sneer, wrenched back on the halter round his neck, causing his eye nearly to pop from its socket.

Faran held up his hand, stopping the guard from repeating the process. "Leave him be," he ordered. The guard stepped back, laying the halter on the ground. Faran returned his gaze to the captive. "Don't you fear death?" he asked.

"What, would you have me beg for my life, like that strumpet?" the Doppelgänger sneered, nodding towards Malliana.

"All men fear pain."

"Not I," the Doppelgänger spat.

"Then what do you fear?"

"That our enemies have escaped, and we stand here waiting to die."

"Our enemies?"

"Aye, both you and I have reason to hate them: Thalassa, Urthred, Jayal, Alanda."

Faran was silent for a moment, listening to the rasping progress of Nekron through a side passage. "Look around you: this is my army. Do you think we can fight the demon with so few?" he asked.

The Doppelgänger took a step forward, the rope trailing in the dust behind him. "It is better to die fighting than like rats trapped in a hole."

"Perhaps," Faran replied torpidly. "But what then? Where will you find these enemies? They fled hours ago; they could be anywhere."

"They carry Dragonstooth, one of Marizian's three magical artefacts. They will have gone to find the other two: the Man of Bronze and the Rod of the Shadows."

Faran feigned disinterest, though he was close to getting the information he desired from the creature. "Perhaps, but where in the world can these objects be found? The Man of Bronze disappeared two thousand years ago, and Illgill took the Rod of the Shadows."

"I have seen the Orb—I know where they are!" the Doppelgänger replied, his single eye bulging from its socket in excitement.

"Then where are they?" Faran said, leaning forward, staring hard at the Doppelgänger.

The creature's face fell, as he realised he had given away too much. "They are in the north," he said reluctantly. "One is in the Nations of the Night, the other further north still, in the ice plains."

"So, now we know where the artefacts are. But

what good is an artefact, or all the magic in the world, if the enemies you would use them against, Thalassa and the others, have disappeared?''

"I have seen them, too." The Doppelgänger fixed him with his single eye again.

"Seen them? Do you carry the Orb with you? How can you see beyond these walls, beyond Thrull?"

The Doppelgänger tossed his head. "I need no Orb. Jayal and I are but halves of one whole. Believe me, I see them even now, through his eyes, as clearly as I see you." He paused as if mentally focusing on the picture in front of him. "Magic took him and the others to the north." The Doppelgänger's face took on a slightly abstracted air as if he gazed on something far away. "He is in a village now, the whore Thalassa and the old lady next to him. A feast is spread before him, half-witted villagers are dancing around them."

"You lie," Faran said, half-rising from his throne.

"No, it is the truth. Ever since he came to the house on the Silver Way, I have seen more and more, as if his two eyes and my one were one. Once before the exorcism our two minds were joined in struggle. Now they do battle again, but this time mine will win. Every day my influence on him will grow stronger. Slowly he will become mad, haunted by that voice he heard when he was a boy, my voice. Then we will be one again, and my spirit will go into him: then I will dominate his mind, just as I did before. And when I have the Rod of the Shadows, I will cast him out from my body and consign him to this crippled thing," he exclaimed, jerking his head at his hunchbacked frame.

Faran slumped back into his throne. Strangely, he believed every word the Doppelgänger had told him, though there was no reason to trust him. The creature's words had been spoken with complete conviction, with a burning zeal. Two hundred years of life had taught Faran how to catch a lie. There was no need to wait for Golon now. A new hope burned in him. Thalassa was alive; he felt it in his bones. He turned, resting his head on his hand, his mind racing.

There was a way to escape: one he had rejected an hour before, a way that was perhaps as much a guarantee of their deaths as waiting here. But now he felt invigorated, suddenly impatient.

He spat to one side, ridding his dried throat of the choking dust, which he now noticed for the first time. Dust, dust, what was man but dust? Suddenly, he was drowning in a sea of particles, of dead men's eyes and ears and brains, of bones pulverised long ago, their hands were in his eyes and throat. Who could live in this sea of dust? He had to leave this place immediately.

He stood abruptly, the guards straightening as he did so.

Then he heard the sound of a stone panel grinding open in the shadows to his left. Without looking, he knew it was Golon. Now the sorcerer could confirm the Doppelgänger's story. His heart thudded painfully in anticipation, and it felt like its dried arteries were sutures holding together an old, festering wound, sutures that would burst then and there. Yet he composed his features and turned to face the sorcerer, who now emerged out of the darkness. Golon's chest rose and fell—he'd obviously been running. His mauve-and-brown robes were caked with white plaster dust. His dark eyes glowered as he fought for breath.

"Well?" Faran asked.

"The demon is very close—I heard it in the galleries of the library." Golon panted.

"Let it come," Faran answered dismissively. "What of the girl?"

Golon looked away, cowed by the look on Faran's face. "I went back to the parapet as you told me," he said. "The mists still hid the marshes, but the pyramid of skulls was visible. . . ."

"And?"

"The sun rose—the Brethren were destroyed—there were still figures on the summit afterwards, but then there was a flash of light, and they were gone."

"Gone?"

Golon dared to look at him again, his eyes hooded and cadaverous in the lychlight. "Sorcery—I felt it even from the city—it was the sword." Another tremor shook the floor, more dust poured down, one of the guards started coughing.

"So, they used its magic to escape?"

Golon was momentarily distracted as there was another crack from above. He glanced up: another chunk of cement and bone as large as a table had separated from the barrel vault and hung by a thread from the ceiling, threatening to come plunging down on their heads.

"Yes," he answered finally, his eyes still on the threat. "Teleportation—it must be that priest of Flame. He knows the sorcery of Reh. He used the sword as a focus for his powers."

"Where would they go?" Faran growled, taking a step closer, though the Doppelgänger had already supplied the answer.

"Like attracts like," Golon said, taking his eyes from the ceiling and looking at Faran. "They would have gone towards the other two artefacts of power, to the north."

"Then we will go there, too," Faran said. "This creature here," he said, reaching forward with his one good arm and seizing the Doppelgänger's collar, "knows where."

Golon stared at the Doppelgänger for a moment, then the lump of masonry he had been staring at broke loose from its feeble mooring and came crashing down. It fell onto one of the slaves. The man didn't even cry out as the mass seemed to swallow him, showering the room with an explosion of dust and bone mould. The other slaves fled to one wall, screaming with fear.

"Enough!" roared Faran, and instantly they fell silent. "You," he said, returning his stare to the Doppelgänger, "I will let live a little longer. Let what you told me be true; otherwise, you will suffer. Now let's be gone from here."

"Where can we go?" Golon observed, a puzzled look on his face. "All the exits are blocked,"

Now it was Faran's turn to smile. "Seven years, Golon—not one moment have I slept while you and the others dreamt the baby sleep of the living. Have you ever thought what one like me who lives in darkness does in the night? The rock of Thrull is deep, and there are many secrets hidden there that not even you know about. Come!" he ordered, gesturing at the guards to drag the Doppelgänger after him.

"But where?" Golon asked again.

"To the oubliettes," he said, striding towards one side of the chamber. The bone facings there looked the same as in the rest of the room, but he raised his remaining hand to the wall, and, like a rising bird, a panel shot up into the air. An unlit passage was revealed beyond. In the dim shadows of the candles burning in the skulls in the throne room, Golon could just make out the forms of Faran's two vampire bodyguards waiting within, their seven-foot frames nearly filling the space. "Come," said Faran. "I will show you a place you never dreamed of."

CHAPTER SIX

✤

Thalassa's Second
Awakening

Thalassa woke. A dull gleam of moonlight fell over her. It came from a slit in a shutter covering a window. She saw that she was lying on a cot. Underneath her was a lumpy mattress stuffed, judging by the pricking on her naked skin, with coarse hair. She turned her head, and in the dull light she could see her surroundings. A room with a low, timbered ceiling, roughly rendered walls and an earth floor. It smelt faintly of animal fur and peat fire. How had she here? All she could remember was that a moment before she'd been having a strange dream.

At first it had been Urthred she had dreamed of. She had been looking at him in the dream, looking at the mask: at the hideous ridges of scar tissue, the noseless void, the ragged lips. But then she saw the face crack into a lipless grin, and she knew the face was flesh, not wood and lacquer. She'd run, over a featureless terrain, pale boulders and dust, like the surface of the moon.

She had run. She had heard him calling her back: his voice had been gentle. But she had not stopped until she was far away and the voice had faded. Then she was on an ice-covered mountainside, the cold stars shining down on her. She was thirsty after the run: she broke off the ice and ate it, feeling it lance the side of her mouth so blood and cold water commingled. She felt a fever in her veins, the fever of the blood that came with the vampire's bite. She had become one of them: her thirst would never be assuaged.

In front of her she saw a lake, and on it two islands. She would go to it and slake her thirst with the lake water, she decided. She walked down to the shore, but before she could even stoop to drink, her feet were carrying her beyond the shore, over the surface of the lake. Now she was on the first of the islands. She began to climb to a palace she could see at its centre. She entered it and went down dark corridors. Ahead she saw a silver light coming from a well set into the floor. She approached it and looked down, and saw in its depths a silver bowl.

A figure joined her in the gloom. She turned: she could dimly see the man's face in the silver glow. It was not the priest, but a white-haired man, his long hair held back by a golden band in which were set many precious gems, alternate red and orange, curiously the colour of each of his eyes. His face was young, unlined and brown, his lips pale. He took her hand and they floated down into the well. There he lifted up the bowl as if he wanted her to drink from it. Suddenly the walls of the well fled away, and she saw behind him an azure sky, great domes of silver and gleaming minarets lancing upwards, and golden dragons that soared across the heavens in fiery trains. She turned once more to the man. The otherworldly eyes, their surfaces sparkling like pyrites, bid her enter them.

"Are you death?" she asked, her voice coming to her ears though she was sure her lips had not moved.

The man's face cracked into a half smile at odds with the alien light of his eyes. "I am not death—I am Reh." The words were in a language she didn't know yet instinctively understood. "Look around you, Thalassa, look at Reh's land—it is called Lorn, a land that has never known death."

And Thalassa looked again upon that vision of the world as it must have been during the Golden Age. She saw the great lake spreading away in the sunlight to distant shores and on it two great islands clothed in white buildings that sparkled in the sunlight, a sunlight stronger than she'd ever known. The vision seemed perfect—yet there lingered a doubt in her mind.

"Where is this place?" she asked.

"It is of this world, yet is not," Reh replied cryptically. "Only my servants live in it, and they will never die, not until the Lightbringer comes."

"All places have known death," she said. "It is the natural order of things. Why is your land exempt?"

A shadow seemed to pass over Reh's face, but it was gone in an instant like a hastening cloud passing over a mountain.

"When the last battle came, I saved my servants," the God said. "All the others fled. But I, though wounded by Iss' trickery, stayed and made this place, Lorn, safe from the fires and madness that raged in the Mortal World at that time. I made the people immortal and beautiful, forever young. The sun in the Mortal World was obscured by black clouds that killed or transformed all who lived under it, so instead of the light of the sun, I set that of my cousin Erewon, God of the Moon, to shine forever." As he said these words, the sunlight dimmed and the scene became night, and where the sun had been, a full moon shone at the highest point of the sky. "So it shines, always full," the God said. "I instructed them to wait for the return of the Light of the Second Dawn. And so they have waited these ten thousand years."

"But the moon like life has its cycles. All things must change. It's the natural order. It must pass like all things." Again, Thalassa didn't know where these words came from. They seemed to rise to her lips unbidden by her mind.

"Yes," Reh replied. "All things must mutate. Even Reh rises at dawn, then sinks again at dusk. Too long my servants have lived under that unchanging moon. You will alter all that. You are the Lightbringer—you will bring the sun again into my land. But first you must drink from the Silver Chalice." Once more the well and silver bowl appeared before her eyes. "It is the antidote to the vampire's bite. It waits for you now in Lorn. But beware, the enemies of Lorn are rising from the Broken Hines: the journey will be dangerous. Make haste, my child. You must be in Lorn in a month." Then the vision faded, and she woke and found herself lying in the bed in the strange room.

It was quite dark. She struggled to remember where she was, then she recalled the first awakening, in the cave up on the hillside: the young girl, the vista of the mountains, the villagers coming to greet them through the ruins of the ancient city. She must have fainted then, for the rest was a complete blank.

Where were her clothes? She looked around and saw, hanging off a crude chair, the thin dress she had donned what seemed a lifetime ago at the Temple of Sutis in Thrull, and next to it, one of the fur-lined cloaks that Alanda and she had packed in their travelling packs before their hasty exit. The rents in the dress had been sewn, albeit crudely.

Next, she explored the twin wounds in her neck: they were upraised and sore to the touch, and the skin around them felt hot. The fear returned. Was she cured? Had the death of the vampire who had bitten her released her? A strange current was running through her veins, as if her blood had thickened, swelling the vessels. And then there was the thirst. There was an earthenware pitcher filled with water and a beaker on a table next to the cot. She poured the water eagerly into the cup and held it to her lips, but just as her lips touched the liquid she knew this was not what she thirsted for; the dead smell of the water repelled her, and she threw it to the floor as if it were acid.

She stifled a cry and swung her long legs out from under the fur coverings. She must find Urthred. He would know what to do, how to find Lorn and the Chalice she had seen in the dream. She had no doubts as to its existence: was it not Reh himself who had shown it to her?

It was cool in the room, and there was no fire.
Clasping her hands around her naked body, she shuffled over to her clothes and quickly threw them over
her head, then straightened her hair as best she could
with her bare hands. Now she heard voices outside.
She went to the window and unhitched the shutter.

The window looked out onto a square of packed
earth and stone shaded by an oak tree, its leaves pale
in the moonlight. Lanterns had been set out and some
brightly coloured rugs had been laid on the ground.
A fire burned at the exact centre of the area. Across
the square were single-story, whitewashed houses, and
beyond she could see the silhouette of the mountains
and the plains laid out in purple-and-brown shades
of night.

A group of about a hundred villagers, man, woman
and child, sat on the rugs. They were clad in simple
woollen jerkins and leggings. In their midst were
Alanda and Jayal. It seemed there was a deep discus-
sion going on between them and the man she recognised as Garadas, the headman of the village. There
was no sign of Urthred anywhere.

She was giddy from the moonlight, as if the light
warred with something in her soul, with the throbbing
from the wound in her neck. She retreated unsteadily
into the room and tried to compose herself. She must
go out, face her friends and these strangers.

She slipped on the cloak and unlatched the door,
steeling herself. Would she smell their blood? Could
she resist it? She stepped out of the room, finding a
corridor lit by a lantern. A door at its end must lead
onto the square. The young girl she had first seen at
the shrine was sitting on her haunches in the corridor,
but the minute Thalassa appeared, she stood up and
smiled.

Thalassa smiled uneasily in return, wanting to tell
her to go away. Did she speak her language even?
She was sure she had heard the villagers talking a
tongue similar to her own.

"Are you rested?" the girl asked. So her memory

was right, they did speak the same language though
it was thick and curiously accented, and she had to
concentrate to understand it.

"How long have I slept?" Thalassa asked.

"A day and a half," Imuni replied.

"So long?" Thalassa wondered aloud. But she had
no sleep the night before last. The two eyed each
other reticently. "Come," she said after the pause.
"Why don't we see what the others are doing outside?" The girl nodded and guilelessly offered her
hand. Thalassa hesitated before taking it. Her eyes
fixed on the blue veins in the child's neck under the
brown tan. Was she tempted? How did vampires feel?
But there was nothing, no covert longing, only that
ill-defined thirst that water could not slake. Her gums
were so dry: she felt her lips drawn back over her
teeth; surely she was baring them in a savage grimace?
She half expected the girl to scream and run away,
but she only looked at her curiously. Thalassa realised
she had been standing staring at her for too long. She
forced a more natural smile onto her face and took
Imuni's hand. They stepped out together into the
night.

Immediately they emerged from the house, all heads
turned towards them, and the hubbub of voices died
out. The villagers rose solemnly from where they were
seated. Garadas made his way through the throng and
bowed low. Some of the other villagers shuffled forward after him and knelt on the cobbles of the square.
A few held crude earthenware dishes and cups, which
they held above their downcast heads, offering her the
food and the drink contained in them. Thalassa looked
at the offerings. She hadn't eaten for two days, but
realised she had no appetite. She felt another wave of
panic and started to sway dizzily. Where had Alanda
gone? Then she saw her standing with Jayal at the
back of the crowd. Both of them were looking at her
guardedly, as if not knowing what to expect.

Thalassa shifted uncomfortably: never before had
she been the centre of such intense scrutiny, not even

in the temple of Thrull, when she had danced before
the clients after the First Lighting.

"Please," she said, after a few moments of silence.
"Return to the feast." The villagers clambered back
to their feet. Garadas held out his hand, and once
again Thalassa hesitated before taking it. The headman glanced from his hand to her face, and it seemed
to her there was a momentary flash of suspicion in his
blue eyes. But the look was gone in a second. She
reached forward and took a grip on his gnarled fingers.
She was led forward by him and Imuni, who still clung
to her other hand, to the only place of note in the
circle of rugs around the fire: a raised platform made
of coarse cushions dyed the same deep orange and
red as the rugs. Here he bade her sit, and the villagers
came forward once again with plates laden with flat
breads and gnarled apples, pulses and grains and a
wooden drinking goblet full of a pale yellow liquid.
Again, the sight of the drink repelled her. Now
Alanda and Jayal were led up and placed to either
side of her. She glanced at them nervously, then
looked down.

"How do you feel?" the old lady whispered.

She looked her old friend in the eye, and she could
see that Alanda knew, knew what she had become. "I
feel rested," she said as neutrally as she could, trying
to still the shaking of her body. She glanced around.
"Where is Urthred?"

"He is nearby," the old lady said.

"Where?" Thalassa repeated, more insistently. "I
must speak to him."

"They wouldn't let him into the village," Alanda
whispered, but then fell silent: the people of Goda
had pushed forward until they were very close to the
throne and settled themselves on the bright rugs
around her. Garadas had taken up a seat in front of
hers. White-haired men and women, the village elders,
placed themselves on either side of him.

"You are the Lightbringer, you must thank them,"
Alanda muttered.

Thalassa hesitated, seeking for something dramatic to say, but in the end the only words that came were: "I thank you for your welcome."

"It is freely given," Garadas replied, his dark face cracking into a smile. "Now my people want to bring you gifts," he continued, clicking his fingers.

Thalassa held up her hand. "The gifts of food and shelter are enough."

"No. We have waited for you for a long time. These are special gifts, ones that we have kept for the Light-bringer." He nodded, and through the circle of on-lookers Thalassa saw Imuni approaching with a large bundle held crooked in her arms. She laid it on the rug at Thalassa's feet and unrolled it. She saw that it was a white cloak, spun from the purest yaks' wool and embroidered at the hem with gold. "It is beautiful," she said.

"Every year over each generation since the founding of the village we have saved a few threads of the best wool, from the youngest of the herd, and each year the women have woven them into this garment."

It looked frighteningly large, and Thalassa imagined it sitting like a tent over her shoulders and trailing like a bridal train on the ground behind her, but she stood, and let the fur cloak fall from her shoulders. There was an intake of breath as the men saw the white slimness of her shoulders in her courtesan's dress. Imuni held the cloak up, and she put her head through the circular opening at the top, allowing it to drop over her body. To her amazement it fitted like a glove. The people saw it, too, for a hubbub of excitement echoed around the square. "Over the centuries we have measured the cloak against the Lightbringer's statue in the shrine," Garadas said. "Only last year was the cloak finally big enough. And now, the very next year, you have come." Thalassa saw a toothless old man next to Garadas nodding enthusiastically, clapping his leathery palms in glee when he caught her eye.

But Garadas continued. "Tradition also has it that

the Lightbringer must have a handmaiden as one of her gifts. . . .''

"I have Alanda; she has always served me faithfully," Thalassa said, looking around at her old friend.

"If your friend will excuse me, the tradition is that the Lightbringer's handmaid will be young, the headman's daughter, if he has one. I give you the services of my daughter, Imuni."

Thalassa looked down at the girl. She was smiling broadly, seemingly unafraid of this new role. Thalassa wondered what being her handmaiden entailed in this humble village, but accepted the offer in the spirit in which it was given. "We will be friends," she said to the young girl, and Imuni's face cracked into an even wider smile.

"Now we will feast," the headman said. Men carrying bundles of firewood had been setting up even more fires in the square, and these were lit, although the air seemed very mild, a gentle warmth sighing in from the plains below. The men next brought out spit roasts and lamb carcasses. Large pitchers of the fermented yaks' milk were being offered around, and a hubbub of conversation filled the air.

Now would be a good time to ask Alanda what had happened to Urthred, but just as she was about to do so, three old men approached. They had with them hand drums, a bagpipe and a bone trumpet as high as the man who carried it. They sat on an adjacent mat and immediately the cow horn and pipes burst into a strange wailing tune that seemed to inspirit the sparks and flames from the fires to rise ever higher into the nighttime air. The man with the hand drum joined in a monosyllabic, syncopated patter at odds, it seemed, with the wailing of the wind instruments. The young girls of the village came forward, their eyes cast down shyly and, led by Imuni, began moving in a stately dance, a type of quadrille in which partners were exchanged, in the pattern of an ever-expanding and -contracting flower petal.

The dance continued for an hour. Thalassa glanced

up. Overhead she saw the moon, the same that had reached its full two nights ago in Thrull, rise up over the snow-covered peaks. Her heart suddenly filled with a spring of well-being, of warmth for her friends; the sullen dread of what she had become could not be forgotten, but somehow the magic of the night drove the anxiety into the background. The people were kind, though she still had the nagging doubt that they would soon see what she was—then she knew what would follow: she would be driven from the village.

Jayal, too, stared at the moon. A deep frown sat on his brow. He seemed barely to notice the dancing or the music. She could guess what was preoccupying him: the double, and his father, these were all-consuming concerns. He must have finally noticed she was looking at him, for he looked around, and their eyes met. There was a strange haunted look in them, and his face twisted almost into a sneer, a sneer she had seen somewhere before. . . . Then she remembered: it was exactly how the Doppelgänger had looked when he had revealed himself to her and Urthred in the Temple of Sutis. She felt a sudden stab of fear as if all this time she had been deceived, that this man wasn't Jayal but the Doppelgänger. Jayal's look held for a fragment of a second, then he looked away hurriedly.

At that moment, the music and the dancing suddenly finished. The villagers clapped their hands against their thighs in appreciation, and the young girls joined the other villagers on the rugs. Imuni seated herself below the dais on which Thalassa sat. Now there was a stream of conversation as the villagers, apparently a garrulous lot, began chattering after the hour of silence enforced by the music.

But Thalassa's sense of well-being had gone with Jayal's look. She turned to Alanda. "Jayal is acting very strangely," she whispered.

Alanda leaned in closely, glancing at Jayal. He was still staring into the night. "Ever since the headman told him of the army in the mountains and the light on the plain, he has been like this." Then Alanda told her all that Garadas had related to them of the events six years before.

"Where did the baron go?" Thalassa asked when she was finished.

"To the north, through those mountains." Thalassa followed the direction of her finger and saw the sinister outline of the Broken Hines and the Black Cloud. Lightning stabbed through the darkness, followed by a long roll of thunder.

"What lies beyond?"

"A land called Lorn."

"Lorn?" Thalassa answered. "I just dreamt of it."

Alanda's blue eyes glimmered in the firelight. "Then there is hope."

"Do you know that place?"

"My people came from near there, driven away by the fires left by the battle of the gods. Some came here to Goda. Others fled to the south, and wandered the earth. They used to be found all over Ormorica, Galastra, Thrulland and Surrenland. They were great magicians."

Thalassa looked at the people of Goda. "But there are none other left here in the north?"

Alanda shook her head. "These folk are all that remain, and the magic left them years ago."

"So what lies to the north?"

"First those mountains, the Broken Hines. A place of evil. Now the Dark Time has come again. Garadas says that fell creatures will appear there soon, this winter or the next."

"And we have to travel over them!" Thalassa said.

"Yes, a great forest lies on the other side, and somewhere in its centre is Lorn, close to the ruined city of my people, Astragal."

Thalassa hung her head. "I remember, back on the marshes when he died, Furtal telling us of Lorn."

Alanda nodded. "He searched for it in his youth, but he was the only one of his party who survived the mountains, and he never found it."

Thalassa smiled sadly. "Sometimes I doubted whether he even crossed the Palisades, you know how he was taken by mad fits of whimsy."

"He got here all right, but no further," Alanda replied. She stared off into the distance for a little while, no doubt remembering her dead friend, Illgill's court musician. Then she seemed to compose herself once more, and turned back to Thalassa.

"Tell me more of this dream you had," Alanda demanded. Thalassa did so, telling her of the islands in the lake and the Silver Chalice and what Reh had told her of bringing the sun once more to that moonlit place.

Alanda nodded her head, as if she had been expecting this. "Beware, child. You may bring the sun again to them, but they will not thank you."

"Why?"

"You will take their guardian from them: Marizian's second artefact, the Man of Bronze. He alone keeps their enemies at bay, the same that even now stir in those mountains yonder."

"I must go there soon, Alanda," Thalassa said, clutching her old friend's hand, "before the month has gone and I become one of the undead."

They were both startled when Jayal, whom they thought oblivious to their conversation, turned to them, his eyes glittering in the moonlight. "Yes, we must go soon," he said urgently. There was the same haunted look on his face that Thalassa had noticed earlier.

"Are you all right?" Alanda asked.

Jayal didn't answer her question directly, but leant in even closer. "You are a seer. You see both as a normal mortal, but also, beyond the doors of ordinary perception, you see other things, do you not?"

"Yes: the past and the future, but only half-glimpsed, as if through a dark glass."

"Then know this," he said fiercely. "This last day and a half I have been sitting here. I should have been happy: food and drink; my father alive, maybe

somewhere close. But here," he said, pointing at the
corner of his right eye, "here there comes a dot, like
a cataract creeping to blot out my vision. I see other
views, confused scenes, panic, running bodies, dark
passages. I feel panic and fear."

"Where do these images come from?"

"From him: the Doppelgänger. He lives: he, too,
has escaped from Thrull. Every passing hour I see
more and more of what he sees. But there is more: it
is not what I see, but what I *feel*. Even though he is a
half a continent away, our minds are locked together,
struggling for domination."

"But how is that possible when he's two hundred
leagues away?"

"Because he's coming, nearer and nearer by the moment." Jayal shook his head vehemently. "Faran is
with him. That is why we have to leave immediately."

"Thalassa is too weak to travel."

"You heard her—her blood is infected. She has only
got a month to find this Silver Chalice. Think about
it." He stood abruptly and, with one more burning
glance at the two women, paced off into the night,
past the villagers who fell silent, startled by his sudden departure.

Thalassa watched him go, any feeling of well-being
destroyed by his words. Now, more than ever, she
realised she needed Urthred's advice. "You said they
wouldn't let Urthred into the village," she said to
Alanda.

Alanda looked about her warily, conscious that the
villagers could now hear them in the silence following
Jayal's departure. "Garadas spoke to him outside the
shrine. He told him he couldn't enter the village wearing his mask."

"And?"

"You know as well as I: he has sworn not to remove
it. Garadas told him of a tower on the outskirts of the
village, he's been there ever since. They have taken
him food and drink."

Thalassa thought of the priest, alone, listening to

the music coming from the village. A chill had settled on her. Safety was an illusion; she had always known it. She had travelled far from Thrull and quicker than a ray of light. But the vampire's curse had come with her. And now, somehow, Faran was hard on her heels. They must run again. She could not stay for the villagers' sakes—for their hope in her, however misplaced, as the Lightbringer; not only for what she would become, but for what she would bring. The long journey seemed to beckon her—miles and miles—mountains, forests and icy deserts, and she felt herself once more on the edge of a void of uncertainty. She must go to Urthred.

She rose suddenly, the movement bringing on a tide of dizziness. Immediately the conversation that had just started stopped again. The villagers' faces turned to her in the firelight, surprised that another of their guests was leaving so soon.

"I am going to see the priest," she said, staring around at them. "Child," she said, turning to Imuni, "will you bring me some food to take to him?" The young girl glanced at her father, who merely nodded, the smile gone from his face. The young girl started piling earthenware dishes onto a cloth that she tied at its four corners. She handed the bundle to Thalassa.

Thalassa looked around the gathering. "I'm going to the tower. Let no one follow me. I will return soon. In the meantime, eat and drink, let the feast continue." She turned to Imuni. "Where is this place?" she asked.

Imuni pointed with a trembling finger down the steep central street of the village, towards the north. "At the end of the path, a mile outside the village," she said.

Thalassa followed the direction indicated. "Good," she said. "Now I will go."

"Let me come with you," Imuni said.

Thalassa stared at her for a little while. "Very well," she answered, "but not to the tower itself; I must speak with the priest alone." She nodded for Imuni to lead off down the cobbled path. Behind her, a profound hush had fallen over the feast, but she was barely aware of it as she hurried between the low stone buildings towards the edge of the precipice.

CHAPTER SEVEN

✦

The Eagle's Perch

The priest had heard the music: it had entered his ears and filled them with the bittersweet yearning of loneliness.

He stood on the platform outside the tower. Below him the plains were black—the moonlight did not penetrate to their inky depths. It seemed that he stared into a void. In the day that Thalassa had slept, he had kept to the shadows of the tower, fretting on many things, his heart in turmoil, the quiet of the mountains no comfort. He was alone, and the solitude grated on him.

His mind was made up. He must go to the northern mountains. His destiny was there. The others could winter here, in the safety of Goda, but he could not wait. He would have left that very day, but thinking of Thalassa had kept him from doing so. He needed to know she was all right. Had the vampire's death cured her of infection? Was it not written in the *Book of Light* that when a vampire was slain, all its blood slaves were released from their thrall?

Yet he remembered her waking in the shrine, the light of the sun hurting her eyes, her dizziness. Was that the effect of the wound, or something worse, something he couldn't even bring himself to think about? He must know. Would she come to the tower? Or, if she was still too weak, maybe Jayal or Alanda would send word, tell him she was all right. He had to be sure she was safe before he left.

He had waited for her all that first day and the

entirety of the second. Now it had been dark for three
hours, and still she hadn't come.

When the music had first started he had gone outside
and looked up at the lights of the village on the shoulder of the hill. He had thought of her again, his spirit
seeking out hers until it seemed that it had shaped
itself into a grey hand winnowing in the air in front
of him, long fingers uncoiling like misty tendrils
through the darkness, stretching the mile to the village. He would touch her, make her come to the
tower. But the hope that she would come had ebbed
away as the evening progressed. The music played on
and on. Melancholy and worry in equal parts coiled
and wreathed around his chest like a restless snake.
A feeling he remembered well from those hours spent
in the tower at Forgeholm, listening to the passing
voices in the courtyard below, the rattle of pots and
pans in the kitchen wing, the solemn sounds of the
rituals in the temple. Life so close, yet so far.

In the darkness, he turned as he had in those hours
of loneliness at Forgeholm to that hidden place in his
inner soul, listened to the sound of his heart drumming
slowly, so its beat added a bass note to the music of
the bagpipes and the drums from up the hillside. At
that moment he hated the people of Goda. But it was
an unreasonable hatred: he was the demon, forever
outcast; who could argue with their fear? If he had
done what the headman had asked and taken off his
mask, what would have happened when they saw what
lay beneath it? Then they would have known the
meaning of terror.

But the irony was that now, for the first time since
the Burning, he had hope that it wouldn't always be
like this: something had happened in these last two
days. He was healing: since that long-ago day in
Forgeholm his face had been frozen into a mask as
rigid as the one he wore; but now he felt it coming to
life, blood flowing through the dead skin. He felt the
change—nearly imperceptible, but yet undeniable.

The suspicion had been confirmed the night before.

He had tossed and turned on his narrow cot in the tower, unable to sleep despite the rigours of the last two days. Eventually he abandoned the hope of sleep altogether and rose and picked up the leech gatherer's staff. It seemed to exert a magnetic pull on him: wherever he put it, even if it was out of sight, it was like an animate thing calling to him. The mutilated stumps of his fingers itched to pick it up. The wood was filled with a life of its own, and when he held it, even through his gloves, he felt energy flowing into him.

That night he struck a flint and lit a rush taper and inspected it once more. Small branches had shot from its gnarled surface, adding to the one that had burst from the bark in the Lightbringer's Shrine. Miniature oak leaves glowed in the taper light, intensely green. He sat on the edge of his cot for a while, staring at the staff in the flickering light, unable to lie down again, his body burning with energy, a strange tingling. After a while he had disassembled the gloves from their harness and stripped off his undershirt. He seized the bough with his mutilated hands. The energy was even greater now, and he noticed a faint green glow coming from the bark. He applied the taper to a tallow candle he had found and went outside into the dark, still midnight hour, naked from the waist up.

Never before, not even in the stillness of the night at Forgeholm, had he heard such silence: not a dog barked and the thunder had ceased rolling in from the north. The only sound was the gentle hum of the wind over the hill. There was a pool, a catchment area for water, at the tower's east side. He went around to it, the candle guttering in the wind. Its surface was matt black, unruffled by the breeze, the candle a flickering star reflected on its surface. He shut his eyes and knelt by its side, not daring to see what would be revealed in its reflection. He played his fingers over his body. For eight years the digits, burned to the first knuckle, had given out only a little feeling, but now, just as when sensation comes back into the legs after a long time kneeling, he felt a strange alien tingling there, and a numbed response as he traced the fingers over his skin, as if he felt another's body, not his. His eyes still closed, he explored the ridged contours of his chest. Had they flattened out somewhat? It was as if the healed skin had peeled away to reveal living flesh.

He opened his eyes and in the reflection of the pool saw that the scars on his chest and limbs were a strange white and red, as blood now coursed through the dead tissue. As he ran his fingers over his body, he was sure there was more sensation in them than there had been since the Burning. Manichee had been right, he was healing. His body had suddenly come back to life like a long dormant root putting out new shoots after the winter. He reached up one of his hands to the mask, then hesitated. He had come to look at his face in the pool, but it was too early. The hand fell back—that would be the final test. He had gone back to the tower and slept soundly until the morning.

He had awoken full of energy. Everything he needed for the journey was in the tower, left no doubt in readiness for the villagers' next descent to the Plain of Ghosts in the spring. There was rope and pitons aplenty, rock hammers, harness, warm clothes, dry rations. He had inspected the wooden stairway and what lay below it: he had had enough experience of climbing the mountains near Forgeholm before the Burning to see that the descent, though not easy, was possible. Manichee's gloves gave him strength greater than any other man's. He could make it to the plains. But he could not go until he had word of Thalassa. The day had worn on until dusk and then night. Had she forgotten him?

He had given up any hope of anyone coming when a sudden chill playing on his spine told him he was not alone. He turned in the direction of the village: the moon was up, and in its wan light he saw a ghostly figure, the colour of ivory, gliding down towards the tower through the walnut groves from the direction of the village. The figure was dressed in a voluminous, white, hooded cloak. He didn't need to see her face to know it was Thalassa. His chest tightened, and he realised he was holding his breath.

He stood motionless at the mountain's edge as she came over the last field and then onto the bare slabs of rock on which the tower stood. She stopped in front of the door to the tower. The moonlight flooded into the hood of the cloak, lighting her face. Her skin was almost translucently white, and the freckles that lightly sprinkled her nose heightened the flawless perfection of the rest of her face. It seemed even more lovely than it had been before. He tried to read her expression. Her lips trembled, but her brow was set: uncertainty, yet determination. He left the edge of the cliff and approached her.

If she was surprised by his sudden appearance, she didn't show it. She smiled nervously, one corner of her mouth puckering slightly.

He needed to know whether she was cured, but he couldn't bring himself to ask the question lest the answer was the one he feared. In the end she spoke first. "I have brought you some food." He looked down: she clutched a bundle to her chest.

"Come," he said, gesturing at the door of the tower. She followed as he pushed the door open and motioned her inside. He caught the slightest whiff of some herbal scent on her skin as she brushed past, and something beneath it, a womanly perfume. He followed her into the tower. Only one tallow candle burned on the makeshift table at its centre. He shut the door, noticing how the interior suddenly seemed cold and untidy, how rumpled the small cot was, how the scraps of last night's meal still stood on the crude table. She placed the bundle down next to the soiled earthenware dishes.

Silently, he went to the fire, which still had a few embers glowing in it, and kicked it into life, throwing more kindling on. As he stared at the fire his mind raced: what should he say?

Finally, the fire blazed, and he threw a log onto the

kindling and turned. She stood silently at the centre
of the room. She had let the cloak fall from her shoulders, and it lay like a spreading white pool around her
ankles. Underneath she wore the same flimsy dress
she had worn at the Temple of Sutis, the rents around
the neck crudely stitched, the wounds purple and
brown on the white column of her neck. The outlines
of her wandlike body were revealed by the candle
behind her. Time stood still as he stared at her. What
was she? They were so different: she had lived so
much in her short life; his life had only seemed to
begin in the last two days, the rest had been erased
by what had happened at Forgeholm.

"There is wine," she said finally, pointing at an
earthenware stoppered jug that now lay revealed
amongst the other pots on the cloth. "Will you drink
with me, Urthred?"

The request was so mundane, it caught him by surprise. He had been expecting some revelation. He
composed himself. "I can't," he said. "I would have
to take off the mask."

"Yes, the mask," she said wistfully. "That is why
you have been sent here. Because of the mask."

There was a lump in his throat, but he knew he
must tell her now. "Not because of the mask, Thalassa. Because of my face. The mask is my face: an
exact replica."

Her eyes never left his. "I know," she said simply.

"How? Did Alanda tell you?"

"No, I saw it in a dream last night. I was afraid.
But now I'm not afraid."

"But I am," he answered. "The mask is my protection." He turned and stared at the fire. "Without it
there is no hiding, no pretence. Everything will be
finished when it is gone," he whispered at the flames.

"You won't cease to exist, Urthred."

"Perhaps not." He took a deep breath. "Come, let's
sit, even if we can't drink together." He pulled back
one of the stools and she perched on it, her naked
shoulders trembling. He reached out one of the gloved

fingers to còmfort her but, just as he had at the shrine, pulled it back. Their talons would rip that delicate flesh. He sat on the stool opposite her.

"I came to tell you of my dream," she began. He looked up at her. "You were in it, as I said. You were trying to help me, but I ran from you. Then a vision came: it was as if I stood on the shores of Lorn. I was thirsty, but I couldn't drink, and then I knew, as if I didn't know already—I am infected. In a month I will become one of them."

On the instant his blood cooled, the atmosphere of the room altered: it was as if he could see the warmth like a physical thing flowing back into the night air outside. "It was only a dream . . ." he began, but she silenced him.

"Forgive me. I know it is difficult, but hear me out." She then told him of what Reh had shown her, the vision of Lorn and the Silver Chalice, how the Light-bringer would make the sun shine again on that land.

When she had finished he could only stare at her. A cure for the vampire's bite? The *Book of Light* had never mentioned such a thing. His heart had been like ice a moment before but now he found he desperately wanted to believe in Thalassa's dream, wanted to believe there was hope. He stood. "If this is true, we have to hurry. We have to leave tomorrow," he said.

"There is more," she said. "Even if I was well, we would have to go. Our enemies, Faran and the Dop-pelgänger, are near."

"But even if they escaped Nekron, it is two hundred leagues to Thrull," Urthred protested. "It would take a man a month to travel that distance on horseback. And that is not taking into account the Palisades. With the mountains it would take much longer, if it was possible at all."

She looked away at the fire. "Do you believe in affinities? That like attracts like?" The priest nodded his head. "The sword brought us here, close to its companion, the second of Marizian's artefacts, the Man of Bronze. They are of the same essence—just as the twin halves of Jayal's soul, light and dark, are but parts of one whole. Would not the Doppelgänger be drawn after its severed half, Jayal?"

He agreed silently: all magic worked by invisible correspondences. If she was right, there was even more danger in remaining in Goda.

"Are you strong enough to leave?" he asked.

"I have no choice, Urthred. I only have a month."

"Believe me, we will find this Silver Chalice before then. The Lightbringer will return the sun to Lorn."

"Aye, they all tell me that: the Lightbringer, I who cannot abide the light," she said wryly, turning away.

"Go back to the village, tell the others. We must go tomorrow, before the winter snow arrives."

"Thank you, Urthred," she said. And with one more frank stare into his mask, she rose. Picking up the fallen cloak, she slipped through the door.

He followed her, but when he got to the door, she had vanished into the night, as mysteriously as she had come.

He stood there for a little while, then went back into the tower. He picked up the flagon of wine and, with the pincers of his glove, pulled out the stopper: a smell of cloves and damsons wafted up under the mask, a smell not unakin to her scent, he thought as he took off his mask and tipped it to his throat, drinking long, hoping that the racing of his heart would stop and sleep would come, but seeing only her eyes in the moonlight.

CHAPTER EIGHT

✤

The Eater of Souls

Golon knew the properties of demons better than any other man who lived at that time on Old Earth. He had summoned them for the last thirty years. He had been born into a family that had the gift, in the far north of Ossia, in the grim windswept steppes south of Valeda. He had six brothers, all of whom, because of their gift, had been taken to Tiré Gand by the Elders at an early age. He was the youngest, but had always been the most methodical of all of them, profiting from his elders' learning, and their mistakes. Now he was the only one of the seven left alive—all his brothers were dead, consumed by their creations, their souls forever walking Shades.

But he had been careful, never rushing into the rituals, as they had done. He had memorised the nature and aspect of each of the three hundred demons in their ranked hierarchies, each painstakingly locked away in his mind. In his career as a summoner, he had called upon all three hundred, demons that came on different days as an ethereal mist, or as shimmering fire, or as a cloud of plague, or in the form of lumbering beetles as big as a horse.

No one could say where the demons came from, for they were not of the gods as humans understood them; neither were they human, if the gods had any understanding of them. They came from another world, one that Golon associated with the wan stars in the sky. The gods lived there, too, having fled to them when they had left the world at the beginning of time. They had vanquished the demons in the new worlds they found there, subjecting them to their will. Over time, man had stolen the magic of the gods from The Books of *Light* and *Worms*. And thus it was that sorcerers like he had learned how to draw the demons down to earth by their conjury.

He had meditated long and hard as he gazed at the dim light of the stars, growing darker and darker as the sun died. The stars' alien beauty mirrored well the strangeness of the creatures he brought.

And, if the demons did live in the stars, it also explained one other thing—their implacable hatred of mankind. How could it be otherwise? Were they not called from their starry thrones to do the bidding of such a low form of life as a mere human? Only in the pentagrams and holy signs was a summoner safe from the creatures he brought from the worlds beyond, and for some only the added sanctuary of a consecrated temple ritually washed with the blood of innocents would give complete protection from the enmity of the things thus brought from the ether.

A lonely life and a dangerous one, that of a summoner of demons. Twenty years of his life had been given to learning the trade. He had spent those years sequestered alone in a tower outside the city walls of Tiré Gand, a safe distance from human habitation. Not more than one in ten survived the first years of learning the demonologist's craft. And of the seven brothers who had begun, god-gifted all, he took a strange pride in knowing he alone was still alive.

In those twenty years, none but the bravest traveller had approached the apprentice summoner's tower, or disturbed his pentagrams if they stumbled across them scorched on the grass of deserted woodland groves or on the turf of the high moors.

He had survived the dangers of those years. At last, each spell had been accomplished and each one had been memorised; each hierarchy, each attribute from the "Book of Night," the part of the *Book of Worms* that dealt with the demonologist's craft. That day, he had emerged from his tower and returned to Tiré

Gand. There were few that denied he had the Craft; though now he had the power, he suspected the temple Elders mistrusted him. Was he not now stronger than they? Men came to him, ready to exchange gold for his services. Many a midnight had found him in lonely graveyards collecting the material for his rituals, lifting the grave soil from the plots, or draining the blood from corpses. For three years he had been famous throughout Ossia. Then Faran had bought his services—not with gold, but with the promise of the Black Chalice: one day it would be his.

They had marched on Thrull with the legions of the undead. On the way he had been called upon three times, and each time he had succeeded. Hdar, the breath of plague, had been called to fall upon a town on their route which had defied his lord: the demon had come in a cloud of poisoned fleas. Two days afterwards the captain of the garrison had surrendered: the battlements were manned only by corpses after the plague had swept through his ranks. Next, Strag, demon of winds, had whipped the white combs of waves upon the Astardian Sea higher than houses at his behest and drowned the navy of Galastra; the shrieking wind had sent many of Faran's men mad with its sound. Lastly, he had raised Lox, the poisoner of rivers, the night of the battle of Thrull. He had come in a green mist and defecated green maggots into the city's drinking cisterns: on the day of the battle many of Illgill's men had not risen from their beds.

He remembered each with an artisan's pride: the power unleashed upon his enemies, then safely contained and banished back to its own world. He had never lost control of a being he had summoned—until tonight.

Now he had brought Nekron, most dire of all the summonings, the most potent of all the pantheon of demons. Golon knew all too well the properties of what he'd called from the ether. Over thirty years of study and practising in the codices of the Worm, only one of the demons had etched itself on his mind with such acuity that he could not forget one fearful detail of its appearance. When he'd been a young novice at the start of his twenty years' study, he remembered the shock that had coursed through him when he'd first seen the demon on the illuminated pages of the "Book of Night," its purple body clear against the silver-and-grey background of the tome. He'd quickly flicked the page over, too scared to dwell longer on even the demon's likeness, but the form of the horned skull had become etched on his retina forever after, like the afterimage of a sudden dazzling light.

He'd never forgotten Nekron, through the slow progression through the minor circles of summonings. Even in the first of them, in a lonely barn where Golon had captured and tied up an itinerant of the steppes, Nekron had been present: after the pentagram had been drawn and the powders flung in the air, he had succeeded in bringing forth a minor demon, named Katin. It had only been a blind, white-bodied worm, some six feet long, a lower aspect of the God. It had approached the sacrifice in a series of jerky undulations of its slick white body—its maw had widened, impossibly wide, its rows of barbed teeth flecked with strings of saliva. It had consumed the sacrifice whole, the man's screams continuing for a long time as he was slowly ingested.

After he had dispelled Katin, Golon stumbled out of the barn. He stood on the rainswept moor, in a cold sweat, his heart beating wildly. He let the rain trickle down his face as he stared unseeing at the clouds. Even in this lowly demon he had seen Nekron, a faint likeness in Golon's mind, a pale reflection of what lay unrealised in the planes beyond.

After that first summoning of Katin he had felt power and revulsion all at the same time, as one who performs a dark act and forever knows the tainted but illicit joy of it. Those who tasted that dark joy could never then abandon it. That was why his six brothers had died, though they had seen the dangers all too well.

It was only years later that he knew he was ready for Nekron. He went to the temple in Tiré Gand and gathered the monks together. They'd descended to the vault of the Temple of Iss, purple-smoking censers in their hands, skull masks underlit by the harsh light. There with trembling hands he'd first drawn out the pentagrams and opened once more that page of the book that had impressed itself so much on his mind all those years before. And there he had first made Nekron flesh.

Now, once more, Nekron was no longer a mere picture in a book: he, Golon, had brought him to earth again. Against all the rules of his craft and after years of circumspection, he had done what he thought he would never do: summoned outside the magical wardings that protected those of his craft. No one in living memory had attempted this with any demon, and to do it with the mightiest of all of them was the rankest of folly.

Alpha and omega, all the darkness of the other demons was found in Nekron. He was the whole of their many parts, was the summation of all the others. He had been there in that first summoning, in that lowly, clumsy, blind worm. Now he was here at the last.

Nekron—eater of souls, Prince of the Dark Labyrinth, Iss incarnate, the serpent that ate its own tail. No warding could stave off its approach, no magic salve the wounds of its thousand teeth. Prayers were ineffectual, would only increase the hollow laughter of the Dark Prince as his avatar consumed the summoner's living soul.

So it was with the weight of one who knows he is doomed that Golon now hurried after his master down the dark corridors under the throne room in Thrull; knowing that the promise of power, and above all the Black Chalice, all those things with which Faran had enticed him into his service, were hollow now. Like his six brothers, he was destined to be destroyed by his own creation.

Golon ran with the others, already lost in the maze-like catacombs beneath the Temple of Iss, wondering how Faran found his way. He had lost sensation in his legs. It seemed he glided over the ancient flagstones down which they fled, only his fear operating his limbs.

Faran was flanked by his two vampire bodyguards, one still clutching the Black Chalice to his chest. Behind them was Calabas, his body servant, then Golon himself, followed by Malliana and the Doppelgänger and a group of nine slaves (all that remained of the hundreds who had once been in the cells); at the back, the corridors were choked with the remaining Reapers of Sorrow, many fewer than the original number. Yet they kept their discipline; when their captain ordered rear guards to fall behind to guard against their pursuer, the men did so without a murmur. But what hope had they against a creature that could pulverise rock? As they went deeper into the labyrinth of tunnels, fewer and fewer ran after them to join them at the next intersection.

It was impossible to tell how near the demon was. Though hidden by the catacombs, the rock that surrounded them magnified every sound, every tremor it made. The walls of the corridors down which they passed, walls quarried from solid rock by Marizian's creatures five thousand years before, quivered and shook as if they were merely jelly, not granite. The corridor floor was like the deck of a wildly plunging ship in a storm; he fell and hauled himself up then fell again as it rocked wildly from side to side. The passageway behind collapsed in a roar of falling rock. He knew some of his fellows had been buried, but miraculously he had not been touched. And though the passage behind was by now filled with rubble, there was no comfort there, for Nekron moved through rock as mortals walked through the air, his thousand barbed teeth grinding the rock to an invisible dust.

Where was Faran leading them? He had said they were going to the oubliettes, a place Golon had never been. They were now in the lowest depths of the Temple of Iss, below the ancient catacombs in which the undead had slept the second sleep for the generations before Faran had come.

At last, Faran halted and Golon guessed they had reached their destination. It was a corridor which ended in a cul-de-sac. He paused, his chest heaving, peering into the gloom. His hope was dashed when he saw there was no exit. They were trapped like rats in a hole. He stared around him, desperately seeking for another way out.

Water dripped down the walls, forming a green slime which glowed in the torchlight. A series of ten steel grates lay at the centre of the corridor. Though he had never been there, he knew of this place: below were the deep pits in which were incarcerated those malefactors whose blood was considered too corrupt even for the refreshing of the Brethren; men whose crimes were such that no pardon would ever be sought or given. Instead they had been consigned to die of hunger, thirst and madness in the never-ending darkness of the oubliettes.

Faran walked purposefully to the last of the openings, and, with his remaining arm, lifted up the grate. He tossed it aside as if it weighed no more than a pillow. It landed with a deafening clang on the stone floor of the corridor, drowning even the noise of the rock tremors behind. Golon briefly heard one of those imprisoned beneath the nearest grate groan out aloud. Perhaps this forgotten servant of Reh hoped that rescue had finally arrived. He watched as a white hand covered with sores stretched up towards the light of the torches. He stepped away from the groping fingers and joined Faran, who was gazing into the open pit.

A dark hole, a vacancy, was revealed below the grate. A cold blast of air rose up from below and played over Golon's bald pate. He intuited an infinite space beneath his feet. Not a pit at all: but a way down into the underworld!

One of Faran's seven-foot bodyguards suddenly materialised from the gloom of a side alcove, dragging behind him an immense coil of thick hemp rope. He tied off one end to a large ringbolt set in the floor, then, silently gesturing for the others to stand back, kicked the coiled end into the blackness below. The rope whiplashed back and forth like a snake as it spooled out, the coils disappearing more and more rapidly so that Golon felt dizzy just watching them unreel. Over and over ran the coils, and with each coil Golon's dread grew: there was a vast depth below them. He knew he would have to descend it using his meagre strength. Where was the levitation spell which he had conjured when he'd rescued Faran in Marizian's maze? But that spell only worked when the summoner could see the object of his descent. There seemed no bottom to the pit, the imagined depth below numbed his mind. The gestures and words of the ritual wouldn't come to him. Another shudder wracked the underworld, and then the sound of approaching thunder. A cry of alarm echoed down the corridors as one of the watching posts behind them was overwhelmed.

He'd have to climb, and his master, too, with his one arm.

Faran seemed unperturbed by the gaping black hole beneath him. While the first rope unwound he snapped the fingers of his remaining hand. The vampire guard fetched another immense coil and a leather-and-wood harness from the alcove. The guard threaded the free end of the new rope through a pulley set into the rock ceiling of the corridor before attaching it to the top of the harness frame. Then he kicked the coil of the second rope over the edge. Golon saw now that the first rope was merely a guide; Faran was going to have himself lowered in the cage, braking his descent with the aid of the first rope. Faran buckled himself into the apparatus, then gestured at the Doppelgänger to step forward.

The creature stood staring at Faran for a moment, a defiant smile on his scarred face. Then one of the guards bundled him forward roughly. Faran reached behind the Doppelgänger and grabbed the rope pinioning his hands.

Pain flashed on the creature's face.

"Into the harness with you, dog!" Faran snarled. "If I knew Jayal Illgill would die with you, I would throw you down the abyss without a second thought."

"And my secret would die with me," the Doppelgänger retorted.

Another tremor rocked the tunnel. Faran nodded at one of the vampire guards, and they thrust the Doppelgänger into the harness, strapping him in until he resembled a trussed chicken, his hands pushed up at an unnatural angle behind his back.

Faran gave the rope attached to the ringbolt a hard yank, and, satisfied that it would take their two weights, nodded at the guards, who pushed the harness closer to the edge. Then he fixed Golon with a stare. "Follow as best as you can; otherwise, may Iss take your soul to the Dark Labyrinth."

Then without another word he pushed the harness out over the edge of the abyss, the slack of the rope taken by the two massive vampire guards, Faran clumsily guiding them down with his single hand. The pulley squealed and groaned in the ceiling. Then he was gone.

Malliana cowered at the brink of the hole, looking into the depths with undisguised fear. "This is madness," she cried. "You see how deep the pit is!" Her eyes darted from one to another of those left in the corridor as if seeking one of their number who would refuse to go, and stay with her and face whatever dangers were coming. But already the first of the Reapers had produced another rope and cast it down into the depths, and after it had finally unravelled, the first seized it and began climbing down. Others laid hold of the hawser-tight rope and followed. Golon, swallowing his fear, thrust another man aside. He would live, of that he was determined. He seized the taut,

vibrating rope and lowered himself hand over hand,
his ankles desperately locking on to the twitching line.

Never before had he had to exert himself in such a
way. Within a few seconds, his shoulders burned and
sweat had burst from his brow—but the fear of the
infinite drop below gave him the strength that he
thought he lacked, though the twitching rope constantly slipped through his hands, burning them raw.
Down and down, the more people climbing onto the
rope above him made its antics wilder and wilder; it
sawed to the left and the right like a pendulum. He
wished that the wild movement would stop. As if in
answer to his wish, there came a sudden whoosh of
air by his shoulder and then a high-pitched scream
as someone plummeted past. For a moment the rope
stopped jerking as all of them climbing down it
stopped, listening to the faller's ever-distant screams.
They never heard him hit the bottom. Golon wondered whether the falling man had struck Faran. But
it was his own self-preservation that was paramount;
he eased his grip and began the slow descent again.

Down and down, for ten minutes or more: until
Golon knew that he would not be able to hold on any
longer and was preparing to let go and fall, for anything was preferable to the agony of his arms and
shoulders. But then, as if by a miracle, solid ground
materialised beneath his feet. He stood there swaying,
so numb that it didn't register for a moment that he
had reached the bottom. Then he came back to his
senses. Nothing had ever felt so good before as that
simple stone floor. Then the next man came sliding
down the rope, knocking him backwards. His feet
slipped on something warm and damp: the remains of
the faller. He stepped away quickly.

It was pitch-dark as the abyss at the bottom of the
pit. He groped about him blindly but found only
empty space with his fingers. He staggered a few
paces, splashing through a large puddle. Finally his
groping hands touched a rock wall a safe distance

from the bottom of the rope. Others would fall, he was certain.

Minutes passed: then he heard another scream. This time the faller must have hit others on the rope, for there came more screams followed by a succession of sickening thuds. Another silence, then he heard urgent whispers in the darkness and the clank of steel. Someone struck a spark from a tinderbox onto a pitch torch. It flared up in orange flame, but the light barely touched the darkness of the place they found themselves in: a huge underground vault, the ceiling hidden in the darkness from which they'd descended. Faran stood at the end of the chamber, holding the Doppelgänger by the collar of his cloak, the abandoned harness by their side. Somehow, the priestess and some forty of the other guards had made it down safely from the invisible heights above. As with Golon, their fear had overridden any physical weakness.

Water dropped monotonously from the ceiling, the drops falling like silver rain through the light, then pattering with loud retorts onto the cavern floor. Black puddles glowed in the feeble torchlight, and in some places there were deep pools such as the one he had waded through in the dark. Golon deduced they must be well below the level of the marsh by now. He wondered if this place had once been the city's artesian well. Rough-hewn tunnels, about twenty feet in circumference, snaked off in all directions. On the cavern walls were smooth plaques chiselled from the rough stone. They bore strange hieroglyphics in a language he didn't recognise.

The rope had stopped twitching a minute or so before. All those who were going to descend had come down. The others had fallen, or were awaiting their fate above. Faran hesitated no longer: he barked a command at those behind and strode off down a steeply descending shaft, still with a steely grip on the Doppelgänger. Two or three of the men lit torches they had carried down, but the illumination was still

only fitful. Stepping past the mangled remains of the
fallers, Golon followed.

For half an hour or more they passed through a
plethora of tunnels and workings deep underground.
The only sound was the harsh breathing of the men
and the rush of water through hidden tunnels. Perhaps
the demon had satisfied itself on those it had found
in the corridor? The underworld went deeper and
deeper. There were more of the ancient hieroglyphics
on the walls, but no other clue as to who had built
this place.

Then Golon sensed an emptiness in the air in front,
different from the close air of the tunnels. The torches
barely penetrated the gloom, but the tunnel wall
abruptly disappeared on either side. Ahead, he could
dimly see another large space and a dipping away of
the ground. In the middle distance he could make out
what appeared to be five or six white lights hanging
motionless in the air. Faran went forward, following a
series of steps that led away to the right around the
ring of the vast chamber. As they approached, Golon
could see he was following a circular rampway that
spiralled slowly down to the centre of the amphitheatre. The silhouettes of ruined buildings appeared
out of the gloom.

The lights in the air got closer and the ruins more
distinct as they circled lower. Golon looked around in
wonder as buildings loomed up out of the darkness: a
buried city, older than the gods themselves. Ancient
rusted steel piers soared up, supporting stone buildings
which must have been here since the gods inhabited
the world, their hollow cores like empty temple naves
from which the ghostly sound of their footsteps
echoed back. Now he could see the source of the lights
more clearly: towers stood drunkenly tilted at odd
angles, light shining from opaque prisms at their tops.
Did ancient magic still live at these depths? Were
there still survivors after all these years? His eyes
strained in the darkness, but no one stirred in the
towers.

The light grew stronger as they passed them, painting the haggard faces of his companions. He found he was next to the High Priestess. She had fallen into a state in which her mind had seized up, leaving only a savage grin on her rouged lips; the rest of her face was vacant, empty. Only the Doppelgänger retained something of his original calm, unbothered by the savage yanking movements with which Faran tugged him along. It seemed the ancient terrors of the place were as nothing to him.

They hurried on for another half an hour. The sorcerer thought he knew the dark byways that riddled the ancient rock of Thrull, but now he realised that his expeditions into the catacombs under the Temple of Iss had barely scratched a hundredth of what lay below. Faran and Faran alone knew this netherworld: now Golon understood how his never sleeping master had made use of the night-time these last seven years; seeking ever darker places in the heart of the world.

As they descended deeper, an ancient and primal fear crept up his spine: surely they were nearing the centre of the world, had gone so deep they were almost at the gloomy entrance to Lord Iss' Purple Halls from which no man had ever returned and from which Reh struggled every night to return for the dawn?

But though they had come so deep that, if Iss himself had reared up out of the shadows, Golon would not have been surprised, they were not safe from Nekron. He heard again a faint rumbling. The demon was still behind them. Nekron had finished feasting on those left above. Now they were the only living souls left. He would not be deflected by mere rock, rock that was like paper to the barbed terror of his mighty jaws. If a vampire could sense a living soul at fifty yards, then a universe could not separate Nekron from that scent. He would travel any distance.

The others heard the noise behind them, and seemed to guess well enough what it meant. They began to run, the torches swinging erratically. Now they were approaching the bottom of the vast hollow.

Details of the ancient ruins flashed past: stone edifices
as tall as the temples of Thrull themselves; vast curtain
walls that hurtled into the upper darkness, skeletons
of steel, each girder a man thick, enough steel to fur-
nish every army that had ever marched over the world.
But all these marvels were merely glimpsed, for the
shakings and shudderings grew louder and louder as
Nekron found their level and came thundering on
through the corridors they had passed earlier. And as
he got ever nearer Golon felt his dark mind reach out
to him, its summoner, lusting for his soul, for did he
not know, above all other men, that this was what all
summoned creatures desired, to destroy those who
had brought them from their plane to this earth?

How much further could they run?

As if in answer to this silent question, Faran stopped,
those following skidding to a halt behind him. The
guards' torches shone wanly on the ruins, but Golon
saw that the road had levelled out: they were at the
bottom of the declivity into which they'd been travelling for the last half hour. He felt the weight of the
ancient ruins rising tier upon tier all around him, right
back to the rim of the hollow where they had entered.
In front of them the road continued, petering out in
a slime-covered pathway bordered by an avenue of
shattered columns. Ancient mausoleums could just be
seen in the dim light ranged each side of the paved
way.

Beyond the tombs he could see the many-pillared
frontage of an old building, built in three tiers, orna-
mented with statues so worn by decrepit age that only
a few fluid features could be seen, as if the statues
were made of nothing more than melted wax. As
Golon drew level with Faran he saw his leader's eyes
travelling high in the darkness as though seeking out
the very pediment of the building hundreds of feet
above them.

"What is this place?" Golon asked despite the
growing fear of what followed them.

Faran thrust the Doppelgänger at one of the guards

and turned to him. "The gods dwelt underground: the whole world is crisscrossed with the canals they built under the earth. Many a time have I come here when you and your like slept, seeking for the magic of the Elder Times." He fell silent, lost in contemplation of the building in front of them, oblivious to the uneasy stirring of his companions as once more they heard the earth tremble at Nekron's approach. Then he laughed. "But all their books and their buildings are ash; the gods destroyed each other, or fled to the stars. We are all that are left, and the gods care not for us—what bitter tears." He sensed that Golon was about to say something and held up his hand. "Enough—how far away is the demon?"

Golon closed his eyes and immediately his mind was full of the dark psyche of the beast approaching at a furious pace through the passageways leading to the ruined city. "It will be here soon, master," he said simply.

"Then we will all die—you the first death, I the second. There is only one hope. Look there!" He gestured. The flickering torchlight of the guards fell on a great trough to their right, where a thin trickle of water flowed reluctantly through ruined piles of masonry.

"The barques of the gods came here in the old times of the world, riding the great silver river that carried them through the land." His words were interrupted by a mighty roar from high above them: Nekron had reached the fringes of the buried city. Everyone turned and stared in that direction. In the ghostly light they saw one of the light towers toppling slowly to one side, and a moment later there came the distant thunder of falling masonry.

A murmur of despair came from the guards and the captives. "Silence!" Faran barked and, instantly, they quietened. He turned to Golon again.

"We have one chance: we need the magic of the old times again."

"What magic, master?"

Faran leaned in even closer, his eyes burning. "Call upon the barge of the God to return. You will find a way: you have studied hard, seen the Dark Labyrinth of our master's heart. You know all the secret summonings of Iss. Fill that channel, Golon. Bring his barge from the Dark Labyrinth of the night!"

"Master, it is beyond my skill. . . ." Golon began.

But Faran seized his arm painfully. "No, you who have brought Nekron upon us can bring us this!" His eyes blazed, and Golon's senses swooned as Faran's mesmeric eyes bored into him.

"Perhaps," he muttered, falling under Faran's spell.

Another mighty shudder wracked the ruins above them, and now Golon could hear the beat of Nekron's thousand feet on the paved way down which they'd come: the demon, gathering power, was ploughing through the ruins. A mile, maybe less; it would be on them in a minute. The demon was coming for him; its power was focused on him, its maker, the most prized soul of all.

Faran's eyes continued to glare into his, flaring red in the torchlight. "Concentrate, man! Bring the river that leads to nothingness—bring Iss' silver barge!"

The sound of breaking masonry, transmitted through hundreds of feet of rock, was ever closer, each succeeding tremor like the aftershock of an earthquake. Then the rocky ceiling a mile or more above them cracked and there came a mighty roar. Thirty seconds later house-sized lumps of rock rained down, impacting the ground with teeth-juddering concussions. The air was full of the shrieking fall of rocks. One the size of a meteorite fell in front of them, sending out a choking cloud of dust, fragments of rock spun through the air—one of the Reapers twisted round and fell to the ground, disembowelled. But somehow none fell directly onto them; otherwise, they would all have been killed in an instant.

Golon for a moment thought that this was the end. He stared up at where the ceiling of the cavern must be, waiting for the rest of it to fall, but, for the moment, it held.

He was a demonologist. He had brought those that the gods had enslaved to their wills when they had fled to the stars. But he had never called upon an aspect of a god. He cleared his mind, brought the image of all the tomes he had studied to his mind. Golon's mind was like a library: locked in its stacks were many grey shelves and alcoves, stuffed with his learning, and beyond were secret doors that he himself barely ever opened. Now he followed a path he had rarely used, through avenues of half-remembered memory. The thrill of the journey possessed him now; his soul was hurrying him on.

He came to a door he had never dared open. Now he was in a forbidden place, an area where obscure spells concerned with the ancient lore of the gods resided. He paused: somewhere on the dark shelves of his mind was the spell that his master had called for, but where? Not on the shelves, not where any mortal could have plucked down the knowledge that only the gods should be privy to. No, where was the secret door that hid the last secrets? Then he found the place. An invisible portal guarded by a mauve-coloured serpent hovering in midair.

A quietness entered his soul, a quietness he'd not experienced since he was a boy. He felt the ancient currents of magic passing all around him; he saw the very shelf and the silver-bound tome in which he had first read of Iss' silver barge. He uttered a word of command and the guardian serpent vanished and there it was, the book, hanging in the darkness of his mind. He sent forth his spirit to it and the covers of the book opened and, instantly, the words were there in front of him, as clear as if he were back during those stolen moments in the library in Tiré Gand. His heart was suddenly full of the mournful song of summoning.

He raised his hands in a supplicatory manner to the empty water channel in front of him, the gesture send-

ing a thrill of power through his veins, a power that
called upon the dust of the grave and the roots that
burrowed beneath the earth, that blazed in the skulls
of dead men and their dying breaths, that lived forever
in the Black Chalice. He forgot the sound of the approaching demon, went beyond dread, to a place beyond fear. He felt his soul draining into that
bottomless well where dwelt the writhed and curled
form of life consuming life, the great snake that was
Iss, the serpent that ate its own tail. And he drew
deep. Then he came back from the depths into which
his mind had plunged, like a diver who rises to the
surface and draws deep lungfuls of air, filling his body
with the void, drawing the God into him.

He felt a smooth vibration under his feet, a contrast
to the jaw-hammering percussions of Nekron's approach. Out in the distance to the left, where the channel disappeared into the darkness, like the white cap
of a mighty wave, hovering on the point of breaking,
he saw a white luminosity against the utter blackness.
Then the whiteness rushed forward toward him, filling
the dry channel that ran in front, like mercury filling
the tube of an alembic, the light becoming ever
brighter. Then with the sound of a wave running up
a flat stretch of sand, the white liquid passed down the
channel and sped on to their right in a silver torrent.

He turned—the faces of his companions were
bathed in the same ghostly luminescence as the river,
their clothes a pearly white. Strangely, though their
lips moved, none of their words could be heard. And
he realised that the sound of the river, far from being
silent, was filling his mind with a white noise higher
pitched than any noise he had ever heard before.
Faran was gesturing off to the left with his one hand
whence the torrent rushed from the utter darkness,
and Golon turned to look.

From far in the distance he saw a dark shape staining the pure silver surface of the river, a dark shape
that became bigger and bigger as he watched until
it took substance and form, drawing level with their

position. The details of it were obscured by the dazzling light of the river. As quickly as it had appeared, it came to a sudden stop, and now, despite the glare, he saw what it was—a boat styled in an ancient manner, some four rods long, its prow shaped like a serpent, its thwarts protruding bones, its hull covered in black scales. And at the back of the vessel he saw a figure dressed all in black, a cowl hiding his face, steering the ship with an oar that was slung through a rollock of bone. And he knew that this figure was greater than even the demon he had summoned.

For had he not searched in his heart, in the grave roots of the earth? Had he not called the greatest summoning of all, greater even than Nekron? And who less than Iss' ferryman, Acharon, had come, he who transported the God through the Dark Labyrinths of the night, who took Iss' dead from the Palace of Grey to the abyss beyond? But all those who were transported by Acharon paid their fare. With a fast and certain dread, Golon stepped towards the barge, knowing what that fare would be.

CHAPTER NINE

The Feast

The feast was still continuing when Thalassa returned to Goda, but the atmosphere was now sombre. The villagers had intuited from her journey to the tower that something was afoot; some of them may have even overheard her whispered conversation with Jayal and Alanda. Rumours were circulating with the fermented yaks' milk.

In the two hours she had been away the warm wind had ceased and the air had grown colder. The square around the whitewashed buildings was now filled with a freezing mist. More wood had been piled on the fires, and they burned high, sending sparks and embers defiantly into the night. What little conversation there had been petered out when they saw her come out of the darkness.

Garadas rose to greet her and led her back to her seat. She saw that Jayal had returned as well and once more sat in abstracted silence. Thalassa was conscious of the villagers' gaze upon her. "Why has it got so cold?" she asked the headman.

He sat heavily on the rug in front of her. "The Dark Time has come," he said gloomily. "Every two generations that cloud on the mountains to the north gathers. Then the warm wind that prolongs the summer and hastens the spring dies away. This winter the frost will pinch; it will be hard for my people.

"So it has been throughout our history, every hundred years. My grandfather told me of the last time: winds that blew the herds over the mountainside, cracks of thunder like the sky being torn apart, snow that drifted as high as the roofs of the houses. The spring was late, and the ground too frozen to plant the summer seeds. Starvation followed. Only a handful survived. Now the cloud has come again, and my people are weak. Perhaps none will survive this time."

As he finished speaking the villagers sat in sombre silence. They had heard the story before, but now there was a greater sense of immediacy to the words. No one feeling the sudden cold could doubt him. Garadas drank long and hard from a bowl, his eyes closed. In the silence, the villagers turned to Thalassa, as if she would have some answer for them. She rose slowly to her feet again and looked at the faces turned expectantly towards her. "I had a friend once, a musician. Like me he was a southerner," she began. "He spoke of a land called Lorn. It lay here, in the north."

Garadas looked up from his drinking bowl. "I have heard of that place: it is one of those names passed on from one headman to the next, though no one from Goda has ever been there," he said. "It is meant to lie beyond the Broken Hines, many leagues from here."

Thalassa nodded. "No human has ever seen it. It is only heard of in ballads as old as the world, and remembered by musicians like my friend."

"What did they say of Lorn in these songs?"

She looked away as she recalled the words she had heard years before in the house on the Silver Way, remembering firelight like this, the courtiers ranged round, Jayal by her side. She glanced at him, to see if he remembered, too, but his attention was fixed once more on the passage of the moon, oblivious to all else.

"They sang of how it was a magical realm," she said, "where it was always summer, where the sweetest lutes were carved from the trunks of the evergreen trees, a place that had never known death."

"A sweet song," Garadas said. "But what of it?"

"It is said that Reh placed a creature called the Man of Bronze in that land. He strikes the Forge with a mighty Hammer, creating the warm winds that bathe these mountains. You are far to the north, the sun is weak. Yet warm winds come. Where do they come from?" She looked around her, but the people were silent, waiting for her next words. "From him. He keeps the light of his Forge burning in the Dark Time of the world. The warm wind that comes to Goda originates from there."

"Yet the darkness comes now," Garadas said. "Why doesn't he drive it away?"

"Like all things in the dotage of time, the Man of Bronze is old. He waits for someone, someone who will make him new again."

"Who is that?"

"The Lightbringer: he waits for the Lightbringer."

A hubbub went up from the crowd.

"I must journey to Lorn," she said, looking levelly into his eyes.

"You speak of old songs," Garadas replied. "But how can you be sure Lorn exists?"

"I have seen it in a dream." Garadas's brow wrinkled, and it looked like he was going to speak again, but she held up her hand. "You speak of Marizian: you believe he existed, built the city on the side of the mountain and set the Lightbringer's Shrine above it. You believed his words when he told your ancestors that the Lightbringer would come. Marizian had three great magical artefacts. One you see before you," she said, pointing at Dragonstooth glinting from Jayal's scabbard. "Another you saw seven years ago, the light that crossed the plain, the Rod of the Shadows. But the third, the Man of Bronze, is in Lorn."

"How can you be so sure he is there?" Garadas asked.

She looked around at the people. "Marizian travelled to the Southern Lands and built a city called Thrull. But even those who are nearly gods must pass from this world: Marizian died there and was buried in a great tomb." There was a collective intake of breath. "I have been in that tomb. I saw many won-

ders there, but the greatest was a scrying device he
left behind to guide the People of Light in the Dark
Times of the world. In it I saw images of the three
objects I have spoken of, as clear as day, showing
where they rested in the world. The Man of Bronze
is not far, just over the Broken Hines, in the middle
of that forest sung of in the old ballads. The Forest
of Lorn."

"The Man of Bronze heats the world, but what is the
purpose of the other two objects?" Garadas asked.

She once more fixed him with a stare. "You saw the
light upon the plain those years ago."

"It was brighter than any star," he answered.

She turned to Jayal, who had left off his abstracted
staring at the moon and now looked at her in a curious
way, as if surprised by the forcefulness of her words.
"Show them the sword," she said. As if in a trance,
he stood and unsheathed Dragonstooth. Immediately
the square was bathed in its blue-white light. "Is this
not like the light you saw?" she asked.

Garadas was staring at the dazzling light of the
blade. "It is very like," he whispered.

"See how the shadows flee before the light. But the
light of the Rod is even stronger. And the magic of
the Man of Bronze is stronger still."

"You can make him drive away the clouds and the
winter?" Garadas asked.

"Maybe," Thalassa said. "But we need to leave soon."

Garadas's expression fell. "Then our hopes are in
vain: no one can travel across the Plain of Ghosts in
winter, and no one has attempted to pass over the
Broken Hines at any time."

"There must be another way."

Once more he was silent before he spoke again.
"There might be. There is a gorge that runs across
the Plain of Ghosts. It comes from this side of the
mountains, from a place called Harken's Lair, and dis-
appears into the Broken Hines. Legend has it that it
used to be a roadway of the gods in the early times

of the world, that it was driven through the rock of the mountains, as straight as an arrow to the north."

"But none of your people have travelled it?"

He shook his head. "Years- ago, some people of Goda went into the tunnel at this end, into Harken's Lair. They spoke of terrible magic: many were slain. Since then, none have ventured near the gorge again."

"Will you lead us to it?"

He rose slowly. "The sun grows weak, the winters longer. Marizian's ghost sent you here to stop the darkness before it destroys the world. If your hope is in Lorn, so is ours. I will take you, tomorrow, before the snow comes and it is too late."

They locked eyes for a moment. "Garadas, you are a brave man," she said, "but there is something else you ought to know. Our enemies from the south are following us."

"We will face them, too, if needs be," he said. He turned to the people of the village. "Tomorrow I will go with the chosen men." He pointed at a group of warriors sitting near the front of the dais. "Be prepared." There was a stifled gasp of despair from some of the womenfolk when they heard his words, but Garadas paid it no heed. "Tomorrow at dawn," he said. "We don't have much time: I smell the snow, it is coming."

"Until tomorrow then," Thalassa said, rising, too. She bade good night to Alanda and Jayal and, taking Imuni's hand, went back across the street to the headman's house.

Her mind was full of misgivings despite Garadas's offer of help. She felt very weak, the wound in her neck throbbed, and she worried how she would react to the sunlight the next day. A next day that seemed not so far away now—it was well past midnight. She still had a month before the moon was full again. Not until then would she join the true Dead in Life. The mountains looked quite close. Lorn couldn't be too far beyond them. There, if her dream could be believed, was not only the Man of Bronze, but the Silver Chalice, too.

When she finally got to her cot and lay down on it, her mind was still whirling with a thousand warring thoughts. But the second her head touched the pillow, sleep surprised her: a deeper sleep than she had the night before, or for many years. No more dreams came to her of ancient gods. No dreams at all.

CHAPTER TEN

The Outland

Beyond the northern ranges of the sandstone mountains known as the Broken Hines lay another great plain, and beyond that the great Forest of Lorn. On its edge stood a watchtower, a mirror image of the one that stood on the cliffs of Goda fifty miles to the south. It was an old weathered construction of black basalt blocks, covered by lichen and limed by rainwater. As the sun rose, two misshapen figures could be seen standing behind the machicolations of its top, watching the southern sky.

Snow had fallen during the night, and the air was bitingly cold. Despite it being very advanced in the season, the fringes of the woods beyond showed only the first signs of autumn. The deciduous trees were just turning orange and gold.

The two creatures who lived in the tower had once been men. They had been exiled from Lorn for a long-ago crime. Their names were Krik and Stikel. Once, like all the people of Lorn, they had been immortal, but for their punishment they had been sent into the Mortal World, the place they called the Outland.

They had known nothing of the Outland before then. Nor had they known time. In Lorn the full moon always shone, and it was always midnight, always still. No shadows moved, no clouds crossed the sky; so the God had ordained it, so it would always be.

But when they came through the Moon Mere into the Outland, the mortal moon first shone on them. And as they stood dripping with the enchanted water of the lake, as quick as the poison of a serpent's bite, the curse of mortality flowed through their veins. Their skins withered and their limbs bowed, their backs crooked. They stared at their old hands, holding them up in front of them as if they belonged to strangers and had been grafted onto their arms. When they saw each other's faces they screamed. Such was the curse that they only recognised each other by their voices. All around they saw the woods and smelled the rank odour of the cycle of life: birth and decay, the sweet stink of rotting leaf mould and the bitter sap of growing things. They sat on the edge of the mere, looking longingly back at its surface, knowing that their master, the Watcher, had cursed them never to return until they saw the comet in the southern skies. The comet that would tell them the Lightbringer had come.

A new world to Krik and Stikel, each gradation of light and shade marking the passage of a moment, of ineffable, unknowable time. The moon rose and fell in the sky: no longer did it always shine at its zenith. They saw the world like the giant face of a clock: the night fled over the horizon, and the purple ball of the sun rose slowly into the sky and sank back again in the evening. Everything was in motion: the clouds moved across the sky, hurried by the hours; the shadows followed the course of the sun, foreshortening and lengthening as the day wore on; animals crashed through the foliage, then became silent.

They went through the forest with heavy hearts to where the Watcher had told them they would find the tower, and there they stayed for many years. The promise of the youth that they should have had forever slowly left them; they forgot even how they came to be here. All they could remember was that they were waiting for the comet and the Lightbringer. They had been told she would come: no one in Lorn had said when, and "when" had not been a concept that either of them had understood before they were exiled. Each hour they sat watching was an infinity to them, they who had only known infinity before.

So time had passed, and they were now very old, nearly too infirm to climb to the top of the tower to resume their watch. The day before yesterday Stikel had got up in the dark ready to relieve Krik's night-long vigil. As was his custom he breakfasted on a frugal meal of grains and pulses, then gone up to the ramparts and stood silently with his old friend.

Stikel was staring to the south, at the skies where they had been told to look by the Watcher. The sinking moon illuminated the scene. They saw in its light the plain stretching away to the Broken Hines. The mountains were the home of the Nations of the Night, the ancient enemies of the people of Lorn. The peaks soared crookedly up into the clouds that had first appeared a year before. The cloud looked like the grey gas spewed from a volcano. Lightning flashed and caught the tortured edges of the razorback ridges and underlit the cloud with angry crimson. The cloud was building as it had over the past year, thicker and thicker, obscuring the ancient ruins at their summits. It was nearly dawn, but as yet the eastern sky was not showing any grey.

But then they saw the comet, arcing through the heavens. It was as if a star hurtled through the thick cloud over the Broken Hines, a bright star that grew and grew in magnitude, its brightness dazzling against the grey of the early-morning sky—a comet falling in a scorching arc, burning a trail of vapour through the darkness. It fell, faster than the fastest kestrel plummeting onto its prey. Then, with a rippling of the air, and a blinding flash of light, it exploded with a white radiance that lit the whole southern horizon. This was the sign. The Lightbringer had come to the Outland; their waiting was over. They could return to Lorn.

But had she come too late? The night before had been the night of the full moon. The gateway through the Moon Mere would be closed for another month. More: now they were released, it seemed hard to leave their home; habit had deadened them. And they were afraid: afraid of what their fellow countrymen would do when they saw their withered faces. They would stay in the tower until the moon was full again and the gateway to Lorn stood open.

On the second morning after the comet, the sky lightened, revealing the newly fallen snow on the plain in front. A wind was blowing hard from the south, contending with the warm breeze at their backs. At each gust, flecks of the cloud were ripped from the mountains and flew like flailing ghosts, grey arms outstretched, over the plain towards their vantage point. They had often seen the mist do this in the last year, but today it looked more substantial, more threatening, as if each shred of mist carried within it a writhing figure. Neither of the old men liked the look of this: never in their many years had it happened before. They wondered what it meant, what was happening in Lorn, for all things that happened in the Outland were mirrored there.

Then it was as if the whole of the Black Cloud over the mountains began to roll towards them like a grey avalanche.

They turned to one another: they needed no words. They hobbled down the stone steps and, without glancing behind or taking any of their possessions, unbolted the tower door and ran for the safety of the forest edge. But they were frail old men, and their wind was gone by the time they reached it. They stopped, gasping for breath, and saw the monstrous wave of mist roll on, devolving in on itself, then spewing forth again, rolling inexorably forward. It was three hundred feet high or more.

Krik and Stikel didn't wait to see any more, but turned and ran again. Krik fell first, and his old friend stopped to try to help him, but Krik waved him on angrily. Stikel looked once more at him, then stumbled down the old path towards the Moon Mere, knowing his friend was going to die.

Somehow he kept going for many hours. But as he neared the lake the mists were close behind him. He reached the lake edge and began to wade into the waters, but he knew it was a futile attempt: the sun was up, the moon long gone from the sky. The first wreaths of mist overtook him and enveloped him. He felt icy fingers ripping at his soul; the world began to spin. He fell facedown into the waters. The mist pulled back like a retreating tide through the trees. Stikel's body floated on the surface, carried gently towards the centre of the lake.

So it was that none in Lorn knew that their hope, the Lightbringer, had come.

CHAPTER ELEVEN

✤

Down to the Plain of Ghosts

The second morning in Goda. In the first pale light of dawn Thalassa's eyes cracked open. Then the pain came, as if sand had been thrown into them. She clenched them shut again, the afterimage of the sun dazzling, as if she had stared into its centre all day. Her heart beat rapidly, and her mind raced. Were her eyes now too sensitive ever to look at the sun again? Cautiously, she opened them fractionally. This time, the light was a little less painful. She reached for her clothes and started dressing, keeping her eyes narrowed.

Outside in the square the sounds of preparation had gone on for most of the night and after the first hour or two's sleep, she had lain on her cot, wide-awake. Only towards dawn had the noise died away. Now it was deadly quiet in contrast: an air of dread hung over the mountain village, the stillness broken only by the distant crying of babies and the barking of dogs. Now and then she heard the calls of the shepherds and the sound of bells hung round the yaks' necks.

But there was a muffled quality to the sound, and she wondered at it. Then she realized: snow, the snow had come in the darkness.

She cautiously opened the shutters to her room. Outside was a white world. Heavy white flakes whirled over the village; the roofs of the houses were covered with a thick virgin layer; a drift a foot deep lay in the square; and the mountains were hidden by a dark grey

cloud that rolled steadily to the north like the underside of a grey sea pouring over the houses of the village. Far away the constant roar of the river seemed
muted, muffled by the white blanket that had been
thrown over the mountains. She flinched back from
the muted glare. Garadas's words came back to her
from the night before: "Going down the mountain will
be easy, but when winter sets in, we'll not be able to
return to Goda until the spring."

She shivered. It was clearly madness to be leaving
in weather like this, but she had no option. She must
get to the Silver Chalice quickly, before the month
was up. The thirst, even now, gnawed at her every
waking moment, a thirst not for water, but for something darker, richer altogether. Her veins were on fire,
throbbing to the beat of her heart.

The square was filling now: all the people of the
village, even the infirm and the sick, were gathering.
As she stood at the window, Alanda appeared like a
ghost from the fog, coming from the direction of the
other side of the square. She heard the sound of busy
preparations elsewhere in the house.

She quickly washed and put on her clothes, a thick
underlayer to go under the woollen cloak, stout shoes
that she had tried the night before. She wondered
whether they wouldn't pinch her feet, they seemed
rather small. Then, despite herself, she smiled: a small
discomfort like this was the least of her problems. All
being ready, she went out into the corridor. Imuni
stood there, dressed also in a woollen cloak, with a
pointed peak, clutching a gnarled staff and with a very
serious expression on her face. "Child, why are you
dressed like that?" Thalassa asked.

"I'm coming with you," she said, a stern frown on
her brow.

Thalassa knelt in front of her. "I told you yesterday," she said kindly. "We will return soon. Besides,
we have your father to look after us."

At this moment Garadas himself came out of a side
door further up the corridor. He was dressed in wool-

len leggings cross-strapped with leather and a hooded cloak almost as voluminous as Thalassa's. He clutched a bow and quiver of arrows in one hand and a leather satchel in the other.

He, too, saw Imuni's dress. "Imuni, I told you that you must stay here with your mother. We will be back in the spring," he said firmly.

Imuni's face puckered. "That's all that adults do—tell you this and that."

"It is good we do; otherwise, who knows what mischief you would get into," Garadas said with a small smile despite himself.

"But Papa, you will not be here for the Festival of Light."

He patted her head. "Don't you forget who we go with. The Lightbringer—she who we thank that day. Will we not be safe with her? Won't we have our own festival, wherever we are?"

Imuni looked down, her mouth set in a sulky pout. "I suppose so," she muttered petulantly.

"Come, you are the headman's daughter," Garadas said gruffly. "I won't have you showing me up in front of the other men's families." At his words, Imuni nodded heavily and, assuming what she seemed to consider a stern grown-up expression, visibly braced herself. Her father put one of his arms around her shoulders, and they went to the front door of the house and threw it open.

In front, the snow-covered square was occupied by the entire population of the village. They stretched away below the steps leading up to the house, waiting expectantly. Their breaths condensed in front of them, creating a cloud on the cold air. The handicapped and sick had been brought out and waited at the base of the steps. Everyone fell silent when Thalassa appeared with the headman and Imuni.

Thalassa saw the dozen men picked out by Garadas standing to one side of the crowd. They were dressed like the headman, with the addition that each of them carried thick coils of hemp rope around their bodies.

Pitons dangled from their belts. Half of them were bowed under the weight of packs nearly as big as themselves. They bore a motley selection of arms. Hunting bows, flanged boar spears, skinning knives. Jayal and Alanda, swathed in woollen capes as capacious as her own, stood next to them.

Garadas turned to her. "Will you bless them?" he said, nodding at the invalids lying on the stretchers in the front of the crowd. She was about to protest, but then she saw the hopeful, yearning looks in the eyes of the sick. They truly looked as if they expected her to touch them and cure them on the instant. She glanced at Alanda, and the old lady gave a small nod. Seeing her old friend standing there gave her courage, and she stepped out into the light. For an instant the increased glare seemed to blind her, and a cold fear ran through her again. But the sun was still hidden behind the snow clouds: the light was tolerable.

She turned to the east, where the sun was struggling to break through the whirling storm clouds and lifted her arms to it, and spoke the words from the *Book of Light* with which she had greeted the sun every day of her life. As she said them she felt for the first time, despite her predicament, an answering call from deep within her blood, a power, a kinship with those who had devoted themselves to the Sun's service.

Then she came down the steps and looked at the figure on the first stretcher. A child lay on it, his face was as grey as whey, and he was trembling despite the heavy layer of blankets. There was a yellowish tinge to his complexion. "What is wrong with him?" she asked Garadas.

"He has the rheumatic fever. Every year, ten or so of our children are taken by it. It's hardest when the children die: every year, the people of Goda become fewer. What hope do we have when we lose our youngest?"

Thalassa reached forward her hands and held them just above the boy's forehead. She felt the heat coming off it, and then, more curious still, it was as if she could see his life force, saw it flowing in wisps away into the cold air. She left her hands over the child's forehead a minute or so, the only sound the whistling of the wind and the low breathing of the expectant crowd, then she placed her palms firmly on his forehead, stemming the heat loss, feeling for the source of his life force. "Take off the rugs," she whispered, closing her eyes, not knowing where her inspiration was coming from, but instinctively knowing what she did was right.

"But it's cold. . . ." Garadas began, but stopped his words, silenced by the look he saw on her face. He came down the steps and slowly peeled back the layer of rugs, revealing the boy's trembling, emaciated body underneath. Slowly Thalassa cupped his head, feeling the heat, then laid it back on to the stretcher again. Then she moved down his body and placed her hands on his chest, stemming the flow, bringing warmth back into his heart. "Be like Reh's furnace," she silently prayed to the heart, "and be like the bellows of his Forge," she said to the lungs. Then she moved her hands to his abdomen, cold and white and swollen, and instilled there life-giving heat like the glowing white Egg that burned at the centre of the World. Then her hands took his cold feet, which felt like marble, and she prayed that they should become like the blazing sandals of Soron, Reh's cohort. The boy stirred as she finished her last prayer.

"How do you feel?" she asked, and the boy smiled weakly, despite the cold.

"I've been on a journey . . . it was very dark. . . ." he whispered. The crowd gasped.

"These are the first words he's spoken in days," Garadas said excitedly.

"Now," Thalassa said smiling down at the boy, "lie on your side, as if you were going to sleep." The child did as he was told, curling into a foetal ball. Then Thalassa pressed one hand on his head and one on his feet. "Let the circle unite, let the day follow the night," she intoned, and she felt energy like a lava

flow in an endless round coursing through the child's
body and through her as well, as if they were united
in one round of fire.

Presently, she lifted her hands away and the child
slept like a baby beneath her; colour had come back
into his limbs, and he breathed regularly. "Cover
him," she said. And a woman, the boy's mother she
guessed, came out of the crowd, mute thanks in her
sad eyes, and gently raised the blankets over the
child's body.

Thalassa rose, and as she did so there was a stirring
in the crowd, a murmur of admiration. But already
Thalassa had moved on to the next person, an old
woman lying on the next stretcher, her legs in
wooden braces.

As so it was for half an hour she passed from one
to another, as the crowd watched in the square, and
the men waiting for her and Garadas rested on their
packs. And each she lay hands upon went away with
their condition seemingly improved. She moved in a
trance, not knowing how or why she did things, just
knowing what she did was right. Finally she realised
she had reached the end of the line. The sun was quite
high by then. Seeing it, the dreaminess that had been
in her all the time she had been laying on her hands
suddenly vanished, as if burned away by its light, and
she felt a sudden impatience to get away.

The figures in the square separated, and she saw
Jayal and Alanda coming towards her, accompanied
by the men of the expedition. "Are you ready?" Jayal
asked, lips tight. She had noticed him from the corner
of her eye pacing the square impatiently for the last
few minutes. His whole being seemed to quiver with
barely suppressed energy. His eyes constantly flickered
to the south as if he expected any minute to see the
Doppelgänger and Faran coming like Fates over the
lip of the mountains.

Thalassa rose to her feet. "Yes," she said. "We have
a long journey."

Garadas gave orders to his men, who embraced

their families, then started down the village street in the direction of the ropeway and the tower. Garadas turned and kissed his wife, then, kneeling, did the same to Imuni.

Thalassa knelt, too, and looked into the girl's eyes. "We will be back in the spring, I promise," she said, and as she rose she slipped into the girl's hands the string of beads she had been wearing that night in Thrull, the only item of jewellery left to her. The girl sucked in her breath as she saw the stones shine in the weak light of the sun.

They stood for a moment in the snow in the square, the three southerners and Garadas and his family. There was a certain light in Garadas's eyes as he looked around at the snow-covered village, a melancholy sheen as if he didn't expect to see it again. Then he turned and, without another word, set off down the road after his men.

The villagers had gone before them and lined the way out of Goda, their heads bowed, but their eyes nevertheless turned up to see the departure of the Lightbringer. Thalassa wondered what thoughts they must have now. The ancient guardians of the place had stayed but two days and now were as abruptly leaving, going on a journey that all acknowledged was extremely dangerous: surely those who remained feared that they would be left leaderless, the wives as widows, the children as orphans.

They quickly caught up with the chosen men. One of them handed Jayal a bow and a pack. The others seemed content to carry Alanda's and Thalassa's supplies for them, so all the two women had to do was wrap their cloaks tighter arond them.

They passed between the ranks of the villagers. Like an omen for the coming journey, the cloud suddenly lifted to the high peaks above them and the road was drenched in sunshine. It was as if she had stepped from a darkened room into the noonday sun. Thalassa's vision gradually adjusted, though the brightness

seared her retinas. Good, she thought, she could still
manage the daylight.

At the end of the road out of the village there was
a white stupa marking its boundary. Here the cobble-
stones stopped abruptly, and various paths meandered
off to the fields. They set off down the path that Imuni
and Thalassa had followed the night before, through
a grove of walnut trees and fields crudely separated
by low drystone walls. Some of the villagers' yaks
grazed in them in the soft morning light. As they approached the end of the valley, the details of the plain
below and the mountains seemed minutely etched in
the shadows of the sun. Marizian's road came down
from the mountains to their right and passed like a
dark charcoal mark across the snow-covered expanse
of the prairie. Ahead they could see the grey tower
perched on its platform. To its left the river roared
over its bed of boulders in a white rage before reaching the sheer edge of the cliff and tumbling into space.
The bass thunder of the waterfall far below could be
heard even from this distance.

As they descended towards the tower the cloud lowered, and the snow began falling again. They hunched
against it. They were already cold by the time the grey
silhouette of the tower loomed in front of them. The
ramshackle wooden door at the tower's base leant
ajar: a sudden dread came to Thalassa, that the priest
had gone already. She called out into the darkness of
the interior, but no response came from within.

Then Urthred appeared from around the corner of
the tower in the swirling snow. He carried the leech
gatherer's staff and a backpack. There was a sudden
intake of breath from the men when they saw him,
and their hands went to their weapons. Thalassa stilled
them with a gesture.

She turned to Garadas. "Remember, the priest is
my friend," she said. "Do not judge him by his mask."

"Superstition dies hard," the headman answered
grimly.

"Nevertheless tell your men to treat him as one of

us now. You will need him. More than you can imagine," she said.

Garadas nodded, gesturing to his followers to put up their weapons. Thalassa turned to Urthred, her eyes narrowed against the glare despite the greyness of the sky. "Are you ready?" she asked.

"Yes, though I wondered whether you would come," he replied, looking at the blizzard.

"If this continues long, it's going to be difficult to find our way," Garadas said.

Urthred took a step towards him. He held up the leech gatherer's staff. "This will guide us, however hard it may snow." The headman looked at it sceptically.

"It was hewn from a tree in Lorn," Urthred continued. "All things have affinities with their place of origin. Its magical virtue will guide us to the forest." He turned to Alanda, who stood to one side, her old face pinched with the cold, despite her fur cloak. "You told me that your people came from this land."

She nodded. "If the Books of the Witch Queens are true, from the borders of Lorn itself."

"Then take the staff," Urthred said. "Yours is the magic of nature and its cycles: you will feel the sap of the wood flow towards the parent tree and," he said, leaning close to her, so none of the others heard, "it will give you strength."

She took the staff, her blue eyes fixed on the eye slits of the mask, and Urthred saw that she understood. She would need it on the arduous journey to come, for she was the weakest of them all. "Thank you," she said.

"Come, let's be on our way, before the snow gets any heavier," Garadas said impatiently.

He led them to the cliff edge and onto the platform at the head of the wooden steps which plunged down the slope of the mountain in front of them. To their left they could just see the edge of the river running a deep black between the rocks in the streambed. Icicles now hung from the rocks where the black waters of the river Goda, compressed into a narrow gorge, thundered over the rapids before launching themselves into space at the edge of the cliff. Such was the volume of its water that it appeared almost solid as it fell downwards, the only movement visible in its mass being fleeting flecks of grey and blue. They followed its fall until it disappeared from sight far below. A faint mist of vaporised water eddied up from the unseen depths of the gorge, and the rocks clinging to its sides were black with condensation.

The wooden steps were covered with a layer of snow. The steps ended at a buttress of rock a hundred feet down the mountain, just visible through the haze of water vapour.

Garadas led off; even on the steps the way was treacherous, the wooden slats beneath slippery, the snow coming up to their ankles, hiding danger spots underneath. They descended slowly until they reached the rock buttress. A wooden gantry with a block and tackle at its head hung over the cliff edge, silhouetted like a scaffold against the grey clouds. Beneath them all that could be seen was a lone pinnacle of rock rising out of the mists.

Garadas hauled the rope hanging from the gantry free of the snow and gave it a tug to see if its end was still secure. Then he turned to the southerners. "It is not too late to go back," he shouted over the noise of the fall. "But after we begin to climb, there can be no return."

Urthred was inspecting the rope in the headman's hand.

"How much rope have you got?" he asked.

"Enough, as long as some of the existing ropes are still sound. We'll replace the rotted sections with the rope we have brought. . . ." His voice trailed off, but his implication was clear: if they ran out before they got to the bottom, they would be stranded, unable to climb up again.

One of the men had produced a small wooden seat. He began to rig the chair to a wooden pulley set into the gantry. "We will lower the women in the chair, the rest will have to climb," Garadas said, explaining the contraption.

Garadas nodded at one of his men, who came forward. He shrugged off his pack and, taking a stout hold on the rope, swung backwards out towards the precipice, finding the cliff edge with his feet. He lowered himself in short, practised drops over the edge of the cliff, paying out the rope, and disappeared into the swirling cloud. In a minute or so, there came a tug on the rope.

"He's reached the bottom," Garadas announced. "Now we'll send down the packs and equipment." While that was being done, some of the other men were working on the seat, arranging its leather straps and threading rope through the eyeholes of the harness. The rope was then attached to the pulley at the head of the gantry. When all was ready they helped Alanda into it. All fourteen men left on the buttress took the end of the rope and gradually lowered her out of sight. After a few seconds there came another tug on the rope, and the men hauled the seat back up, the device careening wildly back into sight now it was virtually weightless.

Thalassa looked at it with misgiving. It was all right for Alanda to use it: she was an old woman. But she herself was young; surely she had the strength to climb down on her own? But it was as if the sunlight had leached her strength. For the moment she would go along with the headman's plan. She hitched her cloak around her and stepped into the harness, buckling herself into it with the leather strap. She nodded at the men, and they began to lower. She descended into the white void, black-and-white cliff faces looming out of the mist beside her.

Back at the top the others waited their turn to make the descent. Urthred stood next to Jayal. The young knight was jumpy, the agitation he'd shown in the village now grown tenfold. He suddenly whirled round towards the head of the steps as if he sensed movement there. And for the briefest of seconds Urthred, who had followed the direction of his gaze, thought that he, too, saw something standing above them in the driving mist. But then a flurry of snow came down and, when it had cleared, whatever it had been was gone.

"Did you see it, too?" he asked.

"A figure," Jayal answered.

Garadas came up at that moment: it was their turn to go down. "Is there anyone out here from the village?" Urthred shouted above the whistling of the wind.

The headman shook his head. "The snow will have driven all the villagers indoors. Why?"

"We thought we saw a figure, at the top of the steps."

The headman narrowed his eyes, squinting up at the cliff top. "There is no one there now," he said. "Come, we must hurry," he said, descending the rope.

Jayal didn't look reassured by his words but went back to where the rope waited for him. He seized it, waiting for Garadas's tug, which soon came. Glancing back one last time at the steps, Jayal did as the first villager had done, inching himself backwards off the cliff face. But Urthred could see before his head disappeared over the edge the wild haunted look in his face. What had he seen in the mist? The Doppelgänger? Faran? Their expedition was in trouble even before it had started.

Another tug on the rope signalled that Jayal had reached the bottom, and now it was his turn. He looked at the rope, realising that the metal talons of his gloves would shred it. He would use other means for his own descent. He went to the edge, ignoring the rope, and gripped the rock face fiercely with his claws and began to climb down quickly. He made good time: his gloves gave him a strength no other man could command. Once already they had saved him from death when he had swayed on the gargoyle above the moat of the Temple of Reh. This was easy in comparison.

He made it down to where the others waited on a narrow ledge. They stood getting their breath, peering down into the white world below. Then, eerily, the dangling rope by their side gave a sudden jerk, and then started vibrating. Someone else was coming down. They stared at one another. Jayal's face was sheet white. "I told you," he hissed. "They are right behind us."

CHAPTER TWELVE

To Iken's Dike

They waited as the rope twitched again, everyone's body tensed and weapons ready. But, after the initial shock, reason returned. If this was an enemy, he would be an easy target as he descended.

A figure emerged from the whirling cloud above. A very small figure it seemed, though the distance was foreshortened. Gradually some details of its dress became apparent, then a scared face peered down at them. The face of a young girl.

Garadas swore under his breath. "Imuni," he said. His daughter had followed them. Garadas went to the rope and seized the end, holding it, as she slithered down the last few feet. "What has possessed you?" he shouted, grabbing her shoulders, his face red. "Didn't I tell you to stay? Your mother will go mad with worry."

"But Papa, I told one of the other girls where I was going," Imuni replied, shaken by her father's rage. "I had to be with the Lightbringer."

The headman looked away, a bitter expression on his face. "Now I see what all this prophecy has done for us. I'm cursed for making you her handmaid." He glared at Thalassa, then turned back to his daughter. "Well, child, you have made a lot of trouble for yourself. Can't you see how dangerous it is?"

"But you have been down here hundreds of times, Father."

"Never in weather like this. No one goes down to the plains in the winter." He looked up the cliff face. "A man might climb up again, but not a child."

Urthred stepped forward. "I could take her back."

Hope registered briefly on the headman's face. Of all of them the priest had enough strength to carry himself and Imuni back to the top. But the young girl had taken a panic-stricken step away when Urthred had spoken. Like all the villagers she was terrified of him, would certainly never allow him to touch her. It was hopeless. Garadas glanced upwards despairingly and shouted, in the vain hope that another of the villagers might have ventured out and was at the top, able to winch Imuni back to safety again. But it was as he had told Urthred and Jayal: everyone was in Goda.

He turned back to his daughter. "You haven't heard the last of this. Your mother will beat you when you get back, and no one ever deserved a thrashing as much as you. But for the moment there's no other option: you'll have to come with us."

The girl tried to suppress a grin. Her father leant down to her eye level. "From now on, never leave my side, is that clear?" he said, wagging his finger in her face. The grin froze on her face, and she merely nodded.

Garadas straightened and took her by the hand and went to where the next rope awaited them.

So the climb down from Goda began, and lasted most of the rest of the day. Cliff after cliff, the waterfall a constant companion, Urthred climbing on his own, disdaining the rope. In midafternoon they heard a howl from far below. The wolves were already out on the plain.

The headman looked grim, his coal black eyes staring down into the mists. "The mountains are full of unquiet spirits who live in the ice and snow: the invisible ones that send avalanches and open crevasses, the banshees of the wind, the ice giants," he said. "Those dangers are behind. But below there are other dangers: these wolves you hear now are nothing to what follows: the Ice Wraiths, the Dark Ones who dwell in the Broken Hines, the demons that live in Iken's Dike;

and then after these wolves will come the greatest of them all: Fenris Wolf."

"What is that?" Thalassa asked.

"It is a creature who appears at the first snows. Some say it is the winter incarnate: none can tell whether it is ice or fur. It is a shadow that passes over the face of the plains, whose breath is the spirit of frost, whose claws are icy talons, whose eyes are the substance of the frozen moon. The wolves you hear now are the size of horses—and it? No one has lived who has got close to Fenris. That is why none of my people remain on the plains after the first snow."

They had reached another cliff face, where stood a pylon of stones crudely cemented together, another roughly made wooden gantry on top of it. Below was a sheer cliff face, even steeper than the ones before, plunging into the white gloom below.

"This is the greatest test," Garadas said, looking down at the drop beneath them. He spoke softly so they could barely hear him over the sound of the fall and soughing of the wind. "It is the longest descent: two ropes joined together barely make it to the bottom."

Jayal, too, peered down into the clouds. His face was ashen.

"There's more danger than just the wolf or the wraiths at the bottom," he said quietly. They all turned to him. "The Doppelgänger," he said, his eyes gazing blindly past their misty surroundings, at what he saw in his mind's eye. "He is near, knows where we are. I can tell. He can see us—as I see him."

"What do you see?" Thalassa asked.

"An underground tunnel, and a white light: he's in a type of barge. It is coming, very quickly."

"Is there any way under the mountains?" Thalassa asked Garadas.

"Perhaps. There is a tunnel, Harken's Lair, where the Dike begins. Legend has it that it goes right through the mountains—perhaps as far as your city in the Southern Lands."

"Then we must avoid it," she said.

But the headman shook his head. "There is only one way down, and the path leads us right to the entrance."

"Let our enemies come," Jayal said grimly. "At least we have had warning."

The men by now had finished unravelling the ropes and had tied the ends of two of them together in a bowline and set up a pulley with the seat. As before, one of the villagers climbed slowly over the edge, inching his way backwards. His descent seemed to take longer than any of the others before. This time it was at least five minutes before the tug of the rope came. The packs were sent down next. The chair was made ready for Alanda.

"Don't look down, whatever you do," Garadas urged, "the depths will mesmerise. Many have fallen who have looked into them." She nodded, looking pale and feeble, no more substance than a puff of wind, as the chair swung this way and that. The others lowered her slowly. It seemed an eternity before the rope slackened and they knew she had reached the bottom safely. All of the men were panting for breath, even though Alanda was no more than skin and bones. The operation was then repeated for Imuni. When she was safely down, the men looked exhausted and incapable of anything more than climbing down themselves.

Thalassa turned to the men: "You cannot go on helping me. I'm young: I'll climb—that way you will have some strength left."

"No," Garadas said. "We will use the chair."

She shook her head. "I'm strong enough."

Garadas was about to protest again when Urthred stepped up. "Let her go: I will be near if she gets into trouble."

Thalassa smiled her thanks, which he returned with a nod. He walked with her to the edge and handed her the rope. They stared at each other for the moment, then he led the way over the edge, climbing

backwards, his boots seeking purchase on the slippery
rock face. Thalassa started down hesitantly, her arms
straining on the rope. Then her feet slipped and the
rope bucked in her hands. Suddenly she was dangling
in space. She clung two-handed to the rope, knowing
the slightest relaxation of her fingers would plunge her
to her death.

She looked over at Urthred, clinging like a limpet
to the rock face two yards away. She stared into the
pitiless eyes of his mask. Suddenly she wondered
whether he wouldn't let her fall. Wasn't he a priest of
Reh, and was she not about to become one of the
Dead in Life? But now she heard his voice, reassuring,
in contrast to the cruel image of the mask. "Hold on,
I'm coming," he called. Then very cautiously he
shifted his grip on the rock and began painfully to
inch over to where she swayed on the rope.

"Take my hand," he grunted, "but be careful, the
claws might hurt you." Gingerly, she reached out and
seized his wrist above the gloves where the harness
attached the apparatus to his arm. She reached up her
other hand and clamped it on his shoulder, then swung
round, so she straddled his back. She heard him grunt
again as he took both of their weights, and the claws
screeched on the rock as he fought for purchase. "You
can't hold us both," she said urgently. But he said
nothing. Slowly, he felt below for the next foothold.
She looked down. A mistake, a fugitive gust of wind
blew away the cloud momentarily and she could see
the drop below them, all the way down to the plains
below, a thousand feet or more, and on a ledge Alanda's white hair, the smallest of dots beneath them. She
felt giddy with vertigo, and clenched her eyes shut.

"Are you all right?" Urthred asked. She nodded
slightly, holding on grimly. Inch by inch they descended until, as if by a miracle, she heard Alanda's
voice and saw that they had reached the bottom. She
let herself slip down the last few feet. Urthred followed. They stood together, breathing heavily, swaying from side to side on the ledge.

She held out her hand and touched the sleeve of his cloak. "Thank you," she said. Urthred smiled under the mask. His heart was beating quickly, but it was not all due to the exertion of the climb.

There came a shout from Garadas's man and they saw Jayal descending. The priest went over to help the villager stay the swaying motion of the rope, which became more and more pronounced as the climber got lower and lower. Jayal reached the ground, and leant against the cliff face, sucking in great gulps of air.

Once they were all safely down, they checked their equipment. There was precious little rope left: much of it had been used on the last descent.

Evening light poured in from a gap in the clouds to the west. There was a small pool on the ledge. All apart from Urthred gratefully leant down and drank from the limpid surface of the water. He, too, was parched, but couldn't take off his mask. Despite his thirst he was happy: his face tingled again. The ragged lines around his mouth, the harsh ridges of the scar tissue that crisscrossed his face, all seemed to him to be easing out: even the cartilage of the nose and ears felt like they were budding, re-forming. Even in the constricting prison of the mask it was as if a face was bursting through the old scars like a butterfly from a chrysalis.

He looked up; the Goda mountains behind were dark. In front, in the temporary abatement of the storm, shadows stretched across the level plains, long fingers groping across it from the western peaks. The Plain of Ghosts: he saw what it was, a place of evil, where dark thoughts and dark deeds had been done at the beginning of time. Marizian's road showed as a dark line in the snow heading arrow straight towards the Broken Hines. Now he was almost on the plain, the mountains opposite seemed much higher; the side shadows of their cornicing accentuated in the slanting light of evening: their shadows reached far towards the east to Shandering Plain. But their summits were lost, hidden in the jet-black clouds coiling around their shattered upper slopes. Lightning flashed in the clouds, and a peal of thunder rolled towards him, borne by the northerly wind.

Garadas called an end to the halt and led them off down a scree slope to the left of the ledge. Below they could see the edge of Iken's Dike looming through the mist, the river bounding over one more cliff, then falling into its depths. The sound of falling rocks disturbed by their feet echoed back from the vast space.

At the bottom of the scree slope, half-buried by fallen rocks, was the beginning of a stairway chiselled from the mountainside. It followed the side of the plunging gorge. To their left they could see a large rectangular opening: the entrance to Harken's Lair.

Jayal unsheathed Dragonstooth and climbed down into the chasm, his eyes fixed on the opening to the Lair. Thalassa took a good grip on Imuni's hand. If it had been dark before, all light seemed to be sucked from the air as they descended. The ground opened beneath their feet, and there were no handholds on the stone steps. A trip would have been fatal. The side of the mountain rose up behind them, swallowing them in shadow. The roar of the fall was deafening, but they couldn't see where it fell in the darkness below. Black crags steepled over their heads, nearly joining at the top from where they had descended.

The steps reached a platform: a narrow ledge ran off to the right following the upper lip of the gorge, while the other steps plunged straight down towards the utter darkness at its bottom. They were now nearly level with Harken's Lair. The cavern was some hundred feet high. A strange odour came from its depths— old metal rusting into decay. Garadas ordered one of his men to light a lantern. Jayal stared intently at the entrance. The cave was shadowed, dark, sinister.

"Who was this Harken?" Thalassa whispered, the place so oppressive she dare not raise her voice.

It was Urthred who answered. "Reh's charioteer," he replied. "He kept the steeds of the God here in the Elder Time. Some say their dragons still sleep, waiting for the God's return."

"Come, let us go," Garadas said, a nervous edge to his usually gravelly voice. He pointed to the ledge on their right. "The path follows the rim of the canyon for a mile or two, then leads out onto the plains."

"What then?" Urthred asked.

"Further on, nearer the Broken Hines, there are more steps that lead back into the gorge. We'll go down them, then follow the Dike through the mountains to the north."

Jayal had been staring fixedly at the opening of the Lair. He turned his haunted eyes to Urthred. "The double is here. I feel his presence. You know the curse— I must go and fight him, even if I am destroyed doing it."

"Why sacrifice yourself? We are nearly in Lorn," Urthred said. "Your father is there with the Rod— with it you will be able to destroy the Doppelgänger forever."

"There are more enemies than yours in the cave— creatures of the gods who hate mankind. Can you fight them, too?" Garadas added.

Jayal wavered, looking from the two men back at the cave mouth. Then the grim set to his features slackened, and he nodded reluctantly. "Very well, then. But our reckoning will not be delayed long," he said, as if addressing his invisible twin far below.

They started down the right hand of the canyon. All their eyes were locked on the last glimmer of light coming from the top of the canyon, fifty feet above their heads. As they proceeded the path rose gradually and the lip of the cliff face slowly fell towards them. They would soon be on the same level as the crags above them. After that they would be out on the Plain of Ghosts.

Each of them was so absorbed by the feeling of doom and the distant prospects of safety offered by the light, that the soul-piercing howl of the wolf pack instantly froze them all to the spot. It came from the north, where their path met the lip of the gorge.

They stood motionless for a moment or two, then the villagers started stringing their bows and nocking arrows onto them. Then the rattle of metal and wood died out and they listened. Silence except the soughing of the wind down the canyon.

"Look after my daughter," Garadas said to Thalassa. He advanced, taking a hunting spear as long as he was from one of the villagers: it had a barbed tip and flanged blade. He peered closely at the ground in front as they emerged from the canyon and followed a slight incline up onto the plain. The snow had stopped. There was the faintest glimmer left in the western sky and nothing more. The plains stretched away to the east, covered in a pristine blanket of snow; the gorge continued as a wide trench to the north.

Garadas suddenly pulled up with a start, staring at something in front of him on the ground. They hurried forward. There was a disturbed area in the snow and several sets of pawprints angling off to the north through the gloom. There was also a strong ammoniac stink, and a yellow patch where the snow had been burned down to the bare ground underneath.

"A wolf pack: Fenris's cubs," Garadas said, squinting down the line of the trail. "They've gone to the north, towards the Broken Hines. Something has driven them off."

They looked about them. The wind whistled eerily, sending up ice devils all around them.

Alanda's voice surprised them. "I feel something— an evil presence. It is close—that is what drove the wolves away."

They all turned to stare at her. Her blue eyes blazed at the light of the lantern, darting hither and thither, as if trying to seek something in the darkness.

"What do you feel?" Thalassa asked.

"Ice Wraiths—don't they call this the Plain of Ghosts? They come in the snow, in the wind, they are all around." And now they all listened, and it seemed over the threnody of the wind they heard another sound, a high-pitched whistling not of this earth. It seemed to grow in intensity as each ice devil whirled into life and fell back to the ground.

"Where are the next steps?" Thalassa asked Garadas.

"A mile or two in front," the headman replied, his eyes quartering the plains ahead, trying to find the source of the unearthly whistling. "Perhaps we should go back into Harken's Lair."

"We can't go back there: you said so yourself," she said. She turned to Urthred. "We have need of your magic."

He nodded grimly. "Leave me when the danger comes," he said. "Fire will defeat the ice: no other magic and no mortal weapon will work against what comes. Find the way into the gorge, I will follow you."

Garadas gave out orders. His men pulled snowshoes from their packs. They were made of a flat ring of wood which had been strung with corded hide. The men passed pairs to Thalassa, Jayal, Alanda and Urthred, showing them as best they could in the feeble light of the lamp how to attach them to their feet. This they finally managed to do despite their numb fingers.

"Close up," Garadas ordered, clutching his daughter with one arm and his spear in another. He motioned Urthred to precede them, and they set off. They gave the patch of evil-smelling ground a wide berth.

The light was nearly gone. The wailing of the ghosts grew stronger as it faded.

CHAPTER THIRTEEN

The Barge
That Ate Time

Acharon stood on the rowing platform at the back of the barge. The only light was the ambient silver glow of the river. His face was shadowed; it might not have even existed, for the area under his hood seemed to contain an infinity of darkness which not even the silver light could penetrate. But yet, even over the noise of falling masonry in the city behind them and the drumming of Nekron's thousand feet, they all heard a voice as cold as the touch of death coming from that area of darkness that was his face.

"Who has called me?" it asked in a bony whisper.

"I have, lord," Golon replied, looking down, not able to stare into the void of Acharon's face.

"You who are not even of the Dead in Life? You who look upon the face of Reh? Those mortals who call on me must pay a price," the ferryman said.

"I know," Golon answered, his heart ice. Acharon only dealt in living human souls. Such as his.

It seemed the ferryman's invisible eye had found the soul of his being; he felt an icy chill, running from the glacier of his heart like meltwater into his veins. With one bony flick of his wrist he knew that Acharon could take his soul as easily as plucking a flower. "You must give up your hope of eternal life; give your soul to Iss, there to live with him, until time ends, in the Palace of Grey."

Golon tried to speak again, but it was as if his tongue had frozen: no words came out.

But now his master stepped towards the barge, shouting over the roar of destruction behind them.

"Acharon, oarsman of the labyrinth. Do you know me?"

The demon turned its head slightly and appraised him. "Faran Gaton Nekron. A true servant."

"If I am as you say I am, give us passage," Faran said, staring defiantly at the creature.

A thin sound that might have been laughter emitted from the void. "I have already spoken: everything has a price—even to a true servant. The price is a soul. Yours the Prince does not need, for he already has it: it was forfeit two hundred years ago, the moment you sipped from the Black Chalice. It is already lodged in the Palace of Lord Iss. If you could see it, there in that inky place, mounted in a pyramid that houses a hundred million more. Row upon row of souls, higher than the sky. Yours is there, captive like a moth, glowing in the eternal darkness."

"Then what can I give?" Faran asked, his shoulders slumping. The men could by now barely stand on the quay, the ground shook so much. They held onto the walls and toppling pillars, just to remain on their feet. Yet curiously, the surface of the silver water in front of them did not stir.

"You will pay with the life of the person you hold most dear. Within a year that person will be dead, carried to the Palace of Grey, there to wait on Lord Iss until the end of time."

"The person I hold most dear?" Faran asked. "Who is that?"

More faint laughter echoed from the shadows of the hood. "Ask not what you already know, Faran. Only agree."

"I will," Faran replied with a spasm of his face, as if the pact was being dragged from his mouth by red-hot pliers.

"Your pain is good, Faran Gaton Nekron," Acharon said. "Iss cares not for light bargains. Mount up, you and your men, enter the barge. Tell me where and when you will go."

"When?" Faran asked.

"Aye: this river is time, it is like the never-ending circle of Iss, finding its beginning in its end and its end in its beginning. Now you have made the sacrifice; speak, you may go forward or back as you wish."

Another deafening concussion came from behind him, but Faran still hesitated, a thousand thoughts going through his head. He was tempted to tell Acharon to take him back to yesterday, when Thrull was still his, when anything had still been possible—when he could have possessed Thalassa; stopped the masked priest at the city gates; never gone to Marizian's tomb . . . there were too many other things: the thousand blunders and omissions of the day. But all that had happened had happened because it was written in the *Book of Worms*. Whatever action he had taken, surely he would have ended up in this very same predicament that he now faced?

A sudden courage entered him; only the future counted now: he would go to the north to track down his old enemy the baron, to finally resolve this war between the temples: one final combat and Illgill would be dead, Reh's light extinguished and Iss' kingdom assured. Then, and only then, the Prince of the Dark Labyrinth might hear his pleas to spare the one he had just offered up to him.

"Take me to that place where the creature known as the Man of Bronze lies."

"And the time?" Acharon asked.

"Let us get there just before our enemies," Faran replied.

"Then enter the barge: I will bring you to that time, and as near to that place as I can."

"You won't take me into Lorn?"

"No; that is a place where no servant of Iss can travel. But I will bring you to its borders."

His voice was nearly drowned by a monstrous roar from the end of the chamber, and the floor shook so hard that it was as if they rode on the back of a moving creature. Some of the guards behind them were buried in a cloud of falling masonry. The rest swallowed whatever fear they might have had of the eerie barge and threw themselves forward over its bony gunwales. Huge masonry blocks fell from the ceiling, crashing onto the quay, tripping some of the men, so they missed their footing and fell into the silver river. They vanished silently into its depths, without so much as a splash.

Faran did not waste a glance behind, but stepped onto the thwart of the barge. Even he felt the bitter cold of the bone gunwale under his booted foot, the freezing air. He looked back. The demon approached the barge swifter than a galloping horse: the buildings of the ancient city dissolving before it in a cloud of pulverised masonry dust. Since the descent which had broken her strength, Malliana had dropped further and further behind. Still a hundred feet from the barge, she fell as a rock landed next to her. She struggled to rise, but it was clear her strength was gone. Faran looked at her indifferently: she had rung the temple gong that had summoned the undead and set in train the events that had brought doom on the city. Now the demon would take her. The demon's maw deviated slightly. Faran saw the High Priestess's mouth open in a scream, but then she was taken into the heart of its purple throat. The demon didn't pause, thundering on towards the barge. Its mouth, like a lightless purple tunnel, filled the whole horizon.

Unconsciously Faran gestured to Acharon. There was a sudden giddy sensation and his feet almost lifted from the ice-cold planks, then the barge was in motion. Smoothly accelerating until, as swift as an arrow flight, yet with no sensation of movement, it hurtled over the shimmering silver river. One moment there was the image of the demon's thousand fangs, then it, and the city, were vanishing specks far away down the silver ribbon of the river. Then they were gone and

there was only darkness behind: they had disappeared
quicker than the mind could comprehend.

Faran turned. He stood right next to Acharon at
the stern of the barge. The ferryman barely moved,
though his finger joints clicked every ten seconds or
so as he flicked the ivory oar behind him, impelling
the craft forward. With each flick of his oar there was
a sudden feeling of weightlessness in the barge, and
unsecured objects that Faran and his men had thrown
into the bottom of the vessel floated up in the air,
settling again before the next oar stroke. Already, the
thread of the river stretched behind them into infinity.
The riverbanks on either side were a blur, so indistinguishable in the swiftness of their passing that they
might have actually stood still, had he not glimpsed
like images suddenly lit up by lightning, ancient struc-
tures, their facades reflected for a split second in the
silver mirror of the river, flashing past. Other craft
could be seen in those milliseconds, moored to ancient
wharves or mooring poles, their dark hulls lifting silently to the wash of Acharon's barge before it hurtled
on into the darkness ahead.

The cold was intense; the humans crouched low on
its bottom boards, their cloaks wrapped around them
in the freezing fog. The barge did not glide upon the
surface of the river, so much as plough through it, the
serpent head of the prow seeming to drink in the river
on which they flew. As if the river *was* time, and the
barge, carved in the effigy of Iss' tail-eating serpent,
consumed future time as it drove forward through the
dark tunnels. Time was a loop: so swiftly did they fly
that surely soon they would return to where they
began: then time would end. The end of the river was
the end of time.

But no. Faran had offered a soul to Iss. Not before
that soul, more precious to the Prince than any jewel,
was taken into Iss' Purple Halls would the end of
time come.

Faran nevertheless sensed a strange dislocation: how
everything that remained in the barge was the same,

but that the universe outside was changed, as if the two inhabited a different space and time. He watched as the hem of his cloak floated about him in the freezing air, like a fringe of underwater reeds. Everything was cut loose from normality—time, place, gravity—even the mind.

For such as he who had endured two hundred years already, the journey that now began, a journey that might take a second or an infinity, was of no account. His mind closed down, submitting to the will of Iss. He dreamed of many things: of his youth, of those days of laughter in Tiré Gand, of the women and song, and the night of the assassin when he'd died the first death. He dreamed of Thalassa's pale-skinned neck, and the blue river of her blood.

Then, curiously, for desire had long dried out in the arid riverbed of his veins, a longing came, a desire so different from the bloodlust of the last two hundred years. Desire, so long untasted . . . he once more savoured his mistress's lips and her body under him as they coupled that moonlight night two hundred years ago. But now it was Thalassa's face underneath him. It was as if he was alive again, alive as he would never be. As if real blood still beat in his heart and his veins, not the thick treacle that now only remained. Alive just as he had been before the first knife, like a mallet blow, had fallen on his back and he had tasted blood for the first time; his own blood filling his lungs and throat.

Hours, a day, a week, all were as one in this dreamtime when he remembered what it was like to once have lived. A heavy darkness settled on his soul, and he felt the circle of Iss growing tighter and tighter. Soon it would all be over. Iss had forgotten his promise. All dreams and wishes were futile: the circle would close, the serpent would squeeze the life out of them. Yet strangely, a peace came with the knowledge.

Yet all the time he dreamed, he was peripherally aware of movement in front of him in the barge. The humans restless in the cold, hunger and thirst gnawing

at them, their heads lowered. Were they lost in the
wretched dreams of their past, as he was? Was it a
long time, or short since they had left the underground
city? In the barge it seemed both. Only the Doppelgänger sat with his head up, staring back at Faran and
Acharon in the stern, impervious to the others. Golon
crouched over one of the Reapers, feeling for a pulse
at the man's neck. Faran knew he was dead without
Golon telling him. He watched as Golon managed to
stir two of the dead man's fellows. Together they
wrapped the corpse in a cloak, leaving his skull mask
free of the garment, an eerie mirror of the state to
come. It gleamed in the silver light as they staggered
to the thwart with their burden and hefted it overboard. The barge rocked slightly from the displacement, then ploughed on relentlessly. . . . Each beat of
the oar like a refrain in Faran's ears: to the end of
time, to the end of time . . .

Now Golon came astern. He looked pinched and
feeble, drained from his summoning, of no more substance than a paper man. He said something, but
Faran was only half-aware of his words: how there
was no food, no water. But something must have registered, for suddenly his own blood thirst started swelling: had the new moon already passed? How long had
this journey taken? a minute or a month? How many
moons had passed and he had not drunk blood? He
scented the rich berry aroma of the living blood about
him, and he felt his dry tongue pass over his parched
lips, and instantly he was awake again, back in the
conscious world.

He stared down the barge. Golon was sitting again
in the place where he had tended the dead man (how
many days ago had he returned to that position?),
struggling to keep the bundles he'd snatched from the
Temple of Iss from floating away in the strange vacuum around the barge. The Reapers, their skull masks
a white glow hiding faces that might have showed sto-
icism or despair, the vampire guards towering over all
the others, the Doppelgänger, a small smile playing

on his scarred visage facing the stern: all their faces underlit by the glow from the silver refulgence all around them. The silence was made even more eerie by the noiselessness of the passage broken only by the intermittent clicking of bone as Acharon twitched the oar in its bone rollock.

For the first time in what seemed days Faran let a tremor of anxiety enter his heart. Each heartbeat brought them nearer extinction, or to their goal. The days that Thalassa had gained on him would now be devoured by the serpent. The barge was its own universe, governed by laws beyond those of the physical world. Yet somehow he knew that, if it could have a destination in the physical world, it would be the north to where so many strands of his fate had conspired to go: Baron Illgill himself, the Rod of the Shadows, Thalassa, Illgill's son, the Man of Bronze . . . Attracted by the old magic and the intersection of the prophecies in that place.

Now he turned to the ferryman and stared into the vacuum of his hood.

"Where does the Man of Bronze lie?" he asked.

There was only silence from the ferryman for what seemed another hundred beats of the oar. Then Acharon turned his head, and Faran stared into the void. "We have a bargain, Faran Gaton Nekron; I will take you as near as I can to him. Do not ask where he is, unless you have another soul to give."

Acharon turned his head away, and the silence returned, punctuated only by the bony click of the oar.

Hours or perhaps seconds passed. Faran lost count of the click, click of the bone oars, like the metronomic ticking of a clock. But then he intuited that some crisis approached; that point where time itself creased to exist, where it folded back into itself, where the serpent consumed its own tail. The river raced by, but far ahead he sensed a vanishing point. Then, as the barge sucked in the silver reel of the river, he saw.

At the end of the silver thread, a hazy silver aura surrounded the far distance. Beyond it he sensed a

grey area, an emptiness. Was this the end of time?
The God had reneged on their agreement, they would
not go to Lorn. Instead they would be consumed by
the maw of time. He must act or face the final darkness. As they approached he saw that the light was a
ring of silver fire, some hundred feet in circumference
which blazed around the tunnel sides and over the
silver liquid. In its light as they hurried towards it, he
caught glimpses of ancient runes etched on the smooth
tunnel walls in serried columns. The writings of the
gods? A final protection against interlopers from the
Mortal World?

A heartbeat passed, then the barge swept into the
aura of silver light and he ducked, throwing his cloak
over his head. He felt an unpleasant blast of an even
greater cold than the one they had endured until now,
the cold of a total vacuum, only dissipated slightly by
the force of their passage and then, through his covering, he heard a scream. He wrenched the cloak back
and noticed that it was coated with a thick layer of ice.

Then his eyes went to the front of the barge. It was
a blaze of blue white light: one of the Reapers was
surrounded by an icy fire that burned like no other
that Faran had ever seen, the flames licking about his
body, his eyeballs bulging from his head like overripe
grapes as his frozen face shrivelled. The scream had
come from one of the man's comrades sitting next to
the burning man; the strange fire and flecks of white
flame were falling onto his armour and the bone
thwarts and tumblehome. They blistered and smouldered but didn't catch light.

Then the second Reaper came to his senses and
shouldered the blazing body over the side. The man
fell into the water without an audible splash, then was
gone. Though that danger was passed, Faran's eyes
had swung back to the prow of the barge. The silver
thread of river had disappeared, leaving an inky blackness that even his eyes found difficult to penetrate.
He glimpsed rough granite walls dripping with condensation flashing towards them. The death struggles

of the Reaper had upset the barge's delicate equilibrium: it had begun to spin, turning on its axis, broadside to the current.

He whirled around: Acharon had disappeared, the bone oar hanging limply from the rollock. They were out of control, heading towards one of the tunnel walls: the rough granite hurtled closer and closer by the second. One of the Reapers had seen the danger; he rushed past Faran and seized the oar, in an attempt to steer the barque back on course. But as his fingers touched it he underwent a terrible transformation—the flesh of his fingers withered before Faran's eyes, and his face shrunk into a mummified mask. The man's mouth opened but no sound came out. Then he swayed and fell over the side.

Cursing, Faran levered himself up and, ignoring what had happened to the Reaper, grasped the oar with his one hand. He felt its intense cold, a cold that seemed to search for his soul, but finding it gone, passed through his body into the hull of the vessel. Faran swung the steering oar violently to the left. The barge keeled hard over, nearly throwing him overboard, too, as his only handhold was the oar. But the prow of the barge was swinging, just in time. With a shriek of splintering bone, it screeched along the tunnel wall, ivory shards flying up in the air from its tumblehome. Faran wrestled for control, swaying precariously. Now one of the vampire bodyguards fought his way back to him and grabbed the oar, too, forcing it around. There were a series of further bumps, then the barge once more sailed straight ahead, its pace slackening.

Faran drew a deep breath into his desiccated lungs. Slowly his eyes swam back into focus. The surface of the water ahead was a matt black. Sound had returned, the keel now splashing through the water. He sat down heavily on the thwart at the end of the boat, his heart hammering slowly in his chest. The barge glided on, slower and slower. His light-sensitive eyes searched the darkness, saw they were entering a vast chamber. It unfolded around them, empty space soaring upwards; galleries ran round it at dizzying heights, and he could see ledges and rock cut dwellings and tombs with elaborate pediments and facades. The barge inched into the middle of it and gradually slowed to a stop, its momentum gone. Faran stood once more: the vampire guard at the oar stroked once or twice at his unspoken order, but the barge barely moved in the dark water.

Golon had also risen to his feet and stood unsteadily as the barge rocked gently under the weight of his displacement. He raised both hands as if holding up a chalice to the invisible ceiling of the chamber, and it seemed for a moment as if there was a vessel of some sort in his hands, for a grey-green light suddenly flowed downwards from it, bathing his hands and the nether regions of the vault.

In the enhanced light, Faran saw with a start that the Doppelgänger, too, had vanished. Where he had been sitting there was just his cloak, and a faint whiff of smoke that eddied away in the still air. He had not gone overboard, Faran was sure: the magic of the portal had worked differently on him. Where was he? In another time and place? Faran cursed again. He'd gone, and with him went the secret of what he had glimpsed in the Orb. Gone, too, was his ability to see into Jayal's mind. The Doppelgänger would have led them straight to the young Illgill and his party. The only hope was that Acharon had kept his side of their bargain, that they were at least close to Lorn.

He looked once more at the looming walls of the cavern. He could see canals snaking off in several directions all around them, each as likely a route as any, if the barge could be persuaded to move again.

"Where is this place?" he asked Golon.

The sorcerer looked at him, his eyes hooded by the green light hovering above their heads. "It is as Acharon promised: we are in our world."

"Then where?"

The sorcerer shrugged his shoulders. "Maybe beneath the Palisades."

"And what of him?" Faran asked, pointing to the spot where the Doppelgänger had been sitting.

"He came from Shades: maybe he has returned there."

Faran sat wearily again. For the moment, though, it was as if he could think rationally again after a long period of despair. There was even a strange tranquillity in sitting quietly in the gently bobbing vessel. There was no danger—yet. Ahead was the unknown. But men had come here before, judging by the worked sides of the tunnels and canals. And where men had come, however deep under the earth, there would be a way back to the surface.

Why had men built these canals? For the gods. Here in these tunnels the giants, dwarves, all the creatures of legend, had delved alongside man, in the darkness for centuries under the gods' cruel reign. Some of their ancient malice might still endure in these abandoned byways, even if they themselves were gone.

"Enough of the light," he ordered, and on the instant, Golon's magical beacon ceased to bathe the scene in its nacreous glow. Faran heard one of the wounded men moaning in the darkness—the sound echoed back off the walls of the chamber, doubly amplified. The noise grated on his mind. He was about to silence the man when, obviously sensing the hidden menace of his presence, he quietened of his own accord. Then the only sound was the waves lapping on the bottom of the boat. The heaviness of the ancient times descended around them like a dark blanket.

CHAPTER FOURTEEN

Harken

One moment the Doppelgänger had been sitting on the thwarts of the barge, the next, as the silver light had enveloped him, he had felt the shock of the water. He struggled in it, but his efforts were in vain. All was dark, no way of knowing which way was up or down. He thrashed his bandaged hands, trying to swim back to the air. Thankfully his cloak had gone; otherwise, he was sure, it would have dragged him down to the bottom.

But even as he struggled for his life, the thought came to him: he couldn't die, not while his double lived on this earth. Let him sink to the bottom: he would lie there in the black depths, a day or a year—it didn't matter: he was indestructible. Once more he was filled with a strange elation. He was immortal. Had he not been as badly wounded as a man could be as he lay on top of the carrion pyres on Thrull field those seven years before? Yet he had been carried away from the battlefield, mistaken for Jayal, by Jayal's sergeant Furisel and survived—as he would now. While Jayal lived he could not die.

He kicked hard and his body rose. He broke the surface and took in a great lungful of air. He trod water. There was a deep and unrelieved darkness on all sides and no sign of the barge or the silver river. The contrast between the former brightness of the river and this darkness was absolute. He heard the lapping of water against stone. Where was he? The barge had been travelling to the north. He sensed rather than knew he was deep underground. The Palisades: he was buried deep under the mountains, in a place that humans had not visited in ten thousand years.

He swam towards the echo of the waves and his hands touched a surface. The smooth side of a canal. At least that was a constant: all that had changed was that Acharon's magic had gone, the silver liquid on which they had travelled had disappeared, and he, for an unknown reason, had been cast from the barge.

During the journey the tunnel sides had been interminably uniform apart from where, in a flash of an eye, they had passed ancient ruins and jetties with stone steps leading out of the water. Was he near one now? Probably not—they had been many leagues apart. Panic seized him, but again he calmed himself. He could not die. What else was left for him anywhere on this world or in Shades apart from the knowledge that while Jayal lived, so, too, would he?

That and the thought of revenge: he breathed it in like air, the hot anger of his thoughts warmed his limbs against the numbing cold. Revenge, that was the thing to concentrate on: revenge on all the Illgills for what he had become. Desire to take what was theirs and make it his own, humiliate the baron and his son. Had he not pledged this for himself?

He clawed his way down the side of the canal, and then, as if by a miracle, his hands felt the beginnings of a slimy stone step, and above it another one. There was a way out of the canal! He hauled himself up onto the step, his naked body dripping. He felt forward: more steps. He dragged himself further upwards until he reached a platform, throwing himself down thankfully on the clammy surface. Then he lost consciousness.

When he awoke, for a moment he'd forgotten where he was and how he had got here. So many strange births in his life. Then he remembered the barge and the end of the silver river flying towards him and the silver arch of light. Faran was gone. Why had he not gone with them? Because he was not a creature of this world, of its laws, of its time; that was why. He

was and always would be on the outside of human
life. He was alone. Loneliness was best for thought.
Companionship was nothing, but an idle buzzing in
his head, a distraction. His thoughts reeled from the
despair that had assailed him on Acharon's barge on
that seemingly endless journey. He had seen that
Faran had felt it, too, the futility of the endless round
of human life. He sat, easing his cramped limbs,
squeezing his broken hands, feasting perversely on the
discomfort. Yes, he and Faran were alike. Both had
tasted of this dish of misery: Faran of the never-ending
life in death, and he, the monotonous place called
Shades, where all pleasures palled.

But though pleasure palled there was one emotion
that did not: pain. He lived for pain; pain reaffirmed
he was alive, had not been sundered completely from
this world all those years ago. Pain, pain alone—the
breath of infant's cries, screams of women at birth,
the puling lament of dying soldiers, or the curses of
old blind men—there was always pain somewhere to
alleviate the greyness of life. Pain was the centre without which nothing else would exist: the first and the
last expression of birth and death. The time between?
A mere vacancy where men waited like cattle; waited
for the hand of their master to fall on them for the
slaughter.

He could have easily laid himself down on the platform again. Sleep was pleasant. But then he remembered: as he had been unconscious, he had found
Jayal. His mind had been liberated, had flown from
this dark place, seeking out the host body from which
he had come seven years before: Jayal. And for a moment he had entered that body, and he had seen with
Jayal's eyes. A scene had come to him. It was a new
one: no longer was he in the village he'd seen before,
the rough folk dressed in yak-wool robes, a strange
festival. Now they were climbing down a snow-covered
mountain, the clouds whirling away to either side.
Something told him that they were on the north face
of the Palisades. He was close to them.

Then another thought came: if he could see with his eyes, was he not nearer Jayal's mind? Would his thoughts not touch his brother? Were they not two halves of the same soul? Would Jayal's mind not give way to him, as it had when they were children before the exorcism: Their battle was not over; it had only just begun. Slowly he would start inhabiting that mind again; the body, his stolen body, would follow. And when they found the Rod, it would be Jayal's soul that was forever cast out from it. He would go to Shades where he, the Doppelgänger, had suffered so long.

Now he noticed that it was curiously warm where he was lying in the tunnel. His maimed hands went out to the rock wall in front of him and quickly withdrew. It was burningly hot. He started up the stone steps away from the canal, careful to keep his hands away from the rock, though he felt the heat fiercely on the soles of his feet. Now his eyes sensed a dim red glow above him and, as he approached, he saw what it was, a red flow of magma like candle wax dripping through a fissure in the tunnel wall onto the steps. Now he could see the stairs climbed steeply upwards. The walls of the stairwell pulsed in and out with the heat as if they were alive. Suddenly a gas bubble burst and a gout of steam shot through the wall, enveloping him. He coughed in the sulphur cloud, fighting his way past, nimbly skipping over the half-molten blobs of lava lying on the steps.

He halted and tied one of his ragged bandages over his mouth. Then he pushed on, higher and higher, the heat becoming more intense. But now there was light glowing through the steam. At the head of the steps he found himself above a huge circular chamber. Lava flows poured through four stone canals into a round depression at its exact centre. A black metal crucible sat on a pedestal, above the boiling magma. A silver liquid bubbled in the crucible. A gantry hung over the centre of the chamber. A forge of some sort, the power of the molten rock harnessed by the gods in

ancient times. There was a passageway leading off on
the opposite side to where he had entered, reached
by a circular balcony that spiralled the chamber. The
ferocious heat was searing his lungs. He went round
it quickly, and entered the far corridor.

It led to another chamber, darker than the first, lit
only by the fires behind him. There were metal racks
built high to an arched ceiling and a dark throne at
the end of a long table at its centre. Strange tackle
hung from the racks: glittering metal bridles, which
shone with the same light as the liquid in the crucible,
their bits cruelly flanged, designed to rip at the
mount's muzzle, break the fiercest creature to the will
of its rider. Below them a rack of lances shone with
a dim blue light. He stepped closer to the table, which
stretched fifty feet or more to the dark throne, and
saw enormous tongs, pincers and a mighty hammer
lying there in a pearly white film of dust.

He strained his eyes to see what lay beyond, on the
throne. No movement. He took a step further, then
with a mighty groan, a figure, eight feet tall, levered
itself in a shower of dust off the throne, the chair itself
disintegrating at the sudden movement into a heap of
worm-eaten planks. The Doppelgänger froze in mid-
stride.

The man that stood before him was human in shape,
dressed in a cuir bouilli of ancient design, with widely
upswept shoulder pieces. His brow was dark as thunder, his face sallow, under a rocklike forehead. His
hair, unnaturally black like a raven's, was covered in
a fine patina of dust that fell slowly onto his shoulders.

The man swayed, gazing past the Doppelgänger's
right shoulder as if he could not see him, and when
the Doppelgänger looked closer, he saw that the creature was, indeed, dead blind. His eyes were milky
white orbs. He could not guess how long the silence
might have continued, but the creature stirred again,
as if recalling that it had heard a noise.

"Who is it that comes?" it said, in a deep bass voice.

"I am a traveller," the Doppelgänger replied.

"A traveller?"

"From the south, from a city called Thrull."

"Thrull? I have never heard of that place."

"It has stood for five thousand years. How could you not know of it?"

"Know then, mortal, that Harken has remained here for twice that time."

"You are Harken?"

"Aye, Keeper of the Steeds. What is it you seek in this place?"

The Doppelgänger hesitated, deciding to tell the truth. There was ancient magic in this place, and he hoped to profit by it, by getting on the ancient's side. "I was brought here against my will—I wish to travel to Lorn. . . ."

"Lorn? Now that is a place I know. My master, Reh, built it before He left the earth. Only the servants of the God may enter it," Harken said dismissively.

The Doppelgänger feared that the man grew impatient with his questions—soon he would discover that he was a creature of darkness and not of Reh. He adopted a petitionary tone: "Lord, I am only an ignorant traveller, tell me, then, how I may get to it."

Harken grunted. "Only through a thousand dangers, for the Nations of the Night lie between here and that place."

"What are these Nations?"

"Traveller, you know very little. In the fire of the last battle all the mortals perished who lived north of the mountains, for none but a god could have abided the light of that day. No human survived that did not change."

"Change?"

"Transformed by the fire that fell from the skies: they took the form of the creatures of the night, of the Dark Ones. All this I saw before the dazzling darkness blinded me."

"But you still know what passes in the world outside?"

"A thousand years is nothing to a god. I grew impatient: I wondered if Reh had forgotten me. Though my own eyes were lost, I still had the eyes of my steeds. I went to the stables and fixed a harness on one and sent him abroad, to scour the country and see what had become of the outside world. I sw through him the sorry world, blackened and covered with smoke. I saw the unfortunates crawling upon the face of the land, metamorphosed, their bodies changing, growing scaly limbs and wings, some whose bones were their skin, others who wore their internal organs like clothes outside their bodies. The dark woods were full of their wailing, some of their souls had been driven into the tortured barks of the trees. All this I saw, and saw, too, the magical realm of Lorn that Reh had made for his true servants."

"I must get there before my enemies," the Doppelgänger said.

"Enemies—what enemies are these?"

"Worshippers of Iss."

"You were brought here by servants of Iss? Where have they gone?"

"To the north, through the tunnels and canals— they, too, want to reach Lorn."

"North, you say? Then they will find the stables! The dragons will wake and fly forth upon the world, spewing fire!" Harken had become agitated beyond belief: he took one pace and then another, wringing his hands. Then he halted and thought for a moment. "You must help me." He pointed at one of the harnesses glittering from the racks overhead, its position familiar to him despite his blindness. "Reach up and take that, and bring me a lance."

The Doppelgänger looked around: the racks were impossibly high, but then he saw an ancient winching mechanism attached to chains at either end of the racks. They could be brought down to a manageable height. He went to it and hauled on the lever of the winch as hard as he could with his injured hands. There came a startling metallic groan of rusty cogs, and the apparatus began to drop towards him in spastic jerks, showering him with the accumulated filth of the millennia. Then one of the fragile chains gave way, and he dodged quickly aside as the whole came crashing down to the floor, with a roar of beaten metal. He seized one of the bridles out of the wreckage. It was a curious affair, a bridle with a harness attached. The harness had stirrups, and metal bolts where spurs should have been. He could only guess at its purpose. A strange tingle ran through his fingers, as if a million bees buzzed in his veins.

Harken seemed unperturbed by the noise. "You have it, now don those gloves," he said, pointing to some heavy lead gloves lying on the table. "You must wear them to touch the lances."

The Doppelgänger picked up the gloves: they were an absolute dead-weight in his hand, solid lead, he guessed. He wondered what practical use they could be. Nevertheless he clumsily slipped a hand into one of them, plans forming in his mind as he did so. He lifted his hand once more: the glove felt lighter now he had it on. It was as if the weight had adjusted itself by magic to his strength and hand size. He seized one of the weirdly glowing lances. More energy passed through the gloves into his body. He looked down, and it was as if he glowed with an inner light. Magic of the gods!

"I have them," he cried. "What now?"

"To the stables. You will destroy our enemies with the lance!" Harken answered, holding up a hand. It was as if half the wall on one side of the room vanished in a roar of air and grinding rock, so swiftly did a hitherto invisible slab of rock soar into the ceiling. Beyond, the Doppelgänger saw an amber-coloured corridor, bordered by glowing red lights, disappearing into the distance.

"What is it?" he asked.

Harken laughed. "The stables are many days' march to a human, but we will be there in minutes." Groping with his hands, he made his way around the table and

stood before the door. "Lead on!" he commanded,
and the Doppelgänger did so, holding the lance close
to him, as if Harken might snatch it from him. He
stepped into the corridor and immediately felt his feet
being carried bodily forward in a strange undulating
motion as if he rode on the back of a galloping horse,
as fast as Acharon's barge had travelled. The red light
of the corridor flashed past at bewildering speed as he
and Harken were drawn inexorably to their destination.

CHAPTER FIFTEEN

❖

Lost in the Snow

Garadas had allowed the single lantern to remain alight at the head of their column. They moved in single file along the edge of Iken's Dike, roped together, seeking the next set of staircases down. The snow had banked, forming a dangerous cornice over the edge of the gorge. Already one of the men had fallen through the fragile layer and ended dangling over the chasm, his life saved by the rope. The wailing of the ghosts increased as total darkness settled on the plains below the Broken Hines, only one solitary bar of red light like a bloodstain on the horizon. Ahead, the sky was as black as Hel, presaging a terrible storm. The cloud was rolling inexorably towards them.

Progress was slow, their feet lifting high in the clumsy snowshoes, their pace restricted to that of Alanda, who communed with the staff, trying to get a fix on the steps Garadas had spoken of. They lay somewhere ahead, hidden by the snow.

Their way was marked every twenty yards or so by small cairns which poked through the covering of virgin snow. But as the black cloud swallowed them, the snow fell even harder, and these became less and less distinct. Each step became more and more of a struggle. Finally they ground to an absolute halt as the wind increased to a shriek and flakes the size of autumn leaves came hurtling into their faces.

The snow speared through the eye slits of Urthred's mask. The storm was coming from the north, from those mountains which had so fascinated him ever since he'd arrived in Goda. But whatever was coming

on its black wings represented nothing good—evil was
coming. Then he saw blue forms in the grey and white
of the snow blizzard, coiling vortices of ice in which,
nevertheless, some vague human form could be
glimpsed. Ice Wraiths—malevolent spirits captured in
spectral bodies. Their touch could freeze a man in an
instant. The wailing reached a deafening level, his ears
rang like crystal, and he felt his inner core quaking.

The edge of the blizzard was only twenty yards
away. The spearman took a step forward and flung his
weapon right into the teeth of the wind. It was a good
throw, travelling arrow straight towards one of the
forms, but as it reached it, the iron tip splintered like
glass into a hundred fragments. The rest of the men
fell back into a circle, but Urthred held his ground.

Their situation was desperate, but they had hope
while there was still a faint afterglow of the sun. He
threw his gloved hands towards the last fleck of red
in the cloud, and closed his eyes. In an instant he felt
his veins begin to hum with coursing life, the heat
passing from him, through his gloves, to the west, following the fugitive sun, the descending chariot of Reh,
where it fell like a comet into the Western Oceans
beyond Galastra, where the world ended and the dark
portico of Iss' Underworld stood gaping, ready to receive their fiery cargo. Like reins of fire he saw the
sunbeams, reins that now he seized and drew back
towards him, back over the horizon so that when he
opened his eyes he saw a field of wavering red light
pulsating in front of him, the snow vaporising as it
struck it, casting a thick mist about them.

He threw his hands towards the nearest of the Ice
Wraiths and the blanket of fire pulsed forward towards
it. As the fire touched the edge of the blizzard, a tornado of ice and flame erupted into the air. Icy fragments smashed into his face mask, knocking him
down. He heard his voice shouting for the others to
run as he struggled back to his feet.

The blizzard was still rolling towards him as if it
and the wraiths within it were being manipulated by

an unnatural power. Some of the creatures had escaped the wall of fire and hurtled towards him. A twisting form brushed against his left arm and instantly his cloak stiffened with frost and he felt his veins turn to ice. More Ice Wraiths swooped towards him. Desperately he willed the flames of the wall of fire to come back to him. A red glow in the blizzard and there they were again, red candles against the white. Fire and ice met together, but the fire was dominant. He felt the ice thawing away, then there was only heat. He was engulfed in flame, the creatures' high-pitched whistling drowned by a series of explosions. He fell to the ground, unconscious, the fire singeing him. He blacked out.

When he came round he found himself lying on a patch of muddy ground, his whole body soaked. He had been saved from the fire by the melting ice. He levered himself into his elbows, staring around him. It was now utterly dark, the snow hurtling into his face, and the wind howling ferociously. But the Ice Wraiths had been destroyed. Only one fiery puddle of the wall of flame still burned on the ground, guttering and nearly extinguishing in the wind, which continued to howl around him. There was no sign of his companions. He struggled to his feet and was driven backwards by the force of the wind. He called out, but his words were whipped away in the gale. There was no point of reference in the maelstrom of flying ice and snow. Without Alanda to guide him, he was lost.

The edge of the Dike must be close. They would have gone there, seeking the way down that Garadas had mentioned. He would need light to find them. He knelt by the remaining pool of fire, sheltering it with his body from the wind. He held out his gloved hands and grasped the flickering tendrils of flame. There was no pain. He manipulated the fire, twisting it as someone who fashions clay, until he had made out of it two snakelike tendrils of fire writhing and squirming in his gloved hands; he stretched his hands up, stand-

ing slowly, and the twin snakes stretched, too, till they
stood as tall as him, their flames like streamers, flickering downwind of the gale. Then he released them,
and they fell back to the ground, where they writhed
and sparked in the snow.

He sent them a silent command to go west, to their
sire, the sinking sun. The serpents turned half circle
and were now pointing back into the teeth of the gale.
So, the wind had backed to the west, as if deliberately
blocking his path. He pushed into the wind but once
more its strength drove him back. He tried again, leaning right into it, yet barely able to keep his feet, let
alone advance. His feet slipped, and he stumbled
back—one step, then another. He was being driven to
the northeast. The struggle against the wind had taken
a lot out of him already. His limbs were frozen, and
his eyelids felt leaden; he was so tired. The cold was
numbing his brain. He would die unless he quit the
struggle soon.

Reluctantly, he turned his back to the wind and let
it blow him and the fire serpents in front of it. Now
he had no control over his feet, but, like a boat before
a storm, he was driven before the wind, the serpents
flying over the ground in front of him, burning through
the hard-banked snow, their power diminishing before
his eyes. When would the storm ease? It seemed to
follow him like a fury, blowing him further and further
towards the Broken Hines. So it continued for an hour
or more. Each time he tried to turn to the west he
was beaten back towards the mountains. He called out
again, but he knew he was too far from the others
now: the only answer was the howling of the wind
over the Plain of Ghosts.

One second the priest had been fashioning the fire
into a fiery tent around him, then he was lost in a
whirling maelstrom of flying ice and snow. Jayal tried
to force his way to Urthred's side but was pushed
back, the vortex of the storm rearing up above them
like a white wall, then spreading outwards, forcing

them back towards the edge of the Dike, separating them from the priest. At the storm's centre they saw the flames flickering for a moment, then all was lost in the whiteout.

Jayal started forward again, but Garadas seized his arm. "No! You heard him," the headman yelled. "He told us to get to safety."

But Jayal shrugged off the arm, starting back into the blizzard.

"We can't let him go alone," Garadas shouted. He waved his men forward, and they followed. But in an instant they were engulfed in the blizzard. They stumbled back, as if spat out by the vortex of snow and wind. Back and back they were driven but, unlike Urthred, they were driven to the west, towards the gaping chasm of Iken's Dike. It was as if the storm was animate, wished to blow them over its edge to destruction. Then a sudden vacancy, the edge of the Dike, appeared at their feet. They threw themselves to the ground, clutching desperately for handholds to prevent themselves being blown over its edge. The wind howled over their backs, plucking at their cloaks.

But then Alanda shouted something: she was pointing with the leech gatherer's staff. Was the staff showing her the way down into the Dike? The steps they'd been heading towards before the storm? Garadas fought his way back to his feet and waded through the snow to her side, helping her up, anchoring both of them against the brute force of the gale. Alanda was pointing back to the south, in the direction they'd come. They must have overshot their mark. He motioned for his men to follow. They stumbled along the side of the gorge, leaning away from its depths, their feet dislodging snow and ice that fell away into the blackness below. Still there was no sign of the steps.

Alanda faltered and fell against him, only Garadas's supporting arm keeping her upright. The staff fell from her nerveless hands into the snow. He snatched it up as two of his men came forward to carry her.

"The steps can't be far away," Garadas shouted at

Thalassa. He struggled through the snow towards the
looming edge of the Dike, careless of the danger of
the fragile cornice collapsing under him. The others
followed as best they could, hampered by their snowshoes, straining in the faint light to see what lay ahead.
Garadas knelt on the very edge of the gorge, staring
down into its depths. The man with the lantern joined
him, dangling it over the abyss, trying to throw light
into the murky depths. All that was visible was an
utter darkness, from which a coiling mist emerged only
to be whipped away by the blustering wind.

Garadas got back to his feet and, his eyes never
leaving it, set off down the side of the Dike, leaning
into the wind. "We have gone too far: the steps must
be behind us," he shouted.

The man with the lantern had shuffled a few feet
down the chasm side. Now he shouted excitely,
pointing downwards. Garadas hurried to him. Set into
the side of the cliff, they could see a set of rock-cut
steps emerging from under the lip of the cornice and
leading down into the gloom. The others congregated
around, eyeing the descent dubiously.

"It is our only hope," Thalassa said.

Garadas nodded and shouted orders. His men
pulled out primitive spades and set to work digging
the head of the steps out of the snow. After a few
minutes one of the spades struck something solid and
they saw the ice-covered stone beneath. They all lent
a hand now, throwing the snow aside with mittened
hands until they had uncovered the steps. Garadas
nodded at the man with the lantern, and he stepped
down into the darkness followed by the others.

They descended only a little way, halting on a ledge
some twenty feet across, sheltered from the blizzard
by an overhanging buttress of rock. The men lit more
lanterns. Their surroundings were revealed in their
flickering light. A black rock cliff face glinted back at
them from the other side of the fifty-foot-wide chasm.
The air between them was filled with steam, tinged
with sulphur. They leant over the side of the ledge,

their eyes streaming in the prickling steam. They could just see, a hundred feet below, the bottom of the ravine, and what looked like a kind of black road, running arrow straight at its bottom. Steam leaked through the sides of the ravine and from the surface of the road.

For the moment they were too exhausted to go any further. Garadas ordered them to eat and then rest as best they could. There was no fuel for a fire, and it was bitterly cold. The men laid Alanda's unconscious body on the platform. Fugitive gusts of snow periodically fell from the lip of the ravine, whirling like confetti before disappearing towards the bottom. The villagers and Thalassa slumped wearily on the icy ledge, breaking out their food supplies from their packs.

But Jayal could not stay still. He paced on the edge of the platform, staring down into the depths, the food in his own pack forgotten. It was clear he would not rest or eat, and Thalassa could not either; she was too shocked. Urthred was gone, sucked into the heart of the storm. She laid down the heel of bread she had been contemplating gloomily and rose and joined Jayal on the side of the platform.

Jayal's hood was open, and snow and ice had matted his eyebrows and the beard that had grown over his chin. It was as if he didn't see the gorge but quite another scene.

"Jayal?" Thalassa asked. "What do you see?"

He shook his head as if recovering from a heavy blow. "The dragons again. A fiery chamber and the dragons."

"Harken's Lair?" They both looked down the dark line of the chasm to their left. "He is so close now," Jayal said. He clutched the salamander hilt of Dragonstooth tightly, his jaw set, his eyes grim. "I'm ready for him," he said. "Though we both go to Shades together, I must finish this!"

She looked back through the darkness towards the entrance to Harken's Lair.

"We must set up a watch," she said.

Jayal nodded, though his sweat-beaded brow was still very pale. "I will watch first."

"Why don't you rest?" Thalassa asked.

He shook his head. "Why deprive others? I will not sleep. Let me watch."

"Others must share the burden: come, I have some food," she said, leading him away from the edge of the platform, to where the scraps of her meal were laid out on a cloth. He sat mechanically, and she handed him some bread. He began to chew, then the movement stopped and he stared once more into the darkness of the opposing wall of the chasm.

She watched him surreptitiously from the corner of her eye. He was changing even as she watched, his mind completely given up to the mental struggle with the Doppelgänger. Worry lines etched what once had been a smooth, youthful brow, and there were bags under his eyes. There was no hope left in them now.

Perhaps her hopes, too, had gone. The wound throbbed in her neck, and her veins seemed slow and sluggish. It was coming. Nothing except the Silver Chalice could save her. What had happened to Urthred? She was sure he was still alive, that she would have felt it in her bones if he had died. He would find a way back to them, she told herself.

Garadas now approached, indicating the man he had detailed to take the first watch. The headman looked sideways at Jayal, his eyebrow raised interrogatively. "I will watch, too," he said quietly. The headman nodded his understanding and gave his orders, and they all settled down for what promised to be an uncomfortable night. Thalassa now knelt by Alanda: she had recovered consciousness. Garadas had given her back the staff, and she clutched it, as if her life depended on it. Her face was ashen and her breathing shallow. Thalassa wondered whether Alanda could survive the night. Only the staff and the promise of Lorn somewhere to the north seemed to sustain her.

CHAPTER SIXTEEN

Marizian's Road

U rthred followed the twin tracks of the fiery serpents, while the blizzard kept up at his back, driving him even further from his friends. Instead of going
to the west, he was being driven to the north, towards
the Broken Hines, straight towards the origins of the
storm.

At around midnight he glimpsed the raised line of
Marizian's road through the driving snow. He climbed
up to its pavement. Its surface glowed in the light of
the fire snakes: strangely, the snow had not settled on
its surface. It might have been built only yesterday.
Its surface was a smooth white marble, completely un-
pitted, each block perfectly aligned with another. He
felt a strange tingling coming from its surface through
the soles of his sandals. Where the snowflakes struck
the road they melted instantly, burned away by a hidden energy. The magic of the wizard was still present
in its ancient stones.

He looked back to the south. The storm still raged,
ice cutting into his mask. He struggled with it a moment, but it was hopeless. He was too weak to fight
the unremitting wind. He relaxed his shoulders and
allowed it to take him up the road. As he progressed
some energy seeped back into his body, his sandalled
feet curiously light. It was as if the road moved as
well as his feet, carrying him northwards at twice the
speed he had made before. The serpents slithered forward on the white marble, burning brightly once more
as if they, too, were reinspirited by the ancient magic
in its stone.

Now the wind died, and he looked back—the edge
of the blizzard stood motionless to the south, like a
wall. On one side a gale, yet above him was the still
night air, the stars shining. He took a step back, but
as he did so the storm pulsed forward once more, a
tendrils of howling wind lashing into him. Now he
knew the storm was indeed animate, possessed of a
malevolent spirit, herding him towards the mountains,
further and further from his friends. He turned and
the blizzard instantly died, as if it sensed that his will
was broken, that he would go the way it wanted him
to go. The fire serpents blazed back to life. He gestured them forward down the road and followed. In
front the mountains loomed, each step towards them
taking him further from his friends.

Three hours later he saw in front the road begin to
lift upwards towards the spurs and foothills of the Broken Hines: the moon shone down, lighting the way. He
could see the black silhouettes of the mountains and the
dark cloud that had spawned the storm hanging over
their summits, shot through with flashes of lightning.
On either side of the road the hitherto flat plain began
to undulate, rising in low ridges. The road cut arrow
straight through them, leading ever up towards where
the first dark basalt buttresses of the mountains began.

He began to climb. Whatever energy was in the
road seemed to dissipate, and his legs began to feel
laden, his head fell, his breathing strangled as the air
thinned. He would have to rest soon, but where? He
lifted his head and peered forward at the terrain in
front. He hadn't noticed it at first, but in the hazy
serpent light in the snow and almost camouflaged by
the grey cliffs, he saw the outline of a tower, slightly
ahead of him. It was similar to the one on the outskirts
of Goda. Even from this distance it seemed to have a
deserted air. He would rest there until dawn.

He left the road and waded through the drifts to
the entrance to the watchtower. Its door had long ago
been blown in by a storm. Inside the circular stone
floor was bare, and there was no tinder in its fireplace.

He sent the serpents before him, into the hearth. With a gesture from him, they coiled up. He wrapped himself in his cloak and propped himself against the wall next the fire. The serpents glowed for a while, heating the room imperceptibly, but their magical life was ordained only to last a limited time, and now it began to leach away. Soon they faded to grey ash.

Despite the hardness of the floor and the intense cold, he drifted off into sleep. An hour later he was woken by a roar of thunder that echoed down from the mountains above. He drifted back to sleep, but the thunder came again and this time he thought he heard a voice in that thunder, a voice that brought a distant memory, a voice of command. The voice spoke to him, telling him to get up and start climbing the mountain. He levered himself away from the wall, half-awake, ready to obey unconsciously, but before he could stand his strength slipped away, and he drifted back into another fitful sleep.

It seemed he had hardly rested when grey light began seeping through the doorway telling him it was dawn. Now he could see a barrel-vaulted ceiling above him, and a circular stone stairway built into the thick sidewall. He rose stiffly, stamping his feet to get his circulation going again, and pushed himself into the narrow confines of the stairway, bending his lanky body as he climbed. He pushed out through the snow covering the top of the tower. Above he could see the Broken Hines intermittently through the driving storm clouds. Back the way he had come the night before there were only fleeting views of Marizian's road through the falling snow. The edge of the blizzard still hung where he had last seen it a few miles back, waiting like a vengeful ghost.

He descended to the chamber below and pulled out his supplies: some bread, now going stale, goats' cheeses and strips of dried meat, plus one or two of the bitter apples, the last of the harvest he had seen clinging to the spindly orchard trees in Goda. He ate sparingly, not knowing where he would find any more.

Then he unstoppered the wine Thalassa had brought
two nights ago; again he caught a fugitive scent of her
perfume as he drank. His thoughts lingered on their
meeting: her cloak on the floor, the outline of her
body silhouetted by the candle . . . He caught himself
staring abstractedly at the ashes of the serpents lying
in the hearth for a few moments. He shook himself:
the day was passing. There was no way back to Iken's
Dike: he could only go forward, over the Broken
Hines. It looked like a long climb.

He packed and, wrapping his cloak around himself,
left the tower and reached the road. Overnight, its
appearance had changed. No longer was it the flat
pavement as it had been then. It was now cracked and
weathered; as his eyes followed its course upwards he
saw it was buried under rockslides. Whatever magical
virtue had maintained it was now gone. He began to
trudge upwards. The Black Cloud still hung like a
solid presence low over the peaks. It was utterly silent
apart from the bluster of the wind in his ears. No bird
sung, no creature moved on the mountainside. He was
climbing into the heart of danger, where no human
had stepped in millennia.

After two hours and many switchbacks he entered
the Black Cloud; it was tinged with a sulphurous stink,
and his eyes began to water. He wrapped a cloth over
the mouthpiece of the mask and pushed forward. The
slope eased, and he entered a natural amphitheatre
surrounded by a ring of jagged peaks which loomed
through the darkness. Scarred ridges and cliffs chiselled by the wind into tortured spires and razorback
cornices rose directly ahead. In front of him the bottom of the hollow of the amphitheatre was filled with
a dark bog a mile wide, completely blocking the way
forward. The remains of the road plunged right into
the black waters of the swamp. On the other side he
could see the road rising up again towards a peak a
thousand feet above him. The summit was surmounted
by a ruin.

First he had to cross the morass in front. Black bubbles rose to its surface with full plops. Rotten tree trunks and branches protruded from the surface of the swamp like skeletons. A drifting fog hung over it.

He felt a sudden displacement, rather like falling, and briefly an image flashed into his mind. This amphitheatre under a blue sky and a warm sun, silver waterfalls falling into a crystal lake spanned by the white arches of a bridge. A white marble pavillion on the other side of the lake, surrounded by trees and a well-planted garden. He saw a woman clad in white moving in the garden, and his heart gave a sudden lurch of recognition. The woman had dark hair. She straightened and turned to face him. His eyes strained to take in her features, but she was too far away. She raised her hand slowly. Was she greeting him or waving him off, warning him? Then the vision was gone and he snapped back to reality and the dismal scene all around returned.

He felt fear for the first time since leaving the tower. What had been the meaning of the vision? But there was no time to worry now. The only way to the summit was through the swamp. He went to its edge and saw the glow of the white marble slabs of the road under the black water. He placed his foot delicately into the cold water onto the first slab. It sank a little beneath his weight, but otherwise seemed firm enough.

He set off, his eyes riveted on the oozing mud and the indistinct trail of sunken marble blocks under the surface. A bubble broke on the surface with a melancholy plop, making him jump. He teetered, and suddenly lost his precarious footing.

He fell into the water: the cold was jarring and he felt the mud sucking him down. He clawed at one of the blocks of the road, trying to drag himself back up. Then, from underneath the water, cold, skeletal hands grabbed his ankles and began to pull him backwards, his gloves scratching on the marbled surface of the block. He struck out with his feet, but the hands would not relinquish their grip. The last lip of the block slipped from his grasp, and he felt the water over his

shoulders. Then, mysteriously, the hands holding him
dropped away and he was left floundering. He struggled back to the block, hauling himself up onto it. He
turned quickly to see if there was any sign of his at-
tacker. Where he had been seized, another bubble
rose to the surface and broke with a dull plop, a blue
wisp of stinking decay visible on the stagnant air, before it blew away.

Urthred shuddered. What lived at the bottom of the
swamp? He didn't wait to find out, but stood rapidly,
pulling his sodden cloak around him, realising that all
his food would have been spoiled by his immersion in
the mud. There were more of the loud explosions in the
mud to either side, but this time he was expecting
them, and he didn't lose his precarious footing. Gratefully he reached the far side of the bog.

In front of him, where he had seen the vision of the
pavillion a few moments before, was a strange sight:
a crudely carved gateway of dark wood, two vertical
beams, joined by a curving timber over the top. The
whole structure was hung with mouldering pieces of
footwear of a strange design, pointed slippers, hanging
by threads to the superstructure. A path led away beneath the archway, through the dark boles of the dead
trees, and continued up the slope. A fine mist of light
rain fell. The thunder rang out, nearly deafening now,
echoing about the amphitheatre. He took the path, a
chill going down his spine as he passed under the archway, looking at the shoes twisting and turning in the
light air, wondering what it meant.

Now he found himself on a slope of volcanic ash,
dry as dust despite the sheen of rain. The slope rose
gradually to a buttressed ridge half a mile ahead, and
this ridge in turn led upwards towards the lowering
mountain peak, now to his left. He hesitated for a
moment, peering upwards. He fancied he saw, high
above in the mists, a shadow flying slowly through the
cloud, but he couldn't tell whether it was his eyes
playing tricks or not. He set off again. Despite the
damp his sandals kicked up little clouds of dust, and

his sodden fur cloak was soon caked with a grey patina.

He climbed slowly until he stood on the ridgeline. Ahead lay the summit. He had nearly made it. The time for thought had long passed, and with only a silent prayer to Reh, he set off upwards again, climbing thus for another hour or more. He was dimly aware of the line of Iken's Dike below, crossing into the mountains beneath him. His world fell away into the depth of the gorge below, and he felt vertigo pulling him down. Spinning mist soared upwards and past him. Were his friends in the gorge? Had they been blocked by the storm? Dark, paranoid thoughts began to race unchecked through his mind. Had they abandoned him? A leaden despondency fell on him the higher he climbed. The villagers of Goda had been right: he was forever exiled from human life. His hopes were dust.

The path narrowed and narrowed until it became only some ten feet wide. The wind threatened to pluck him over the side. He gazed forward, trying to see the end of the ridge and the summit. Then he saw a figure further up it, blocking his way.

He stopped dead. Its features were indistinct in the dark mist, but he glimpsed a helmet with wide horns reaching out to either side, the dull glint of a halberd held in front of it. It wore a shaggy pelt that fell to its knees. It seemed to occupy the whole width of the narrow ridge. There was no way forward. He glanced behind. Another figure had materialised out of the mist, blocking his retreat. He was trapped.

He gathered his courage once more and sought for a spell: a summoned creature from the fiery heart of the world that would precede him and drive the guardian in front away, or a fiery dart that he could fling at it, blowing it to atoms. But he suddenly realised that his heart and his veins were cold, as cold as they had ever been, chilled by the immersion in the swamp, by the feeling of being utterly deserted. Never before in his life had his faith seemed so remote. All he had now were the gloves, and even they felt heavier: metal weights, rather than levers of great power, their hinges stiff from their dousing in the marsh water.

This was the end then: the long journey would finish here. He would die, and Thalassa would never know what had happened to him. Perhaps she wouldn't care. His brief life outside Foregeholm had been a failure. He hadn't found the Silver Chalice, or the Man of Bronze, or Lorn.

He shook his head. What was this despair? The very mist seemed pregnant with it, starving him of hope. He rallied himself: he would go down fighting at least. He stepped forward, clicking the stud on his glove that unleashed the blade from the heel of his right hand. Closer and closer he got to the figure in front, stealing a glance over his shoulder at the figure behind to see if it followed him, but it was now lost in the mist. He would only have to confront this one foe: but that surely would be enough?

Then he stood in front of it. It was some ten feet high. He saw its coat was made of pelts of human hair, one or two still showing the pink skin of the scalps of its victims. Its face was a horror to freeze a man's blood, if that blood was not already frozen as his most surely was. It was as if it had been flayed, the features obscured by clotted blood. Only a little skin clung to what must once have been the face; otherwise, it was all bone. Yet life still glimmered from behind the thing's eye sockets.

But as he approached, the creature made no move but stood rigidly still. Now he was only a foot away and he could smell its odour, yet still it hadn't moved. Then he understood. He was no different from this thing: was not *his* face as hideous as this creature's? He was one of them, one of these Nations. He held his breath and drew abreast of it, but it was as if the thing didn't register his existence, and he slipped past, scrambling up the path, casting a nervous look behind him. The creature remained where he had left it, staring down the ridge, the only movement its decorative scalps blowing in the faint breeze.

He had nearly reached the summit. He stared down into the mists to his left. The sides of the mountain were sheer, dropping an incalculable distance into the depths of Iken's Dike. Closer he saw another ridgeline rising up, arcing around a black tarn set into a col and disappearing into a cave mouth. The black clouds that covered the summit roiled up from the seething surface of the tarn. The mist seemed to boil with hidden life, and he glimpsed the outline of a creature with leathery wings and extended jaws flying over it in wide circles. He stood motionless, and he heard the creature shriek as it circled low over the water. He heard another sound, a high threnody, undisguised by the moaning of the wind: the same eerie whistle as he had heard from the Ice Wraiths on the Plain of Ghosts. This truly was a place of the damned.

He realised it was nearly sunset. The sky all around was a slaty grey, full of snow, but one stray sunbeam broke through a crack in the overcast sky, and like a finger from heaven bathed the summit to which he climbed in a coral glow so that the red sandstone of the rock shone against the darkness of the sky. Now he could see the ruins more clearly. The central building was a round keep, surmounting the very peak of the mountain, with narrow slit windows looking out over the spires and tortured rock and battlements of the range. Curtain walls surrounded it, rearing up from the sides of the mountain.

This was the place he had been drawn to, even from faraway Goda. It seemed familiar to him. It was as if its ancient rock was part of him, the threshold of an undiscovered land, yet also the land of his birth, the place he had come from before Forgeholm. Manichee had told him he would discover the secrets of his past here.

The thunder rolled again, and in it he heard the voice of the night before. But now he heard what the thunder said—one word, as clearly as if it had been shouted into his ear.

Ravenspur.

It came over and over. The place he had been named for. Was it his imagination? No, the thunder had a voice. This was it. This summit—Ravenspur.

If he had been cold before, nothing now remained in his veins but ice. So cold, he was no different from the frost-shattered rocks that lay around him, as if he had once more become part of this wilderness from which he had come twenty years before.

What would he find here? Something had happened to him here, before his first conscious thought. But what? His mind was racing; why hadn't Manichee told him everything?

He would know everything now.

CHAPTER SEVENTEEN

Harken's Lair

Deep under the Palisades they waited in darkness greater than any of them had ever known. The undead lord ordered the barge to be steered around the underground chamber in a wide circle. There were several canals leading away from it in a radical pattern.

He glanced at Golon, who seemed to have withdrawn into himself, his gaunt head pressed to the dark cloak at his chest, his brow furrowed.

"Well?" he asked.

The sorcerer's yellow eyes flickered up like a lizard's. "It is as I thought. We are at the mountain's heart."

"Under the Palisades?"

Golon nodded. "With my inner eye I can see the traceries of ancient magic which carved these chambers. They are faint: the afterimage of a power spent aeons ago, but I may be able to follow them to the surface."

"Why did the gods dig so deep?" Faran asked, almost of himself.

"This is where Harken kept the God's dragon steeds."

"So far from the sky?"

"They were creatures of flame, formed from the very fire of the Heart of the World. They were kept penned here for the safety of all those who dwelt on the surface of the land."

"A hard penance."

"Aye—I feel their ancient malice brooding here. They were no friend of man. We have to be careful."

"You've found a route out of here?"

The sorcerer nodded. "It is faint, but it will do."

"Good," Faran said distantly. "But you know what must be done before we go."

Golon inclined his head again.

Now Faran steeled himself for what was to come, and pulled back the cloak hiding the wound. He glimpsed the shattered stump of yellow bone protruding from his shoulder and felt the cold of the chamber infect its exposed marrow. The vampire guards and the Reapers looked on impassively.

Golon grunted and rummaged at the bottom of the barge, producing a long cloth-wrapped bundle which had been strapped on his back all through the flight from Thrull. He removed a small black pouch from his belt and opened it, revealing a curious selection of hooks and needles and various kinds of twine and cat-gut. If anything, it looked like part of a fisherman's tackle kit, but its real use was revealed as he rolled the cloth bundle slowly across the deck of the barge. Faran's severed arm rolled gently loose, its hand slightly cupped, the fingers tapered to long nails. It looked strange anywhere but where it should be, and Faran almost involuntarily tried to flex the severed limb, to prove that it was indeed separate from him, that it was not still part of his body. But the arm remained inert. Golon picked it up and laid it on the thwart, then busied himself with a wickedly curving needle and some black gut which he unravelled from a ball. He threaded the gut and glanced up at his master. Faran merely nodded, then looked away down the boat.

He heard Golon approach, then felt the first prick of the needle at his shoulder. It was as if Golon worked on anaesthetised flesh, so deadened were Faran's nerve endings, but nevertheless the sensation was an unpleasant one, as much psychological as physical. Faran closed his eyes.

When the final clumsy knot was tied, Faran lifted his head. He only had command of the stump at the moment; the rest of the arm was as floppy and wilful as the arm of a marionette. But he knew the nerve endings would slowly grow again, white tree roots seeking blindly for that dark core to his being that had been fertilised by the Black Chalice. He looked dispassionately at the join. The job was a clumsy one, the catgut barely trimmed off at the edges of the flesh which was raised up in crude red ridges around the wound. Now his arm, like so much of the rest of him, would bear testimony that inside this patchwork of skin and suture lived a man of straw, dried, empty. How many more years of this existence? Until the sun went out. So Iss had proclaimed, then there would be darkness and only such as he would live. Even Golon, the summoner of demons, would perish. But beyond the death of the sun, he, Faran would live. For what? To perpetuate this mockery of a body, this hollow life?

He looked up unseeing at his sorcerer, wondering again why men like this desired what he had attained. This empty life which had no meaning but mere existence prolonged indefinitely without release. The Life in Death: how weak they were desiring it! For what would be left when the sun finally went out but endless night, arctic wastes and the howling wind scouring the dead world? Man would gradually die, but Iss' servants would live forever beneath the ground, asleep, no blood to drink. Why did they desire this? Through weakness, with the belief that any existence was better than none at all. Fools! Yet, even now, the remaining vampire guard carried the Black Chalice taken from the reliquary by his throne chamber: this was why Golon and the Reapers followed him so loyally. They yearned to drink the coppery gall of its contents, so, though their souls would be sent to extinction, their bodies at least would be immortal.

Yet however dim the lamp of his own desire had become, he still counted the days ahead as he had always done by the mental subtraction of tasks to be

done, hurdles to be surmounted, debts of blood to be
paid. Meaning did not exist without time: but these
landmarks gave his endless journey some relevance,
some completion. So now, as the barge described a
lazy circle of the cavern deep beneath the Palisades,
he took a mental inventory of what was to come on
this journey, dreading perversely that he would find
nothing, but the futility of what he did would be
brought home to him, lost in an endless desert where
even attainment of one goal was illusory, endlessly
replicated by another thousand futile acts.

Too long he had stared at Golon, for the sorcerer
had cast down his eyes; Faran sensed him teetering
on the edge of his mesmerism, his soul swooning in
his gaze like so many thousands before him, moths to
the candle of those dark flames. With an imperious
gesture he indicated that Golon should snuff the magical blue light that had been hanging like a ghost over
the serpent-headed prow of the barge. Darkness came
instantly like a balm, and his thoughts journeyed into
the heart of that darkness, deep into the core of his
mind, where light was forever extinct.

First there was the question of Illgill: though Thrull
was now finally destroyed, the baron still lived. With
him he carried one of Marizian's artefacts, the Rod of
the Shadows. What was this thing? The Doppelgänger
had spoken of it as an instrument of resurrection, of
it being a bridge between this world and the world of
Shades. One thing was sure, while it existed Iss' purposes were thwarted and the slow precipitation of his
will into the dark liquid of the future halted. The
baron must be found, the Rod destroyed.

But this journey had another purpose: he must have
Thalassa in his power once more. Faran was accus-
tomed to mastery—prized the power of being able to
possess what he wanted over the possession itself. So,
now Thalassa was gone, it was not that she had become more valuable to him, only that her loss diminished his power, and that diminished him. How many
times at a whim could he have had her sent from the

temple, possessed her finally? But the knowledge of this power had not excited him then, only now that he had lost it did it begin to dominate his mind and overwhelm all other thoughts. Though the course of his blood was slow and sluggish, yet it quickened imperceptibly when he thought of her. Was she now like him, one of the undead? If so, he had destroyed that which he now, and only now, most desired. She to live as a human. She the promise of that life so long ago in Tiré Gand, now lost. Yet still there might be hope. All the vampires on the marshes had been slain: Golon had told him. Was it not said in the *Book of Worms* that when the Dominant died, the subject would be freed?

But instinctively Faran knew otherwise: corrupted blood would not die, but would spread like a disease, wider and wider. He felt this as an undeniable truth, in his atrophied heart and in his veins, the veins that carried that selfsame blood.

These twin purposes were all he knew: beyond the here and now of his desires there was nothing on the endless road to eternity with which to comfort himself.

He flung his cloak back over the mutilated shoulder and looked up to where the vault of the cavern should be, but though his eyes had seen in what men called darkness for two hundred years, no particle of natural light had ever penetrated this deep, not one wandering scintilla had ever for a millisecond cast its feeble being onto a speck of the ancient rock that hung above them in the darkness since Reh first forged these mountains at the beginning of time.

"Light," he called, and once more the ball of blue light was there hanging at the prow of the barge, and he could see in the misty purple heights some vague indication that a thousand feet above there might be some ceiling to this underground world. High up on the rock faces he could now see carved stone niches with savage effigies of the old guardians of this place: gargoyle statues, their eyes bulging, half wings raised above their shoulders, their tongues spitting and lashing out in front of their faces. Maybe Harken had been one like these, half flesh, half stone, to have lived in this place so far from the light of humanity.

He turned to Golon, one eyebrow raised interrogatively.

Golon pointed towards one of the looming cavern mouths. Faran saw there the rusty tracings of metal stains on the ancient rock. "I feel a faint trail: magic, power—I know not what it is. We must be careful."

Faran nodded and drew his sword. The barge was now no more than an unwieldy mass of wood and bone, wallowing in the oily black water. He motioned for the remaining vampire guard to take Acharon's vacated rowing perch. The undead seized the oar in its bone rollock. The Reapers meanwhile took up serpent-shaped oars which they had discovered lying under the thwarts and set to paddling. The barge slowly picked up headway as they glided towards the arch, the underside of its vast coping lit up by the hovering blue ball of flame at the prow as they glided under it. There was only the languid sound of the oars in the oily black water echoing back from the tunnel walls.

The walls were virtually unmarked, although every hundred yards or so ancient runes had been scored into the rock. Faran could find no meaning in the signs but gradually he noticed a change. The water around them began to turn a rusty colour. Now, rather than seeing danger, he smelt it. The air, drawn into the leathery expanses of his lungs and slowly percolating to his deadened nerves, was corrosive, acrid. It had a taste of metallic decay, of power grown rancid and corrupt.

"Stop," he called, and instantly the rowers ceased, and they silently glided on. The bottom of the barge grounded on something which slithered slowly down its length, but, whatever it was, was hidden by the opaque, blood-red water. Ahead he saw another archway and an emptiness beyond it. The smell grew heavier and heavier so even his deadened eyes began to tear. His companions held their cloaks in front of their mouths and eyes: all of them struggled for breath in the poisoned air. Then they entered the chamber beyond.

Tiers upon tiers of stone ledges nearly as far as his eyes could see rose up on either side of the stone canal down which they glided. And on each one in row upon immobile row they saw the dragons.

They stood upright and erect. Fifty feet tall, their metal black wings silently crossed in front of their gleaming dark torsos, their heads lowered to their broadly muscled chests, which were covered with an iridescent plumage. Their eyes forever closed, their dark heads giving back to the lonely light of the barge a solitary reflection. Harken's charges. The Dragons of Elder Times, the steeds of the gods, whose breath was fire, whose talons could cut adamantine, whose eyes could burn stone. Now Faran knew where the poisoned air came from. It was the slow leaking of their blood from their armoured bodies, a fluid which over the centuries he saw had carved deep runnels into the ledges on which they stood. Now all sound was stifled in the barge, no one dared breathe let alone exclaim at the sheer numbers of them. Faran counted some two hundred of the creatures, but there were even more, he knew, lost in the upper tiers beyond his vision.

Golon, too, was staring with a burning avidity at the silent rows. Faran knew what the sorcerer desired: to alight on the edge of the canal, to climb to the first ledge, to discover the mysteries hidden in the dragon's sleeping bodies. But even Golon could sense the heavy scent of danger: he remained silent as they drifted on. Now in the silence they heard another sound, a low hum which grew in intensity the farther they glided towards the end of the chamber some half mile away. The surface of the rust-red canal shivered from an unseen tremor, then there came the grinding of stone like the rolling of thunder. And the rock into which the stone canal eventually disappeared suddenly cracked open, revealing a gap into a world of light, a huge ever-widening gap that grew and grew until it

was a hundred feet wide. Instantly the light flooded
down the chamber, filling it to its furthest ends with
a dazzling radiance against which Faran flung his
arms protectively.

The heat was fierce, but not scorching. He struggled
to see what lay in that vast expanse of light beyond,
but as he did so he heard over the hum a new sound,
a metallic groaning, and he saw some of the silent
shapes of the dragons woken by the light shuddering
into life, their wings unfolding, raining acid onto the
surface of the canal, which frothed and seethed as
if alive.

"Row!" he yelled, and instantly as if woken from a
dream, all his men leant on their oars and the barge
slowly began to pick up speed through the red waters.
Faran clambered down from his vantage point at the
stern and ran forward, exhorting his men, casting his
eyes back as one then two, then it seemed dozens of
the bowed heads of the dragons swung up abruptly
and their closed eyes snapped open. Red beams of
light crisscrossed the darkness. He swung round; a
hundred yards to the gaping portals beyond. A soaring
column of light fell into a circular pool at its far end.
The waters where the light struck it frothed whitely.
There seemed no exit beyond it.

He thought for a moment of ordering his men to
turn the barge, but it was too unwieldy to manoeuvre
in the confined width of the canal. Besides, there now
came a mighty roar from right at the end of the chamber where they had first entered. His eyes were
blinded by the light, so he saw only indistinctly a sudden eruption of orange flame and, beyond, movement.
One of the dragons stood on its perch, its wings extended, its beak open. An orange geyser burst from
it. Then there was a whole series of fiery eruptions as
orange flame rolled silently at first, enveloping more
of the dragons, causing a chain of explosions.

Then the noise of the explosion was on them, the
stern of the barge was lifted up by the shock wave
and propelled forward at an even greater pace. The

wave of rusty water overtook them, swamping the stern. The barge swung, out of control, slewing into the side of the canal: bony splinters from its thwarts whistled past Faran's face as they were scythed off.

Somehow the barge straightened just as another shock wave lifted them. The white light in front grew in intensity as they were sucked into it, the water boiling and hissing. Faran grabbed desperately at the thwart to keep his balance, but as they entered the light a curious thing happened, for suddenly his feet left the planking of the barge and he felt himself float up weightless into the shaft of light. He saw the others drifting upwards, too, clutching desperately at handholds. Then they were accelerating, pulled by the light, past series after series of glowing beacons which flashed past faster and faster.

He hung from the thwart with his only good arm, and looked down: vertigo took hold as the receding pool fell away with breathtaking speed. But even then he saw movement at the bottom of the shaft, the black bodies of dragons flying after them, snatched up by the white light, soaring after them. He looked up: they were hurtling towards a circular opening, a blue-white opaqueness covering the circle. Then, at the last split second, he saw what it was. The exit to the shaft was covered in a thick layer of ice. The light beyond must be the light of the sun, a light that could destroy him in seconds.

He shouted at his men, but the noise of their passage was so deafening that he had no idea whether they heard him or not as he dragged himself under the thwart of the barge, which a millisecond later crashed through the ice and hurtled upwards.

Daylight, but not daylight, a daylight muffled by a black roiling cloud which saved him from the mist of extinction, though it was piercing enough that the extremities of his flesh began to sizzle and char. He clamped shut his eyes and felt a sudden deceleration, the barge slow to a hover, wobble precariously in the air, then fall backwards sickeningly. There was a teeth-chattering crash as it fell to the ground and began to slide on its keel. There was an accompanying hissing noise which he wondered at, then recognised. Ice—they were sliding downwards rapidly on an ice field.

Even through his shut eyes, he caught the gleam of an orange fireball behind him as there was another explosion at the mouth of Harken's Lair, then the prow of the barge crashed into something in front. There was a splintering noise, and he sensed branches whipping away overhead. There was another bang; his eyes sprang open involuntarily in time to see the keel of the barge split open from stem to stern, bodies tumbling like broken puppets onto the ground. Once more he felt weightlessness, but the weightlessness of sudden deceleration. For a brief second he flew in the air, before landing in a bank of snow.

It took him a few seconds to clear his vision. He saw that it was that moment of dusk when only the slightest taint of light remains. Then more pain in his eyes. Orange explosions flared in the dark fog, and then there came a roaring noise that sounded like a waterfall and the tearing of fabric at the same time: the dragons were loose, hurtling through the air. How many? The air was momentarily full of their flame and noise just overhead; he steeled himself for a blast of their fiery breath. Instead he was knocked to the ground by the force of one passing just above him. Then they were gone, soaring upward, no doubt in search of the sight of the dying sun which they had been denied for so many millennia.

He levered himself back off the snow. His eyes returned to the ruins of the barge. Shattered bone planks lay scattered down a steep, tree-lined slope. A tree stood next to him: one of the Reapers hung in it, his bronze armour impaled by a branch, his skull mask twisted round at a 180-degree angle, grinning even in its owner's death. One or two more of his men were struggling to disentangle themselves from the remains; others were ominously still. He counted only about half the company that had been in the barge—the others had been lost, no doubt thrown to their deaths as they soared out of the tunnel.

Now he saw Golon rising slowly from a section of the barge, his cloak ripped, his white hairless chest exposed. The sorcerer's teeth were chattering in the intense cold, which Faran only now began to register as it seeped through his own atrophied nerve endings.

He got down from the snowbank that had cushioned his fall, annoyed to find that his reattached arm was still beyond his voluntary control but hung uselessly by his side. His legs, too, were more unstable than he had thought, for he stumbled in the snowdrift and would have fallen if his good arm had not clamped around the bole of one of the trees that had arrested their progress. Golon was wading through the drift towards him, but his eyes were fixed on the air overhead. Faran heard the muffled roaring of the dragons from the clouds. They seemed to be quartering the area, searching.

"We must get into the trees," he shouted, as Golon staggered up to him. There was more cover there. Golon nodded. Faran pushed himself drunkenly off the bole he'd been leaning against and hurried down to the shattered barge, giving orders to those who had struggled to their feet. Those too injured to stand up he ignored. He began to run clumsily downhill, conscious that at least some of his men had fallen in behind and were following. But the roaring of the dragons was coming closer and closer, and he heard the heavy beat of wings through the cloud base. There was a blinding gout of flame which lit up everything in a shifting silhouette for the briefest of seconds. Smouldering charcoal twigs rained down from the stump of tree which blazed like a Roman candle. He swerved round it, conscious of more dragons diving through the darkness.

Then light burst out all around him: light so dazzling that it was whiter than white, and all stood for a moment revealed in stark outline before his oversensitive eyes shut down and a veil of darkness descended.

Arms grabbed him, and he heard Golon's voice exhorting him to get up, to hurry. As he was helped along by the sorcerer, there was another explosion and this time a roar such as he had never heard in his life. He crashed into something solid and unmoving in front: a huge expanse of embossed metal, that twisted and shrieked. A blow sent him to the ground.

His vision slowly returned, his eyelids contending with a gluey substance gumming them together. Now he saw dim outlines again, and one that blotted out all others looming above him in the darkness. Crackling blue-and-white energy played around it like a ruff . . . a dragon, on the ground, right in front of him.

He fumbled for his sword, still in its scabbard, as the creature's maw opened wide. He felt the heat shimmering at its mouth ready to explode over him in a fiery geyser. But then the ground shifted beneath him and he slipped down, as the earth opened in front of him, and the creature, its wings thrashing, was swallowed in a raging quagmire of rock and earth that seethed like madly boiling water.

Golon stood next to Faran, his arms held out and down. The sorcerer had cast a spell: an ancient summoning of Iss' element earth. Interment. But the dragon was only half-buried. It flapped its metal wings, half-struggling out of the pit, close to flight again. Faran leapt to his feet and swung the sword, finally free of its scabbard. The blade lanced into one of the dragon's glowing red eyeballs, and the creature flung its head to one side, twisting the hilt from Faran's grasp and sending it soaring away through the mist. But the damage had been enough: the thing's spastic movements became even more accentuated, its wings beating with the force of a hurricane, throwing up gouts of mud and rock, before it sank beneath the level of the pit. Golon reversed the position of his palm and made an abrupt shovelling movement; the lips of the crater caved in on themselves, burying the dragon.

Faran stared at the ground. So close, never had he

been so close to death. He thought of his dry skin bursting into flame. What would the end be like: a fleeting moment of incandescent agony, then nothing?

He sensed other figures moving about them on the mountainside, and presently they were joined by one of the vampire guards and two of the Reapers. One of their masks was scorched black, and the man's upper torso was badly burned, shreds of cloak sticking to raw patches of flesh. Faran guessed he wouldn't live very long in this cold. More of his men came down the slope through the mist, some twenty of the fifty men he'd had in the barge. For the moment the dragons had gone again. They had to get away from this place as quickly as possible. He looked around.

Some physical features of the landscape around them appeared fleetingly through the drifting clouds. They were on an ice field forming a treacherous glacis, broken only by the stumps of the trees that the barge had collided with. Below them he saw a deep gorge running along the side of the mountain, its cliffs utterly sheer. If the barge had slid another hundred feet, it would have hurtled to destruction over the lip of the gorge. Steep mountains ringed them. The only way out was up, there was no way down into the gorge.

He nodded to the left, and the surviving men began to traverse up the treacherous ice slope. They hadn't got far when the burned man, already weak from his wounds, slipped and started sliding down the ice slope. He flung out his hands, trying to arrest his fall, but they slithered over the smooth surface, the ice like a funnel sucking him down to the cliff face below. Faran heard a faint scream, and he was gone. The other Reapers kicked their armoured boots into the ice field, making a trail for Faran and Golon to follow.

Night came as they climbed. They reached the end of the ice and found a jagged rock buttress breaking through the glacis and soaring up into the clouds above them. Now there were rock handholds, the going was slightly easier. They struggled upwards for an hour or so, each treacherous handhold threatening

death as much as promising safety. They reached the
top of the buttress, and saw in front of them a flat
boulder-strewn plain. There was a hint of distant
mountains ringing them, but once more the clouds obscured the view. An inspection of the edge of the buttress they had just climbed confirmed their worst fears.
The buttress was part of a sheer cliff face, plunging
down to the bottom of the gorge, two thousand feet
or more below them. There was no way down it, only
apparently to the north and west, where moonlight
showed through dark, sinister cloud. They set out in
that direction. Far overhead, thousands of feet up,
Faran heard the calls of the dragons, seeking the last
beams of the departed sun.

Ahead he saw the cliff face swing round in front of
their path, forcing them to the west. The ground began
to rise slightly. He saw dark shadows ahead, and saw
that they were trees. More trees and at this height?
He called a halt, peering forward: a dense thicket of
thorn trees dead and black, their boughs like groping
talons. They would have to go through them: there
was no other route to take.

They pushed on upwards, struggling with the thorns,
blinded by the mist, which seemed to grow thicker
and thicker as they ascended. The air was as corrupt
as it had been in Harken's Lair. Golon and the other
humans were wracked by troubling coughs: soon all
of them held the hems of their cloaks over their faces
once more.

The lands beyond the Palisades were unknown:
even in the library of the Temple of Iss there had
been very little written of them, for nothing hard-and-
fast was known about this part of the world. Had it
not been razed at the God's departure? And the Palisades were a barrier that no man could pass. But
Faran knew enough: he looked at Golon. His face was
partially masked by his cloak, but he could see that
the sorcerer had come to the same conclusion. He
knew where they were. Faran motioned to a halt. The

black trees hung dripping motionlessly around them, hunched as if waiting to spring.

"We are in the Nations of the Night," he said flatly.

Golon lifted the cloak away from his mouth so he could reply. "Aye, it is the Nations." He pointed to the east. "Over there is Shandering Plain, to the north the Forest of Lorn. The gorge below is called Iken's Dike."

"Then Acharon has brought us to an evil pass. Those that dwell here hate mankind, whether they be of the Worm or Reh."

"Yet he promised to bring us near our enemies," Golon said. He reached into the leather satchel in which he carried the accoutrements of his craft, withdrawing a small purple bead held on a string. He dangled it in front of him. The bead swung imperceptibly in the dead air, the sorcerer eyeing it intently. There was a silence in the thorn forest as the others watched him, broken only by the black condensation that dripped slowly from the fog-steeped trees.

"I sense the magic of Dragonstooth to the east, below us near the Dike," he said finally.

"So Acharon did keep his promise. The Illgill pup is this side of the mountains. Thalassa, too . . ." Faran mused. But then he noticed a strange stillness had crept over Golon, who was looking hard at the shadowy trees. "What is it?" he hissed.

"More magic." There was a slight tremor in the sorcerer's voice, a tremor of fear that sent an answering shiver like slow glacial ice through the thick blood of Faran's veins.

"What magic?" he demanded.

Golon indicated the silent branches all around them. "The trees: they are alive."

Faran stepped back, but snagged his cloak on a trailing thorn bough as he did so. He ripped it away, staring intently at the thorn. It did seem to him that there was something watchful in the crooked boles of the trees, an air of inherent malice. And like animate beings, the trees had seemed to bunch and block their

route as if guided by a dark intelligence rather than
by the whims of nature. "We'll go on," he said, almost
as much to Golon as to the trees themselves, which,
in the thick gloom of the mist, seemed to lean in on
them farther, as if preying upon their words.

Golon nodded silently, and they took some steps in
the direction where there seemed some hope of
squeezing between the ripping barbs. They struggled
through, losing threads of their cloaks to the thorns,
only to find their way blocked again and again. The
barrier of thorns in front of them was like a maze
with many dead endings, and passages where they
turned back on themselves. Golon consulted the purple bead many more times and each time his findings
were the same: they were being driven further and
further to the north. Their attempts to turn to the east
were met with more ripped cloaks and scratched
hands.

Finally they came to a gap in the thorn thicket.
Above them Faran could see looming peaks through
clouds. A thick black fog hung on the ground in front.

He turned to Golon and saw in the sorcerer's eyes
what he already knew: despite their efforts to turn to
the east, they had arrived at the very heart of the
danger. "Draw up," he ordered the others. They
pressed closely behind him, weapons ready. Then he
stepped out into the fog. Instantly there came a rattling of wood all around.

Gaunt figures slipped from the trees behind them
and to either side. They were of the substance of the
trees: skeletally thin, their bones and muscle made for
a seasoned darkness, of the essence of the trees, with
barbed points protruding from their skins, narrow
faces, reaching to a sharp point, in which dark eyes
burned. Their claws were many-fingered talons of
thorn, and they carried pointed weapons made of the
wood. The creatures surrounded them, compressing
Faran's party into an ever-tighter circle. Then he was
aware of another figure coming through the mist from

the direction of the mountain. The creatures allowed a small gap in the circle to open to let it through.

It stopped, its body, it seemed, drawing the mist around it in a thick caul, hiding it from view. A voice came to them from it, a voice that spoke their language, but with a dry rasp much like the sound of a slithering serpent. "It is wise not to struggle," it said. The figure moved closer, but it was still hidden by the mists.

"Who are you?" Faran returned.

"I come to greet you: you are called Faran Gaton Nekron. My lord saw your coming. It is not every day that humans emerge from Harken's Lair."

"You have followed us?"

"Followed? No, the forest has followed you, held you in its embrace, a league or more you have come, and it has come with you, to the gates of Ravenspur."

Now the creature fully emerged from the mist. It was six feet, the same height as Faran. Green of skin it was, a green skin like a toad's mottled with black, its neck bulbous and folded into a hundred chins. Its face might have been human, though it lacked a lower jaw, and its words were emitted from a gaping pink hole that lay in its throat below its yellow eyes, so that when it spoke it was as if the words came from a hideously distended smiling mouth. Though it had two arms and two legs and walked as a human would walk, those appendages and its body were covered with a green-and-brown scaly carapace that looked as sturdy as forged steel. It carried a human head in its hand, still with a skull mask attached: one of the Reapers. It tossed it to the ground in front of Faran's feet.

"I bring you one of your men," it said tonelessly, but its eyes were laughing.

Faran coldly regarded the head which had rolled to a stop by his boots, then looked back at the creature, his good hand twitching, its fingers unconsciously searching for the hilt of his lost sword. His eyes regarded the creature's, but the thing was immune to their mesmerism; they bore no influence with such as these.

"What is your name?" Faran asked.

The creature's yellow eyes never blinked. "My name is Smiler," it said, and indeed the wide opening at its throat gave life to the name, however adapted it might have been for the human's tongue. "Come," the creature said, waving one of its stunted arms behind it in an imitation of a courtly gesture, turning its carapaced body stiffly as it pivoted.

"Where?" Faran asked.

The creature chuckled. "Why to Ravenspur, as I have said." Suddenly the dark fog that had been veiling the scene divided as if drawn to one side by a string, and they saw in front the slate grey of a scree slope and, looming above it, the lower reaches of a mountain, its upper reaches lost still in the mist and the night. Faran could see a precipitate path zigzagging up the mountainside until it reached a saddle over which it disappeared, only to reappear far up the side of the looming bulk of the mountain.

The creature turned once more. "Follow," it said. "My master waits for you."

So saying, it turned its back and strode towards the slopes. Behind them, there was a rattle of hard wooden limbs, and the forest of tree men pushed in at their backs, driving them on.

CHAPTER EIGHTEEN

The Master

Urthred turned one last time as he reached the summit of Ravenspur and looked back at the southern mountains. The tips of the Palisades, lit by the moon, were just visible above the snowstorm swirling on the plains and the dark thunderclouds below. He wavered for a moment. The leaden despondency he had felt ever since he had begun to climb fell on him again. Not even in the tower at Forgeholm had he felt so utterly alone. A dark voice spoke to him. He had been abandoned by his friends in the snow, left to die. In Forgeholm he had known his place, had hidden in the tower all those years; never even coming to the window in case one of those waiting in the courtyard below had caught a glimpse of his face. Yet, since Thrull, he had been in human company; Thalassa, Alanda and Jayal—they had accepted him. Or had they? A nagging doubt ate at his mind. Here he was an outcast, forgotten already, his usefulness over. A vision came to him: Jayal and Thalassa, in an embrace, laughing together, laughing at him, the circus freak. A cold hatred entered his mind. He had been deceived: Thalassa had never even liked him. The villagers of Goda had been more honest in response to him than his so-called friends; they had never shown him anything else but undisguised horror.

Then he tried to reason with himself. These were not rational thoughts. The Black Cloud hanging over the mountain was affecting his mind; his friends had not abandoned him. There was a sacred bond between them all. Then why was he alone? Again the worm of doubt. The cycle began again. His mind whirled in the grip of a fever that warped and bent every argument back on itself.

He composed himself, tried to sort out his priorities. He must find the others. Prove these delusions were nothing more than that. They were going through the Dike to Lorn. The quickest way to rejoin them was to go up to the ruins on the summit and find the way down on the other side.

And yet still he stared at the mountains as the wind set up a weird harmonic off the rutted face of the mask. The only focal point to his existence had been the certain knowledge that something would be revealed in this place. The waiting was finally over, twenty-one years of it gone in a flash. This was Ravenspur, the place he was named after. Now he would know the truth.

Yet he couldn't move, still held as the tide of contending emotions warred in his heart and mind. And so he might have stood forever until the wind had blown him to the depths below. But then suddenly red explosions of light blossomed in the air far away to the south, underlighting the clouds. Again and again they came, where the entrance to Harken's Lair was hidden by the snowstorm. Not the flash of lightning, of that he was sure. But of what? And then, though he was many miles away and the wind howled and moaned all about him, he heard faintly a triumphant screech, echoing about the gullies and buttresses. He watched as the explosions rose higher and higher into the air, then swooped again. He strained his eyes to see more, but the distance and the clouds prevented him.

Once more the red lights rose in the air, and they grew brighter and brighter as they hurtled through the grey towards him, as swift as light. Then the clouds cleared momentarily and a moonbeam caught them, and he saw their glittering forms. Mighty winged creatures, the moon glinting off their scaly sides in every prismatic hue: blue, red and orange. Their wings crushed the air beneath them, their glittering eyes fixed upon the north: they thundered past, a mile or two to the west, the very air around him whipped up by the force of their passing, so his cloak was blown straight out behind him and he had to clutch at the rock face to save himself from falling.

Dragons. Released from Harken's Lair. His heart went out to the soaring beasts as they disappeared into the cloud, longing to follow them, to go with them. Reh's creatures, alive once more on the earth. What need for the *Book of Light,* when the power of the God was once more incarnated in these creatures of the Flame? For a moment all his doubts fled away: the God still lived. All things would be right again, the darkness defeated. The evil in the land purged.

Then another thought came, one that cast a shadow over his exultation. The dragons were alive, but where had they come from? Nothing had stirred for millennia from the depths of Harken's Lair; Garadas had said so. So what now had disturbed them? Had someone or something passed through their resting place? He remembered Jayal's visions. Who would come through the bowels of the earth, Iss' dominion? Who but Faran himself? The Undead Lord had found a way through from Thrull and was on this side of the Palisades already. He was certain of it. Urthred had seen the work of Golon, his sorcerer, had seen the man's power when they had met so briefly on the roadway in Thrull the night he had entered the city. Golon had done it: had brought Faran here not in the three months he had imagined, but in three days. They had run out of time. And still he had to reach the summit and find a way down the other side to the northern entrance of the Dike.

His mind suddenly made up, he turned and climbed the last few steps through the ruined curtain walls. The round keep loomed above him. On each side the mountain fell away in sheer cliff faces. There was a dark rectangular opening in the front of the tower, some twenty feet high. He entered, his footsteps echo-

ing in the empty space in front of him, Moonlight
streamed in from the west through the evenly spaced
windows of the keep. A circular staircase rose up to
the next level of the building to his right. It was the
only visible feature. It was cold in the hall, the cold
of ancient stone; he guessed that the stone would re-
tain this chill even if the sun had blazed outside. He
peered into the darkness and saw an exit on the opposite side of the immense floor. All he had to do was
hurry across, and he would be free of this place and
the dark thoughts weighing on his mind. But something held him back, fixed him like a glue that he
could not escape. The mystery. The name of this place.
His name.

Instead of heading towards the exit, he started up
the set of stairs in front of him. A faint light surrounded him, though he could not see its source. It
seemed to move as he moved. Once more he had the
feeling of déjà vu, of having been here before. No sign
of any guardians here, no signs of life at all. He passed
down a corridor and found another stairway leading
up. He began to climb, high into the upper reaches of
the keep.

Once more his surroundings struck him as strangely
familiar, like an image of a scene which, briefly
glimpsed, returns again and again to the mind. He
halted and closed his eyes, and the memories, if anything, grew even more intense. First the recollection
of being carried in soft arms, carried so it was like
he was cocooned from the world and saw everything
through a faint mist. All was warm and comfortable
even in this harsh place it seemed. Then voices echoing in the halls, a baby's anguished cries, his own and
another's—Randel's? Then a void, filled with howling
arctic winds and whiteness and the creak of saddle
leather; then his first conscious thoughts at Forgeholm.

He opened his eyes. How could he remember anything from that time? He had only been a few weeks
old. It was like when he had first seen Ravenspur from
Goda, as if the recognition had been planted there by

another force. Then the revelation dawned on him. These were not his own recollections: the memories lived independent of him, were here, lodged in the walls of the place, in every stone. They lived and breathed, remembered everything; he merely heard the cry of the stone, saw what it had seen. He reached out a hand and touched the wall: there it was, as if there was a slight rising and falling, the swelling of breath through the palm of his glove. The walls lived. He started climbing again.

Darkness ahead at the head of the stairs: the voices, confused and angry, began to multiply in his head, became a cacophony of conflicting sound. He heard a woman's voice shouting and the infant's cries louder and louder. Then the noise was abruptly cut off, in an instant, and all was deadly silent as he took the last two steps. As he did so, the light disappeared, as if a door had been shut.

Now he was blind. Unlike in the room below, there were no windows here. A place with no view, yet it stood at the top of the mountain. Dark. A place of brooding thought, of thoughts so many times turned over that they had gone sour, of lost hopes turned bad: a faint scent hung in the air, as if the taint of those failed prospects had turned into the ether.

Never before, not even in the confining bounds of the mask, had he experienced such darkness. Only that sour smell was left.

He felt a presence in the room, a presence immune from sight or sound, a thing of pure thought, that had survived for years as others would suck on the air to live. It had slept in the stone all these years, exerting a subtle attraction, like a lodestone to metal, that had brought him here. Was this his enemy?

Then he heard a voice. Where had it come from? The words were carried away as light is drawn off the edges of the world at the end of day, in the entropy of all positive things, things for the good carried to the peripheries. Dissipated, annihilated.

It came from the darkness.

"Urthred of Ravenspur . . ." Then it died away, like a dying wail as if no energy was left in it to speak anymore.

"Yes," Urthred answered. "Who calls?"

"Urthred . . ." Once more the voice died away, as if uncertain, as if rehearsing the speech of humans, a tongue long unfamiliar to it.

"Who calls?" Urthred said again, whirling in the darkness. He could have spun like a top, but the world in this utter darkness would have remained infinitely still.

"One who is like you," finally came the answer.

"What is your name?"

"Do not worry about names. Call me the master of Ravenspur, if you like. Yet I have no name, only memories. Memories of bitter times, when the sky caught fire and the gods destroyed themselves."

"Where do you live?"

"In the shadows, in the rocks, in the ice: wherever my spirit now finds rest, I am there. Watching for those with souls of light to come."

"And what do you do with those when they come?"

"You saw the guardian on the ridge. All have perished, all who have come to the Nations."

"All, except me."

"I have spared you, Urthred. Your friends are in the gorge beneath the mountain, yet I brought you here, sent the Ice Wraiths onto the plain, sent the storm that cut you off from the others."

"Why?"

"You will never be as they are, Urthred."

"As who is?" Urthred answered, though suddenly he was absolutely persuaded by the voice: the despondency filled his soul as it had outside. He was outcast, would forever be excluded from human congress, just like the Master.

"Humans, souls of light: beware them. They betray the deformed and broken. I know. My people suffered as you have suffered after the fires that destroyed the world. Our enemies in Lorn had no pity on us when we came to their land; though we died in hundreds, they drove us away. They claim to need us, but they love only those whose figures are straight and faces unscarred."

"No, you are wrong. Even a wretch like me can find human warmth," Urthred replied. But the words sounded hollow even to his ears.

"You think Thalassa and Alanda and Jayal feel anything for you? No, Urthred, you are no more than a puppet to them: you have great magic. They will use you, and when the world is theirs again, they will send you away, just like the Nations were turned away. You will always be alone."

The words were soft, persuasive, the feeling of despondency hung like lead in Urthred's veins. Images came into his mind: Thalassa and Jayal, together, locked in an embrace, naked, their perfect bodies so different from his; the look of Imuni when she had first seen the mask; in Thrull, the High Priest Varash's look when he had peeled it off and shown him what lay behind: the sight had killed him. Outcast, outcast, forever. The voice was right, he was damned. He would never be part of that other world. His dreams were nothing.

Silence, then the voice came again, very gentle now. "You asked me why I brought you here. To give you a choice, Urthred: renounce your friends. You see, don't you? How they mock you behind your back. Join me. The Dark Time has come again. The guardian of Lorn, the Man of Bronze, grows weak. Only Thalassa can save them. But she has betrayed you." Once more a vision came to Urthred: Thalassa laughing with Jayal, her head thrown back, exposing her alabaster neck . . . desire and the knowledge of its unattainability stung his heart.

The Master's voice continued, a bass drone. "In two weeks my armies will be ready. Then we will go into Lorn and slay the people there and take that land and live in a paradise. You are one of us, scarred by the fire. Renounce your humanity: you will never be accepted by their kind. Return to your people and live in peace finally. Below, Urthred, there are so many like you, scarred and deformed, as they have been since they were born. The seed of fire the gods cursed them with turned and corrupted their bitter limbs. The same seed you carry in your veins."

Urthred was silent, the words of the ghost of this place echoing in his ears. Had he come from here? Was he not named after it? Perhaps it wasn't the threshold of something else: there was no revelation waiting for him in Lorn. This was it. The sum of all his expectations. He was born of one of these corrupted creatures.

Once more his mind struggled against the torpor overcoming him. Instinctively he knew this wasn't so: he had come from somewhere beyond here. This place was merely symbolic of something. What had been the meaning of the woman by the lake in the vision? It had been a warning, he was sure: she knew that he would have to face this temptation.

"You are silent," the voice said.

"I was not born in this place," Urthred said. "I had a vision down the mountain. It was my mother, wasn't it?"

The voice was silent once more.

"She came from Lorn, didn't she?" he continued, suddenly sure, a new and brighter vision like a ray of sunlight coming into his mind, dissipating the fog that hung there. "She came from Lorn and stopped here." He closed his eyes, the image of sunlight becoming stronger. He saw her: she was travelling to the south, with the children, there was another creature with her, hunchbacked and misshapen, yet still not like one of the damned who lived here.

It had been just over twenty years ago. Before this cloud had hung upon Ravenspur. But something had happened here. Then he cried out as the revelation came to him. She had died on the mountaintop. She could not go farther into the mortal land. She had come from Lorn. She had sacrificed herself. Why?

He heard a wailing noise, and his eyes sprang open. White forms like hands spinning a web to hold him hovered around him in the darkness. It had been a trap, to tempt him with despair; a few more moments and he would have fallen into the thrall of the voice, but he had beaten it off. The icy fingers were reaching out for him, but once more he felt his veins light with fire, and his hands swept up, sending a circle of flame shooting up around him which the icy fingers could not penetrate. He would have to get out of here soon, but before then he needed to know more. His mother had died here. Where was she buried? And again the answer came unbidden. Deep in the mountain, they had carried her deep down, the creatures that dwelt on the mountain. While they had her body, they had part of his soul, part of what he had lost.

But he couldn't go to her now: he felt the evil below, the evil he would have become if he had listened to the voice anymore. He must go, and quickly, to the north to help his friends. He swivelled his arms around him, the circle of fire whirled ever quicker, becoming a tornado into which he was sucked. He heard the voice snarling like a wild beast.

There was a spinning sensation, then the darkness abruptly lifted and instead of smooth stone, Urthred felt jagged rocks under his feet, and he saw that once more he stood on the mountainside below the keep. But he was now on the northern side. He could see a jagged path leading downwards towards another dark plain. It was as if he had been in a dream, a nightmare in which he had been ensorcelled by the Master's voice. But he saw the moon had sped across the sky. Many hours had passed. What he had heard had been real enough. He had to get off the mountain and warn the others. He looked down towards the plains, but the layer of whirling clouds still hid them. Only up here did there seem calm, the moon almost full, shining down onto the jagged peaks and the undulating cloud below.

He began to run downwards, reckless of the darkness and the uneven path, feeling the evil reaching out to him, trying to pull him back.

He would return and recover his mother's body, he swore. But first he must get to Lorn, warn them of what was coming.

CHAPTER NINETEEN

Ravenspur

Faran followed the shambling figure of Smiler into the clouds. It hauled itself up the near-vertical slope with a ponderous tread. Black snow lay in hollows to the left and right of the razorback ridge they were ascending, and the wind howled and moaned like a creature in its death throes. They made a strange sight: the mottled being with its gaping mouth, dragging its carapace like a coracle on its back, the Undead Lord, tall and erect, clad all in black, caked with plaster dust and torn to shreds, one hand dangling uselessly by his side, and behind them Golon, his bald gnomic head all that could be seen over the purple-and-brown robes of Iss. The remaining men followed close behind, urged forward by the line of thorn creatures.

No words were spoken, but every now and then Smiler turned its heavy frame towards them, as if seeing if they followed. Then, seemingly content, it continued its slow progress upwards. They climbed high and far. The Black Cloud and night hid the landscape until the moon finally broke through, and they saw, far below, a lake, its surface bubbling and seething as if it burned with a black fire.

There were no other signs of the inhabitants of the wasteland, though once or twice Faran thought he saw dark shapes pass over the face of the obscured light of the moon. The track narrowed even further, they were on the narrowest of spines of rock. Now he could see jagged toothlike crags looming through the driving mist far below to the left and right. He kept his eyes

lowered to the two-foot-wide path. So fixated on the
path was he that he was surprised when it terminated
in a rock buttress in front. The ridgeline led directly
into a gaping cave mouth like a wide gash. Torches in
metal brackets on either side of the entry sent fiery
cinders whirling through the turbulent air.

Smiler advanced into the darkness of the cave
mouth. Shapes awaited within. To one such as Faran,
no body or face could be considered so misshapen or
horrible as to make him quail, but even he shuddered
at what emerged from the shadows. First he saw a
grey creature, hewn, it seemed, of the rock itself, with
a low forehead: it scuttled on four limbs the size of
tree boughs, like an ape with its foreknuckles close to
the ground, but its eyes set deep into its rocky forehead were all too human. Smiler led them past it as
it stared balefully upon them.

The multitude pressed in on them, their babble in-
comprehensible, of a legion tongues or more: feath-
ered creatures with the heads of birds but the bodies
of naked women, creatures whose bodies were made
of shadow and whose voices were like the howling of
the wind outside, grey-faced basilisks that Golon
looked away from but whose gaze Faran returned
evenly, unaffected by their petrifying stare. But of all
of them there was still one that made even him start
and take a step back: the exoskeleton of human bone,
whose face was a skull, but with living eyes dwelling
in the sockets, its sinews exposed like creeping red
vines over the pallor of its bones. Even Faran hurried
past that one, wondering how the thing lived in its
mutilated state.

The cavern stretched back to a broad series of
stone-cut stairs, a bowshot away. They passed towards
them, through the hellish occupants of the antechamber. Faran shut out as best he could the cacophony of
sighs and moans and imprecations, and the kaleido-
scope of brown and grey and red bodies, arms and
claws outstretched as if trying to pluck him into their
midst. Instead he fixed his eyes upon Smiler's back.

Where the creature advanced, there opened behind him a two-yard-wide passage into which none of the grabbing fingers and claws dared trespass, though the stink of the corrupt creatures filled the chamber to choking point.

They reached the staircase and climbed up out of the bedlam. At the head of the stairs were double doors made entirely of bone. These were opened inwards, seemingly by invisible hands, and they passed into a silent corridor. The doors shut with an eerie screech behind them. The corridor ahead was carved from black schist and lined with skulls mounted on metal poles. But like everything else in this hell, there were particles of life even in them: for, as Smiler passed, suddenly, as one, they screeched and gibbered and spat out a black bile. A globule landed on Faran's cloak, sizzling like acid. He wiped it away contemptuously with the gauntlet of his good hand, feeling the black cold seep even through the thick leather of his glove.

There was another set of double doors at the end. These, too, groaned open, and Smiler lumbered through into a chamber hewn, it seemed, from the very fabric of the mountain. It was shaped like a vault, some hundred feet high, with its upper reaches lost in the gloom. To the left and right there were large jagged openings that gave out onto boiling cloud and empty air. The wind whistled from right to left across their path, laced with shreds of black cloud. There was a sense of pent-up energy in the futile battering of the wind and its deafening noise, as if all the anger of this benighted world was contained and brought to a roaring head in this one spot.

Smiler advanced, and Golon and Faran followed, fighting the wind which threatened to sweep them off into the howling void outside. Now, at the furthest reaches of the chamber, Faran could see a plain stone throne. It was carved from a ten-foot-high granite block. A figure was sitting there, motionless despite the chaos which surrounded it. The figure was cowled

in a brown cloak, its folds curiously unruffled by the
wind. Its hands were bunched up inside the voluminous sleeves, and nothing could be seen of its face
under the gloom of its hood. Faran might have
thought the cloak empty—even when he had followed
Smiler across the roaring space between the cavern
mouth and was nearly in front of it, it didn't stir.

But then the figure raised its head, revealing what
lay beneath the cowl. Faran came to a complete stop.
Beneath the hood he saw not a face, as he had expected, something perhaps equal in horror to all those
he had seen in the antechamber far below. What he
saw went beyond that.

A mass of flickering flames blossoming into life then
fading again, much like the glowing red embers of a
fire which only flare up when a breeze passes over
them. Beyond the shifting mass of red and orange
were what might have been indistinct human features,
much like burned paper turned to grey ash which yet
holds a shape before it is blown away.

Golon, too, had stopped, and Faran could hear his
breathing low and strangled by his side, even over the
howling of the wind and the buzzing of the hidden
energies that seemed to live in the figure on the throne
like a hive of furious anger. He turned: Smiler had
retreated and now stood at the ivory doors at the far
side of the chamber; it was strange that even the sight
of the misshapen creature was a comfort in comparison to the vision in front of them. He forced himself
to look again at the figure on the throne.

The apparition now raised one of its arms, and they
saw that the sleeve was indeed a black void, and it,
too, flickered with a magical light, giving only the merest hint of a hand.

The voice came not from the face itself, but from a
space perhaps just behind the hood. As if the words
originated not from the being at all, but from a long
distance away, almost as if from another plane. Faran
did not know it, but it was the same voice that Urthred
had heard a few minutes earlier. The Master of Ra-

venspur. Present here, as he was everywhere under the dun cloud that sat on the summit of the mountain.

"So," it said, "a creature of the Life in Death, one of those that would live forever." Silence again, save for the sound of the void howling from beyond the mask. "You see what this world is," said the Master of Ravenspur. "You see how this land is inimical to humankind. The Nations of the Night: only the shadows can dwell here. The world fears us, for we have abandoned human hopes. You and I are alike, Faran."

Its face flared once more into incandescence as the wind crossed it, fanning the inner flames that seemed to fuel its being. "All that come from the lands of the humans, any that the gods did not curse as they cursed us, are our enemies. But you are different. You have given up the God's balm, the hope of death, and in this you are a brother, for none who live in the Nations of the Night have tasted death since the gods left the earth.

"The light of the sun is inimical to you: to I and my people too, any light is hateful, the light of the moon also. None of us can stand the radiance which reminds us of our more blessed state. Only one thing sets us apart: you worship a God, a God of darkness it is true, but one of the gods that brought us to this pass. And in this land all gods are cursed. Soon you will know that all the heavens that you and your fellow priests hawk to the credulous are but hells like these: there is no zone in the skies or the heart of the earth or in Shades or any other place where there is comfort and happiness for eternity.

"So welcome to the Nations of the Night, and let your soul soon be as godless and empty as mine: then, and only then, will you be truly welcome, not like those who in ages past came across the Palisades thinking to wage war upon this land—those who died in the mountains and the few who limped on and were slaughtered before they even saw the Broken Hines. Those were madmen, but you have resources; how else would you have come through dragon's lair?"

There was silence then as if an answer was expected. Faran stirred, seeking for words, but none came.

Now, as if the thing in front of them had picked up on his inner thoughts, there was what might have been a hint of laughter in that space where his voice came from. "Speak, tell me why you have come. I will listen, for strange things, strange even in this place which I come to only every hundred years, must be spoken quickly."

"Lord"—the word came with difficulty to Faran's lips, for he had not uttered it to any man or being these last two hundred years, save only to Iss and his servant Acharon—not even to the Elders in Tiré Gand—"we came not knowing where we travelled to, but followed a magical trail that was begun back in the lands to the south."

"No one comes here *knowingly*." Again the laughter from the abyss. "Tell on, this tale of what humans call magic amuses me, but tell a true tale."

"Lord, there was a magician, named Marizian, who built in the Southern lands a city called Thrull. He carried there with him three artefacts and the books of the gods, of Reh and Iss. . . ."

"Speak not of them." The voice sounded again, this time with angry inflection.

Faran continued quickly, as he was bidden. "The artefacts remained there for centuries, and nothing disturbed their rest until one of them, the Man of Bronze, left Marizian's tomb and came to the Northern lands. Then the other two, a sword and a magic rod, were taken. We seek these items in the name of our God. . . ."

"A name I will not hear again," the voice cut in. "Your tale, though, is familiar. Many have come seeking the Man of Bronze, but none have found him, nor Lorn the country it rests in either, for both lie beyond human eye. Lorn is a kingdom created by him you call the God of Flame long ago, a heaven for his servants. They should be like us, creatures of shadow. But where we were damned, they live in a paradise where they never grow old. For millennia it has been preserved against our just wrath: first by the magic left behind by the God, deposited in the person of the king of the land. Thereafter, as that magic died, by this magical creature, this Man of Bronze, who came to their aid.

"He was set to work in the Smithy left behind by the God; there his Anvil strikes the Heart of the World: magical currents flow from it, keeping the gateway to Lorn shut against their enemies, warming the air, keeping the moon always frozen in an unmoving sky . . . But now the Man of Bronze grows weak: soon the gate that protects the kingdom will open once more, and we will flood through and destroy them." His voice trailed off, and if mere particles of molten air could be said to scrutinise anything deeply, so they did Faran.

"Yes?" Faran asked over the howling of the wind.

"Yet, again, Lorn may survive. Faran, you have told a true story thus far, but you have left out the heart of the story. Yours is not a tale only of lost artefacts. The living: they are what have brought you to the north. Do not think I don't have knowledge of all those who have passed near my borders. First, the doomed humans, servants of the Flame who came from the south seven years ago. Your old enemy, Baron Illgill: that is his name, is it not? He came with a handful of his men, carrying one of those objects that you have spoken of: the Rod of the Shadows. The blue light of it was like a star over the Plain of Ghosts. It was before my armies had gathered again as they gather now; otherwise, he would have died like the legions before him. He passed through the mountains and into the Forest of Lorn. Then, but two days ago, there was early in the morning, just as dawn was breaking, a comet from the south. It overarched heaven and fell upon the valley yonder where those peasants live, descendants of the sons of men, but now so interbred they would be unrecognisable to you. In that comet were four humans. The son of the baron, a priest of Flame, an old lady, and, finally, a young girl. Are these not who you truly seek?''

Faran nodded. "They are my enemies, as was the baron.''

"Good, then you may be of service. But first I must tell you of Lorn. Reh set a dome over that place, a powerful illusion, that hides the city. He also set a full moon at the zenith of the sky, which shines down on the city always. The city is only visible to humans every month, when the moon in this world corresponds with that in Lorn. When the two are in agreement in the skies, the gateway will open and the city be revealed. And then, for a brief time only, men can travel over to the island on which the city stands.''

"The moon is not yet one week old,'' Faran said.

"True: more than three weeks then before the gateway is opened. My armies are gathering, as they have gathered before, every hundred years since the gods left the earth. And through the millennia, every hundred years, we have marched on Lorn. But each time the God's magic has destroyed us right on the borders. Each time it has taken a hundred years for the Nations to gather again.

"But, over time, the magic that Reh left behind grew weak. A thousand years ago, it died away altogether and it looked like Lorn would fall. Then I summoned the Black Cloud that is our people's tent, the same Black Cloud that you see here, for as I have said, our people cannot walk in the light of the sun or the moon. But then, from over the Palisades as our armies gathered, I saw the glint of metal high on the Palisades one morning; the mountains trembled and avalanches fell like white curtains from the mountainsides. The roar was like a thousand lions roaring, and the snow swept right across the Plain of Ghosts to the mountain's edge. Then we saw his ruby eyes, his limbs of adamantine: the Man of Bronze. He came on, through the snow that boiled about him like foam on a storm-tossed shore, his eyes like lava, his fists rocks of iron. The rearguard of my army threw themselves in his way, but the gaze turned some to stone, others he crushed to particles of shadow with his fists. He came on over the mountains, scattering all those who stood in front of him, and travelled on to the lake. And there, just as the moon reached the zenith in the sky, he stepped over and went into the kingdom. There already the main body of my army waited, ready for the last assault on Lorn. And there they died, when Lorn was in sight at last."

The Master halted, and turned his head towards the hurtling cloud. "Soon after, the magic resumed as strong as it ever was, a hot wind that rose up from the surface of the lake and blew over the forest. And every time the Black Cloud gathered over Ravenspur, that wind blew it to shreds, scattering the Nations once more. So it has been for a thousand years, until recently, when the wind has become weaker and weaker."

"What has caused this change?"

"Many true things were written in the twilight of the world, though written by the hands of men. But those of us who dwelt here at the beginning of time heard the words of the gods directly. To us they are more than prophecy. So it is that I have seen our many defeats, the fruitless gathering of the armies, saw even the coming of the Man of Bronze. Yet it was our destiny to continue trying to take Lorn. But now that era that the gods spoke of is at an end: a new era has begun. They saw how the Man of Bronze would grow weak after a thousand years in Lorn; for growing tired of the dying sun, he waits for one to come and redeem him. She alone will he obey."

"Who is this person?"

"One the gods call the Lightbringer."

"Thalassa," Faran breathed. The *Book of Worms* had been true. She had come, the prophecies were being fulfilled, here in this remote land.

The Master was silent. Perhaps he had picked up on Faran's thoughts. "Our desires are as one," he said eventually. "Your enemies are coming through Iken's

Dike, into the heart of the mountains. You, and you alone, can stop them. My armies are not yet born from the Black Tarn. Go now with Smiler and the others. Destroy them."

"Their magic is strong," Faran said.

"Yes it is strong—but it is nothing to the Nations. In a few days they would have been destroyed by us. But for now only Smiler and the others you have seen are in this world. They are all we have, that and the despair that gnaws a man's heart and the dark sendings that I will send into their minds. Go with Smiler. I ask you only one thing."

"What is that?"

"Spare one of the humans."

"Thalassa?"

"Why would I wish to save our greatest enemy? No, Urthred, the priest of Flame. I want him alive. He is mine and mine alone."

"Why spare him, a priest of Reh?"

"No more questions. I will show you one more thing; a warning of what will happen if you fail. Then Smiler will lead you into the underworld, where Iken's Dike passes under these mountains."

With a sputtering of flame, it rose and glided forward, the cloak hiding what should have been its legs, unperturbed by the winds that roared through the jagged openings in the mountainside. It approached the one to the east, and looked out, flames licking around the brown cloak, which nevertheless didn't burn under its cold fire. It raised one of its hands, and suddenly the soughing of the winds stopped completely, and the clouds drifted away, and a vast panorama stood revealed below them.

A semicircle of jagged peaks surrounded a wilderness of black scree slopes and glacial valleys filled with jumbled moraines. Two hundred feet below them was the col that Faran had glimpsed during the ascent. The black waters of the tarn glimmered in the moonlight.

"The Black Tarn," he murmured. "All the Nations are born in its waters. Tonight, the first of those from the world beyond will emerge from it. He who comes every winter: the Great Wolf." He gestured, and immediately the strands of mist hanging on the mountainsides seemed to be sucked towards the black waters of the tarn, tumbling like ghosts. A thick white layer of mist bloomed in an instant on the lake surface. Below the white appeared a blue glow that grew slowly in intensity until, like a foetus in an embryonic sac, it twitched with a short spastic motion as if it had suddenly come to consciousness. The mists over the tarn began to churn as if being drawn into the water.

"He breathes; he is the spirit of corrosive winter, the ice that breaks a rock in half, the frost that pinches a finger from a hand. Its howl is an arctic gale, it runs faster than the wind." Now a huge form hauled itself slowly from the waters. It turned its massive head towards the opening in the mountain face high above it, red eyes gleaming like dark rubies. Even in the dim light and the foreshortened perspective, Faran saw perfectly its huge frame, as large as a temple, its face, the white tongue hanging from its mouth, the blue cavern of its mouth, its fur, a glowing white as if made of the ice itself. Its dripping jaws seemed to fill the valley below.

Then the Master of Ravenspur lifted his burning hand and pointed towards the head of the valley, where a glacier vomited out towards the eastern slopes in a spew of boulders and chaotic moraines. The creature laid back its head. Faran looked down into its gaping throat—an ice tunnel snaking away to the centre of the earth—and heard the suck of the void and the mists as they were gathered into its being.

Its howl filled the night air and the mountains, like the ripping of iron, a voice beyond sound which almost split Faran's eardrums. Then the wolf was gone, in the blink of an eye, vanishing, leaving only the layer of mist undulating like a turbulent sea.

"Go," the Master ordered, "and if you fail, the wolf will follow after. Be watchful then. For the wolf will

destroy everything of this world it finds, you
included."

Now, it seemed, Faran heard the voice of mocking
laughter in his head. He turned, but the brown cloak
no longer held any flames, falling as if suddenly cut
from strings to the floor. He sprang forward, but the
cloak was empty. He turned. The ivory doors at the
end of the chamber had opened. Smiler stood by
them.

Faran approached the creature. It looked at him
stonily, with reptilian eyes, then the gap at the base
of its neck opened pinkly. "Come," it said. "I will
take you into the underworld." It turned and walked
down the corridor. Faran's hand went to where his
sword had been, but then he remembered: it was gone.

He followed the lumbering creature. The hall below
was still full of the nightmarish creatures he had seen
before. Smiler gestured, and they fell in behind Faran.
Smiler led them down a dark twisting staircase that
descended into the stone heart of the mountains.
Somewhere, not too far away, was Thalassa.

CHAPTER TWENTY

❧

Riding the Dragon

The Doppelgänger followed Harken along the glowing corridor. He had been expecting a long passage through the mountains, yet, just as soon as they had set foot on it, the forward motion of the corridor slowed slightly, and he saw a granite wall hurtling towards them at an alarming speed. He flinched, expecting to be crushed, but just as they reached it, the wall suddenly rose up and they rushed underneath, the Doppelgänger feeling the rock door only inches from the top of his head. They slowed further and came to a complete stop. They were in a semicircular steel chamber. Behind was the opening to the corridor of eerie lights, but this closed as he watched, and he felt a sudden weightlessness which must have continued for two or three seconds. Then the sensation passed and a steel door in front ground open.

A scene from Hel confronted them. Before them the door gave onto a metal gantry perched halfway up the side of a gigantic chamber. Serried ledges rose up into the darkness. There were more ledges below, dropping towards the dark surface of a canal which ran down the centre of the chamber three hundred feet below. The ledges were full of dark glinting metal bodies, arms furled over their torsos like sleeping bats, their eyes glinting redly in the dark. A hundred, a thousand, who could count? Several spots on the ledges were empty. Fires raged on the floor below, where lava pools smouldered on the surface of the river. Molten pools of metal, the remains of the dragons which had fallen, turned silver then black in the flames. Caustic fumes rose into the air. The far end of the tunnel was a solid sheet of flame, and the Doppelgänger could see the creatures at that end begin to bubble and melt like wax statues. Even at this distance from the fire, the heat of the conflagration was intense. He felt the metal gantry below his feet begin to buckle and his clothes beginning to scorch.

Harken stared blindly at the scene as if indeed he did see, though the roar of the fires would have told him enough. He groaned as if struck a physical blow.

"The enemies have been and gone. The fire cannot be doused. All will be destroyed."

"And we, too, if we don't escape," the Doppelgänger said urgently.

"Escape?" Harken seemed to have come back to his senses. "Aye, escape. We must escape. You have the bridle?"

"Yes," the Doppelgänger shouted back, for the roar of the fire increased in intensity second by second.

"Good, then come with me." The blind stable master set off to the left, where the gantry gave directly onto one of the ledges. One of the creatures stood twenty feet away, its claws clutching the edge of the ledge, its ruby eyes glittering, its metalled chest and plumage a dun bronze in the flickering fires.

"Vercotrix, my mount, I have come," Harken called, holding his hands out to the creature. An aura of orange light bloomed from them and fell on the dragon's face which had hitherto been lost in the darkness. "Come, Vercotrix, though all your brethren be lost, I will save you at least." He turned to the Doppelgänger. "Give me the bridle," he ordered.

The Doppelgänger did so, seeing how the metal suddenly coruscated with a dazzling light as the old man touched it. Harken fumbled forward to a set of steel rungs set next to Vercotrix's perch. He began to climb these, followed by the Doppelgänger, past the dragon's body towards its head some thirty feet above them. The end of the stables was rocked by explosions, threatening to blow the Doppelgänger from the swaying ladder into the void. Somehow both men made it to a small steel platform at the top.

Harken threw the bridle and stirrups over the creature's shoulders, feeling forward so he ran his fingers down the creature's fire-blackened steel teeth, the energy in his fingers forcing the teeth apart. He pushed in the flanged bit. Immediately the dragon stirred, the eyes glowing a deeper red, its mighty shoulders heaving, then dropping. Harken swiftly swung himself onto its back, clutching the reins, his feet fixed into the stirrups, which had clamped to the creature's sides with a metallic clank.

He turned his blind eyes back on the Doppelgänger. "Pass me the lance," he ordered.

"But what of me?" the Doppelgänger asked.

"What of you?" Harken laughed. "Do you think you can ride one of the God's steeds?"

"But I will die."

Harken didn't reply, merely reached out one of his hands towards him, trying to snatch the lance from him. But the Doppelgänger had other ideas: with one swift thrust he plunged the needlelike point of the lance into Harken's chest. It passed through his sternum as if it were no more than tissue paper. There was the sound of sizzling flesh, then a flash of white light. When it cleared, Harken had disappeared, vaporised.

Vercotrix bucked and spasmed, sensing his master was gone from his back, and its mighty wings flared out to either side, crushing the steel platform against the sidewall of the chamber. The Doppelgänger lost his footing, and the lance spun from his hand. It fell, ricocheting off each of the lower ledges of the chamber in succession. And each time it struck one there was another explosion of white light and more of the dragons were blown from their perches, falling to the chamber floor, where they erupted in balls of red-orange flame. The Doppelgänger managed to grab a trailing handrail as he plunged downwards, swinging in space over the three-hundred-foot drop.

He saw Vercotrix's taloned feet tensing, as if it were
preparing to launch itself into flight. He had one last
chance. He flung himself at the dragon, clamping onto
the creature's back and snatching the reins as it thrust
itself forward into the air. The dragon fell like a stone,
the Doppelgänger falling with it, unable to get his feet
into the stirrups because of the force of the rushing
air on either side of him, seeing the burning chamber
floor hurtling towards him. Then the dragon flapped
its wings once and there was sudden uplift as it levelled out, swooping to the left, towards the burning
inferno at the chamber's mouth. Only the energy of
the glove that the Doppelgänger still wore seemed to
keep him attached to the dragon's neck; otherwise,
surely he would have fallen helplessly to his death.

Through the arch at the end of the canal, he saw a
shaft of light in front, beyond it, a rock face. Vercotrix
was hurting towards it at breakneck speed. Now it
would all end. . . . But at the very last second the
dragon gave another mighty beat of its wings and
soared upwards, up the column of white light. A blast
of supercharged air, and they were through into the
night sky, and he saw the dim moon and steep gorges
rushing past on either side. Below he saw in the blink
of an eye the smashed remains of Faran's barge, bodies scattered around it. But then they were gone, Vercotrix twisting and bucking its head, trying to rid itself
of the interloper on its back, only the glove keeping
the Doppelgänger attached to the dragon as each beat
of its mighty wings threatened to cast him off. Ahead,
he saw a line of broken summits.

But there was something wrong with the dragon's
flight. It was losing height rapidly. It headed towards
a gap between the approaching peaks, the ground was
rushing up: he saw each rock on the slope below in
minute detail. Then Vercotrix beat his wings again and
they lifted. He felt his foot brush the side of the mountain, then they were in clear air again.

Vercotrix beat onwards over a dark chasm beneath
their feet. The dragon was still losing height and the

Doppelgänger could see it was unlikely they were going to clear the other lip of the chasm. He hauled back on the creature's bridle, trying to get it to raise its head. The flanges ripped into its mouth: a bitter acid spewed from the wound, flying back and burning the Doppelgänger's face.

Now the lip of the gorge was right in front. Vercotrix thrashed its head and the Doppelgänger fell from his perch, dangling from the bridle. Vercotrix rose for the last time. It cleared the chasm edge, its taloned feet trailing on the boulders at the lip. Sparks flew from them as from a lathe. The Doppelgänger slipped further. He felt dead bushes and rocks dragging at his feet, and his clothes were ripped from his body. Then his hand slipped out of the glove and he fell. He hit the ground rolling, over and over, a series of bone-juddering impacts with boulders. Vercotrix screeched triumphantly as it at last felt its unwelcome burden fall from its back. The last thing the Doppelgänger remembered was the dragon soaring back into the air, beating its wings slowly, and turning its head towards the north.

CHAPTER TWENTY-ONE

The Heart of Ravenspur

All night and the next day the wind howled over the top of the Dike. Thalassa and the others crouched on the cold platform, their breaths freezing in the air, hoping against hope that Urthred would find them, but knowing that, as the blizzard continued, the likelihood became more and more remote.

Since the first watch Jayal had refused to rest. He stood staring into the darkness to the south, occasionally pacing the small space of the platform. But as darkness fell over the narrow crack above them that second day, he abruptly stopped his pacing and went very still.

"What is it?" Thalassa asked, scrambling back to her feet.

His eyes had that faraway, abstracted look again as if he saw scenes a long way away. "Fire, a hall of fire." Jayal's hands went to his face, as if warding off an intense heat. His face was beaded with sweat, despite the intense cold in the chasm. After a moment, he seemed to rally slightly and turned his blue eyes on her. "Each step, Thalassa, each step, he is coming closer."

Thalassa stared down the dark ravine, back towards the south. Absolutely nothing could be seen in that direction, and, as it ran arrow straight, a light would have been visible for miles in the inky blackness. But as she watched there came an orange flash as of a lightning strike seen through thick cloud. It seemed far off, but as they all waited and listened no noise of thunder came to their ears. Then, suddenly, there came a whole sequence of flashes, lighting up the hurtling clouds above them in the ravine.

"What is it?" Garadas murmured. Alanda had woken and had raised herself feebly, supporting herself shakily on the leech gatherer's staff. She turned to her companions. "The dragons have woken."

At that moment there came a roar as of the sky being ripped apart right above their heads. "Let the spirits protect us," Garadas muttered. The roaring passed, and they heard heavy bodies hurtling through the night sky overhead.

"Someone has unleashed them," Garadas said, staring upwards. His men had crouched low on the ground as if ducking the passing creatures though they were hundreds of feet above them. Then the noise was gone.

All eyes followed the glow of the creatures in the snow-filled sky as they beat towards the north. "Where are they going?" Thalassa asked finally.

"Maybe to Iskiard, or someplace where they were stabled by the gods in Elder Times," Alanda answered.

"What of the Doppelgänger?" Thalassa asked Jayal. "Do you see him?"

"He is in Harken's Lair," the young knight replied. His eyes closed, so he could focus better on the distant scene. "But now he's coming." His eyes popped open in surprise. "He's riding one of the creatures." Their heads flew up as they heard a single dragon approaching, its giant wings beating like the clap of thunder. It lumbered through the air above them, heading towards the mountains.

"It is him!" Jayal exclaimed. They traced the progress of the solitary creature as it flew to the north, then the sound died away.

"He's in front of us, but where are Faran and the others?" Thalassa asked.

Jayal shook his head. "I only see my double. Perhaps Faran is still in the Lair."

"Or in the gorge," Thalassa added, peering down into the darkness.

"We have to go down into it sooner or later," Garadas said. "There's no point delaying any further."

"We can't leave Urthred," Thalassa said. "He might be looking for us." Garadas fixed her with his dark eyes. His expression said everything: it was unlikely the priest was still alive.

"I'll go and see what is at the bottom of the steps," Jayal said. "If he hasn't found us by the time I'm back, we'll have to leave without him."

Garadas nodded. He told two of the villagers to go with the young Illgill. The three men wrapped scarves around their mouths against the sulphurous fumes and descended towards the distant roadway far below. Gradually the light of their lantern faded from view.

The others settled down again to await their return, their ears straining for any sound over the howling of the wind.

It was getting on for midnight before they saw in the darkness the glow of the lamp again deep in the chasm and then the sound of equipment chinking against rock. Soon they saw Jayal and the other two climbing wearily up the flight of steps from the depths.

The expression on Jayal's face was grim. "We went south, a league or two, and saw the mouth of Harken's Lair: we were a long way away, but still we could see the flames."

"Was there any sign of Faran?" Thalassa asked.

Jayal shook his head. "Pray that the fire has destroyed him."

"There are other ways out of the Lair," Garadas said. "He may still be alive."

Jayal turned to Thalassa. "The priest has not come— we have to leave now."

Thalassa glanced up at the lip of the chasm, at the whirling snow, willing Urthred to appear. But she knew he wouldn't. Garadas was right: he was either a long way from here now, or dead. "Yes, let's go," she said reluctantly.

"Are you sure the Dike will take us through the Broken Hines?" Jayal asked.

"No one knows where any path leads," Garadas said. "All is fate. But I believe the legends, that it will take us through the mountains to Lorn."

"Then let's find out," Jayal answered.

Garadas issued a string of orders, and his men slowly gathered up their equipment, the tension evident. Perhaps most of them only now appreciated the dangers of what they were doing.

Finally, all was ready, and at a nod from the headman they descended into the black depths of Iken's Dike. They trod carefully, for the stone steps were at first slick with ice. From below the sulphurous fumes rose and pricked at their lungs. As they got lower, the ice began to melt. The air became oppressively hot. In the gloom of the lanterns, they saw the black surface of the roadway at the bottom of the chasm. It ran straight as an arrow to their left and to their right. To the south, far away like a distant bonfire, they could now see the yellow flames that marked the entrance to Harken's Lair. They descended the last few feet. The roadway bubbled and heaved in places, melted by a hidden heat beneath its surface, and their boots sank into it.

They turned to their right, away from the fires at the entrance of the Lair. They were swiftly enveloped by the gloom. Garadas ordered all but a single lantern to be doused. Its tiny illumination only further accentuated the crushing weight of the cliff faces on both sides of them. They were dwarfed by the vast heights to either side. Snow eddied down from the lip of the canyon high above, fizzling away into drops of rain when it met the warm air below.

"Where does the road go?" Imuni whispered to Thalassa, who clutched her hand.

Thalassa squeezed it, forcing a smile, though in truth she felt chilled by the knowledge that Faran was likely to be very close. "To the magical realms of the north," she answered, "to Lorn and Iskiard." The answer seemed to satisfy the child, who seemed the only one unaffected by the gloom of that place, and she proceeded silently.

They walked for two hours, the monotony of the road relieved only by the passage of the rough rock faces to either side. The heat underfoot slowly died away, the road surface becoming solid again.

"We are very close to the mountains now," Alanda said suddenly. They halted and turned to her. Once more her eyes were clenched shut and she gripped the staff tightly, then raised it slowly and pointed in front. The darkness was suddenly shot through with green light. Not far ahead they saw the Dike narrow and disappear into a rectangular opening, the counterpart to the one leading into Harken's Lair.

"After that gateway," Garadas said, "we are in the Nations of the Night."

Up to this point Jayal had left Dragonstooth in its scabbard, but now he unsheathed it. Even its brilliance was lost in that vast space. "We need more light," he said.

"Then let the darkness see this," Alanda said. She held up her hands just as another sprinkling of snow fell from above. The particles suddenly froze in mid-air, and the air glittered with a green fairy light that washed the harsh canyon walls. With a gesture of her staff the cloud of glowing particles flowed forward, preceding them.

The villagers seemed in better heart now they saw Dragonstooth and Alanda's magic. The young Illgill stepped to the head of the party, and the villagers fell in behind him. He was full of purpose now, the fits and waking nightmares of an hour or two before forgotten.

They passed under the opening of the cave. Two monolithic statues fifty feet high stood on either side, their hands crossed at their chests, their carved eyes staring towards the Southern Lands: ancient guardians, weathered beyond recognition. Looking up in the light of the glowing particles, the humans saw that the rough walls of the gorge were succeeded here by a series of barrel vaults stretching away into the darkness. The road began to rise slightly, and they saw side tunnels snaking off to their left and right. A distant moaning sound could be heard from them as they passed. No one dared speak, and the only other sound was their footsteps in the vast echoing hall.

The road rose for another mile, and the feeling of gloom grew. Alanda's light began to fade, as if the atmosphere of the place was stifling it. In the semidark they saw the road opened into a round chamber in front of them. The path broke to the left and right and described a circle around another statue, twenty feet high and shaped like a gorgon's head, with bulging eyes and a gaping mouth wide and deep enough to hide a man in. The path rejoined on the far side of the chamber before plunging into another tunnel beyond. From the sides, two curved stone stairways swept in dramatic arcs to a higher level.

They had all halted, staring. Alanda once more stood with the staff upraised, her eyes shut in concentration.

"What is it?" Thalassa asked, sensing her stillness.

"Magic," the old lady replied.

"What sort?"

"Magic of the grave, child: Faran is here."

They whirled around, but as yet the road behind was empty.

"He is very close," the old lady said.

"Let's go on," Garadas said.

But as he spoke, there came a rustling from behind, and they turned once more to see some twenty of the Reapers of Sorrow exiting from the tunnels behind them. The sight of their skull masks froze Garadas and his men to the spot. Imuni screamed, then hid her face. The Reapers came forward in a solid phalanx, their maces beating on their copper shields, the din almost deafening. They turned as one, but then stopped stone dead again. From the mouth of the gorgon ahead, Faran, Golon and Smiler appeared: more figures appeared on the stairways, hurrying down. A despairing

moan came from the villagers when their features fell
into the light, and some of them dropped their weapons from frozen hands. The ravaged faces, the bone
exoskeletons, the twisted limbs. It seemed the contents
of Hel had been emptied into this one place.

"The Nations," Garadas whispered.

Faran came on, gesturing for the creatures to stay
back. His eyes were locked on Thalassa's. He stopped
twenty feet away from her. As he halted, the Reapers
abruptly ceased beating their maces on their shields.
There was a sudden silence.

A small smile broke out on Faran's face. "You see,"
he said, his gaze never leaving Thalassa's face, "nothing escapes me ever; no matter what prayer or magic
you employ." His eyes bored into hers, mesmerising,
and she felt herself being pulled into the vertiginous
depths. And it was as if her corrupted blood sang in
her veins: was she not like him? Soon she would be
one of the Dead in Life. What use was struggle? She
should surrender to the power. He was her Dominant
now, the vampire who owned her. She must give herself to him.

Faran took a step nearer, sensing her will giving
way. "Yes, you are one of us. Tell your friends to lay
down their arms, Thalassa: I only want you and the
young Illgill. The rest can go free."

She was sinking slowly in the web of his spidery voice,
being dragged away from the light. . . . Then she remembered. Urthred. He had promised her they would find
the Silver Chalice: it was in Lorn just beyond this mountain. There was still hope. Her eyes broke contact with
Faran's, and she heard him growl, low, feral, like a
dog denied a bone. And she saw what he was, what
life lay ahead for her, if she fell. But she wouldn't:
she would live to see the sun reborn again.

The noise, too, seemed to galvanise Jayal. He
stepped forward, Dragonstooth upraised. It was a futile gesture, for they were totally outnumbered. Behind Faran, the creatures swarmed forward.

But Faran stayed them with a gesture. "Leave him

for me," he said. He gestured towards Golon, his palm out. In the background Thalassa saw the sorcerer fashion a spell, and suddenly in the Undead Lord's outstretched hand appeared a dark rod, like a column of soot that winnowed as Faran moved his arm: a weapon of sorts, but nothing that looked a match for Dragonstooth. Jayal flung himself forward and swung down with a mighty two-handed blow. Faran lifted his hand in what appeared to be a futile gesture, but as the dark magic touched Dragonstooth the light bled from the sword and in a blink of an eye, dark tendrils sprang like serpents from the blade and twisted around Jayal's arms, pinioning them together.

But still he struggled forward, trying to strike Faran in short-armed jabs despite the magical bonds on his arms. "Help me," he cried. Faran lifted the rod, ready for a killing blow, as Jayal struggled ineffectually to free his pinioned arms.

Thalassa had been in a daze, only half-taking in what was happening, but his cry snapped her back to consciousness. Suddenly she realised that light flowed in her veins again: she had the magic to break Faran's spell, to defeat him. She stretched out her hands. The light flowed from them as if dawn had come. Faran and the creatures were bathed in its glare, and the dark bonds pinioning Jayal seared away.

He swung Dragonstooth at Faran, who threw himself backwards at the last instant, then pandemonium broke out as the villagers suddenly took heart at the sudden reversal of fortunes. The ones who had dropped their weapons snatched them up again and weapon met weapon in a deafening clash of metal. Some struck hide or bone, and the creatures of the Night shrieked. Screams and oaths came from the humans.

Thalassa dragged Imuni forward, sensing the Reapers running forward behind them. She glanced back. Alanda had turned and, holding the staff above her head, called out in a loud voice: the earth shook and rocks began to tumble from the ceiling and the sides of the tunnel, crashing down on their pursuers. They disappeared in the rain of black rock. Now Alanda hurried up to Thalassa, the staff held like a weapon. One of the creatures of the Night was bearing down on her, but then it seemed to hit a solid wall, just in front of the staff, and dissolved into a bubbling pulp, its innards spreading on the floor much like those of a crushed cockroach.

"Creatures of Shadows, illusions only," Alanda muttered, stepping forward and whirling the staff in front of her. Instantly the creatures around Faran and Golon began to melt away into pools of slime, only Smiler making good its escape back into the gaping mouth of the gorgon.

Suddenly Faran and Golon were nearly cut off, and they, too, retreated. Jayal pressed forward with a berserk look upon his face, transformed by rage. Now he would have revenge for all the dead of Thrull field and those slaughtered afterwards. Faran's dark rod still held for a moment, despite the blinding light.

"Magic, Golon," Faran ordered through gritted teeth as he parried another blow from Dragonstooth. "Bring me more magic."

Golon's face was a study of concentration, staring at the leech gatherer's staff. Sweat beaded his sallow brow, his hands shaping a spell that never came. "The staff," he shouted. "It is too strong." Faran was still stumbling back. The two of them had reached the entrance of the statue's mouth. They fell back into the interior. Jayal made as if to follow, then suddenly its extended upper jaw fell. Jayal would have been crushed, but he flung himself back at the last moment. The stone slammed down with an earsplitting crash, sending up a great cloud of dust. When it cleared, they saw that the mouth was fast shut. Faran, Golon and Smiler had escaped.

The villagers set up a ragged cheer, their eyes mad with fighting spirit. They hadn't lost a single man, though one had had his arm ripped open by one of the creature's claws. Alanda hastened to the man's side and applied the tip of the staff to the wound. The man yelped as the wound was cauterised by the glowing end of the staff, but Alanda paid him no heed.

Jayal slowly picked himself up from the floor. "So near," he whispered. "I was so near to killing him."

"And he us. The leech gatherer's staff saved us," Thalassa said. She was shivering. Faran had seen what she had become. At the end of the month she would be like him.

Jayal stared for a moment longer at the titanic mouth of the gorgon as if his eyes could bore through its solid rock and find Faran.

But Alanda wasn't going to let them linger. "Quickly," she yelled. "The darkness is all around us—we're not safe yet." She raised the staff high above her head and led them further into the depths of the mountain.

In the gorgon's mouth Faran stared bleakly at the sealed entrance. The remaining vampire guard and a handful of the Reapers were all that were left, and he had been close to death at the young Illgill's hands. He cursed, cursed with the knowledge of two hundred years' imprecations which came like a black bile from his mouth. Then he rounded on Smiler. The creature stood impassively, the wide slit at its throat opened as ever in a mocking grin.

"So, human, the Lightbringer has escaped Ravenspur—the Master will not be pleased," it said.

Faran approached to within a foot and stared at it threateningly. "Your fellow creatures were nothing more than mist. Perhaps you are mist as well."

Smiler merely grinned back. "Oh, I am real enough. Besides, what would you do? Attack me? Here in these tunnels? You would never find your way out without me."

Faran held its gaze for a moment longer. "Very well: we both want the same thing. We will have to follow them, attack them when they're weakened."

"Then follow me," Smiler said. "The Master will unleash the wolf upon the plains. We will follow with the Thorn Men. Our enemies won't reach Lorn."

Faran nodded slowly. "So be it," he said. "They won't escape us a second time." But in his heart he had already begun to plot the creature's death. Smiler wanted Thalassa dead, but he needed her alive. Sooner or later he and Golon would have to wipe that grin from the creature's face forever.

CHAPTER TWENTY-TWO

❧

The Plain
of Wolves

After the clamour of the fight, an oppressive silence fell on Thalassa and her companions. They left the chamber in which the battle had taken place, and followed the road onwards through the heart of the mountain. For the moment they needed no guidance from Alanda and the staff.

Only the passing corridors on either side told them that they were indeed making progress through the Broken Hines. Rustling sounds echoed from the passages into the darkness of the seemingly endless nave. Now and again, ragged wisps of mist blew out from the side tunnels. The mist hovered, wavering halfway between substance and form, then was blown away by the icy stream of wind which blew down the road. The very rock seemed to brood around them. But, as yet, there were no signs of a more substantial enemy. Perhaps the Nations were no more than shadows? Perhaps the danger had been destroyed by the leech gatherer's staff? But, if any of them nurtured this hope, they did not articulate it. In their hearts, they knew the Nations could not be defeated so easily, and certainly not Faran. The euphoria they had felt after the battle quickly evaporated.

It was in the darkest time of the night when they saw ahead the ragged opening on the northern side of the mountain. They had passed under Ravenspur. They halted, uncertain, not daring to believe they were so close to safety.

"How much further is it to Lorn?" Jayal asked Alanda. The old woman, who had shown such fire before, was leaning against the tunnel wall, exhausted. She didn't respond to Jayal's question. Thalassa turned and looked at her old friend. "Alanda," she said, tugging gently at the sleeve of the old lady's cloak. Alanda stirred slightly and lifted her head. The blue eyes were washed-out and weak, and her face was deathly pale, but she managed a thin smile.

"I heard him, child," she said, pushing herself slowly off the wall. She stood, swaying slightly. Her eyes creased, concentrating on the staff. "It is close. There is another plain in front. It will take an hour or two to cross, then we will be in the forest."

"You need help, my friend," Thalassa said. She looked round, and two of the villagers came forward and supported Alanda.

"My thanks," the old woman murmured.

They pushed forward. Outside the chasm was alive with flying snowflakes, and a bitter wind was blowing. There were steep ice-covered steps to their right. Alanda pointed up them, and they cautiously began to climb, their feet struggling for purchase, the snow matting their cloaks. They emerged into the blizzard at the top of the steps. In front the ground was flat the little distance they could see in the driving snow. Behind they sensed the mountain rearing up into the storm. Alanda pointed ahead with the staff. "That is the way," she said, raising her voice. The wind once more shrieked and howled like a thing possessed.

Garadas now began issuing orders, telling them to rope themselves together and don their snowshoes. But as they were doing so, the wind suddenly died, and as if in answer to its noise there came a howl from behind them, from up the slopes of Ravenspur. They all stopped what they were doing. "Fenris," Garadas whispered. "Quickly," he said. "It will be here soon."

He motioned at one of the men, who broke away from the others sorting through their equipment and came over. The man carried a resin-soaked torch, its handle made of white wood that looked like ash. There was a brass holder at its end, etched with the fire rune.

"My lady," he said, turning to Thalassa. "I have kept this until last, for though we have survived great dangers already, the greatest is now upon us. Fenris comes. Only Marizian's magic will help us against him."

Thalassa looked at the torch again, then back at Garadas. "It was left us by Marizian," he said, "and ever since the headman of the village has kept it."

"What is it?" she asked.

"It is said that when the Lightbringer holds it, it will cast a light that no mortal man, let alone beast, can bear to look at. But it will only work for a little time. Vernigen here will have it ready when it becomes necessary," Garadas explained.

"Then stay close," she said to the sandy-haired villager. He smiled nervously back at her.

Jayal now came up holding the end of the rope so she could tie herself to the line. She helped loop the rope through Alanda's and Imuni's belts, then fixed it to her own.

"Are you ready?" she asked the old woman. Alanda merely nodded, too weak, it seemed, to speak anymore. Garadas waited at the head of the column. He had told the men to take out all the lanterns. Even so their light barely made an impression on the icy gloom. Their breaths fogged the air. When he saw all was ready he turned and led them off over the plain in front, stepping high over the snowdrifts.

The wind returned, blowing lustily into their faces from the north. The lanterns flickered, the candles threatening to snuff out. Behind they could hear the howling of the wolf coming down the mountainside, ever closer.

They struggled on for over an hour, stopping periodically for Alanda to commune with the staff, trying to determine how far they were from their objective.

Each time it seemed they had made little progress. Their eyes strained ahead, desperately trying to spot the edge of the forest. But at least the strength of the gale lessened slightly the further they got from Ravenspur.

Suddenly the line came to a jerking halt. Thalassa squinted forward through the snow. The point man had stopped, his hand held up. She strained her eyes, trying to see what he had seen. They all heard it at once over the soughing of the wind, a low growling noise. But it was no growl that any of them recognised: it seemed to come from the depths of the earth; a low grinding of cartilage and bone and hatred which rose and fell in pitch.

The point man eased back, the lantern held high in his hand. Into its fitful light, its eyes red as a furnace, came a wolf. It growled and all around there were answering growls: the creature was not alone. Thalassa had seen wolves before, carcasses brought back after one of the many hunting trips her father used to make to the Fire Mountains. But this was like none of those, though she had heard of their like: a Dire Wolf. Four feet high, the size of a small pony, its exposed canines were some six inches or longer. Its breath was a dense fog in front of it. But stranger still, its pelt was a blue-grey, as if it were both fur and ice commingled.

"It is one of Fenris's cubs," Garadas shouted. "Watch out; he cannot be far away."

It stalked forward towards the lantern held in the man's hand. Now other shapes could be seen in the dim light. There was a whole pack of them, closing in. But it was as if they were biding time, inching forward only, waiting, perhaps, for Fenris himself to appear.

Garadas quickly issued more orders. The men readied their bows and spears. Vernigen crouched low against the wind, trying to get a spark from his tinder-box for the torch. But the wolves were moving in, their feral stench, the smell of blood and wet fur, thick in the air.

"Don't shoot," Garadas warned. Thalassa wondered

why not. Wouldn't they be overrun in seconds if they didn't act? The nearest was only twenty feet, quite clear in the light of the lantern.

It was then she saw Jayal make a sudden movement in front of her. He had been stumbling along, apparently unconscious of the snow and his fellows, no doubt engrossed in another waking vision. He had barely roused himself even when the line had stopped so abruptly. But now he seemed to come alive again as he had in the tunnel beneath Ravenspur; he reached behind him and took the bow from his back and notched an arrow to it. He raised it until it was levelled at the first wolf, a strange light, as untamed as the look in the wolf's eye, in his own. Thalassa could see the tension in his forearms as he pulled back on the bow.

Garadas opened his mouth, trying to stop him, but the bow thrummed with the energy of release before the first word was out. There was a smacking noise, like wet leather hit with a metal bar, and the arrow quicker than a blink of an eye buried deep in the creature's neck. The wolf leapt into the air, then buckled and rolled onto its back, thrashing on the snow, its teeth reaching back, ineffectually worrying at the arrow in its neck, bright red blood geysering from the wound.

A blur of movement and the other wolves sprang towards them, leaping past their wounded companion, enraged by the smell of blood. Thalassa threw her arms protectively around Imuni as one of them bounded towards them, its jaws open, its purple tongue and yellow teeth quite visible in the dim lantern light. Then at the last instant a spark finally caught the resin torch that Vernigen had been trying to light, and it flared into life. A dazzling whiteness bathed the scene, a strange sizzling noise in the air as much electricity as light.

The sudden brilliance caused the leading wolf to come to a slithering halt some ten feet from Thalassa and the others. It blinked, blinded by the light. The others simi-

larly had halted, growling and snarling, the noise blend-
ing with the enraged frenzy of the wounded animal,
which rolled over and over, still trying to bite the
arrow that was killing it. But the respite would only
be brief, Thalassa knew. One torch could not ward
them off for long.

She caught a flicker of movement out of the corner
of her eyes. Vernigen was holding the torch out to
her. There seemed a roaring noise in her head, the
sound of blood, and the soughing of the wind and the
howling of the wolves, and she couldn't hear his
words, but there was a strange look in his eyes.

"Take the torch!" Garadas shouted, the words suddenly breaking through to her consciousness over all
the other white noise. Then she understood. She was
the Lightbringer: only her magic could save them now.

She reached out. On the instant her fingers touched
it, the torch seemed to explode into an even whiter
incandescent light which sent shadows stretching far
over the plain despite the driving snow. The wolves
stood momentarily in silhouette and then with a hideous yowl they turned and became bounding shadows
on the face of the snow, running away to the north.

Thalassa stood staring at the torch: never before
had she seen anything like the blue-white light that
burned from it. She looked right into the heart of the
light, though she saw the villagers around her averting
their gazes, shielding their eyes with their hands.
Where had such magic come from? They might have
stood there all night, but the brightness of the torch
began to fade and with it the energy tingling in her
veins began to subside, and virtual darkness returned
to the desolate plain.

"They've gone," Garadas said. Thalassa stared at
the brass handle: though the torch had burned so
brightly, the handle itself was still curiously cool to
the touch. The magic was gone from it. Apart from
their physical weapons, they were now defenseless
against further attacks.

"Why did you tell your men not to shoot?" Thalassa asked.

"Those wolves were not the greatest threat: they were waiting for Fenris to come. But he will be here soon, for these wolves are his children. He feels their pain, will have felt this one's death," he said, kicking at the dying animal. It was clearly in its last throes, its head lying on the snow, a purplish pool of blood on the snow by its mouth, its chest heaving slowly. One of Garadas's men stepped forward and drove the point of his spear deep into its chest.

"Listen!" Garadas said. They heard a far-distant howling much like the one they had heard earlier on the mountainside of Goda. It came from the south, much nearer now. "Fenris comes, as swift as the arctic wind."

Thalassa turned to Alanda, who sat on her haunches in the snow, and helped her back to her feet. "It is not far now, child," Alanda said. "Soon we'll be in the forest," but her words were so weak that they scarcely brought any comfort to her friend.

Garadas issued more orders and they resumed their lines. After the light of the torch, the boundaries of the world through the swirling snow seemed even more confined. They strained their eyes forward, hoping to see the tree line of the forest in front. The tracks of the fleeing wolf pack led away to the north, the direction they had to go. Reluctantly, they followed the trail, pursued by the howling of Fenris.

CHAPTER TWENTY-THREE

✤

The Thorn Men

It took two hours for Smiler to lead Faran and the survivors of his party out of the mountain. They found the Thorn Men waiting for them at the exit, standing like a dark and silent hedge, blocking the cave mouth. But they stirred and then rattled to either side as Smiler emerged.

It silently gestured for them to move off. The path led straight down from the cave mouth. Below they could see the shores of the Black Tarn, the place that the Master had pointed out to them earlier. Its shores were covered in a dense fog. They followed a path around its edge, the water black through the thick mist. They heard bubbling far off in its centre and splashing noises, and groans that reverberated off the invisible rocks that ringed them.

Faran's surviving men kept their faces steadfastly to the front, not daring to look at what was being born in the dark waters of the lake; but Faran looked: it was as if the lake's surface was a viscous tar—in it he saw the shadows of limbs and heads, struggling with the surface, struggling to the shore. He saw a skull of one of the damned only some twenty feet distant, its eyes ablaze with a green light. The Nations, born once more from this lake as the apparition in the mountain had promised.

There was a sudden movement in the air, and the mist over the tarn twisted upwards as if a tornado had suddenly materialised there. Freezing fog began to be sucked into the vortex, and the surface of the water churned even more fiercely than before. Even from the side of the lake, they could feel the deep cold rising below, the frozen souls of the disenfranchised, fixed in the glacial depths, re-forming. Smiler halted and stared down at the surface, raising its short arms to either side, as if itself raising the creatures from the depths.

It stood thus for a moment. Thick snow began to fall. Faran stood hedged in by the Thorn Men, cursing the cold flakes striking at his unprotected head. Then Smiler dropped its arms, and turned, gesturing for them to follow it.

At the end of the lake they found a gully leading down, choked with bones and flanked by beetling crags. They followed the path of the stream that fell slowly like an icy treacle over the rocks and falls until they came to a series of huge boulders in front of which the dark water pooled once more. The wind was getting fiercer and fiercer as it was sucked back up the mountainside to the tarn. Then they heard an ear-splitting howl from below: the wolf was ready to do its master's bidding.

They clambered over the man-high boulders. But just then there was a sudden break in the snowstorm and the plains could be seen stretching away. Immediately below them they saw a tunnel mouth, the northern extension of Iken's Dike carved from the face of the mountain. The gorge ran arrow straight to the northwest. Smiler gestured across the chasm. That was evidently the direction they had to go, but how were they meant to cross the Dike? Faran was about to ask Smiler that question, but the creature had already set off again. Where the glacier ended, a blue bridge of ice and snow some twenty yards across overarched the void beneath. Smiler scrambled down and walked over the icy bridge, apparently heedless of the groans of the fragile span and the cascades of ice that fell as it took its weight.

Faran followed more cautiously. He tested its surface before he stepped onto it: the snow was powdery and brittle on the top and fell away into the indefinable depths of the blackness below as he kicked at it. His booted feet met verglas beneath, smooth and treacherous. His eyes went up to Smiler. The creature stood on the other side of the chasm, the smile still open at its neck. The bridge was the only route across. Faran spread his hands out to either side, the severed nerves of his right hand still not responding well to his mental commands, but at least proving some counterbalance. He slipped and slithered across, his efforts clumsy compared to Smiler's. The others followed as best they could, some crawling painfully on their hands and knees. The Thorn Men rustled across, though one or two of their number slipped and fell uncomplainingly into the blackness below.

When all were on its side, Smiler gestured, and with a roar the ice span fell into the depths. The bridge had only been kept in place by this hairsbreadth of magic. Mini avalanches fell from the higher slopes of the mountain, as if in sympathy for the fallen bridge.

Smiler motioned them forward and they set off across the plain. The creature's bulging legs made short work of the snow, but the humans struggled through the knee-high drifts. The slush worked into Faran's clothes, and he felt the moisture begin to attack his desiccated skin. He tried to shrug off the discomfort, forcing his mind into a trance. The scene when he'd confronted Thalassa below the mountain came back into his mind. She had been so close. He had felt her will bend to his mesmerism. He had seen she was one of his now, one of the Dead in Life. Had seen it in her eyes, yet still her soul was alive, and, as she had in Thrull, she had resisted his dominance. But a few moments more, and she would have been his, he was sure.

So he trudged on across the plain, until his surroundings gradually came back to him and he became aware once more of the endless snowdrifts, and the meltwater in his boots, rubbing his dried limbs. Water, inimical to the undead. He thought to stop Smiler and ask where they were going: were they trying to intercept Thalassa and the others? Or was the wolf going after them? The wolf's howling got closer, and he felt it coming swiftly down the mountainside. Fenris. He would reach them first. Then there would be no saving Thalassa. His last chance had gone.

Before he was aware of it properly, the first branches of the forest loomed out of the night, and they passed under them. Faran noted that some green leaves still clung to them in defiance of the cold. The snow was lighter under the trees. Smiler halted. Faran looked back. The Thorn Men had disappeared. He looked around: they had been right behind him, but now there was no sign. Then there came a dry rustle, the creaky sound of old branches rubbing together, and he saw one and then another of them, nearly invisible, moving forward into the forest, a shadow rustling between the boughs of the trees.

Smiler gestured, and the creatures moved off to either side, becoming invisible again. Faran strained his ears to hear the wolf. Nothing now. Had Thalassa escaped?

Smiler interrupted his thoughts: "Lorn lies to the northeast," it said.

"What of the humans?" Faran asked.

"The wolf will follow them—perhaps do our job for us," Smiler answered. "If not, we will complete what we failed to do in the tunnels."

"Very well," Faran answered, looking to the south. She was out there somewhere, perhaps unaware of what was coming. He longed to order his remaining men to attack Smiler, but they would have no chance, not with the Thorn Men invisible in the trees.

He felt the presence of the Thorn Men pressing around, urging him on into the depths of the forest. Very well, he would go into the forest, towards this city of Lorn that the baron was meant to have travelled to—there they would find the second artefact and destroy it. The world once more would start to sink towards eternal darkness: Iss' kingdom would reign.

And yet it was as if that long-denied life still squirmed in his traitorous heart. What joy in the eternal kingdom of the night without her, her lily-white flesh, the promise of her blood?

A coldness, a coldness greater even than the cold blood that leaked slowly through his body, or the freezing wind, settled slowly upon him.

CHAPTER TWENTY-FOUR

The Last Watchtower

Though the weather had been oddly calm at the summit of the mountain, the storm clouds rose up to meet Urthred as he descended its north face, and soon he was struggling against the howling blizzard. Still he ran as if Iss himself was on his heels. But all that followed was the eerie howling of the wolf from high above.

The steep rocky path eased, and he clambered over a last few boulders. Now the ground in front was level, covered knee high in snow. He was on the northern plain. How was he to find Thalassa and the others in the storm? He was blinded by the driving flakes, knowing only that somewhere over to his left ran the continuation of Iken's Dike and to the north was the forest. Surely they would have reached the forest by now? He had to keep heading north.

His magic was gone, and there was nothing to guide him in the darkness, but Reh must have been with him, for after several hours of struggle through the drifts, he reached the edge of the forest. A gust of warm air, the first for many hours, came through the trees from the north, momentarily dispelling the snow, and in the sudden respite he saw the outline of another tower looming in the darkness—a companion to the ones south of Ravenspur and in Goda. He stared at it, wondering whether the tower was inhabited. In appearance it looked abandoned, but as he watched,

a wisp of smoke was plucked through its open doorway and whipped away. Yet he could see no light
inside. He clicked at the stud on his glove which released the hidden knife and approached cautiously,
edging up to the jamb of the door, which creaked
eerily on its hinges in the blustering wind. He peered
in: the last embers of a fire glowed in a grate on the
far side of the room. There was a table and other
furniture, covered by a thin layer of the snow which
had been driven in by the wind.

It was the mirror image of the tower this morning,
except that instead of a stone staircase leading to the
top of the tower, there was a wooden one. The place
was empty now, but it hadn't been abandoned long
ago. He stepped inside, closing the door behind him,
his nerve ends prickling, and cautiously approached
the fire. There was a pot hanging over it with a ladle
in it. He lifted the ladle and sniffed: a vegetable stew
of some sort. Suddenly he realised how hungry he was:
he wrenched off his mask and applied the ladle to his
ravaged lips. The stew was tepid, but he ate it greedily.
It was good—mushrooms and pulses and roots. He
took another ladle and then another. Then he thought:
what if the food was poisoned? But his hunger took
over once more, and he ate again. Next he kicked the
embers of the fire, and seeing a stack of logs next to
the grate, threw some of these on, too. The firewood
was dry, and quickly he had a roaring blaze going. His
limbs began to thaw. Then he sat at the oak table and
emptied his backpack. The food in it had been spoiled
by his immersion in the marsh water earlier, but the
flask of wine was unharmed. He uncorked it and took
a swig.

He was very tired, and his limbs were heavy after
the climb first up, then down Ravenspur. His eyelids
drooped. Anxious thoughts raced through his mind.
His meeting with the Master, his companions out on
the plain . . .

His eyes snapped open; he had slept for only a few
seconds, he was sure. He got back to his feet and went

to the wooden ladder leading up to the battlements. He climbed up it groggily, pushing open the wooden trapdoor at the top. Snow drove in on him, the cold reviving him. He looked to the south. Nothing except the darkness and driving snow. But he persevered, staring steadfastly towards the south, almost willing himself to pick up any glimmer, any sign of life. He felt in his bones that his friends were alive, were coming. Now all was quiet, the snow falling gently: a sinister quiet. His eyes began to droop again, and he forced himself back to consciousness with an effort.

It was after an hour that he saw the sudden white light flaring to the south. A mile or two, maybe further he guessed. It was no physical flame, of that he was sure. Magic. His friends out there alone, no doubt lost in the blizzard. He tried to get a bearing on the light, then hurried down the ladder again and flung open the door to the tower. But when he emerged, the light on the plain was gone as if it had never been. He took a few steps forward through the drifts, but the darkness swallowed him completely. Looking back, he couldn't even see the tower, and he had only travelled a few yards.

He retraced his steps, seeing with relief the glow of the fire through the door. He pulled the door to and threw a wooden bar over it, securing it. A deep chill had settled on his spine. He felt evil very close now.

Once more he climbed to the battlements. He heard a new sound, a strange whispering noise, and peering down at the snow below the tower he saw a black mist begin to steal into view from the direction of the mountains, mist that twisted and turned as if struggling to take shape. Where had it come from? It hadn't been present a moment before, but now the whole white plain was stained by the spreading darkness.

Then a shiver went down his spine and he knew: this was the wolf. The creature that the Master had told him he would send. It was not a thing of blood and sinew, but of the ice and shadows, of the realms beyond, one moment substantial, the next a mist. It

was not fully manifest, yet. But before his eyes it
began to take shape, solidify. There he saw a back,
there a flashing image of a snaggle-toothed mouth,
rent apart by a gust of wind, but re-forming, resolidify-
ing every second—its growth couldn't be denied. Already its outline was the height of the tower. And
where its shadow fell, he saw the snow turning to
black ice. A heavy fall of snow blanked out the scene.
He looked out again, and it was gone.

Then there was an earsplitting howl, right by his ear
it seemed, and he turned. There was the mouth of Hel,
purple and black rimmed by a thousand rotten teeth,
looming right above him tall as a house, its breath smell-
ing of bitterness, of black ice. He flung himself back as
the thing exhaled and the battlements were covered by
black ice. They cracked and broke away as they froze,
suddenly as brittle as glass. A large hunk of masonry
crashed down from the parapet. He seized the top of
the ladder and threw himself down it. He fell the last
few feet to the flagstones of the room, jarring his shoulder. He leapt to his feet painfully and staggered to the
door. He must warn the others. He flung down the bar
and rushed outside, staring back fearfully at the tower.

But he had gone only a step or two before he halted
abruptly. The monstrous shadow had disappeared.
The wolf was gone, gone into the darkness. Where?
Once more there was a lull in the blizzard and far
away he saw lanterns bobbing towards him from the
south. His companions! Then he realised where the
wolf had gone. It was heading towards them. Urthred
flung himself forward, wading clumsily through the
snowdrifts towards the lights, yelling out a warning.

CHAPTER TWENTY-FIVE

Finding the
Dragon Within

Since the howl they had heard after they had fought
the cubs, there had been no more sound from the
direction of Ravenspur. A faint hope dawned that they
had escaped Fenris.

But still they hurried. Now more than ever the rope
binding them together was necessary. The leading man
fell into a side gully covered by a thin crust of snow
and was hauled up, bruised and battered. Another
man took over his duty, but now visibility was only a
few feet, the light of the lanterns tiny glowworms in
the blizzard. Their breath was a cloud of condensed
air, their lips blue and chafed, their faces pinched and
red. They navigated only by the length of rope binding
them to the person in front and when Alanda, after
communing with the staff, shouted out changes of
direction.

"I'm afraid," Imuni whispered to Thalassa, gripping
her hand fiercely.

"Don't be afraid: the staff will lead us to Lorn,"
she whispered back in a voice barely audible over the
howl of the wind.

"How?" Imuni asked. She was blue in the face and
chattering from the cold.

"It came from a tree in the forest ahead," Thalassa
answered. "The leech gatherer gave it to us."

"The leech gatherer?"

"A creature that lived in the warm Heart of the

World, whose forebears swam like salmon in the molten rivers at the beginning of time. Think of it," Thalassa said, smiling. "Think of that heat; it will make you warm."

"Nothing will make me warm," Imuni said despondently, though her mouth had turned up into a small smile at Thalassa's story.

They hurried as best they could, but progress was slow in the clumsy snowshoes. Alanda stopped often to recheck her bearings, her eyes tightly shut, her brow creased in concentration. Then, after each pause, she would make a small adjustment to the direction and set off again.

Half an hour passed in this way. The wind from the south began to slacken, though the snowfall, if anything, became even thicker. Then they heard a new sound. At first it was as if they heard the howl of the wind again, a low soughing sound, rising and falling, but by now the wind had completely disappeared, and the snow fell straight down. They stopped and listened. It came again, a lost, haunting sound, perhaps slightly nearer, though it was impossible to tell from which direction it came through the muffling effect of the wind.

"What is it?" Jayal asked.

"The wolf," Garadas said. "It has found the dead cub. Now it will find us." His men stirred uneasily, casting their eyes nervously about them into the snow.

"How?" Jayal said. "Can it have followed us through the blizzard?"

"You don't understand: it is everywhere on this plain. This is its kingdom, the Plain of Wolves," Garadas answered. And indeed the sound seemed to come from all directions at once, was part of the icy wind, the desolation.

"Then we will fight it," Jayal said, holding up Dragonstooth.

"Your prayers would be better," the headman said, casting a despairing glance at his child, who stared at the adults around her with innocent incomprehension.

"It is only half of this world: its eyes were taken from the dying coals of the gods' hearts, its body is ice and mist, its breath is poison to breathe, its claws stronger than the talons even of the priest's gloves, it runs as fast as the wind."

"How far is it to the edge of the forest?" Thalassa asked Alanda.

"We must be close to it now; but the staff tells me only in which direction to go, not how near it is."

They moved off again, wading as quickly as they could through the drifts. Now all their eyes quartered the area around them. A sharp iodine smell filled the air, and the snow in front even in the dim light could be seen turning a faint yellow colour.

Then there was another howl, its reverberation shaking their bones. Much closer now, fifty yards perhaps, immediately behind them, and they felt even through the cushion of the snow a tremble in the earth beneath their feet.

There was confusion now in the line of the men, the rope twisting back and forwards. Garadas shouted out orders, but some of his men seemed to have lost their reason, throwing off their belts, or cutting the rope that bound them. Some clutched still their weapons, but half had begun to wade away from the source of the sound. Those that remained fell back into a tight circle. Jayal, who had been tugged to the ground by the rope, struggled back to his feet. "There!" he said under his breath, and then, in the brilliance of Dragonstooth, they could all see it: a dark form, it seemed higher than a house, looming in the falling snow. It moved with a strange loping stride towards them, twin red coals like lanterns advancing jerkily through the air—the creature's eyes, high above the ground. It leant its head back, ready to howl.

Urthred could see the glow of the lanterns—a white ambient light through the snow. He had followed a line of stained yellow spoor to the south, hoping against hope that he would get to them before the

wolf. But he was too late; it was materialising ahead,
between him and the lights.

He ran forward through the drifts. Now he needed
Reh's magic fire more than ever. The air was full of
the creature's smell, then he was right on it: it loomed
out of the blizzard, higher than a house. He slithered
to a halt and raised his gloves, clenching his eyes shut.
Where was that molten spark that had burned so
brightly in Thrull? There was a warm tingling in his
finger stumps, as if somewhere the God had dimly
heard his call, but somewhere in the arctic night or
maybe on the mountaintop, the spirit had been lost,
so though molten flames seethed and slipped through
his veins, only a red ball like a bubble of fire welled
slowly from his fingertips, hanging gelatinously there.
He flung it in the direction of the creature. The glob
fell with a hiss of evaporating snow at its feet.

It turned, the light of the molten fire for the first
time illuminating it properly. He saw the white crystals
of its hide; the red wells of its eyes turned in his direction, then the corrupt stink of its breath rolled over
him, like the smell of metal long drowned in a pond,
rusty and virulent. Black ice formed on his cloak in
an instant, like a lead sheet, the weight making his
knees buckle. The ice penetrated the eyeslits of his
mask. His eyes, unlidded, glazed as the frost descended on him. He fought to keep on his feet. Dimly,
through the thin coating of ice, he could see a huddle
of people: Thalassa's face, the glow of Dragonstooth,
some eight villagers.

He fought the ice entombing his limbs. Where was
that molten dragon, or the Wall of Fire?

And somewhere, from some hidden source, the heat
did come, pervading his body. Gradually his sight
swam back as his eyes unfroze. More fire burst from
his fingertips and he flung it forward, this time the
molten lava striking the creature's side, shredding it
so the fire passed through it, and a vast hole appeared
in its middle. He saw that Thalassa and the others had
somehow skirted around it and were running clumsily

towards him. There was something curious about their feet: then he saw what it was—they wore snowshoes.

"To the tower!" he yelled at the top of his voice. He turned and saw in the light of Dragonstooth that it was closer than he dared have hoped. Not more than fifty feet off, and, beyond it, the bare boughs of the forest edge. The others were alongside him now, but the creature had recovered and came forward like an avalanche of ice crystals and mist. Its features briefly glimpsed, then vanishing, only to materialise again much closer as, step by step, it ran them down.

Then the edge of its body flowed over him and he felt a terrible numbing cold. He slashed out to left and right with his gloves.

The creature howled with pain and rage; a giant claw materialised out of the ice and scythed at Urthred, who ducked at the last second. He stumbled back and found himself free of the choking ice cloud. His cloak was stiff as steel; and as he ripped it free with his talons, it shattered with an earsplitting crack. All the others had reached the door of the tower. Jayal stood at the threshold, holding it open: Urthred stumbled towards him. The creature must have been just behind, for as he threw himself past Jayal into the tower and the door was slammed shut, the chamber was filled with a freezing cloud of vapour.

Garadas and Jayal had already put their weight behind the door and thrown the bar down. Then the howl came again: it was as if the air had been ripped from his ears and the surrounding ether as the creature enveloped the tower, and it was filled with a white, blinding mist as the temperature plummeted. All he could see was the white light of Dragonstooth, and the lanterns and shapes moving around it. His hands met something hard and he realised it was a table at the centre of the room. He grabbed its edge and dragged it to the door, the two men stepping aside as he thrust the table into place. Already Jayal and Garadas were pulling other items of furniture to build

up the barricade. It looked like the door would hold—
for a while.

There was another prolonged howl, as cold and
chilling as the arctic wind, then a rough scraping sound
of ice against stone as the creature circled the tower,
the corrupt stink of its breath leaking through the
arrow slits, frosting every inch of exposed stone with
ice.

In the light that filtered through the choking fog,
Urthred could see that another column of thick mist
was falling slowly down the shaft from the open trapdoor above them. Then he felt a numbing cold on his
ankles and looked down: wisps of mist had begun to
filter in through the narrow crack between the lintel
and the door, and had begun spreading out in an undulating fan covering the floor by the threshold to the
depth of two or three inches. Danger from below and
above. Fenris: insubstantial as the winter wind, a
breath, an exhalation, manifesting itself right in the
midst of them. No stone could deny him: soon his
form would materialise in the tower itself. Then they
would all die. Just as the Master had promised.

The air was becoming colder and colder. He stepped
back and looked behind him wildly. The very fire in
his veins was beginning to slow. Yet now he needed
that fire more than ever, not just the fire that had
destroyed the vampires in the temple square, but the
greater fire, the fire of creation, with which to conjure
a creature commensurate with Fenris's dark force. The
fire that had been in the dragon steeds thundering
through the air beneath Ravenspur Peak, the magic
of an older time.

Only once before had he summoned that power,
and then inadvertently, when he was twelve, in the
Hearth Fire of Forgeholm Monastery. Could one will
such a spell of creation? Or was it a natural force,
impossible to be willed? The summoning of spirits: the
highest level of the five arts of pyromancy. The serpents he summoned on the Plain of Ghosts had been
only the smallest manifestation of the greater hierar-

chies of creatures: the Dragon was the greatest. Hours of study would not help if the faith deep within was not there. What had he learned in Marizian's tomb? That the *Book of Light* was dust, the very book from which he had learned his conjuries of Flame. Yet there was a greater faith, a faith that lived within and not in books.

He clenched his eyes shut and sought out the seed of fire buried deep in his soul, seeking it in the dark byways of his mind. It seemed he searched for a long time, peripherally aware of how the cold outside grew and grew; but he was away from it now, on a long inner journey. Distant memories, childhood innocence long corrupted by his scars and his loneliness swam unbidden to his mind, and then the dark words of the Master, as if in that one person all the betrayals of his life were made manifest. Slowly the temperature fell in the tower, until everything, even the light of Dragonstooth, was swallowed up in the white mist and the talons of ice. . . .

There came a growl, not from outside but from within the tower, and he knew that Fenris was there, and then, just as this knowledge came, so came the fire he sought, as it had that one time long before, in the Hearth Chamber at Forgeholm. His soul stretched towards it, yearning for its heat in the cold. Now he saw in his inner mind a red penumbra of fire and within it a writhing orange form, in a red embryonic sac, a being waiting to be given life by the seed of fire which he brought. And then he entered the red light and remembered that this was how it had been when he was a child, within the heart of the creature he had created yet outside it at the same time. Now he rushed towards it, the fire and the egg he had created from his heart, down the roaring red torrents of his blood, the roar of his blood and its fire uniting to fill his ears with the music of the Flame, and then it reached the end of its journey and he raised his gloves and unleashed the thing.

The white mist transformed of an instant to orange, and there it stood before his eyes.

A Dragon, a thing of indistinct mass some ten feet tall, its body ablaze with orange-and-red flame, its eyes carbuncles set into an iguana-shaped head, ruffed with gills that puffed out like leather bellows at either side of its bulbous neck. Shimmering silver wings made of a fiery lace spanned the width of the tower, its taloned claws were made of gleaming steel. The very same apparition that he had conjured at Forgeholm.

His companions cowered at the far edges of the room, their hands raised, warding off the intense heat that spewed off the creature in an aura of white flame. Stray flecks of straw and other debris whirled into the air and ignited in brief explosions of flame. The pool of white mist on the floor and the shapes in the column of light boiled away in a thick vapour that pooled like black treacle on the floor. There was an agonised howl from within the room as the icy heart of the wolf began to melt. The mist of which it was formed began to evaporate, then was driven up through the trapdoor opening above, flying before the white-hot fire. But the tower was too confined for the Dragon. Its shifting mass of flames and scales soared upwards after the retreating mist, the ladder igniting like a candle up its entire length as it soared past it, a fiery stairway to the heavens, the Dragon chasing the fleeing shadows with its flame.

Urthred felt its pull as it soared away as if he were the living heart of the thing he had created. Then he *was* the Dragon, the ground no longer beneath his feet as his being followed up the shaft. In a beating of a heart the walls of the tower blurred past on either side as he flew upwards through the floors of the structure and burst through the trapdoor at its top in an explosion of timber and boiling vapour. He glimpsed in its fiery light the lichen-covered crenellations on the parapet. Then he was flying out into the driving snow, which misted suddenly as the heat turned it to vapour, an aurora of moisture spread like a halo around him.

Below he glimpsed the snow-covered moorland and the dark line of the Dike.

He was powerless, carried by the Dragon through the dark to the north, as if it sensed where its fellows, those he had seen at dusk, had gone. It flew, beating its mighty wings, thrusting down the air beneath. He felt an exhilaration that he had never felt before as the wings bore him soaring upwards, giddy as the earth dropped below him. Then he was above the snow clouds and the night was crystal clear, the clouds like fleecy wool below, spinning into a vortex around the watchtower where the Dragon had erupted into the air. The sky was empty in front of him to the south, he could now see the mountains of the Broken Hines, their razorback peaks exposed at their centre, Ravenspur. Beyond them the Palisades.

His senses took on the characteristics of the creature he had become: his sight, his smell, his hearing, all were enhanced. He smelt the trail of Harken's dragons, a whiff of metal and fire. He turned his head to the north, in the direction he had seen them fly, and his spirit followed. Below, he saw the forest stretching away. Suddenly he wanted to stop the Dragon, turn its head back towards the watchtower— but it was too late—the Dragon was the essence of pure will, a thing of Reh which had been spawned in the heart of the sun: once set on its course there was no turning the creature back. All he could so was ride it forward, over the forest, the earth rushing past. A glimpse of another mountain range and ruins and a lake and, far beyond, a glimpse of the cold empty tundra, Iken's Dike a dark line running straight through it. Now the ground beneath was a blur. A hundred miles were shredded by the urgently beating wings in a minute. But the further from the tower and the epicentre of the summoning he got, so he felt his power over the Dragon diminish. Its strength was giving out, its wings began to beat slower and slower. Then he felt weightlessness as it began to sink. Suddenly, he was dropping fast. He fought for control, trying to stop the vertical plummet towards the earth. But its will and his had been separated.

The fire began to chill in his veins, and the Dragon fell faster and faster, in giddy circles, like a bird winged in flight by an arrow. As vertiginous as the flight had been, it was nothing to the sudden onset of vertigo as the thing suddenly plunged straight down like a falling stone towards the icy plains below.

He looked down at the ground rushing up towards him and knew he was going to die. . . .

CHAPTER TWENTY-SIX

❖

The Man of Bronze

He dreamt. As he had dreamt for a thousand years. He dreamt of past times when he had been almost a god, and the golden towers of Shandering Plain had sparkled in the bright sun and the steeds of the gods arced in graceful flight between them, through the azure sky. And he dreamt of the arena whose sides rose in silver banks higher than a mountain: whose jousting place was ten miles across. Here he had fought as the God's champion. Of all of them he had been the greatest; undefeated, indestructible. Until that final day.

It had been a tourney and they'd brought him forth to brassy music that had washed the plains and the grandstands and the far mountains. Almost a god—even he knew it then, the favourite of him who had made him: Reh. On one side of the arena far away was a golden shimmering presence that was like the sun: somewhere in it, invisible, sat the God. The being that no mortal would ever see, but he, the Talos, had seen. From the morning light he had fought all day. He had smitten the rival God's champions: one after the other they had fallen until the penultimate: the spider of the Moon God, which he had throttled with its own adamantine web.

Then only one champion remained: the serpent of Iss. The day was nearly ended. Darkness fell on the arena as he had waited for it, and still it didn't come. He scanned the open field with eyes that could see through plate steel. The light of Reh in his distant grandstand was growing dim. Then, suddenly, the serpent exploded from the earth. Why had he not looked beneath the ground? But the serpent of Iss was of the earth and not of the air, and it was the earth which now opened beneath his feet and he was carried down deep into the ground, to the lair in which the serpent had hidden all day long. He felt the venom of its bite burning his neck. And then its talons struck him a mortal blow, the steel plates of his head wrenched from their hinges.

The blackness of a thousand years descended. He had been left there, buried on the Plain of Glass, only a tiny spark of consciousness remaining in his titanic form. Centuries went by, then the final battle of the gods was fought: the sky caught fire and everything on the surface of the world was incinerated. His shattered body lay buried deep beneath the earth, well away from the fires that otherwise would have destroyed him. Yet his eyes still saw what happened in the world above. The sky was black for a thousand years, then cleared, and he saw the plains and the mountains covered with soot. He saw the few human survivors and those that had been changed by the fires.

Years later he'd felt the roar of Iskiard's destruction, and then had seen the lonely man who came across the plains, one of the few survivors of that doomed place. He came with a giant, Adamanstor, one of the monsters that had come with the gods from the stars. They approached, right to the spot where he lay, as if the man knew exactly where the Talos was buried. And the giant had scooped away the isinglass and thrown it in brittle fountains to the sky. And the Talos had been uncovered and the light of the sun struck him for the first time in five thousand years.

The man was called Marizian. He climbed into the pit that Adamanstor had dug. There he knelt and laid his hands on the Talos, by magic and physical skill bringing him back to life. He had felt the burned-out synapses welded back together and the metal thews reknitted by salves of flame. He'd felt the winch that lifted him from the pit and felt the sorcerer working on his legs, rebuilding them. He had glanced down and seen the man far beneath him looking up at him, and Marizian's voice had come, unbidden, into his mind, words of command. It seemed his legs began to move of their own volition, and he followed his new master over the mountains, Marizian raising a road that rose magically in front of them where he walked. The sorcerer left a city in the mountains and called it Goda. He gave them the *Book of Light* and made a shrine above the city telling them that this is where the Lightbringer would come.

But Marizian didn't stay in Goda. All the time he was there, his eyes went constantly to the north, as if he feared someone or something pursued him from Iskiard. They left soon after the city's founding and for many months wandered through the mountains. Eventually they reached the southern slopes of the Palisades and saw a granite mountain sitting amidst a great plain beneath them. They had crossed the plain and stood before the mountain. The sorcerer raised his hands to the sky and called upon the gods to bless his new city, the place he named Thrull. Then he had called forth all the creatures that lived in the rocks thereabouts and sent them down to the place and there they built a great city on the mountain, its palaces rivalling even the dwelling places of the gods. The Man of Bronze worked alongside the others: the giants and dwarves and other warped humans. His will was no longer his, but Marizian's.

And he listened as Marizian spoke to the people of the gods, the same that he, the Man of Bronze, had served all those years before, and heard the wizard lay down the laws to the people of this city as if he himself was a god. Anger boiled in the Talos's molten chest and the red beams of the eyes burned with hatred: beams that had once melted the polar ice cap and drowned the world at the whim of the God. Yet now he was powerless: he could not turn his ire upon Marizian. The wizard held him in thrall.

Years passed, but they were only a blink of an eye to the Man of Bronze. And the wizard, having grown old and feeble, led him to a chamber deep below the rock, and the Talos saw that it was both a tomb and a prison. There Marizian had died. Then as the magical sarcophagus had closed for the final time on the wizard's corpse, it was as if the Talos woke from his thrall. But he was trapped: his limbs could not move, nor his groans be heard, and he had slept again a thousand years, or maybe more: he could not tell. The bellows of his lungs filled with old dust, and the fire of his veins didn't burn but only glowed. How long would he have to stay, in the darkness once more?

Then one night, many years later, he felt the power outside; and he stirred. He sensed a lightning storm sent by the gods raging outside, then a bolt struck the tomb like a root delving deep under the earth right into the chamber. It burst into the tomb and struck him, finding its way to his heart. He woke: once more he heard the God's voice, telling him to flee, to go back to the north. He had risen up and marched from the tomb, toppling walls and ceiling as he went. On the surface, the men who now lived in Thrull ran before his earth-pummelling strides. He strode across the plains to the north, to where the gods had lived. Through Harken's echoing caves he strode, battering down the stable doors behind which the God's steeds had been penned, lighting with the flame within him the ancient darkness of that place so it was as if noon had come to midnight and the inside of the mountain had glowed transparent with his fires. Then he had marched on Ravenspur—there he had found the first of the Nations and slain them. Then he had gone into the forest and found his way to Lorn, where the enemies of Reh, the Nations of the Night, were massing on its borders. They stood in his way, but he had slain them in their thousands as he had their comrades below Ravenspur. And after the battle he had gone to the smithy on the Isle of Winds, the place where he had been forged by Reh's own hand, where the God had told him to wait.

And there the servants of the God came to him and bound him to their service. They harnessed him to the

Forge, mighty levers strapped to his arms and a belt about his torso, and in front of him where the unwavering beam of his eyes would forever fuel it, the Egg of the World from which he had been forged burned with a coruscating light that was never dimmed. And since, each and every day and night the sparks had flown and the warm wind had kept the enemies of man at bay.

Only once since then had he seen the outside world again, when the Nations of the Night had come to the borders of Lorn once more and he had been released from his harness. Once again, he had driven back the tide of darkness, burning away the warped creatures that came in the mist.

But now he knew he would soon leave this place. She was coming: the one whom Reh had seen, the one whom Marizian had hinted at in his prophecies but had barely understood, for in the end he had been but a mortal. The one who was not human but bore in her part of the godhead: the Lightbringer. Then he would go with her, to the north, to Iskiard, and discover the mystery that Marizian had left in that cursed place.

And the thing he had fled from those five thousand years before.

CHAPTER TWENTY-SEVEN

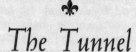

The Tunnel

"Priest!" Alanda's voice. He had given himself to the fall, his limbs slack, his vision spinning over and over as he had fallen through the night sky until he had become dizzy and shut his eyes waiting for the moment of bone-shattering impact.

Instead, the old lady's voice. His eyes sprang open. He was swaying unsteadily on his feet on the rough brick floor of the watchtower. Alanda was tugging urgently at his sleeve. He blinked his eyes, disoriented, his limbs clammy with cold sweat as if he were coming round from a terrible fever.

"What happened?" he whispered.

"You went with the spell, and nearly died with it," Alanda said, her eyes creased in concern.

Of course—Manichee had warned him—keep a distance from the magic, never let it take you over; otherwise, you would die when it died. Had he forgotten those rules so quickly? But it had been eight years since he'd last used the spell. The exhilaration of the summoning had been too much.

He saw a stool next to him, and he sat on it shakily. His head was still whirling. He stared at the ground and gradually his head stopped spinning. Now his hearing returned again: first the soughing of the wind against the walls of the watchtower, then a hissing sound as the snow crystals blew past, the sound amplified by the walls. He looked up: his three companions stood around him in a semicircle, all with looks of concern on their faces. Garadas and the six surviving villagers stood behind, looking at him warily. He smiled despite his dizziness. Only a few hours before on Ravenspur he had been convinced that his friends had abandoned him, had forgotten him.

Thalassa knelt in front of him. "How do you feel?" she asked. For a moment he couldn't answer. Her grey eyes, so close to his, seemed to rob him of speech.

"Better," he said eventually. "Better for being back with friends. I had a long journey over the mountains."

"What happened to you?" Jayal asked.

"The storm was not a natural thing—it was sent," he answered.

"By whom?"

Urthred rose shakily. "By the king of the Nations. He wanted to separate me from you. After I fought the Ice Wraiths I was driven to the north. I followed Marizian's road, right to the summit of the Broken Hines. There I met the ruler of these lands, or rather his ghost."

"And he didn't kill you?"

Urthred pointed at the mask. "He took me for one of his own—told me that you had abandoned me. I was tempted to believe him, Jayal, sorely tempted. As it is with you and the Doppelgänger, so it was with me: his voice was in my mind. It was so persuasive. But I fought it. Then the vision disappeared, and I hurried down from the summit and came to this tower."

"But I still don't understand why he spared you."

Urthred looked away. "Nor I—it's a mystery: a mystery that belongs to my past." He turned to face them again. "The chief of the mountains is called Ravenspur: part of my name. Whoever took me and my brother to the Southern Lands came from it. I had another vision while I was up there. A woman clad in white, by a lake. My mother. She died there. Perhaps the Master knew I would one day come to this land and, hearing the mountain's name, travel there. And there try to tempt me to do his bidding."

"What did he want you to do?"

Urthred now turned to Thalassa. "He wanted me to stop the Lightbringer. You have seen the Black Cloud. There is a tarn up in the lakes, a gateway to the Master's world. Every hundred years his army forms in the waters of the lake. As Garadas told us, that time has come again. Soon they will go to Lorn—only Thalassa can stop them."

Jayal nodded his head grimly. "We met some of his creatures in the underworld." He told Urthred of all that had happened to them in Iken's Dike, the appearance of Faran and Golon, the battle. "Creatures of Shadows that the light destroyed, but Faran and one or two others survived," he concluded.

"Then we haven't much time," Urthred said. He cocked his head and listened. All of them could hear the raging of the storm outside: the wind was mounting in intensity by the second.

"The storm will not end—not while we are here. It is like the Plain of Ghosts again. Even the winds do the Master's bidding."

He turned to Alanda. "Can you tell how far it is to the city?"

The old lady's face was pale and drawn, but she stirred at his question. She pulled aside her cloak and revealed the staff hidden under its folds.

"My powers are weak. All I can tell you is that the city lies somewhere in the forest. It might be a bowshot from here, or a month's travel."

As one they turned to the north, to that imagined point where they would find the city of Lorn. It could be so near: if so, they might risk a short journey through the storm. But if it was far, then they would all perish in it. No one spoke: all no doubt hoped to hear the storm subsiding, but it seemed to rage with even more power than it had a few minutes before, funnelling down from the mountains and then, in an ever-diminishing spiral, circling the tower. It grew and grew in intensity, like a top reaching the height of its spin.

Something had to be done. Jayal thrust aside the

barricade, dropped the bolt and pulled open the door. He was nearly ripped from his feet. Outside, all that could be seen was a white wall of driving snow and nothing else. Garadas helped him push the door shut again and they once more threw the heavy wooden bolt lying to one side across it. The headman cursed, his face downcast: no doubt he was thinking of the villagers who had fled from Fenris. They would stand no chance of surviving in weather like this. But there was something else on his mind as well. "The wolf will return," he said.

"How?" Jayal asked. "The priest has destroyed it."

Garadas turned to him. "It is not so easy to destroy the winter: for that is what it is. The storm is its harbinger. He will be back soon."

Urthred could only nod his agreement. The wind had now reached bansheelike proportions, and it was as if he could feel the tower trying to rip itself off its foundations. Already he felt the cold begin to fill the tower like an invisible liquid, the chill infecting his bones. Even the flames of the fire in the hearth began to subside, as if pushed down by the cold air forcing itself like a plunger into the room. The burning logs turned before their eyes to dull embers and grey ash. It was as if this eye of the storm was a giant centrifuge in which heat was cast out, leaving only a fathomless and absolute cold.

Thalassa, who had stood quietly by all this time, looking pinched and frozen despite her furs, suddenly held up her hand. "Do you hear that?" she whispered.

And now all of them did. The outside walls of the tower echoed with muffled bumps, as if heavy objects were blindly working their way around them, seeking an opening. It was unclear whether they heard shrieks and growls or whether the noises were merely products of the winds whirling around outside.

"What is it?" Jayal asked, the sword gripped so tightly that his knuckles glinted ivory white.

"More of the Master's creatures," Urthred said.

"How can they live in a storm like this?"

"They *are* the storm: it is as Garadas says."

Urthred's eyes went to the door. The oak spar stood
in place: it looked like it could have withstood the
blows of a siege engine for an hour or two before
giving way. "The door may hold them yet." But as if
to show the hollowness of his words, there came that
instant a splintering crash from that direction, and one
of the ancient oak panels visibly bent inwards under
a huge pressure from outside: now there came a con-
certed hammering on the door as if all of the invisible
creatures outside had congregated there.

They all fell back to the wall furthest from the door.
Urthred glanced up: cold mist fell from the trapdoor
above them again, curling into strange twisting shapes,
like those he had seen emerging from the Black Tarn.
He yelled at the others to stand back and they did
so, confused. Urthred thrust his gloved hands in the
direction of the dying fire, feeling the familiar tingling
in his veins, seeking the remaining spark of warmth
in its grey ashes, teasing it up in his mind to a moun-
tainous flame that would fill the room.

There was a sudden absence in the air, then it happened in a second: suddenly all the air in the chamber
was sucked towards the fire and erupted, the grey of
the ashes transformed to a glowing magma before
their eyes. The flames shot high into the room, up the
shaft, where they lashed into the writhing shapes
which burned away like mist. Drops of dark moisture
hissed and spat as they fell to the flagstoned floor of
the tower. One of the villagers cried out as the black
liquid bubbled on his cheek, burning it.

Then, after his cries stopped, there was another momentary silence as if whatever was outside gave pause,
then there came another mighty boom from the barri-
caded door, and white splinters of wood flew from it
into the room.

"We need to barricade the door again," Urthred
yelled. At once everyone was in motion, seizing the
furniture around the tower. The priest looked around
and, seeing one of the cots he had noticed earlier,

began dragging it across the floor with his gloves. Then he saw what lay beneath it: a trapdoor with a ringbolt set into it. He stopped what he was doing and called to the others.

Even over the noise of the howling wind outside, they heard his shout and turned and saw what he had found. Urthred motioned to Jayal. The young warrior thrust the table he had been carrying against the door and hurried over. Urthred seized the ringbolt of the trapdoor and heaved it back, revealing a dark space beneath. The scent of cold earth and mould wafted up from below. A crude wooden ladder descended into the darkness. Jayal swung himself over the lip of the hole, descending clumsily with his sword in one hand as he clutched the edge of the ladder with the other.

Urthred followed down the first few steps. He saw Jayal drop to a packed-earth floor some ten feet below. He glanced down, but the faint light in the room above didn't penetrate for more than a few feet, and the light of Dragonstooth had dimmed. It looked to be a storage area, with old barrels and stacks of firewood taking up much of the available space. He heard Jayal banging and crashing about in the darkness, overturning objects. Urthred was about to shout up the ladder for light, but there was no need. Thalassa had snatched a brand from the still-smouldering fire and thrust it down the hatchway towards him. He took it, the sparks not troubling his gloved hands, and held it out into the darkness.

Now he could see that the area was indeed a cellar, with huge wooden pillars holding up the flagstoned floor above. At the same instant, Urthred glimpsed a tunnel about four feet high snaking away to the northeast of the chamber. He felt a breath of cold wind coming down the tunnel mouth. It led to the open: but where? He oriented himself as best as he could. It seemed to lead to the forest.

Jayal was crouching by its entrance, peering into it. Gasping for breath in the frigid air, Urthred joined

him: tendrils of roots and frosted spider's webs partly
obscured the view, but he could see that the tunnel
might be serviceable. Jayal pushed his head into the
opening, and crouching low, started to worm his way
down it.

Urthred needed no further prompting and shouted
for the others to join them. The seven surviving villagers and the two women and Imuni scrambled down
quickly. Garadas was last: he slammed the trapdoor
shut behind him. Urthred ushered them into the tunnel in front of him, shouting at them to hurry. Finally,
only he remained in the cellar.

He was about to take a first step down the tunnel
when he heard another sudden roaring in the air outside
the tower, and a great crack as the front door to the
tower imploded. The air pressure dropped, making his
ears pop: barrels and boxes started dragging towards
the trapdoor, which flew open above him. His torch
blew out and suddenly he was fighting the tug of the
wind, which dragged him backwards as if an invisible
hand had seized him. He desperately grabbed hold of
the wooden supports that held up the roof above
them. His single free glove clamped into the timber,
biting into the wood. He looked back at the trapdoor
and saw tendrils of mist forming there, pulsing down
into the darkness of the chamber. He glanced desperately up the tunnel: Garadas had stopped and turned.
Urthred could see his mouth shaping silent words
ripped away by the wind. With one mighty effort he
struggled half-blind into the tunnel mouth and the
utter darkness. It was as if the chamber behind him
had become a vacuum, for now he found a gale whistling straight into his face.

Then he felt Garadas grabbing his shoulders and
hauling him up the tunnel. Together they clawed their
way down the shaft, debris from the tunnel mouth
cracking like slingshot into his mask. His back scraped
the earth of the tunnel ceiling and it trickled uncomfortably down his neck. He struggled down it, it
seemed for an age, his head constantly wanting to

twist 180 degrees to see what was following behind, but such was the restriction of movement that all he could do was stare ahead at Garadas's back. He staggered forward at a crouch until his thigh and calf muscles screamed out in pain. Then he became conscious of a minute lightening at the end of the tunnel in front of him, and emerged into a well, choked with fallen leaves. He sensed trees swaying above him and the others, crowding round.

Then the darkness was suddenly shot through with light: Alanda held the leech gatherer's staff aloft—it was giving off a brilliant green light, as green as midday sun through a covering of leaves. Urthred could only wonder at what force the old lady had awoken in the bough, but now they had a second light source. In the light of the staff, he saw moss-covered steps and trees ringing them. They hurried up the steps.

He saw, through eyes misted by the freezing wind, that they had emerged in what was effectively no more than a hole in the ground in a forest clearing, a bowshot from the tower. Oak and beech trees towered overhead, their bare branches waving starkly in the green light of the staff, but even the largest of the trees was bent almost double by the wind. The last of the season's leaves flew past in brown-and-yellow shoals towards the vortex of the tower. Far away, where the storm touched the edge of the forest, he saw saplings uprooted bodily and hurled through the air; the mature trees buckled and ripped at their roots with groans that could be heard even above the wind.

Jayal tugged at his sleeve and pointed into the wind. Urthred could just make out in the light of the staff and the sword an indistinct track winding away into the darkness of the forest. He gestured for Garadas to lead off, he and Jayal to form the rear guard.

Then Jayal shouted a warning and he looked back. He could see in the dim light of the staff that the blizzard had begun to roll forward into the forest. He saw its edge touch an ash tree: its silver-and-white bark and branches were instantly encased in ice.

Shapes moved in the mist, but at its middle was an area of greater darkness, a lumbering shape that seemed to be the centre of the ice and mist that swept down towards them.

As this happened, there came a howl: the sound of the wind incarnate—the spirit of the icy north wind, wind of the arctic wastes, a wind so sheer and savage that polar cliffs would be excised by its knifelike blast. What was his magic against it? It was the howl of the wolf that would devour the blood-red sun and set the land into everlasting darkness. Fenris Wolf, spirit of winter, had returned.

CHAPTER TWENTY-EIGHT

Into the
Forest of Lorn

The dark forest was a tornado of flying leaves and twigs ripped from the trees by the howling arctic wind. Urthred and the others were driven forward by its force, rebounding off tree trunks and being swiped by low-lying branches. At first they had followed the rough track, but it soon became lost in the undergrowth. Behind them, the white-blue wall of the blizzard inched ever closer. For every two steps forward they were blown back one. However hard they struggled it seemed they went slower than what came behind, hidden by the storm.

But then Garadas turned, his dark eyes alive with excitement, and shouted something at Urthred and Jayal. They pushed through the barrier of the wind and there it was: the remains of a roadway, broad flagstones some three feet square, overgrown by saplings growing from the cracks, flagstones riven apart here and there, but nevertheless an easier way than the one they had been following. It led roughly to the north. They ran down it—the woods on either side like a tunnel, a dark world of tangled roots and low canopies of interlatticed bare branches.

Urthred had no idea how long they ran: a half hour or more it seemed. His eyes were filled with sweat which blinded him. He noticed that the road began to mount a shallow rise, and that the trees were beginning to thin out on either side.

He nearly ran into Jayal, who crouched, sheltering his face from flying twigs and the icy wind. He realised he couldn't take another step, and crouched, too, his back to the wind, hazarding a glance backwards, his face taking a flying branch as he turned. Back to the south was a vision of hell: the spinning epicentre of the storm rose some thousand feet into the air, so he had to crane his neck backwards to see its zenith where it overarched them, fingers of black sleet shooting from its summit and raining down on the branches above their heads. But they had outrun it for the moment: in front, to the north, he could see the moon and the stars in the night sky.

Then he felt a touch on his arm. It was Jayal, urging him on again. He scrambled back to his feet and the two set off after the others, their heads bent low as hail and sleet as big as stones fell like missiles about them.

Some minutes passed and the moon and starlight got dimmer and dimmer as the black sleet continued to rain down: driven snow whirled into dervishlike figures on the road before being whipped away behind them. He sensed shadowy figures beginning to form where the sleet had fallen, struggling into life. How long they continued, he had no idea, for the noise of the wind scything through the trees was so deafening that it drove all other thoughts from his mind. All he could concentrate on was his own laboured breathing, the pain in his legs and lungs.

There came one more deafening blast that nearly knocked them off their feet, and then a sudden quiet. He heard the noise of the wind like a wave breaking through the trees far away to the south. Now came the merest zephyr, a light breeze from the north, and with it the tiniest hint of warmth that spread like a balm over his frozen skin—such a contrast it was to what had gone before.

They had all stopped at the last great gust of wind, and now looked at each other in surprise, their chests heaving for breath. There it came again, warmer now, as warm, perhaps, as the wind ever got on this earth with its dying sun, bringing with it the scent of forest foliage. The snow began to melt, the air condensed into a thin mist, and there was a shower of meltwater from every tree. Then the snow was quite gone, yet when Urthred turned, he could see patches of it glimmering where it had fallen only a few yards back. As for the blizzard there was no sign: he could see back to the south a good mile or more. The silence was almost eerie after what had preceded it.

Branches had fallen all around them in that last moment, but some bore green leaves still, and he looked up and saw a canopy of leaves above. Light was feeding through them: the light of the moon.

It was the young girl Imuni who spoke first. "Are we safe, Father?"

The headman got his breath and put his arm round his daughter. "Aye, for the moment."

"It is like the warm breeze in Goda," Imuni continued.

The headman turned to Alanda. "Are we in Lorn?"

Alanda had taken longer than any of them to recover, and she still leaned weakly against the villagers who had helped her. "No," she said, feebly pointing the staff at the sky. They all followed its direction, and saw the moon, four days beyond the full, shining through the trees. "See, the moon is not full." She turned her blue eyes, which flashed in the light of the staff. "Legend has it that the moon always shines full in Lorn."

"Then where is this land?" Garadas asked.

Alanda shook her head. "It lies ahead, somewhere down this road; but how far, I cannot tell."

"Then we better go on," Garadas said wearily.

"Are you rested?" Thalassa asked her old friend.

Alanda nodded. "For the moment. And afterwards? There will be rest enough in Lorn."

Those who had sat on the roadside now stirred themselves, forcing their tired limbs into action. At

least the warmth was a welcome friend after the battle
with the freezing blizzard.

They set off again, picking their way through the
fallen branches and twigs that littered the roadway.
Their progress was dreamlike: again and again the
pulse of warm air came from the north, and they could
see the edge of the Black Cloud that marked the limit
of the storm blown further and further behind them.
Now they had another enemy: fatigue. To a man and
a woman their eyelids drooped, lulled by soporific
warmth. Above them, the diamondlike stars glimmered through the thick canopy of leaves, which became thicker and thicker the further they progressed
down the road.

An hour or so passed, and their pace had slackened
to a shuffle. Jayal led, swathed in the blue-white light
of Dragonstooth that surrounded him like an aura. It
shone brighter now, reenergized by the light of the
moon. A cloud of breath condensation surrounded
them, for here, too, it seemed that the snow had fallen
earlier. Water drops fell from the branches of the trees
and were sucked back into the air by the warmth,
making it very humid.

Suddenly, Jayal stopped, listening intently. Urthred
stopped, too, and for the first time the utter silence of
the forest over the dripping water entered his consciousness.

"What do you hear?" he asked.

Jayal didn't answer directly. He turned to face
Urthred. "All this time, have you heard any animal,
any bird in the trees?"

Urthred shook his head. He listened again. The
breeze had by then entirely died out. Patches of moonlight dappled the mossy banks of the road. Only from
far off did he hear again, miles to the south, but still
piercing through the stillness, a faint howl, the same
howl that they had heard in front of the tower. The
wolf.

"Only Fenris," he said eventually.

Jayal shook his head. "No, I heard a sound ahead, a rustling."

"It could have been an animal."

"There are no animals here—they have all been driven off by the storm."

Garadas now interrupted them. "We must rest," he said. "We have come far enough."

Jayal stared ahead into the forest again. "Very well, but something is out there."

"The Doppelgänger?" Thalassa asked.

"Maybe," he said, his eyes darting this way and that.

They had stopped by an aged holm oak, its leaves hanging on the branch, as if it were high midsummer.

"No need for fire at least," Garadas said, gesturing to his surviving men, who set down their packs. Their fear and their lost comrades were temporarily forgotten with the prospect of rest. They started distributing blankets and food.

Alanda sank gratefully down onto the ground. As she sat the light of the staff dimmed as whatever magical sustaining force within her died away. Urthred wondered how she survived the flight through the forest—how she had survived any of the events of the past few hours, her old body thrust through one ordeal after another.

Jayal was the only one who had not sat down. His head was cocked to one side, his face tense and alert as if trying to hear something beyond the distant baying which still echoed from far behind.

The others by now were eating and drinking their meagre supplies and Urthred sat with them, taking from his backpack Thalassa's flagon of wine. He handed it to her. "Drink," he said. "It kept me well these last two nights."

"You still have it?" she asked, with a small smile.

He looked away, momentarily ashamed. "It helped me below Ravenspur," he answered, then turned the mask back to her. She knew what he was—there was no room for pretence left. "When things were at their bleakest, it was as if you were still with me."

The moonlight seemed to wash the rest of expression from her pale features. It was as if she were a ghost or a creature from another sphere, but her smile never faded even though she stared at the mask.

"Tell me what happened on the mountain," she asked.

He thought for a little while. "The first morning in Goda when I saw the Broken Hines, I recognised them. It was as if I had been there before. After I was separated from you I found another tower like the ones in Goda and at the forest's edge. I spent the night there. The thunder sounded all night, and it seemed to have a voice—telling me the name of the mountain. Ravenspur." He paused. "My name and my brother's." She was silent, willing for him to go on.

"Whoever brought Randel and me to Forgeholm, came from there. And knew I would return."

"But what of the vision of your mother?"

"At the summit I heard the Master's voice, tempting me. . . ." He halted, not daring to articulate all the dark thoughts that had assailed him. "But then the vision came to me," he continued after a few seconds. "And I knew the Master of Ravenspur was lying to me. That I came from the light, from Lorn."

"And your mother sent you from that land to fetch me?"

"Strange as it seems. But we have heard and seen stranger things, Thalassa. We live the book of prophecies, however tarnished and dimmed they are with age."

While they had been speaking, Garadas had approached them and looked down at them, his face ruddy in the light of the lanterns which had been lit around the perimeter of their camp.

"Lorn," he said with an almost audible sigh. "You've spoken of it before, but tell us more before we sleep, for tomorrow we may reach it, and we won't know what is waiting for us."

Urthred shook his head. "I know nothing. Though

Manichee left me books in which all the world was described, nothing was ever written of it in them."

Alanda had looked to be asleep. But now she opened her eyes and lifted herself up on her elbows. "You ask of Lorn. How long have your people lived in their mountain valley, Garadas?"

The headman looked blank: time it seemed had no meaning for those in Goda.

She didn't wait for his reply. "Marizian built the city above the present village. That must have been five thousand years ago. Lorn has existed twice as long as that, or even longer, for it was a city when the gods lived on earth."

"How do you know all this?"

"My people were distant ancestors of yours. They came from this land in that long-ago time and carried to the south the books of their people and their magic."

"What magic did they have?"

"Why the very same that I use now to guide you." She pointed to the staff leaning against the bole of the oak. "The staff was cut from one of the trees on the fringes of this land, the land of the Witch Queens that stood on the borders of Lorn—Astragal. It is as I said both magical and cursed. First the magic: all things are bound together in sympathy, the cut branch wishes to be reknit to the tree. So it is with this bough, for it was hewn from a tree in my homeland ten thousand years ago. Don't you see how it gives me life? How could I have journeyed with you for so long? I am old, but it makes me young."

Thalassa took her old friend's mittened hand as though to offer support.

"Bless you child," Alanda said, smiling. "I'll live a little while longer, but you must be strong, for them," she said quietly, nodding at the sleeping villagers. "You are the Lightbringer. One day you will understand. Though you have seen with your own eyes, you don't comprehend what is in front of you. Magic is in everything, buried deep. But first you must know something of this land and Lorn.

"Thousands of years ago, ten thousand or more, as I have said, the gods lived on this earth, and there in Lorn, upon an island in a mighty lake, Reh set his mighty furnace that heats the earth."

"The lake we saw in the Orb," Thalassa said.

"The same: the furnace heats the earth: you feel it even now in the warm air that comes from the north. But when the battle of the gods was over and Reh saw that the sun would not shine again for a hundred years, he took his people into the kingdom and set over it a mighty canopy and decreed that no one living under it would ever age, but would remain young forever. Erewon, the God of the Moon, worshipped by my people, had been slain in the battle. The moon is the symbol of change and mutability. With his death the source of our magic was cut off. Reh buried him there in Lorn and because he was dead and his people needed light and the sun was dark, set the full moon always to shine on that land. And so the servants of Reh have lived all these thousands of years under the reflected light of their god, the light of his brother moon. They do not die, merely sleep to be reborn again. They wait for Reh to return with the reborn sun."

"As we wait, too," Urthred added.

"It is said in the prophecies that the Lightbringer will liberate Reh's servants and lead them forth again into the day," Alanda continued. "And great magic is hidden there: the Man of Bronze and the Silver Chalice."

Urthred stared at the staff in her hands. "You say that the tree that was hewn from still exists?"

"Yes, the tree still stands. It is called the Dedication Tree. Its roots go to the centre of the earth. As I said, my people are not of the fire and the Flame, but of the natural cycles, and so we worshipped Erewon, the Moon God, on a sacred hill shaded by this Dedication Tree in the city called Astragal. It is said you can see

Lorn from that place. So, the staff leads me onwards, to my home. And from there we will have what we want: a prospect of Lorn."

With that, her eyes closed and she slumped back against the oak.

The four still awake began readying themselves for the night, sharing out the blankets, though the air was mild enough for them to dispense with any covering. Garadas and Thalassa lay down and were instantly asleep, but Urthred continued to stare at Alanda. Again, the old lady had fooled them into thinking she was asleep. She opened her eyes and saw him. She beckoned to him surreptitiously, and he went over and knelt by her.

"You know the magic of this staff, Urthred," she whispered. "It helps me for the moment, but soon its magic will be gone. That is the curse which I told you of, for I think it merely flatters me with this vigour: soon both its power and mine will die." She peered up at him through the fur hood of her cloak; her eyes once a piercing blue were now washed out and dim. "Then I will die. You must leave me when I can't go on."

And Urthred did see the glimmer of mortality in the old lady's eyes, so clearly that a shudder passed involuntarily up his spine. But he shook his head: "You forget, without you and the staff, we would be lost: would be dead already—we need you."

"The road ahead is plain, priest: you will find Lorn. Yet . . ." Her voice trailed off.

"Yet what?" he asked.

"The headman may speak wiser words than he knows."

"How so?"

She looked about her, but all the others, apart from the two villagers detailed to keep watch and Jayal who sat on a tree stump a few yards off, seemed to have fallen into an enchanted sleep. "I don't think it will be so simple getting to Lorn as you think. No one knows where it is."

"But I saw it in the Orb; Thalassa, too!"

"Yes, you saw it in a magical object. And it is a magical kingdom. But do you expect to find it so easily?"

Urthred shrugged. "It is hidden," Alanda continued. "Like Marizian's tomb, tucked away beyond the visible world on another plane. The staff may get you to its borders but no further."

"Then how will we enter it?"

"With faith, just as you showed in Marizian's tomb—you will find a way. And, if not by faith, you have your own magic, priest. The dragon! I never thought I would see it in my lifetime. Manichee taught you well. I know you will finish what he began—crush the Worm, find what you are seeking with Thalassa."

"My powers are nothing compared to Manichee's."

"No, priest—in each generation there will be an adept. He recognised it in you. But remember, these artefacts that Marizian brought into our world have corrupted as well as empowered. The baron used the Rod—now Jayal is haunted by his double, and Manichee is consigned to Shades."

"Aye, it all began with Illgill, and his lust for Marizian's power. The Rod began all this woe—it destroyed Manichee surely enough."

"And the Rod may still destroy Jayal. His shadow will follow him to the ends of the earth." She glanced at Jayal, who still kept his lonely vigil at the perimeter of the camp. "The Doppelgänger must be banished back to Shades; otherwise, both will be destroyed."

"The Rod is a long way away," Urthred said. "Illgill, or someone else, has taken it to Iskiard."

A dark shadow passed over the forest, and, looking up through the branches, they could see another dark tendril of cloud hurrying across the night sky from the south. It swooped over the light of the moon like a bird of prey dropping on its quarry, but as it threatened to overwhelm the feeble light altogether, the warm wind came again from the north and the darkness shredded and the moon beams shone once more through the leafy branches of the trees.

The old lady was clearly exhausted. "You must rest—for it can't be long before dawn: we will need all our strength," Urthred said.

"Then Reh watch over you, priest." She lifted her liver-spotted hand to his masked face. "You chose rightly back on Ravenspur. You are one of us. If only I knew the mystery of your name . . ."

"Tomorrow or the next day I may discover it for myself," he said.

"Look after Thalassa when I am gone," she said, the last of her strength ebbing away. "Remember: you will heal, you will love: have faith, Urthred, this world needs the likes of you."

"Let Reh protect you, too," he answered, a warm glow from the old lady's touch seeming to kindle some long-lost sentiment inside him, so buried that he wondered where it came from. He rose and, with one last look at Thalassa's sleeping form, strode to where a blanket awaited him.

CHAPTER TWENTY-NINE

Smiler

For the first hour, the frozen forest edge had been full of the howling of the wolf. Faran was not sure where the creature was: it seemed everywhere and nowhere at the same time, its baying whipped round in the air by the blizzard raging down from the summit of Ravenspur. Smiler had paid it no attention, plodding steadfastly forward, the Thorn Men nearly invisible shadows in the gloom of the trees.

Then the howling cut off abruptly, and Smiler stopped, tilting its head, listening. It nodded slowly and turned to Faran.

"The wolf cannot go any further into the forest. We are the only ones left who can pursue the Lightbringer."

"What of the other creatures your master promised us: those from the Black Tarn?"

"You have had your answer," the creature replied. "When the moon is full, you will see them. Then you will see the legions as they were at the last day."

"How is it that you alone have physical form?" Faran said.

Smiler stared at him. "There are some of us who live in physical form, those who found other bodies to dwell in when their human ones were destroyed. I was once straight like you, Faran Gaton, but that body died. This I borrowed from elsewhere. I and the Thorn Men and a few others live in this world. But the rest of the Nations are more powerful yet; they are things of pure spirit who dwell in Shades—they grow stronger minute by minute. In three weeks they will be unde-

featable." Then it gestured into the forest, where the
Thorn Men waited nearly invisible, and Faran could
see them now turning to the right, towards the source
of the howling and he guessed that they were now
moving to intercept the human party. They followed,
Faran drifting towards Golon, who held the purple
gemstone close to his body, tracking the movement of
Dragonstooth. He caught his master's eye. "They are
heading to the northeast," he whispered.

Faran nodded, and stepped away. His thoughts now
they were away from Ravenspur were more positive.
They were close to Thalassa and the others. They
would have a second chance. His party was still strong.
The strength was returning to his severed arm and he
still had some of his men left: the campfire guard, the
two Reapers, and Golon. They could free themselves
of Smiler and the Thorn Men, then do as they pleased,
armed with the knowledge that the Master had given
them.

They continued through the forest until Smiler
called a sudden halt. Faran could see something hanging in the trees ahead of them in the moonlight. He
pressed forward so he stood next to Smiler.

The Thorn Men had found one of the humans. The
body hung between two young saplings: sharp wooden
pegs had been driven through the neck and arms. As
Faran inspected the pegs closer they proved to be
thorns taken from the creatures' bodies, holding the
thing upright between the trees. The skin had been
flayed from the corpse, and now hung flapping in the
wind over some nearby branches. Judging from its
stature, it was a peasant, one of the villagers he had
seen in the tunnel under Ravenspur: a short man, unlike the tall southerners.

Smiler stared at the corpse, too, the jagged pink
gash under its chin once more giving its mottled toad
face the appearance of great levity.

"Where are the others?" Faran asked.

Smiler turned to him, the eyes dead and flat despite
the pink grin of its mouth. "This is one who was sepa-

rated from the main party—the others are ahead. There is only one way to go. Into the interior, towards Lorn: that is their only hope."

Smiler looked back. They were still close to the edge of the forest, and the moon and all the sky were totally obscured by the dense Black Cloud that hung from the heights of Ravenspur. Black hail fell from the skies, spattering their cloaks, but it was not frozen rain, but something altogether different. Evil-smelling, plastic to the touch. Wriggling wormlike shapes could be seen forming where it fell, coalescing. And the shapes as yet unformed began to crawl slowly towards the interior of the forest. From the west they could see green ghostlike lights flitting northwards.

"The cloud is the Master's dominion," Smiler said. "Soon it will cover the whole forest. The creatures that spawn here are but the vanguard of what follows."

"But they need the shelter of the cloud," Faran said. "Your master told me so."

The creature inclined its head slowly, its gaze never leaving Faran's face. "We are enough. Do not forget," it said, gesturing at the hanging corpse, "what the Thorn Men can do. Besides, the wolf is returning." And Faran did see in a clearing to their right a huge shadow on the white of the snow, involved mist spinning around it, the snow at the peripheries bubbling and turning a tarry black. "As I said, we are the vanguard, but we are terrible enough."

Faran didn't reply. Already plans were forming in his head. It would take only a few words to Golon, and then this creature and the Thorn Men would be destroyed. All he needed was patience. "Lead on," he growled. "This night will not last forever."

"Oh, believe me, this night," Smiler said, gesturing at the cloud, "will last forever when Lorn is destroyed."

There was a rustle from a nearby tree, and Faran suddenly saw one of the Thorn Men standing there. The creatures could creep up to a man without a sound. A silent communication passed between Smiler and the thing, then Smiler turned back to Faran. "Tracks, leading into the interior."

"How many?"

"A dozen or so. Come, dawn will be here soon: creatures of the Night must rest during the day." It gestured and the Thorn Men melted back into the camouflage of the frozen woods. Smiler set off with its ponderous gait in a northerly direction. Soon they found the remains of the road, and there, in the snow, they saw a confused pattern of footsteps. Whoever had passed that way had done so in a hurry. Golon knelt by them, holding his hand a foot above the snow. Then he rose abruptly to his feet, and his hooded eyes caught Faran's. They were warm: the quarry was only just ahead. Faran nodded slightly. He could see that the sorcerer had intuited what would have to be done to Smiler and its command. But not yet: they still needed a guide through the forest.

They hurried forward as quickly as they could, and soon passed from under the looming balcony of cloud into warmer air, where the snow had not settled.

They were not far behind the party from Goda, but the first light was beginning to leak into the eastern sky. Reluctantly, Smiler called a halt. It gestured into the forest, and like an invisible wave, Faran and the others sensed rather than saw the Thorn Men moving forward, through the trees to the north.

"They will keep watch while we rest," Smiler said. Then it broke off from the path. In front of a ridgeline ran like a wave through the wood. The ridge was broken by a fault line in which they could see a dark cave opening. Smiler led them into it. The walls of the cavern were daubed with strange sigils. Faran scented the air. They were painted in blood. He wondered what strange rituals Smiler and such as it had seen in this place.

But soon Smiler's world would be at an end. He nodded to Golon. When he gave the signal, they would kill Smiler.

CHAPTER THIRTY

✦

Healing Waters

The next morning dawned as mild and beautiful as any Urthred could remember. Though the newly risen sun shone as weakly as it did in the lands of the south, the warm air from the north heated the woodland. Steam rose from the emerald foliage all around.

His companions stirred, as amazed as he was at the contrast between the terrors of the frozen night and the smiling day into which they woke. Soon the sound of their voices echoed gaily around the roadside by the holm oak and a fire was started and packs they had brought from Goda were reopened: dried oats to make porridge and a herb tea made from mountain sage, dried meat and cheese. They all ate as if it were the most delicious food they had ever tasted.

But not all of them were in such a lighthearted mood. Garadas had not joined in the conversation, standing to one side, looking towards the south. Perhaps he was thinking of the men lost out on the plain. Urthred followed the direction of his stare and saw there was even more cause for worry: though the sky was clear overhead, to the south it was an ugly slate grey.

Garadas presently roused himself from whatever thoughts had been occupying him and gave an order to one of his men. The villager got up reluctantly from his breakfast and shinned up a tree. A few moments later he was back. He reported that the cloud hung stationary over the forest some ten miles back, but, where it rested, the trees had turned an autumnal colour. Breakfast was hastily concluded in silence, and the party readied themselves to set out again.

Alanda, at least, looked refreshed. Once more the staff seemed to have revitalised her. She had drunk and eaten with the rest of them, some colour coming back into her sunken cheeks. She levered herself to her feet and stared down the line of the ancient way, which ran like a green tunnel straight ahead towards a series of wooded ridges to the north. Even from here they could see niches in the ridgetops where the road cut through the trees. The staff twitched in her hand until it pointed down its length. Lorn must be ahead.

They departed; even at this early hour it was warm enough just for shirtsleeves. All of them had put their cloaks away, apart from Urthred, who dared not bare his scarred arms.

Presently they saw a river, its emerald light sparkling through the trees, running alongside the road. Its source seemed to be ahead, where a low line of hills cut across their path. The banks of the river were choked with brambles and hawthorns, the blossom of which glowed whitely in the green twilight of the forest.

They walked all morning, then began to climb the line of hills. The river now fell in a series of waterfalls, then rushed past them to the south. They reached a pass at the summit of the ridge between two eminences. The source of the river must have been on the slopes high above them to the right, for they could hear water splashing through the hanging woods above them. They stopped in the gully formed by the hills. The open space gave them views in both directions. To the north the forest rolled on in a series of green waves, but far, far in the distance they could see low mountains, and a series of bald, rocky summits.

Alanda held up the staff, and again it seemed to move of its own volition towards the distant mountains.

"Is that Lorn?" Urthred asked.

The old lady shook her head. "Not Lorn, but Astragal. Those mountains are where the staff was taken from. Lorn can't be much further.''

They turned to the south, where there was a more sinister view. The mountains of Goda, the Palisades and the Broken Hines were all hidden behind the dark cloud that soared upwards into the heavens, tendrils curling over the forest as if seeking out the life of the sun itself. But it seemed to have advanced no further into the forest since the morning. Now they could see what the villager had reported. Where the cloud touched the ground, the forest had turned a golden brown.

But at noon even the sun's heat was oppressive, particularly after the stiff climb up the slope of the ridge, and the sound of the falling water was very tempting. Garadas shrugged off his backpack and sank to the ground, indicating they should all rest.

Once more, the dangers seemed to be temporarily forgotten. While he and another villager prepared food, the others went down to the river to replenish their water bottles and bathe. As the others knelt before the stream, the men stripping to the waist and washing themselves, Urthred—conscious of the scars under his cloak—walked off a little way up the stream to where the first of the waterfalls cascaded into a pool.

The sound of Imuni's cries of laughter rang off the steep rocky slopes below as he climbed upstream. Was this how a man was meant to live? Under a warm sun, with the sound of laughter in his ears? If so, the world couldn't be a bad place. He stopped and looked up at the sun. Even at noon, a haze seemed to obscure its face, as if a permanent overcast hung there. That was the reason for the misery of his age: that inexplicable shadow over the sun, a shadow that had oppressed men ever since it had first appeared, when Marizian had come to the south. In that shadow was the reason why some turned to Iss, and others, like him, longed for the sun's rebirth. But whatever religion a man had, one thing was sure—there was not much happiness in this world, and the sound of a child's laughter was an unusual one.

He set off again. As he walked, another warm gust of wind came from the north, and, he realised he almost felt at peace for the first time in his life. He had made his choice: rejected the Master's temptation. He paused and shivered involuntarily. He had been tempted. But it had strengthened rather than weakened him. He was not one of those that lived in the darkness. His companions hadn't shunned him. Manichee had been right, they had grown used to the mask. But were they ready for what lay beneath?

Now he was high above the road, his companions lost in the foliage below. He stood at the foot of another waterfall beside a deep pool. It fell over a mossy lip in a green cascade, the falling water seemed almost motionless so smooth was the flow. He climbed the side of the fall, further and further from his friends. There in front of him was another pool fed by a small stream from higher up the rocky slope. Trees overhung the water, mirrored exactly in their still surface. Dragonflies hummed over the lily pads at the pool's centre, and he saw orange fish flitting over the pebbles at its clear bottom.

He was suddenly conscious of the quiet. Had he gone too far? But it seemed to him that Garadas would not set out for a little while yet. He could see the cloud to the south in a break in the trees—it still hung motionless, as if it, too, was becalmed in the warm air. For the moment at least they had outstripped the Master of Ravenspur. As for Faran, the sun would have driven him underground.

Here in this lull was a feeling he'd seldom enjoyed in his long years at Forgeholm—contentment: a man should live in this warm air, not miserably huddled in the endless cold that Urthred had known ever since he was a child. The scent of the forest was strong, and he wondered again about this strange land. Here the tang of pine, the smell of grass and flowers came swarming in like a heady perfume. Had he ever felt

so alive? His heart beat strongly in his chest, each
vein seemed to sing, his scars felt as if a balm had
been spread upon them, so where the burned skin had
stretched and pulled at every nerve ending these last
eight years, there was now an unfamiliar ease.

He did not doubt that the magic that Manichee had
promised had fallen upon him like manna: the Trial of
Fire, the contact with the leech gatherer's staff. That
accounted for the outer change, the healing. But there
was another change too—inside him. The quickening
power of Thalassa: she had given him an appreciation
for life he had never had before. He had fought it,
railed against himself for succumbing to it, for being
attracted to her. Now he knew it had been futile. It
would have done as good to argue against a natural
force such as the wind: you could not tell it which way
to blow or how strongly, so it was with his heart. All
mankind through history had been hostage to this
force, no matter how the mind contended with its
existence.

He became conscious that he'd been standing stock-
still for several minutes. The water sang as it fell into
the deep pool under the waterfall. Without thinking
he disassembled the harness of his gloves, the old
leather and metal so aged that even the sunlight threw
no reflection off them. He flexed the mutilated digits
of his hands. Once more he felt life at the end of his
fingers, a painful life, as if his fingertips had grown
again and flames tingled and burned at their ends. He
studied the stumps. Was it his imagination, or had the
flesh mushroomed at their ends, growing imperceptibly since he'd last inspected them at the tower near
Goda?

The fact he could feel anything in them except pain
was enough. He threw off the cloak and his short tunic
and waded into the clear water of the pool. He had
not washed in two days. The warm air played over his
body. The water was cool, but refreshing, and Urthred
ducked down into its depths, letting the water wash
him clean. In his mind's eye he felt the grime of

Thrull, that insidious smell of death that had lain like a pall over the city, the sulphurous stink that had clung around Ravenspur, dissolve away into the water and be washed away downstream. He wished his brother could have been with him. Sadness settled on him anew. Thrull had destroyed Randel as it had destroyed everything else that was good in this world.

Chastened by the memory of his brother, he climbed out of the pool, the silver water cascading from his scarred body. He looked at it—a familiar sight, but today was there something different about it? He stared at his chest. Eight years ago, when the Hearth Fire had laid bare muscles and bones, some of the cloak he had been wearing had been burned into the flesh. He remembered Manichee painstakingly removing fibre by fibre with a pair of tweezers, he in a world beyond pain. But today the red upraised weals looked almost benign, less fierce than he could ever remember them.

He reached out his fingers to touch one of them: he felt the ghost of sensation from the touch. Quickly his fingers explored the rest of the body—barely noticeable, but surely every area burned less fiercely? He knelt by a stretch of water undisturbed by the cascade and looked down: the reflection of his face came back at him from the light of the noonday sun. There was change there, too. The angry weals on his cheeks seemed flattened out, the torn flesh of his nose and mouth less ragged. He raised his hands to his head and felt a soft down—hair was growing for the first time in eight years.

He might have lingered here for the rest of the day had he not at that moment heard a splash of water from the pool downstream. He quickly snatched up his clothes and gloves and hurriedly started dressing himself. He listened, but now there was only the slightest sound from below. He wondered what it could have been. A fish leaping in the water? Still damp underneath his tunic, he retraced his steps cautiously, climbing down the side of the fall.

There was a stand of ash trees by the bank of the first pool and he peered through them at the water. Like the water in the one above, it was almost green in its limpidity, and every stone at its bottom was revealed. But this is not what caused his breath to catch and his heart stop beating. For something white, as graceful to his eyes as a swan, moved on the surface, long golden brown tresses flowing like seaweed in the water behind. He caught a glimpse of a back more dazzling than white marble in the sun and long legs flicked languorously as the figure swam to the further bank. There it rose half out of the water, bracing pale arms on the rocks there, holding its face to the sun. Thalassa.

He was suspended, beyond time, beyond feeling even, for a few slow and painful heartbeats. What was a man's soul when beauty robbed him of his reason in a second? He would have torn his eyes away, but it was as if they had been welded to that white back, strangely elongated in the green water. Further accentuating the grace of her long, tapering body, one of her breasts hung suspended downwards, perfectly convex.

Then reason finally returned: Thrulland, the abominations she had suffered there, the vampire's bite. This was a moment of ritual ablution, he had trespassed upon it. His healing face blushed, yet still he could not avert his gaze. Then she turned in the water, the ripples hiding her body. The spell was broken. He stumbled back, bidding his frozen limbs to be quiet, but still he heard branches snap beneath his feet, and he heard a surprised cry from the pool.

He was shamed. He hurried downstream, past the first waterfall, his idyllic mood shattered.

Then his footsteps slowed and he halted. He would have to confront her sooner or later. She would know it was he who had made the noise. He sat on a rock, staring into the trees, yet seeing nothing. Minutes passed, and the warm wind continued to sough through the branches. Life continued, he was surprised to find.

Then he heard a light footstep, and he looked up. It was her, in her grey dress, her wet hair tied in a loose braid. She was coming down the rocky path from the pool. And strangest of all, she smiled down at him, almost shyly, her lips slightly puckering into an enigmatic smile.

"Ah, priest, so it was you?"

He nodded. "I heard a noise . . . forgive me."

She knelt by him and laid a hand on the sleeve of his tunic. He almost jumped as if he had received a charge from her touch.

"You have been too long removed from others, and I"—she sighed— "have lived too much with them. For a moment, I just wanted to be alone—like you."

"I did not choose to be alone, Thalassa. This dictates that it is so," he said, pointing at his mask.

It was as if she didn't hear him, didn't see the mask. She stared ahead abstractedly.

"For the moment I forgot the vampire's bite, and the thirst. The shade was soothing. It was so peaceful," she said, looking at the glade, at its dappled light. "I could stay here forever." She turned to him again. "And you? Could you stay here?"

He nearly said "I would stay with you." Instead he sought for the right words. "I seek new things, Thalassa. We both saw the books of law—they were dust; so, too, are my vows. I must make my way as a man now, not as a priest."

"You're right: vows made to the dead letter of the law mean nothing. But Reh lives nevertheless," she said, pointing skywards. "For the moment he is my enemy. But when we find the Silver Chalice, once more he will be the sun, and all of life. That is all that matters."

"So be it," he said, his heart hammering wildly at the gentle squeeze she gave his arm. Her mouth cracked into a smile, and his dark thoughts blew away in an instant, like smoke. He could barely look into the perfect grey of her eyes; how could eyes the colour of winter be so warm?

But then he heard another noise, off in the trees.
A rattle, of hard wood knocking together. Then there
was silence. An animal moving through the undergrowth? But it suddenly struck him again how they
had heard no bird or beast all the time they had been
in the forest: it was as if all the wildlife had fled far
away to the north. A chill crept up his spine. They
were being watched, he was certain. He glanced at
Thalassa. Her head was cocked to one side: she had
heard it, too.

"What do you think it is?" she whispered.

"I don't know," he replied. His ears were straining
to catch any more sound. But there was now a complete silence except the sound of the waterfall. The
Doppelgänger? He suddenly realised how foolish they
had been, straying so far from the others.

"Come on," he whispered, taking her hand and
pulling her to her feet. They hurried down to the point
where the others had been washing, but it was now
deserted. A sudden shadow passed over the forest,
and they looked up. A tendril of black cloud had
flown across the sky from the south. Suddenly the very
area of the forest where they stood was in shadow,
although only a few hundred yards away, the trees
still basked in sunshine. It was as if the Master of
Ravenspur had thrown a dark finger over their heads,
reminding them of his presence. They climbed up the
riverbank, and there at last they saw the others: Jayal,
Alanda, Garadas, his six men and Imuni waiting for
them anxiously.

They climbed up the slope and Urthred quickly described what they had heard.

"We heard it, too," Jayal answered.

"What could it have been?" Thalassa asked. "There
are no animals in the forest."

One of the villagers cried out and pointed. Something had left a tree branch swinging further downstream, and from far off they heard another of the
rattles that they had heard by the pool. "Something
is following us, and it's not Faran," Urthred said.

"Then let's go," Garadas said, gesturing for his men to pick up their packs and move off. He took his daughter's hand.

They quickly pushed on down the road out of the shadow and deep into the green heart of the forest. Every now and again they caught the faintest sound of the rattle again, and the chill on Urthred's spine seemed to have permanently settled there.

They hurried forward for two hours, conscious of the shadow pressing them. They flew over rocky gullies and through the many different stands of trees: birch in the ravines, firs on the rocky hills and in between the deep swaths of ancient oaks and beeches. As the sun passed through its zenith they reached another ridgetop, and stopped to regain their breath. In front, the mountains of Astragal looked nearer now. Then they turned to look back. More tendrils of cloud had detached from the darkness to the south and, like dark fingers, flew towards the westering sun. Where the tendrils darkened the forest, the trees turned from their summer green to orange and brown. The shadows were getting closer and closer. Then from the north came a sound. At first it resembled the noise of a wave roaring on a shingle beach. It grew louder and louder. Then in the distance the tops of the forest trees bent back like corn, and the air took on a brassy sheen. Then they saw what it was: a mighty wind approached faster than even the swiftest horse. It would reach them in a second. They flung themselves down, and the gale was upon them—a wall of sound, flying leaves and twigs. Then the wind was past, roaring away to the south. They turned and saw it shredding the tendrils of cloud attacking the face of the sun, then rolling back the larger bank from which the tendrils had come.

They stood, brushing twigs and leaves from their clothes.

"What was that?" Garadas asked, looking at the roiling mass of the storm being rolled almost out of sight by the blast of air. But despite its force, they saw the cloud still survived, twisting and turning in the warm gale as if wrestling with it as for life itself.

"The Man of Bronze," Alanda said. "He still works his magic in Lorn, sending life to the Outland. But see how even he cannot destroy the cloud."

Garadas nodded. "Aye, so my grandfather said it was, the last time the Dark Time came. But then the cloud was destroyed."

"Will mother be safe, Papa?" Imuni asked.

He patted her on the shoulder. "Yes, child; the people of Goda are safer than us. The cloud is following us to the north."

The commotion had now settled on the horizon. Once more the slate grey bank of cloud rolled after them.

"How long do you think before it catches up with us?" Urthred asked Garadas.

The headman narrowed his eyes, calculating the distance and the edge of the storm. "It will overtake us by the evening."

They turned and looked at the ridges off to the north. Perhaps Lorn lay just over them, but they would have to hurry. They set off quickly again.

CHAPTER THIRTY-ONE

A Prospect
of Astragal

The half-moon crossed the sky, casting long shadows over the forest and over the ancient road. Soon its light would be lost—since afternoon the storm front had been catching up with them. Now the fatigue was obvious in all of them. Not a word was said. The air had become very cold again, with brief eddies of snow. The colour of the foliage in the trees had changed before their eyes: from green, to gold, to brown in the time it took to hurry past them. A severe frost had settled underfoot, the memory of the balmy morning long forgotten now.

As they glanced back they saw ice devils spinning on the ridgetops they had just passed over. What was more, as the sky had darkened, they had heard the strange noise from the trees again for the first time since the blast of hot air from the north. Not a single sound, but a long, continuous rattle. They bunched together for security, keeping to the middle of the road, as far as possible from the forest fringe.

The villagers and Jayal were at the front, Garadas close by his side. Next the women. Urthred at the back. It was Jayal who spotted the footprints on the light scattering of snow on the road. He came to a halt with a cry, the villagers bumping into his back. They congregated around him, peering over his shoulder. The footprints were clearly visible in the light of the moon: human tracks leading away down the road—

way in a northerly direction. Strangely, whoever had
been there must have stood there for some time, at
least from when the snow had begun falling, for there
was no trail to spot where they started, only the footprints leading away.

Jayal placed his boot in the footprint: it exactly fitted his. "The Doppelgänger," he whispered, looking
down the line of the road. "He's very close." They
all peered forward. In the distance the low range of
mountains they had seen at midday seemed much
closer, although still several hours' walk away.

Garadas hefted his spear, his eyes quartering the
forest. Then he motioned for his men to go forward
again. They needed no encouragement: the wind was
getting stronger and colder by the second.

The women followed, but Jayal hung back, grabbing
the sleeve of Urthred's cloak and drawing close. His
teeth were shining in the half-light of Dragonstooth,
his lips fixed in an unnatural grin. Only the left side
of his face showed in the light. For a moment Urthred
saw before him not Jayal, but the very image of the
Doppelgänger. His blood froze.

But then Jayal spoke. "Since this morning, I have
seen the road in my mind's eye, every yard, just before
we reached it. It is like every step I take, I have taken
it before, as if I had stood there a moment before.
And now this," he said, pointing at the print.

"The only power he has is over your mind, Jayal,"
Urthred said. Another blast of the wind set their
cloaks whirling about their heads, and they staggered
to keep their balance. Above the ridge to the south,
all light seemed to have been sucked from the sky.

"The mind is the most powerful thing of all," Jayal
answered, staring at the glimmering blade of the sword
as if hypnotised.

But Urthred wasn't listening to him anymore. Instead, he had glimpsed movement in the forest behind
Jayal. It was as if there was a strange displacement in
the vertical plane of the trees. Then he realised what

it was. It was the trees themselves that were moving.

"There!" he cried. "Do you see?"

Jayal snapped out of his trance and turned—and saw the movement now. The strangest sight: the upright bole of a tree moving laterally past the other forest trees. His fists bunched on the hilt of Dragonstooth. The others were now nearly invisible further up the road. "Come on," he said. Both men set off at a run.

Garadas turned when he heard their urgent footsteps. But no words of warning were needed: he, too, saw the movement: tree-figures swarming through the true trees on either side. He urged the others on and fell back to form a rear guard with Urthred and Jayal.

But the creatures swarmed past and, with a rustling of branches, were gone. The entire party halted.

"Where have they gone?" Garadas murmured.

"Waiting ahead," Urthred answered.

"So, we're trapped," Garadas said. "There is no going back." A look of grim determination fixed on his face. "Form up," he ordered.

Jayal took the lead, flanked by Urthred and Garadas. Jayal held Dragonstooth out, Urthred his gloves, Garadas his spear. They pushed on until, as if by a trick of the light, they saw that the road ahead disappeared into a thick bank of thorn trees. They halted, the gale harder and harder at their backs. The trees to either side of the road bent at the renewed onslaught of the wind, but the phalanx of thorns moved forward in opposition to the wind. Now they could see eyes peering from boles at the top of their trunks, the swaying branches so much like limbs, the thorn-clawed feet. They would engulf them or drive them back into the storm. Either way they would die.

"I will open a way," Alanda said, moving forward. She held up the staff and it burst into green light, making plainer the horror of what confronted them. But the light had no effect: these things had passed from the natural world aeons before. They obeyed no magic that she had command of. Her companions began to fall back, the wooden rattle of the creatures' limbs like a snake's. Urthred turned in the gloom, and saw there were more of the Thorn Men behind them. The road was closed in both directions: they were completely surrounded.

CHAPTER THIRTY-TWO

✦

The Spider's Kiss

In the darkness Faran saw clearly. He wondered if Smiler saw, too, or if, like a human, the darkness impaired its vision. Whatever: soon the creature would have no use of eyes. Perhaps the Master would feel his servant's death. Perhaps he was, as he had claimed, everywhere the Black Cloud sat. All the better. He would know that he, Faran Gaton Nekron, was greater still than the Master of Ravenspur.

Smiler's death would be easily achieved. The cave it had led them into seemed an ancient excavation: the ceiling and floor were smooth, and rock-cut steps descended to a lower level. Maybe it was part of the complex of tunnels leading to Iken's Dike. It was dark enough though the sun shone outside, for its weak beams barely penetrated the shrubbery veiling the entrance of the cave.

Smiler had planted its misshapen body on a throne cut in the stone wall of the cave a few yards away from Faran. Its eyes glimmered in the darkness. As far as Faran could tell the creature had not closed them once all the time they had remained in the cave. The rest of Faran's party, except the vampire guard, slept. In the gloom he studied the creature: he wondered why Smiler had left itself like this, unattended, the Thorn Men far away.

Smiler evidently had felt Faran's gaze upon it. "Why don't you rest?" it growled.

"I need no sleep," Faran countered. "There will be sleep enough when the sun goes out."

"As you wish," the creature answered. "Soon we will continue."

"Continue? How? You know I cannot be in the sun."

Smiler indicated the steps, confirming Faran's suspicions. "Iken's Dike. It passes under the forest. One of the old roadways of the gods. It goes due north, to Iskiard. But if we follow it a little way, it will take us a little closer to Lorn."

"Very well," Faran said. He snapped his fingers, and instantly he felt Golon awake. "My sorcerer must dress my wound," he said, indicating his right arm, which he had allowed to dangle uselessly by his side. Smiler shrugged and rested its head against the rock of the throne. There were dark stains on it and the floor all around it, but Smiler sat indifferently, its reptilian eyes never leaving Faran. It was clear it would not or could not sleep.

Golon crouched by him as Faran rolled up the sleeve of his cloak and revealed the line of crude stitches running around his shoulder. "Does it hurt you, my lord?" the sorcerer said loud enough for Smiler to hear him, his eyes not leaving Faran's face.

"We must kill the creature," Faran said out of the corner of his mouth.

"When?" Golon said, busying himself in some imaginary task on the wound.

"Later, when it has grown dusk and we can go to the surface again. Make sure you have something that is fast—you see how powerful it is."

Golon nodded. "It will have the Kiss of the Spider, if I can find one in this place." Faran nodded, and the sorcerer rolled down his sleeve and stood. He walked past the vampire guard, who stood next to a pillar, his unsleeping eyes focused on his master. Golon crouched in the shadows, his eyes darting hither and thither in the gloom until he saw what he wanted. A scuttling form on the ground. Quick as a lizard's tongue, his hand shot out and trapped the insect. He felt it wriggling next to his palm and felt an exultant thrill run through his body as he conjured from deep in his esophagus a bitter bile. Then he spat silently onto the spider. Instantly its writhing stopped. The creature was his. It would do his bidding; its poison would be deadly enough.

He glanced over at Smiler, still sitting on its throne. There was a gap between the black carapace of its body armour and its flesh. That is where he would put the spider, that is where it would do its work. . . . With that thought Golon let his own weariness take over and slumped uncomfortably against the wall, the spider still clutched in his hand.

He woke three hours later; the light still glimmered beyond the foliage at the tunnel's mouth. At first he wondered what had woken him. Then he saw Smiler standing over him in the half-light. For a moment he wondered whether the creature had guessed his plan, but it merely jerked its head, indicating that it was time to move off. Already the others were stirring. Faran was already standing next to the vampire guard. Their eyes caught each other's, and as Smiler turned he gave his master a silent nod, showing that he was ready.

"I will go last," Smiler announced. "Remember, your tricks will be of no use to you down here. The tunnels are a labyrinth, and I alone know the way out." Golon conjured the purple ball of flame so that the humans could see in the dark, and they descended the steps and entered, as Smiler had promised, a series of mazelike tunnels. Smiler gave orders from the back for them to turn one way and then another. It was clear the creature had spoken truthfully: the tunnels were a labyrinth in which they would have been lost in no time without it. Faran congratulated himself for telling Golon to hold back.

After an hour they entered from a side passage what must have been the continuation of Iken's Dike: a straight, smooth roadway that led to the northwest, about forty-five degrees away from the direction in which Lorn lay.

They continued down the featureless tunnel for the rest of the day, their footsteps echoing off the high ceilings, the purple ball floating before them, leaving a violet cloud that drifted down to the ground behind them. At intervals they passed more of the skulls set on posts that they had seen in Ravenspur which spat and chattered strange obscenities as they went past. In between, the only sounds were the noise of their footsteps echoing off the concrete and Smiler's stentorian breathing behind them.

It was what Faran guessed was the early evening when Smiler finally called a halt. The motley collections of humans came to rest, grousing and complaining, but were silenced by one dark look from Faran. Smiler walked to what appeared to be a featureless section of the tunnel wall. It pushed at one of the blocks, which swung inwards, revealing a passage behind. They saw a set of concrete spiral steps circling upwards. Faran felt the touch of fresh air on his face: they were near the surface. He nodded imperceptibly to Golon: it was nearly time.

Smiler jerked its head, and they preceded it up the steps, Golon the last, just in front of the creature. When they emerged they saw the sky overhead was as black as coal, and the wind howled like a banshee. They were at the head of stone steps emerging at the centre of a hollow shaped like an amphitheatre. Autumn leaves whirled around their heads. In the gloom they could see white marble ruins on a series of terraces leading up to a distant tree-fringed ridge.

The spider was still clutched in Golon's hand. He felt Smiler right behind him in the dark, pulling up short when it realised that Golon was still blocking the entranceway. Golon swivelled; in the purple light of the hanging ball he glimpsed the gap between Smiler's muscled neck and the armoured carapace and lunged forward, thrusting the spider into it.

Smiler's mouth opened in surprise, and its arm reached out for Golon. The sorcerer threw himself back into the clearing, but Smiler's hand clamped onto his trailing ankle. The hand was like a metal vice. He felt the trapped bones begin to crack. But then the creature's mouth opened even further as Golon sensed the spider's bloated body burst apart and a thousand siblings explode, running like liquid all over the monster's body, maddened at the confined space, biting it, infecting it with their venom.

Smiler gave a strangled cry. "Treachery," it hissed, its grip unrelenting on Golon's ankle. Faran had been ready: he snatched one of the Reapers' maces and brought it down on Smiler's wrist with a tremendous blow. Even then the flanged blades did not sever the trunklike thickness of the wrist, merely biting halfway through the bones and tendons. Green blood exploded from the wound. But it was enough: Golon felt his ankle released, and he scrambled back to safety.

But Smiler wasn't finished yet. Somehow, despite the poison coursing through its veins, it struggled up the remaining steps. Another blow from Faran rang off the thick armour of its carapace. The vampire guard was also at the top of the steps, his two-handed sword swinging down, but it caught an edge of the creature's armour, and the weapon spun off into the darkness.

But Smiler had sensed the power of the blow, he knew the greatest danger lay with the bodyguard. The creature turned on him, grappling with his chest, and Golon heard the vampire's ribs snapping one after another, like dry branches breaking. Then Golon remembered: the vampire had the Black Chalice in his backpack. He lunged forward. The pack was hanging free, and he ripped it bodily from the vampire's shoulders. The vampire swivelled, its mouth opening in a snaggle-toothed snarl as it felt its treasure being taken, but then the rest of his rib cage must have given way, for the air in his lungs exploded and black bile frothed from his mouth, splattering Golon's shoes.

The sorcerer backed away. Even the spider venom was not enough to kill this creature. He shouted out a warning and with Faran and the others began climbing hastily out of the hollow, up the serried terraces. The vampire guard still clung to Smiler, who lumbered after them, hampered by the undead's dead grip on its neck. They reached the lip of the hollow. Now Smiler had ripped the vampire free and tossed him to one side, but the venom was at last beginning to work, for it faltered and sank to its knees. The last Golon saw of it, Smiler was inching upwards, as slow as a turtle, weighed down by its carapace, yet still alive.

Golon and Faran and the others found themselves on a ridgetop. They could see from a hasty assessment that they were in the middle of the forest. The ridge led off towards the northeast. The air was bitingly cold, and the moon was obscured by a bank of dark cloud. Golon grabbed Faran's cloak and pointed. The Undead Lord followed the direction of his finger and nodded. They set off at a run along the bald summit of the ridge.

CHAPTER THIRTY-THREE

❦

A Wolf
in the River

The Thorn Men closed in on Urthred's party, the bony rattle of their limbs almost deafening, even in the howling of the wind.

"Stand back!" Urthred yelled, and threw forward his arms. A fireball streaked out, dazzling all of them with the sudden light. It fell between two of the creatures and exploded in flame. Their limbs were dry and they ignited like resin-soaked torches. The fire carried to their neighbours; the night was lit up by the orange flames flickering on their limbs. But the creatures still came on, even as the fire spread down their ranks: their thorny limbs outstretched, a wave of heat preceding. The humans fell back, but the Thorn Men got closer and closer, until Urthred felt a sudden stab at his back and turned. A branch lashed at his face, glancing off his mask. Some of the Thorn Men had come up behind: they had been pushed right back into them! He swung his glove, snapping the branch. Black sap gushed from the wound as the thing's other talon scraped him along the back, ripping his cloak to shreds and drawing blood.

Garadas, Jayal and the others were fighting like demons to either side of him. From the corner of his eye, Urthred saw one of the villagers fall, his face flayed open. Another's cloak had caught fire; the villager flapped at it, letting down his guard. Before he could protect himself he was run through the middle by a barbed spike.

Their situation was hopeless; they were being
pushed back into a tighter and tighter ring: soon the
circle would close and there would be no escaping
the spikes. Urthred lashed out again, his metal gloves
breaking another limb in two, but in turn his arm was
ripped by another thorny talon, the thorns hooking in
the harness, hampering his movement.

But then something strange happened: the rattling
of the creatures' limbs suddenly quietened and they
ceased to press in. They stood only inches away from
the tight knot of humans, so close that their burning
limbs singed their cloaks. The fire had quickly run
around the circle of the Thorn Men jumping from one
to another. The acrid smoke was choking them. Then,
as if in response to a distant signal, the circle began
to fall back, two falling in geysers of sparks as the fire
burned away the dark sorcery that animated them.
The rest inched away, their rootlike legs jerking spas-
tically, their dry chatter starting up again, intensifying.

Their movement quickened, and soon all of them,
save the ones left burning on the ground, had retreated back into the forest, to the west. More of them
fell as they made their way through the forest, but the
others continued deeper into the greenwood, the wind
fanning the flames so they shot high into the air, casting the trees into silhouette, making the emerald
leaves glow.

"Why did they spare us?" Thalassa asked, batting
at the burning cinders in her hair and on her cloak.

Urthred shook his head. "The Master has called
them away." He was still gasping for breath, fumbling
to reattach the damaged harness to his arm. They had
been on the point of killing them, destroying the
Lightbringer, Lorn's last hope. Why had the Master
called them off?

He felt blood running down his back from the
wound, and knelt on the ground, his head spinning.
Thalassa knelt next to him, pulling up his shirt to in-
spect the wound. He heard her gasp as she saw his
fire-scarred back. He turned, wanting to stop her, but

she was already ripping a swath of material from the bottom of her undershirt. "Hold still," she said, as she applied it to the wound.

Urthred could only glance around at the others as she tended to him. Garadas was by his two wounded men. The man who had been impaled seemed to be in his death throes, but the one with his face laid open moaned and writhed on the ground. Garadas looked up desperately as Alanda hobbled forward and knelt by the man. His face was cut open, revealing his cheekbone.

"Step back," she ordered, and Garadas did so, surprised. The leech gatherer's staff flared with light and she knelt and placed it against the man's cheek. There was a flash and the smell of cauterised flesh and when she lifted it away, Urthred saw that the wound had been closed by the heat of the staff. He also saw that Alanda's face had gone deadly pale, and she rocked on her heels: she had given up some of the last energy in the staff to save the man. "He'll live," she said, pushing herself unsteadily to her feet with the staff. She swayed precariously, the staff alone preventing her from falling over.

The other villagers were trying to comfort Imuni, but she was sobbing uncontrollably: the journey had turned more and more into one protracted nightmare.

Urthred looked up. The edge of the cloud was very near, but still they had a little time before they were completely swallowed by its shadow. He asked himself again why they had been saved. Urthred could see just the merest glimmer of one of the burning Thorn Men far away, on a distant ridgeline, blazing like a strange beacon.

"Come on," he said, ignoring the cold damp settling on his back through Thalassa's bandage: only now did he realise how badly he had been wounded. He prayed that the creature's thorns hadn't been poisoned.

Garadas helped the wounded man to his feet. He was dazed but seemed capable of walking unaided. The face of the moon at that moment disappeared

completely behind the cloud, and they were left in
near darkness apart from the light of the staff and
Dragonstooth.

"Close up," Garadas yelled to those who followed.
"There will be more fighting tonight." As if in answer
to this there was a mournful howl from the dark wall
of cloud to the south that made them all pause in
mid-stride: Fenris had returned. Only one day after
Urthred had seemingly destroyed it, the monster was
back.

Now all sight was blotted out by snow, wind and
leaves, as the hurricane overtook them. They came to
a halt, huddled together, unable to guess which direction to go. Soon whatever followed would be on them
and they were blind. Urthred turned to face the imagined threat, but his eyes even behind the mask teared
in the knife-cold wind. Then he sensed a presence next
to him, and he dimly made out Alanda holding up the
glowing staff towards the south. Her face beneath the
hood of the cloak had gone a shocking, transparent
white, each vein standing out clearly. It was as if she
had passed into another realm altogether and he
watched her ghost.

He shouted to her, but she was far away, and didn't
hear, her lips moving in some prayer. The edge of the
cloud roiled with a sudden light, a sudden commotion
as if one force contended with another. Then the edge
of the storm fell away slightly to the south. The wind
moaned once or twice, and all was still again.

"Gone for now," she whispered, then her eyes
turned up and she fell against him, the staff falling to
the ground. The others crowded round as Urthred laid
her gently down. Thalassa knelt by her, feeling for her
pulse. Her eyes sought Urthred's.

"She is very weak," she said. "We have to get her
to some shelter quickly."

But Alanda was stirring, as if she had heard Thalas-
sas' words. Her eyes fluttered open. "Give me the
staff," she whispered. "That will give me strength."
Urthred put it into her hands. "Thanks, priest," she

said, swallowing painfully, trying to lever herself up onto her elbows. "The staff is strong, but the wind will return, and then I will not be able to help. The wolf is close, I feel him."

"What should we do?" Urthred asked.

"We cannot get to Lorn. But we can get to Astragal," she said. "The Dedication Tree is there."

As if in answer to the old woman's words, they looked up. There, now only two miles or so away, the hills they had seen earlier rose up blackly in the moonlight, which had returned to bathe the scene. The storm had hidden how close they had got to them. Their hearts rose as one: there was hope yet.

They turned to Alanda. She nodded slowly. "We're nearly there." As one they turned and looked back. Each of them thought of the storm as an animate thing now, informed by a malevolent presence, a roiling mass of black cloud in which it seemed they saw faces of the damned, snarling and tearing at the air with insubstantial fangs as it rolled towards them. The mist hung on the crest of the nearest ridge, as the creature within watched and waited to see what they would do, then pulsed forward once more. Once more tendrils of black mist overarched them, hurrying over the face of the moon like bats, and a spatter of black hail sent them scurrying for cover. An ash tree just off the road suddenly shed its leaves as if an invisible line holding them to it had been cut: they fell around it only to be plucked up into the air again by an eddy of the wind.

No further encouragement was needed. The party set off again, running towards the line of hills. Urthred and one of the villagers now helped Alanda, whose legs trailed uselessly along the ground behind her. The night grew darker as they entered a part of the forest where green leaves still hung thickly on the trees, though even as they watched the hail and sleet turned their colours in an instant to autumn and winter.

The road began climbing steeply again, up one final ridge before the hills, now zigzagging to left and right. As they crested the next rise, they saw a dark gorge

ahead of them, spanned by the ruins of an old stone
bridge, the first human building they had seen since
the tower at the edge of the forest. Only its two end
spans were left, the centre had fallen into the ravine.
A sullen roar from its depths told them that it was
filled with a torrent. They broke to their right off the
road, realising that instead of walking away from the
storm they were now running parallel to it.

The storm fell on them in seconds. The branches of
the trees bent back at the full force of the gale, and
a white blanket enveloped them. Fist-sized hailstones
crashed about them: some found their mark. They
cowered beneath a huge spreading oak tree as the air
was rent with the howl of the storm's passing. Minutes
passed in which the wind eddied and shifted, sending
branches crashing about their heads, as if the wind
itself was alive and seeking them. Then the noise
abated slightly, and they struggled back to their feet.
They heard the storm progressing to the north, as if
their unwitting diversion had finally shrugged the thing
from their tracks, for though the sky was black all
around them, the wind was gone. It was as if the wolf
was still following their original path, over the ravine.
They were safe for the moment.

They fought their way up the side of the ravine,
looking for a crossing point. Two hundred yards along
its side, they found where the centre of the storm had
passed: a thirty-foot-wide swath of desolation carved
in the forest. On either side of it, the trees were still
intact, but in the middle the trees had been driven to
the ground, broken like matchwood. Some overhung
the ravine at precarious angles: a thick hoarfrost covered the ground, glowing dimly in the dark. The track
passed up the side of the river. They hurried back
across the path of devastation, but not before
Urthred noticed the pair of foot marks, dark smudges
in the frosty ground in front of them: the Doppelgänger. He was only just ahead of them; had somehow escaped the destruction. Jayal paused, his brow

furrowing, his eyes darting up to the eye slits of Urthred's mask.

"He is very near," he whispered, nervously glancing around him.

Twin threats: one just ahead, the other moving to the north. The cold of the frost-covered ground crept through the soles of Urthred's sandals and into his heart as they passed over it. After the patch of hoarfrost, there was no further indication which way the Doppelgänger had gone. The side of the ravine got progressively less steep, and they cut down it diagonally until they could see the river at its bottom rushing over the rocks in a white torrent. They picked their way amongst the boulders, trying to see a way across.

"There!" Jayal said suddenly, and Urthred caught a glimpse of a dark figure picking its way over a line of rocks that formed a dam over the river. Jayal rushed forward, Dragonstooth's glimmering blade describing mad arcs through the air as he ran. Garadas and Urthred followed. But when they reached the end of the dam, it was empty, and the figure had disappeared into the undergrowth on the other bank. Thalassa and Alanda joined them, the old woman leaning wearily on two of the villagers' arms.

Jayal glared into the darkness. "It was him, the Doppelgänger."

"Where is he going?" Garadas asked.

"He saw what we saw in the Orb; he is going to Lorn," Urthred replied.

Alanda gestured wearily with the staff. "We must go across," she said, "and find the road again."

They inched over the dam; the rushing torrent white in the darkness. One slip and they would have been swept downstream, but the twin lights of Dragonstooth and the staff gave them just enough light.

As they crossed the river the black clouds cleared and the sky ahead became crystal clear with the stars shining brightly in the sky. There was no sound, the wind had died away completely again. But the silence was as sinister as the roaring storm: each of them felt

its threat. It was as if the storm had vanished into the
air, or into the earth. They struggled up another ridge,
fighting their way through a tangle of branches, and
saw at the top the low hills towards which they had
been travelling all night, their summits surmounted by
what looked like jumbled rocks. In front of them the
river swooped around in a vast curve before thundering away to the east behind them. They made their
way down to the rocky shore where they halted.

It looked an hour or two's climb to the summit of
the hills, and by then all of them were very tired. A
warm blast of air came from the north again, as if
reassuring them that the danger had passed. Once
more the guiding spirit of Lorn was with them. They
were safe.

There was no sign of the Doppelgänger on the opposite bank of the river. They decided to rest for a
moment and fill their water bottles. As the others busied
themselves with backpacks and water bottles, Urthred
and Jayal went to its shore and stared across. The
Doppelgänger was there somewhere, watching. But
what could he do? There were ten of them. For the
moment he merely shadowed them, no doubt hoping
to catch one or two of them alone. As long as they
kept together, he was impotent.

Jayal was a few feet away from Urthred. The priest
turned from him. His wounded back was throbbing
dully, and his lips were parched. He wondered how
much blood he'd lost. He slipped off the mask, barely
caring if Jayal saw his face in the dim light. He knelt
to scoop up some water to his parched lips: as his
fingers touched the surface, he let out a murmur of
surprise. It was almost warm to the touch, as if fed
from the source of the warm breezes feeding from
the north.

Behind them, Garadas had ordered the lanterns to
be relit and placed on the shore, throwing out a perimeter of light. With the moon, they could now clearly
see the trees and the river. All of them knelt and
drank, heedless of Jayal, who still stared rigidly at the

opposite bank, apparently careless of thirst or weariness. Then he stirred and moved away, past the kneeling figure of the priest.

Jayal felt himself drifting slowly, his legs moving as if they belonged to another.

The light of the lanterns had spoilt his night vision just when he needed it more than ever. For the last two days it was as if he had seen the world that the Doppelgänger saw. But now the visions had suddenly stopped. And something else had begun. The voice. The voice that drowned his conscious thoughts filled his mind with an unending litany of hatred. He could not drown it out. And as his feet carried him away from his friends, it began to control his body, too. The Doppelgänger was close, but closer than in the physical sense. He was in his mind. His double possessed him, had entered his soul: for a few seconds their wills contended as they once had when he had been a child in Thrull. But soon that voice would dominate him completely: the same voice that had commanded him when he had been a child, driven him to evil acts, before the exorcism.

Here it was again: the mocking, wheedling tongue. The voice told him, in a sly, confiding way, there was no need for them to fight, no battle was required. His double would tell him what to do. Turn on the others and slay them. Together they would go to the north, find their father and kill him, too. He felt hatred against his companions. Why strive to do good? Everything was corrupt—Iss' reign was coming, even the good had turned to bad. He had believed Thalassa to be the Lightbringer, but now he saw what she was: a drab, staining his honour. His father had abandoned him, taking his one hope, the Rod, far away where he would never find it. The world had turned bad, was corrupt, like a pure white egg, addled at the middle.

His feet carried him beyond the perimeter of light: the other Jayal was gone, swallowed up in the dark vision. He would take Dragonstooth to his brother. He sheathed the sword. Its brightness hurt his eyes:

the things of Reh were abominable to him. He must
find his brother. He was here somewhere in the dark.
He went a little way down the river.

Suddenly Jayal returned to his senses and realised
what he was doing, and the voice abruptly was silenced. His thoughts snapped into his own: once more
he had control of them. He had been so close to being
taken over, possessed once more. But he was still
Jayal Illgill, still knew right and wrong, still had control of his mind and of his limbs. His heart was beating
quickly: none of the others had noticed he had gone.
But would the Doppelgänger realise that he was himself again and not under his domination? Surely he
would come, when he was alone: they would finish
what they had started in Marizian's tomb.

He went further and further down the river, until
the lights of the lanterns were only a glow through
the trees, his eyes straining in the darkness. He didn't
draw Dragonstooth: he wanted the Doppelgänger to
think he was still under his spell.

"Come," he whispered to himself, "come and let us
end it, and we will have peace at last." But there was
no answering sound. He would have to tease him out.

He went to the side of the river and knelt as if
about to drink in a small pool of water in the lee of
a rock. An icy prickle played on his neck, but when
he glanced behind: nothing. Perhaps the Doppelgänger had gone, realising he no longer had control
of Jayal's mind.

He suddenly realised how thirsty he was. He drank
long and furiously, slaking the thirst of the mountain
descent and the flight through the forest. The gurgle
of the water over the rocks filled his ears. His mind
went blank, as if for the first time since Goda he no
longer saw anything: neither his own sight, nor the
Doppelgänger's. What peace there was suddenly in
this basic act, this animal slaking of thirst!

Then he heard another sound: not so much a gurgle
as a chuckle. He lifted his head and his vision came
back: there superimposed upon it, he saw the dark

river of his own sight, and another picture: he, Jayal, leaning over the moonlit surface. The Doppelgänger was behind him! He tried to stand and turn in one movement, but his legs were cramped from kneeling, and he lost his balance, falling to one side, his hand groping for Dragonstooth.

He was there: standing right behind him, a rock held over his head in two hands. Jayal scrambled back, on his elbows, into the shallows, the Doppelgänger taking a step after him. What was he going to do? He couldn't kill him: then both of them, tied together as they were, would die.

The Doppelgänger threw the rock down towards his head. He flinched away and it glanced off his shoulder. He threw out his arm as the Doppelgänger leapt forward and lashed out, landing another blow on Jayal's chin. He reeled back into the water. The Doppelgänger's strength was superhuman, a strength greater than Jayal's even though his body was crippled. Jayal began to squirm backwards, his body now partially immersed in the river.

But as the water covered him, he felt something strange: his legs and back went numb as if an icy poison was stealing through his limbs. He quickly forced himself up into a half crouch as the Doppelgänger came forward again. He blocked another blow with one hand, his other trying to grapple with his opponent. But just at that moment he realised what was wrong with the water. It had been warm when he drank from it, but now it was ice-cold—glacial. The Doppelgänger pushed him back, and he lost his balance and he fell once more into the shallows. His back broke through a thin coating of ice. Then the Doppelgänger brought his fist down again. Jayal twisted to one side, the blow hammering into his damaged shoulder. He dived off to the side while the Doppelgänger was off-balance and scrambled to his feet, ignoring the pain.

Below him he saw his feet were being swallowed up by the spreading layer of ice. The river noise had

stopped as abruptly as if a tap had been turned off.
He stood motionless, his hand arrested over the hilt
of the sword. The Doppelgänger, too, hadn't moved.
He was staring at the surface of the river, now a white
sheet of ice. Then there came a scream from upriver
and an earsplitting howl.

It was Garadas who noticed it first: he had marvelled
at how the air in the centre of the forest was warmer
than even in Goda, how the trees still bore leaves
here. But none of this had pleased him: nothing that
went against the natural course ever did. It was winter.
Goda would remain buried in the drifts for the next
five months. Then why this unseasonable warmth?
And the temperature of the river water wasn't right
either: as if it had sprung from a warm underground
spring.

   He cursed himself for leaving his wife, and cursed
himself for not making sure that Idora had taken care
of Imuni. He had known his daughter was headstrong
and rash, should have guessed that she would follow
him. Now she had witnessed things that no child
should have ever seen and, what was more, she was
in mortal danger. He longed to be back in Goda, in
the low stone house that had been his father's and
father's father's: no one should leave the mountains
at this time of year. Idora would be in front of a
blazing fire, the room shifting and warping in the orange light. The image was such a contrast to the one
in front of him. Here it was dark save for the setting
moon and the lantern, and he was at the centre of the
Haunted Forest. The southerners told him there was
an old city here, but apart from the tower and the
bridge, it seemed to him there was no evidence that
anyone had ever lived in this place, at least not since
the time of the gods.

   He looked once more at the Lightbringer and her
people. Their arrival was a great enough miracle, but
others had followed: the healing in the village square
on the day of their departure, the fire magic of the

priest, the summoning of the great wind from Lorn: magic that he had never imagined or dreamed he would ever witness. Without it he had no doubt that they would be dead by now.

But whatever the miracles that had saved them, they were nothing to a simple man, who lived to be at peace with himself and the world. If only there had been a holy man to guide him. But the responsibility for his people's care had fallen on his shoulders—it had been his decision to let the Lightbringer into the village, and that decision had brought them, inexorably, to this—the middle of the Haunted Forest, pursued by demons. He was afraid, afraid for himself, for his child, for his men, for his wife if he failed to return.

He watched the Lightbringer: she had drunk from the river and was now talking in urgent whispers with the old woman who lay resting underneath a tree nearby. They would have to get to the sanctuary in the hills soon, this place Alanda called Astragal. The quiet was sinister. Where was the wolf? Surely it couldn't lose their scent so easily?

He called to his men, and they rose wearily to their feet. Then he realised one of the party was missing. Jayal had disappeared while they had been drinking from the river. There was something else, too—the sound of the river had changed: a moment before it had been loud, but now it was muted, as if on the instant its water had slowed.

He went to its edge, motioning one of his men to follow, and peered at the surface of the river. Only a moment before the water had been gurgling over its bed, but now it moved as slowly and sluggishly as treacle. The man knelt and touched its surface. "It's cold," he said, looking back at Garadas, but Garadas was staring upstream.

A faint trace of mist curled off the surface of the water, and, further away, a thin sheen of ice was forming.

Then he knew why he hadn't heard the wolf, for the wolf had passed into the north in the heart of the storm, but then sensed they had gone, and had turned back, entering the river near its source, inhabiting the water with its spirit. Then it had swum downstream. The water, turning to a blue-white ice in its wake, had poured like molten glass over the falls, until it had sensed the heat of their hearts.

Garadas's eyes turned to the man kneeling by the river. . . .

His hand was still touching the water and his mouth was open, but the words he was about to speak had frozen on his lips. The man's bare flesh had gone white, the river behind a white, churning mass of ice. Then the scream erupted from his mouth, as the moisture of his eyes froze over and his blood, too. He died where he knelt, frozen into his position as his blood turned to ice and his skin cracked and expanded before the headman's eyes.

Urthred had noticed Jayal passing him, but had stayed by the river, drinking. Eventually, he rose, fitting the mask back onto his face. He was staring down the riverbank to see if he could make out where the young Illgill had gone when he heard the scream. He whirled round. He saw the moving surface of the water suddenly freeze as if time itself had stopped, the kneeling villager's body go rigid.

His eyes turned to the others, locking on Thalassa. She had leapt to her feet at the noise, then the whole surface of the river exploded upwards in a huge fountain of ice. A whirlwind of freezing air and hurtling shards of ice burst from it and from its centre came a howl that took away his senses. He glimpsed the looming form of the wolf even as the ice smashed into his mask and ripped at his fur cloak. Then he leapt forward, towards where Thalassa had been standing. Back into the maelstrom. But he was blind: the breath of the wolf had frozen the air all around them, the breath in Urthred's lungs turning to ice.

*   *   *

Alanda woke with a start. A moment before it seemed it had been warm, and the warmth of the air and the furs made her feel drowsy. She had been talking to Thalassa, but had drifted off, dreaming of Astragal. She knew it was very close now, just at the top of the rise of the next hill. She was finally coming home. But then a cold shadow fell over her and Astragal vanished. Now she saw the same vision that she had had in Thrull, of the city lost in the ice and Urthred strangely transformed and Thalassa . . . Iskiard—its name as cold as the air she suddenly breathed.

Her eyes snapped open, and she saw in an instant the villager bending by the river, the water turn to ice in the blink of an eye and its surface explode upwards. Abruptly the scene was obliterated as the sudden cold meeting the warm air condensed into a white mist. She called out, but the fog killed all sound. She felt something stirring in front of her, growing in size and power by the second. She scrambled to her feet and began running downriver, calling out to her friends.

CHAPTER THIRTY-FOUR

✦

Smiler Redux

Faran halted his men a bowshot down the ridgeline, Smiler's screams echoing from the hollow below them. The sound reminded Faran of a baying fox calling in the night, on and on without remission: unearthly, high-pitched. He doubted he would have to endure it long. Golon's poison must surely kill the creature soon.

He turned to Golon. "Where are we?"

The sorcerer had the little purple gem out on its string. It trembled in his grip. Smiler's tenacious hold on life had unnerved him. "I feel the sword: over there," he said, pointing to the east.

"How far?"

The sorcerer shook his head. "Very near." Faran glanced up at the balcony of cloud hanging over half the sky. Ugly black streamers fell from it, bringing with them more creatures of the Night. The Master of Ravenspur: no doubt he was as much the cloud as the burning image he had seen in the throne room. And as with all beings omnipresent, he, too, would be omniscient, knowing that his servant Smiler was dying, in the hollow behind. And soon he would send retribution.

His mouth opened to order his men to move out when he saw the strange vision appear. Suddenly, there was light over the ridge to the east, where Golon had detected their quarry. The light increased as if a dawn were breaking there, and then, marching through the trees, burning bodies of what must once have been the Thorn Men, their bodies geysering sparks and flames. Their fire ignited the forest, the dry timber bursting alight and the wind from the north fanning the fires, so a roiling mass of flame rolled towards them at breakneck speed. Faran's sluggish blood felt like glacial ice: death by fire, his desiccated body like a resin-soaked torch that would burn brighter than even one of these . . .

So fixated was he on the strange sight that he barely heard the fall of rock behind him. He turned. There was Smiler teetering on the edge of the path, its green face a mottled purple mask, mucus dripping from the gash in its throat.

It eyes stared into Faran's. "Creature of Death," it managed to choke. "My master has seen your betrayal. Now you, too, will die." They stood there spellbound, not even Golon moving, amazed that the poison hadn't killed the creature. It was one of the last two Reapers who moved first, springing forward with his mace and smashing it into the fleshy folds of Smiler's skull. It impacted with a soft sound, but Smiler's head barely moved: Smiler threw up its hand and grasped the Reaper's and bent it back until it snapped with an audible crack. The man screamed in agony, before Smiler flung him behind him and over the edge of the drop. It lumbered forward towards Faran and Golon, a green ichor flowing down its mottled face. Faran still had the other Reaper's mace but he knew it would be powerless against the creature's strength. He stood paralysed, but Golon still had his wits about him. He gestured, and there came a rumble like thunder beneath their feet, then the whole lip of the ridge began to crumble. The advancing edge of the landslide caught the creature's feet. It threw out its hands, but it was too late. It fell backwards in an avalanche of rock and earth.

Faran stared at the sheer cliff face that had opened not two feet from where he stood. Turning again, he saw the whole forest ablaze, the wall of flame marching towards them. He could already feel the heat on his face. Was this the final death? But then he felt Golon

tug his sleeve, gesturing down towards the tunnel
mouth and Iken's Dike. That was their only hope, he
realised. The two of them began to scramble down
the crumbling slope as the fire raced towards them.

CHAPTER THIRTY-FIVE

A Meeting of
Dark and Light

The thick mist still hid the Doppelgänger, but Jayal knew he was close. He knew he might die in the sudden whiteout. So be it: if the Ice Wolf killed him first, then his twin would be destroyed as well. And then—what? Oblivion? Shades? Would his being blink out like a snuffed candle as his shadow died, or would life leech away slowly? Where would his soul go? To Hel no doubt, where all the damned went.

He drew Dragonstooth, the light flaring in the mist, and shouted out into the frozen air. No reply. The others had been up the river, but he had no way of telling where they were now. He went to the right, following the frozen course of the river, feeling the ice beneath his feet, Dragonstooth in front of him. His enemy would see him, he knew. If he came, he would come like a moth to a candle. He would die upon its blade. A howl split the air. There came a sinister cracking of ice from upstream.

The light of the moon was smothered completely, and he felt the cold weighing heavy upon him, so heavy that his feet slowed and his eyes seemed to be forced down by leaden weights. He stopped, shaking his head. Then it came, a sharp stab of pain in the palm of his hand, Dragonstooth warning him, as it had before when danger was near. The Doppelgänger was close. He could smell his presence. He swung Dragonstooth in a drunken arc, meeting only empty air.

Then a hand clamped down on his sword wrist,

holding it there with vicelike pressure, and out of the
fog there it was, in the halo of light cast by the sword,
the face of his nightmares again, the single eye blue
and malevolent, the face puckered and scarred,
twisted in exertion as he struggled for the blade. He
swung his free hand round, but somehow it was as if
the Doppelgänger had already anticipated the movement and caught it effortlessly, so they now staggered
backwards and forwards in a grim dance of death like
preying mantises locking their horns.

"Ah, cousin, cousin," the Doppelgänger said, his
words harsh and forced through exertion. "You want
to kill me, but save your breath. Look into my eye—
you'll see I'm right."

And Jayal did look into the single blue orb and once
more it was as if his soul was being sucked away into
the darkness of the Doppelgänger's mind. "The gods
curse you as an abomination," Jayal spat. All the time
he was aware of the growing cold, numbing his limbs.
The wolf was close. Why didn't the Doppelgänger
care?

The Doppelgänger seemed to sense his failing
power, and thrust Jayal back, so he sank to his knees,
his arms pressed further and further towards his chest.
The Doppelgänger spoke softly, cajoling, as he would
have a troublesome horse. "Lie down, and rest. You
will need your strength where I am taking you, to the
north, to your father. Your mind will be mine, like it
was when we were young, and soon the Rod will be
mine as well. Justice—a dish I thought I'd never taste,
but it is sweet, my cousin, sweeter than nectar."

"We will both die," Jayal spat. "Can't you feel it?
The wolf . . ."

"Pooh, a little cold and you mewl like a child," he
sneered, wrenching Jayal's wrist with such renewed
vigour that Jayal's legs finally buckled completely, and
he fell to one side. The sword was wrenched from his
grip and held at his throat.

"You cannot kill me," Jayal whispered. "Cannot
even injure me."

"And I will not have to," the Doppelgänger said, kneeling by his side. "You feel it, too, don't you? How every day I grow stronger? How I'm stronger than you now? Soon I will dominate your mind; your thoughts will be mine, as they should have been when we were children. You won then, because of that cursed wizard Manichee, but now, it is my time."

"You have turned from Reh!" Jayal spat.

"Reh? Who cares for him? The sun is guttering like an old candle burned to the wick. Soon all men will be dead. But while it burns, I will not sleep, Jayal Illgill. Soon you will do everything I ask. Soon you will become me."

"Never . . . I won't give up," Jayal answered through clenched teeth.

The Doppelgänger merely laughed. "Now I will leave you. I will kill the others in this mist. All except Thalassa. You know what I will do with her. And then I'll return. I will be with you, on your journey, in your mind, until we find the Rod. I am you, and you are me, forever, until we die. Only you can kill me, cousin—and you haven't the courage for that!"

"No!" Jayal cried, lashing out with his feet, toppling the Doppelgänger to the ground. The sword spun away, skidding over the icy surface of the river. Both of them scrambled after it, but Jayal got to it first. He rolled, bouncing back to his feet, and turned. The Doppelgänger was gone—lost in the blanket of mist.

He struck out in the direction he guessed the Doppelgänger had gone, but encountered only empty air, the sword darting this way and that, its light revealing the frozen trunks of trees, and the drifting fog. As quickly as he'd arrived, the Doppelgänger had vanished. Seconds passed, and all he heard was his own laboured breathing and the groaning of the frozen surface of the river.

But it was not the growing cold, a cold that was more intense than any he had ever experienced, but the Doppelgänger's words that sat like ice on his heart. The creature was right. Already he was in possession. Already their souls were merging back into one. The

Doppelgänger did not need to master him physically, because already Jayal's mind was infected with his double's words. Did he not see through the creature's eyes? Did he not feel the darkness growing like a stain on his soul? Did his thoughts not turn to dark, unmentionable deeds? How soon would he inherit all its dark appetites? How soon before his heart became as black as his? When they had found the Rod?

Just as it had separated them, would not the Rod join them so they merged back into one, and his being ceased to exist altogether? If that was the case, better the wolf take him now, let him be destroyed forever and with him his double. He hallooed into the darkness, shouted louder and louder, calling for the wolf to come, his arms down by his sides, Dragonstooth resting in his hand. But his words were killed in the thick mist, so even to his own ears they sounded distant, deadened. How could the wolf hear him? He set off at a stumble, praying that he went towards it.

Was that the noise of something slithering over the ground? The wolf? He smelt its acrid breath. He had killed its cub. Surely it would kill him now? He turned to face it, but then the noise came from another direction and then another and then all around. Whatever it was so close . . . "Take me!" he screamed. But nothing came.

He set off blindly again. He felt his feet slither on the icy surface of the river, then he was on a path, climbing upwards. . . .

CHAPTER THIRTY-SIX

❧

In the Mists

Thalassa had been sitting next to Imuni on the river-bank when the river froze over. The mist condensed as quickly as breath on a windowpane, then her sight was gone. She heard Imuni cry out next to her. She groped in her direction and, finding the young girl's hand, seized it.

In front of her she heard the ice cracking under huge pressure, and the acrid odour of the wolf wafted to her, staining the white mist yellow.

She stood, groping blindly in the mist, trying to find a landmark. Here was the gnarled trunk of the holm oak against which Alanda had been lying, but the space beneath was empty: she had vanished. There was more cracking of ice and what sounded like gnawing bones, then an earsplitting howl. "Come on!" she screamed, pulling Imuni away from the noise.

They fled, Thalassa using her little strength to drag Imuni, who was no better than a dead weight, stumbling on the boulders of the riverbed. Then her feet were slipping on the ice. She stopped abruptly, trying to get her bearings. Now there was no sound except Imuni's sobbing. Now they had stopped moving she found it almost impossible to breathe, it was so cold in the freezing fog; the ice particles settled on her lungs.

"Quiet, child," she whispered. She heard a growl from nearby, and the ice shook under their feet. The wolf was approaching them. Was she facing towards Astragal or away from it? There was no time to think; there came another howl, and the sound wave almost parted the fog so near was the wolf to them. She

turned and ran, pulling Imuni after her again. Her free
hand groped blindly until it met a frozen branch hanging in front of her. There was a steep bank behind:
she had reached the other side of the river. She pulled
herself and the girl up it with the help of the branch,
and peered anxiously around her in the gloom.

"Where's my father?" moaned Imuni.

"Hush, he'll be all right," Thalassa said, wishing she
believed her own words. Her ears strained for any
sound. Here on the opposite bank the fog was just as
dense, cold and spiritless, sapping the very soul from
her body into the frozen ground. She must move; the
ground sloped upwards: Astragal was in that direction.
That was the way to go.

"Come," she said, taking Imuni's hand, and they
started struggling through the tangle of trees, the frozen branches snapping off with sharp cracks.

Up and up she went, pulling Imuni behind her until
the fog began to thin slightly. She felt a diffuse white
glow through it. The moon. She blundered into a tree,
her free hand feeling for a way round it. Its back was
so frozen it felt like metal. Here was another branch
she could use to haul herself up; she clawed forward,
grabbing for another handhold. . . .

An arm. She had touched an arm. As quick as this
thought entered her mind, a hand had grabbed her.
Urthred? But the priest wore those gloves. It must
be Jayal. "Jayal?" she whispered, more in hope than
expectation, for the grip became even stronger. Imuni
sensed something was wrong and pulled Thalassa back
so her feet slipped on the steep bank. But the arm
above her would not let go.

Then the face loomed through the mist and the
moonglow right in front of her. The Doppelgänger:
the lopsided scar puckered the side of his mouth.

"Ha! Maybe there is a god after all," he exclaimed,
pushing himself close to her, his spittle sprinkling her
cheek. "The little virgin whore from the temple!" His
face split into a parody of a grin. He pulled Thalassa
right up next to him, and Imuni, whose fingers were

rigid in Thalassa's, was dragged up, too. "And who is this?" the Doppelgänger asked, his single eye glowering at the child.

"Run!" Thalassa shouted to Imuni, but the girl's fingers were locked rigidly in her own. Her eyes, already mad with fear, were riveted on the Doppelgänger.

"Good," he hissed, yanking Thalassa towards him and throwing his arm around her neck, choking off her breath. "At least she knows what's good for her." Thalassa lashed out with her free hand, but at such close quarters the Doppelgänger barely noticed her blow. He reached out and grabbed Imuni's hair with his other hand. "Don't struggle," he spat, tightening his hold on both of them, so Thalassa nearly choked and Imuni, finally snapping out of her paralysis, yelped in pain.

The Doppelgänger ignored her cries, and another blow from Thalassa, staring intently into the fog beneath them. Even he, it seemed, sensed the danger of the wolf. He began dragging them upwards, through the mist.

But Imuni had returned to her senses: the villagers of Goda were a tough race, and she had been in her fair share of scraps. She twisted her head one way and then another until it was free, then she bit the Doppelgänger's hand between the webbing of his thumb and forefinger. He released her abruptly with a yelp of pain, and with nothing keeping her on the steep slope, she fell like a stone backwards into the fog.

"The little whore!" the Doppelgänger cursed, shaking his wounded hand, the other gripping Thalassa's neck even more tightly.

Thalassa wrenched hard against his grip, desperately calling out the girl's name.

"Let the wolf have her. Come!" He pulled Thalassa towards his chest. Her head bent backwards, trying to catch a glimpse of the girl, but the Doppelgänger was having none of it. He dragged her up the slope. They continued their crabbed progress through the thicket, the Doppelgänger muttering and cursing all the time.

"You can't let her die," Thalassa begged, but he only snarled, feral, half-insane, and in that inarticulate sound Thalassa had her answer. They would all die. She had seen it in his glittering eyes in the Temple of Sutis, and now he was here, halfway around the world, like a ghost that could not be appeased.

He shifted position and wrenched her arm behind her back, then pushed her up the slope, the icy branches scratching her face. Eventually they climbed above the dense layer of the fog. Only a few rippling eddies of it hung in the air. The baying of the wolf still sounded from the river valley below.

The Doppelgänger paused to get his breath. "Safe, my beauty; safe enough."

"What do you want with me?" Thalassa asked, again struggling ineffectually in his vicelike grip.

"A little companionship, then what you denied me in Thrull. Then we will see. . . ." She felt his breath heavy and sour on her neck as he playfully nuzzled at her ear.

"Where are we going?" she asked, hoping to distract him, but he still leaned into her, and she could feel his groin pressing into her back. He was aroused despite the bitter cold.

"Tush, my beauty," he whispered, "I am going with you. To Lorn and then to the north, where the baron went, there to find the instrument that cast me into Shades." He let out a dismissive laugh, pushing her away slightly, and took one last look back into the valley. "Say good-bye to your friends: that creature will kill them all; all of them but Jayal." Where his voice had been savage a moment before, it now seemed ruminative, bitter.

"Come," he said, leading her upwards. "I will tell you how I came here, came here when you thought yourself safe. You will learn, whore: nowhere is safe. Bury yourself under a mountain, soar to Reh's fiery paradise: you will be found. But my story: Faran captured me; a fine journey we had, under Thrull. His magician brought forth one of his god's avatars, a creature that ate time, and so though it should have taken us months to reach this place, here I am. And Faran, too, scenting you out, my lovely, for he needs you as much as I. Touching, no? His blood cries out for yours. But my appetites are more humble, more basic."

He must have felt her tense, for he stopped and once more thrust his face at her through the gloom. "Oh, yes, my cold beauty, he is here, too. And what will the full moon of Lorn do to him, eh? Will it not burn in his veins and make him want you even more? Here, where there is so little blood? Will he not go mad? Maybe his lusts will be the end of him. Good, there will be one less pursuing the baron." He threw his head back and stared at the moon. "It is as cold as this in Shades. Not the cold of the flesh, but of the mind. Nothing ever touches you. Can you imagine what that is like: the coldness of never touching, or being loved; knowing that your soul has gone, lives in another man's body?" His mouth was close to her ear now. She remained absolutely still, not breathing even as he ground his body against hers again, like a dog. But when she didn't respond, he, too, went still, and twisting her arm again, he pushed her before him.

Up and up they went, her eyes fixed on the half moon, filled with tears, though she was beyond self-pity. She was beyond caring what happened to her. They were on the shoulder of one of the hills they had seen earlier. A cliff plunged into the forest below. To their left, there was a steep, tree-lined slope. She could make out crags and jumbled ruins five hundred feet or more above them. They seemed to be on some ancient track, though the going was rough, and the surface was covered with fallen boulders and partially blocked by overhanging trees.

She felt her fur cloak, already rent a hundred times, catch on a frozen branch and rip, but the Doppelgänger paid her discomfort no heed.

Where was Urthred? Dead? No, she was sure he was still alive, just as when they had been separated on the Plain of Ghosts—she sensed his presence not far away.

Then she felt a tingling on the nape of her neck, as if he had answered her call, even here, in this lost place, when she was so near to death. *Impossible,* she thought, *impossible.*

She twisted her head around; and there he was, coming out from the freezing mists below, his cloak glimmering in the moonlight, starched white by frost and snow. And there was Imuni as well, miraculously alive, clutching one of his steel-clawed gloves. She pulled up abruptly and the Doppelgänger swung around. He let out a curse when he saw Urthred. "So it's you, priest," he said, his voice was half mocking laughter, half growl.

He hauled Thalassa back into his chest, stepping close to the edge of the steep slope. "I'll kill the whore if you come any closer," he snarled, thrusting Thalassa towards the drop.

Urthred stopped, releasing Imuni's hand. He motioned for her to stay where she was. Then he stepped up the path towards the Doppelgänger. "Kill her, and you too will die," he said in a quiet voice.

"Hah! You forget, my friend. I cannot die while Jayal lives."

"So you say," Urthred replied. "But I wouldn't advise putting it to the test."

The Doppelgänger took a step back, even closer to the cliff edge. "No, I cannot die," he said, though there was now a small quaver in his voice. No doubt he remembered their previous battle in the Temple of Sutis, the strength of the priest's gloves. "Where would my soul go? Back to Shades? Only magic or the God's malediction can send me there again. Look at me: I am proof the dead can walk."

"Fire cures all things. The Fire of the Rod despatched your spirit to Shades in the first place," Urthred said. "It will burn the evil from the world at the end of time. See, here is fire." He held his right hand up and from the steel claws burst tongues of flame that flickered, underlighting his face in the darkness.

"A fairground trick," the Doppelgänger answered, though his voice was uncertain.

"These are no tricks," Urthred said with steel in his voice. He drew his left hand up the spire of flickering light, elongating it, making it taper to a fine point, so it looked for anything like the blade of a fiery dagger. Then, quick as lightning, the priest brought his gloved hand behind his back, and threw it forward. The fiery blade shot straight from it towards the tiny part of the Doppelgänger's face not obscured by Thalassa. It blossomed before her startled eyes, then with a searing heat passed her cheek. The creature twisted his head at the last moment, but the fiery dart still struck a glancing blow above the Doppelgänger's one good eye. He let out a scream, letting go of Thalassa and staggering back, his hands holding his wound. Then he lost his balance and fell over the edge of the cliff into the darkness.

Urthred ran forward. "Are you all right?" he asked Thalassa. She held her cheek. It was untouched, the only sign of the passage of the dart a faint singeing of her hair. She nodded mutely. Urthred strode to the edge of the cliff and peered down. There was no sign of the Doppelgänger in the Stygian darkness below. But he saw although the slope was steep, it was not that steep. The creature would most likely have survived the fall, if not without some injury.

Next he looked back down the slope towards the river—there was nothing visible there, neither their companions nor the wolf. He turned to Thalassa, who had once more taken Imuni's hand.

"Where is my father?" the girl whispered.

Thalassa bent down to her. "He'll be all right, child. We'll find him."

She looked up the mountain. The bald summit was visible above the tree line. It must be Astragal. That was where Alanda had told them to go. If she and the others were alive, that is where they would be heading.

Urthred went to Imuni and picked her up in one arm, making light weight of the load. "Come, I have strength for all of us," he said, offering his free arm. Thalassa took it, and they began to climb the path. Imuni shifted in his grip, then suddenly went still, and when he looked down he saw she had fallen into an exhausted sleep.

The climb was long and slow, the way strewn with boulders. As they rose higher, he suddenly saw a glimmering on the northeast horizon as if another moon rose there. He stopped, then realised what it was he saw: the lake, the same he had seen during the Dragon's flight, stretching away as far as the eye could see, a broad band of moonlight running down its centre.

Thalassa had stopped too.

"The Lake of Lorn," he whispered.

But she shook her head. "Didn't Alanda tell us that the moon always shone full in Lorn? Here it is only half-full." She was right, the moon was partly obscured, turning to a coppery red as it sank towards the tree-fringed horizon. There was no island like the one they had seen in the Orb in the middle of the inland sea either; just the pearly white of the water, almost dazzling as the moon set over it.

He turned to Thalassa, who still clung to his arm. Her face was white, and she was trembling, staring at the moon, a faint sheen of perspiration on her lip.

"What's the matter?" he asked.

"I was so sure we would find the city," she said.

"It is here somewhere," he answered. "It is hidden by Reh's magic, but we'll find it."

"There are only three weeks left," she whispered, her eyes not leaving the sinking orb as it fell over the lake.

"You saw it in your dream: the Silver Chalice is here, close."

"There is no Island of Lorn, priest, it was only a dream."

Urthred felt a sudden emptiness, a vertigo as if he were falling. She was right. They had put all their hopes on that vision. He had believed it. But had it only been an illusion? He turned once more to the glittering surface of the lake. It was empty and featureless. Had they both been deceived?

He remembered Thrull, how the full moon had sent the vampires into a blood frenzy. This moon was a week into its cycle of decay: in a week it would disappear altogether. Then the real thirst would begin, mounting through the new moon until it shone in the full again. Then she would be one of them, suffering that craving that could never be fully satisfied.

He sensed her eyes on him: she must have guessed what was going through his mind, sensed his despair. She abruptly shrugged off his arm and stepped away, a wild look on her face. Imuni moaned in his arms at the sudden movement, but as yet she didn't wake.

Thalassa took two stumbling paces backwards down the path. "Go; leave me, priest. Take the girl. Save yourself."

He stepped after her but she retreated even farther. "Remember me as I was, not for what I will become."

"I can't lose you now," he said.

Her shoulders slumped—the fight gone out of her. "Let me go. I will wander these forests until I die, or the wolf finds me, or Faran," she said plaintively, though there was no conviction in her words. She needed him.

He took another step nearer her. She didn't flinch away, but stared at him evenly, though her body was still as tense as a spring.

"Listen to what I have to say, Thalassa." He kept his voice low, not wishing to wake Imuni. "I swear on my master's memory that I will do everything to help you. We will find the Silver Chalice before the moon is full again."

She seemed calmer for the moment, and smiled faintly. "I wish I had known you before this, Urthred. Before the Temple of Sutis, before the bite . . ."

"And I, too: before this." He gestured at his face.
"But we have our time now. Come, let us go to the
top of the mountain; Reh willing, the others will be
there already."

Comforted by his words, she offered him her hand.
He extended the leather and metal monstrosity that
covered his fingers and took her fingers into his as
delicately as he would a flower.

So it was that as they climbed to the top of the
mountain, with the sleeping child, a strange peace was
on them, despite all the dangers and the uncertainty
over what had happened to their companions.

They climbed higher and higher up the fir-cloaked
slopes of the ancient granite mountain, passing lonely piles
of stones on either side of the path. Even in the moonlight, he could see that the rock was fire blackened,
friable and powdery, as if it had been subjected to
intense heat. He thought of the destruction that had
swept over this world ten thousand years before. The
same fire that had made the Nations what they were
had destroyed this place, this Astragal.

Further up the slope they found better-preserved
remains of what once must have been a considerable
city. A rampway passed diagonally up a steep slope
to the ruins of an entranceway, guarded by the stumps
of time-weathered towers. The smooth stones of the
rampway were still intact, though saplings grew in the
cracks between them.

Now the moon was very low and it glowed blood
red on the surface of the inland sea.

They passed through the narrow entry between the
towers. The steep stairway turned at right angles to
the wall and climbed up an avenue bordered by ruins,
jumbles of fallen stone blocks bound together by ancient tree roots.

They climbed up the street until they saw the summit opening out before them. In front was a flat
square, to the left, two more towers, flanking broad
steps which led up to a platform on which stood the
ruins of what looked to be a temple. They went up

the steps. The platform was a circular stone area made of ancient paving stones, some seventy feet across with unobstructed views in all directions. The temple stood at the centre of the platform. A rectangular stone building, its pediment held up by fire-blackened columns, it was the only semi-intact building anywhere in the city. Preserved miraculously despite age and the destruction that had laid everything else to waste. It seemed a quiet place in the cold light, and he wondered what its purpose had been. Into his mind came a vision of travellers of old resting here in their long journey through the forest, journeying from one golden city to another, the skies crisscrossed with the white trails of the God's steeds.

On each side of the platform the land plunged down perpendicular cliffs to the undulating canopy of treetops a hundred feet below: beyond it the lake was now fading into darkness as the moon set. To the south, the land was still cloaked in icy fog.

At the eastern extreme of the platform stood a spreading oak some fifty feet high, gnarled and lightning-blasted, but still in leaf. A low stone plinth a foot high stood in front of it, right at the edge of the precipice. The tree stood silhouetted by the sinking moon, its branches casting a deep midnight shade over the temple in its lee. There was such solitude here, as if time had taken on a physical form and sat heavily in the ancient wood.

"The Dedication Tree," Urthred whispered. "The tree that the leech gatherer's staff was taken from."

"Exactly as Alanda told us it would be," Thalassa said.

"The staff will bring her here," he said, "I'm certain."

Thalassa looked back down the mountain. "I hope so, Urthred," she said quietly.

"Come," he said, walking under the canopy of the tree. She followed him. He laid Imuni gently on the ground and pulled off his right-hand glove. In the moonlight, Thalassa could see the mutilated fingers, burned to the first knuckle. He pressed his hand against the an-

cient bark of the tree, and stood with his head bowed.
Tentatively, she put her own hand on it, too. She felt
a tingle, and for a moment the fever that had been
burning her body all day seemed soothed away. She
felt her spirit descend, deep into the earth, following
the tree's roots down and down, through the cool
rock. Knowledge of the quiet places of the mountain
entered her heart, and she felt her soul soothed by
the ancient rock, rock that had never changed since
the fiery birth of the world.

She could have remained thus forever, until her
flesh and bones had crumbled to dust, and she would
have been content. But presently she heard Urthred
sigh and draw away his hand. She opened her eyes
and did the same, and the pressing anxiety came back
onto her. She looked to the east, at the sinking moon.
Soon the sun would rise. With a sickness in her heart,
she realised that for the first time in her life, she
feared the coming of the dawn.

Urthred walked to the southern edge of the platform. He seemed suddenly absorbed. She followed,
wondering what he was about to do. He stood there
outlined by the white fog. It had drifted slowly up
towards them so that some tendrils of it drifted over
the edge of the parapet. He raised his hand, still uncovered, to the sky. A small red mote appeared in the
air above his hand, then suddenly the sky seemed to
erupt into flame, throwing the scene into harsh shadows, driving the mist away from the edge of the platform. Thalassa flinched back, her eyes aching from the
light. He turned and, seeing her distress, steered her
back to the temple.

"It will be darker inside," he said. He crouched and
lifted Imuni, and together they climbed steps to what
must once have been the wooden doors of the temple.
Inside the portico there was no sound except the endless noise of the breeze through the columns. The ancient wood of the doorway had long ago been reduced
to a red dust by termites and the weather, and all they

could see within was darkness and a gleam at the far end where a stray moonbeam fell on an ancient altar.

Imuni half opened her eyes, but Urthred could see she was asleep still, then her eyes closed again. Thalassa, too, suddenly felt very weary and sank to the floor. Urthred knelt beside her.

"Already the light is too much," she said.

He was silent for a moment. "We have three weeks," he said eventually.

"I fear the dawn, Urthred."

"Then you must stay here, where it is dark." He refastened his glove to its harness, then, using the pincers, pulled back the left sleeve of his cloak, exposing the veins in his arms. He flicked his right hand and a knife, quicker than the eye could register, flashed out. The blade shone coldly in the blue light.

"What are you doing?" she asked.

"You must have blood," he said. "Let it be mine."

She flung out her hand, grabbing his wrist. "No! Once I have tasted your blood, then mere tasting will not be enough." A film of sweat covered her brow, and her lips trembled.

"I'm not afraid," he said evenly so as not to wake the girl.

Thalassa sank back onto the floor. "Not yet: there's still time. Let us try to find the Silver Chalice first."

He slowly retracted the knife back into his glove. "Very well. We will wait for the others. They will see the beacon—they will come. Rest: I'll watch for them."

She nodded and lay down on the cold slabs of the temple floor, bunching her hands under her head to make a rudimentary pillow.

He got slowly to his feet, still looking at her. She smiled back at him, then her eyes closed and she was instantly asleep. He stared at her for a moment as if drawing strength from the sight and went outside again.

CHAPTER THIRTY-SEVEN

✦

By the Light
of the Dog Star

Alanda had no illusions: she was near dead anyway, the staff had only given her a deception of life, a life borrowed from its magic. With the last of her strength she drew on the green sap in the ancient bough and, through it, from the earth itself. She felt it sucked up from the soil into her veins: she felt every root and every artery of life beneath the earth flow into her, become her blood. Once more she felt its magic: she was young again, the stored sunlight of those roots flowed through her and burst from the end of the staff in a green phosphorescent light. Images of her childhood came back, of her husband Theodric, his hair golden in the light, their wedding day, the street strewn with nuptial flowers. . . .

Her eyes snapped open and she woke from her reverie. She had to remember that the staff only flattered to deceive. She was an empty husk—it gave her life only for a little while longer.

But she had to get to Astragal: the others needed her help. She set off blindly, the staff tugging her forward.

She crossed over the rutted waves of the frozen river and began to climb the far bank. Up and up she went through a thicket of trees, calling out again, but the fog muffled all sound. How far had she come? A mile or more, she guessed, from where the villager had met his death. The river was far below her. If the

others were alive, they would be going in this direction, heading for the ruins of Astragal.

Everything was dampened and deadened in the
chill mist, and, as the cold intensified, the light of
the staff began to die. She knew she would die when
the light was gone: her hour was coming. The fog eased
slightly as she got higher up the slope. It was then she
found the first sign that the others had survived. A
tattered fragment of dress; Thalassa's dress, the one
she had been wearing under her fur cloak. Her hopes
rose. Thalassa must live, she was the Lightbringer.

She stooped and inspected the patch of cloth in her
narrow circle of illumination. There were another two
sets of footprints in a crazy pattern at the base of the
tree. She placed her hands on them and called upon
the magic of her people, called for the earth to tell
her who had passed this way, and she felt a responding
warm tingle: whoever had passed here had done so
only a little time before. She knew Thalassa was one
of them, but whose were the other set of tracks? There
was no warmth coming from them. Cold, nullity.
Alanda crouched over them, taut as a spring. The
Doppelgänger? The last she had seen him was across
the loop of the river an hour or so before. He was
either following one of them, or had captured them,
judging by the churned footprints on the ground.

She followed the trail. Though the air was cold, the
staff gave her old bones warmth. Again, she heard the
howling of the wolf, but this time the sound seemed
closer. And with the sound came a fetid waft of de-
composing matter, of matted fur and skin and sores,
eddying up from below. She hobbled on as quickly as
she could, but her haste was her undoing; her bond
with the earth was broken. The light of the staff fell
to a mere pinprick with a sudden hiss as if nearly
extinguished by the stink that had settled in the dark
mist. But there was a little magic in it yet, for she felt
its pull on her hands like a diviner's rod, telling her
where the path was. One side she felt the brush of

pine needles, on the other empty space, as the path dropped away over the river gorge.

After an hour she emerged from the freezing cloud of fog: the moon was near setting and dawn could not be far away.

Her fatigue was growing by the second, and she began to stumble on the rocky path, teetering close to the edge of the cliff. She knew she must fall soon, her balance was going. But she couldn't rest here. She pressed on and sensed rather than saw the path open up into a small plateau set into the mountainside: she felt the brittleness of frozen grass under her feet. She rested on the staff, and now she was stationary it began to glow again. Its radiance seemed to give her back her sight, and she looked around the small clearing. There was a ring of lightning-blackened stumps and a tangle of fallen trunks on the plateau. They lay in a tangled heap of branch and stem, their mighty trunks rotting slowly back into the ground. Her eyes went up, and though they were rheumy, she saw the faint glimmering of the lake in the distance: the Lake of Lorn.

She sat on a fallen tree trunk, its bark polyped with mushrooms, and listened again, hoping to hear Urthred, Thalassa or Jayal calling for her. But she knew they wouldn't call—if they were alive, they would be silent, waiting for the day to come.

Since her childhood she had had control of the rhythms of nature, had commanded animals and birds to do her bidding, called upon the plants to bend and twist to her directions, as she had ordered the marsh reeds at Furtal's death, or the lilies which had formed a bridge across the moat at Thrull. And was this not Astragal, the place of her people, where nature had once been most powerful?

She'd heard no beast all the time they'd spent in the forest and guessed that winter had driven them far away. Her mind went out to the tree stumps surrounding her, like silent spectres in the clearing. She addressed them in prayer. She felt in response a dark brooding, as if they mourned their deaths all those years before, a mute sorrowing.

Her books had told her of the sacred lyres fashioned from the boughs of these trees, palaces erected from its ancient wood: the books had said that their very walls would sing and the whole forest would carol from dawn to dusk. There was no sign of that magic now. Then the end of the world had come: the Witches driven from their capital, the Nations changed into the shapes they inhabited now, and the magic had been driven away. Only one people had survived as they had before: the people of Lorn. Had Illgill found their land?

But then it seemed that she heard song, song that seemed to come both from the staff in her hands and from far away, from an area of the forest, on a saddle between the summit of the mountain and a lower peak. She looked down, and once more, as it had done earlier on in the day, she saw that the staff glowed with a green light. The glow increased until there was a circle of emerald light around the tree trunk.

She stood then, her weariness forgotten, and set off, leaving the path to the summit, now traversing across the mountainside on what seemed to be a subsidiary track. Not far away, she saw an answering glow from the saddle between the two peaks. She crossed a rushing brook and found the traces of a path winding upwards. Presently she came to a green lawn stretching between the two crests, with various standing stones arranged around it. Beyond it, she saw a low lodge on the top of the hill: the first human habitation she had seen since the tower at the edge of the forest. Long, bowed chimneystacks rose into the night air like the crooked limbs of trees, its eaves fell nearly to the ground in front of the house. In front of it stood three totem poles hung with the furs and skulls of forest animals looped to leather thongs, swinging in the slight breeze. The house had small round windows through which green light poured. The sound of song came from within, and as she stepped up to the front door she peered into the brightly lit interior.

The world was animate: the seed of life was in all things, from inert stone to human flesh. And in all the world, Reh's light was made manifest in different ways. Yet the sight that met Alanda's old blue eyes was even in her long lifetime unexpected. The spirits of the woods were here incarnate in flitting shadowy figures, tall and gracious, creatures of green light that flitted about the room that now stood revealed. It was a dwelling place carved from the living hearts of trees, notched with runes and symbols in the old Fire Tongue. Each nook and cranny of it was planed from wood that glowed a honey light. The figures of light were human in appearance, willowy and tall, fair folk, men and women in their prime, the ghosts of her people, welcoming her home. They sang as they swooped and dived about the room, and Alanda felt herself beguiled by the sound of their music. The door swung open and she entered, the staff held high in front of her. The celerity of the woods spirits increased to a frenzy.

The room was laid out as for a banquet, with a long table stretching away down its length. She sat upon an old carved oaken chair at its end. As she touched it, the knots in its wood budded into leaf, acorns grew in the centre of the leaf cluster. The whirling figures come closer and closer until she was lost in a whirlwind of light: strange visions came then, of the forest shining in the dawn of the world, and her people working their magic as the God's chariots pulled by fire-spitting dragons crossed the sky. And she saw the dwelling places of the gods, the cloud-piercing towers and walls that forever shone like brilliant steel, in the east on Shandering Plain. All this she saw as if in a flash of time, two or three seconds long but as if every second was an eternity long, so it seemed she had lived the aeons of the visions.

And she saw the end of this earthly paradise in the fiery holocaust of the gods' final battle, and how the new race of people were born from the stinking pools that was all that was left of the rivers and lakes of Lorn. An impure people: the Nations of the Night.

And she saw the place where it was always high summer and the moon always shone: the kingdom called Lorn.

Yet she knew that the vision of Lorn was not of this plane: it was somewhere remote. She heard the voices tell her that it was the moon: the moon was the gateway to Lorn. But no further clue as how to get there was offered.

The singing of the spirits, quick and vital a few moments before, had now quieted and slowed, and Alanda felt a drowsiness begin to steal over her, and she thought how nice it would be to lean back for a moment on the headrest behind her. Her head sank onto it and it was as if the wood reached out and cradled it, like a mother who takes her sleeping child's head into her arms and sings quietly of long-lost days. She felt herself slowly slide down a gentle dark slope and she slept the soundest sleep she had slept in seven years.

She woke: her head was cradled on the same fallen tree trunk that she had been sitting on in the lightning-blasted clearing, the staff still clutched in one hand. The setting moon still hung on the tree-lined ridge to the east, and she realised that only a few seconds had passed. The vision had been but that—a vision, but the numbing weariness had gone. She once more marvelled at the power of the staff, feeling so refreshed from the magical sleep into which she'd fallen that she wanted to be on her way immediately. She must find the others, tell them what she had dreamed: that the moon was the key to finding Lorn.

She got to her feet and started up the mountain. The staff burned brightly once more, and she needed it once the moon sank beneath the ridge, only leaving an afterglow behind. She found a place where the path forked. One branch rose up steeply directly to the summit, the other looped around the mountain to the south on a gentler slope, overlooking the river valley below. Ahead through the limbs of spruce trees she saw that the whole of the mountainside up to the sum-

mit was cloaked in the freezing white fog. The wolf
had become insubstantial again, had crept upwards in
the mist, seeking her out. She was about to take the
left-hand fork when she felt the staff tingle in her
hand, telling her to take the second path, into the
danger. Why? She was afraid, but the staff had led
her faithfully ever since Goda—she must obey. She
set off down the right-hand fork.

The air was getting noticeably colder, in front of
her the limbs of the fir trees were veiled in the thick,
choking mist. She passed into the dense bank of fog.
The staff lit the way, keeping her away from the
deadly drop to her right. The ground under foot was
starched with ice crystals, and her feet crackled loudly
as she stepped on its surface. Vast cobwebs hung between the trees, steel-white as if cast in metal, and
strange growths, like cocoons, hung from the ice-
encased boughs, like giant wasps' nests made of ice.

There came a yowl from ahead, and thick snow crystals, bitter like ash on her lips, eddied in the wind.
She saw a sudden spurt of reddish light, swiftly extinguished, and a whistling noise came back to her muffled on a heavy fall of snow. Despite her fear, she
went forward, blinking the snow from her eyes. Once
more the air became thick and fetid with the yellow
rot of acid decay.

Then she saw it. A figure as tall as the surrounding
trees hunched on the path, part-wolf, part-human, for
it stood on its hind legs, holding two clawed hands in
front of it. Whatever Fenris had been before, now it
was metamorphosed, assuming the human appearance
that it must once have had before it had slunk into
the waters of the Black Tarn. So tall it was, it looked
like it occupied the place between earth and sky.

Her feet seemed to have taken on a life of their own:
she kept moving, closer and closer to Fenris. The wolf
was facing away from her: its freezing exhalations burning the ground black in front of it. It threw forward its
gnarled fingers and the ground ahead was instantly
spidered with a web of hoarfrost. Then she saw the

figure struggling desperately in the icy web in front of it. The pulse of red light lit up the interior of the web, and she saw what it was, the glow of Dragonstooth: Jayal. But the young Illgill was already embedded in ice and the sword's light was dim, as if coming from a great distance. As she watched, the wolf drew deeply of the frigid air all around it, ready for a killing blast.

But before its breath could be exhaled, Alanda had swept the staff through the air in a half circle. As the hollow and the wolf were bathed in a stark white light, the creature turned, its eyes lit up like hellfire, its jaws stretching, its acid saliva falling from its teeth and burning the ground. Time seemed to stop in the light: the snowflakes froze in mid-flight, the wind that had been blowing died away instantly.

Then Alanda looked up, above the looming jaws. The fog parted before her gaze, creating a tunnel upwards to the sky. There were the stars, the home of the distant gods, glittering through the unmoving snow and the motionless boughs of the trees. She sought out one of them: Sirius, the Dog Star, the brightest in all the constellations. Her soul vaulted up, through space, through the many-textured blues and purples of the sky, higher and higher, until the earth was left far below. The deepest black of space surrounded her, and the brightly burning star grew and grew until she stood before its shifting yellow-and-orange gas clouds, clouds that sent great gouts of flames thousands of miles into space, and then the star filled all her vision and she drew its power into her staff. . . .

White light exploded from it, pure light refined from a temperature beyond the imagining of man. In a second of incandescent flight quicker than the blinking of an eye it struck the wolf's side with a white explosion of flame. Alanda clamped shut her eyes, but the brightness burned on and on, inside her mind.

Then, silence. When she opened her eyes again, the wolf was gone, the snow had disappeared. Though the forest remained frozen all around, she felt a breath of warmer air on her cheek. The wind from the north had returned, and already the ice had begun to thaw; meltwater fell from the surrounding trees with a quiet patter like a shower of rain.

She hurried forward. Jayal knelt in the hollow, the sword held up, frozen in his hands in the same position as when he'd attempted a last desperate parry. Though the explosion had thawed the trees, his face and armour were matted in a thick coat of hoarfrost, and no movement came from him, nor breath: he looked, if anything, like a grey statue.

Alanda knelt, laying the staff on the ground beside her, feeling the life begin to drain from her as her fingers relinquished it. She cupped her hands to the warrior's frozen cheeks. They felt like marble exposed to a northern wind: as cold as death itself. Panic set in—had she lost him? Had she been too late? Her fingers dug under the collar of his chain-mail vest, seeking the carotid artery—there it was, and the faintest perceptible beat penetrated even to her frozen fingers telling him he was still alive, but only just.

Her magic had drained her, but she knew she had to act fast. Though the warm wind from the interior had returned, she knew it would be too late to save Jayal: other measures were called for. Despite the chill that still lingered in the hollow, she pulled off her cloak, exposing her frail old bones to the damp. She held it up to the air—the invisible atoms seemed to obey her—a warm breeze sprang up, so that the cloak billowed out, filling up with life-giving warmth. She closed her eyes, communing with the wind, praying for it to return warmth to Jayal's frozen limbs. The cloak filled like a sail, nearly bearing her bird-like body up to the sky, but she wrestled with its corners, as if it were a recalcitrant creature that had to be tamed. She brought it back to Jayal, wrapping it around his shoulders. The warmth surrounded him, and after a second or two, she saw him exhale once, then twice, his breath condensing in the moisture-filled air. His eyelids cracked the layer of frost covering them, and for a moment he stared at her without comprehending.

"The wolf . . ." he mumbled.

"It's gone—you're safe," soothed Alanda. "Rest for a moment: your circulation will get going in a minute."

"Where are the others?" Jayal asked, his teeth chattering together.

"I don't know," she replied. "I found two tracks leading up to the summit. . . ."

"The Doppelgänger was waiting, back by the river. . . ." Jayal gasped. "We fought; but I lost him. Then the wolf followed me."

"You're safe now," Alanda said, trying to quiet him.

But Jayal's eyes were alive with a strange light, and he could not be silenced. "I should be dead. Look at me, my blood has frozen in my veins, yet I live. I am immortal, Alanda: as long as he lives, I must live, too. Such is the magic that separated us, and brought him back. Think of it: only the gods understand this, this knowledge of life everlasting."

"And the Dead in Life."

A shadow passed over his frozen face. "The Dead in Life," he whispered. "Aye, they, too. I am not so different from one who is infected, knowing that my master, like a shadow just on the outside of sight, is always there, dominating my mind. Just as I know the day will come when he will control me, and I will be lost."

"That's why you have to find your father; the Rod will defeat your shadow, trust me," she said, picking up the staff again. Its energy was nearly spent, only the merest flicker of green light coming from its surface. She was very near the end, but she hid it from him as she rose stiffly to her feet. "Can you walk?"

Jayal tried to move his frozen limbs. "Maybe," he mumbled eventually. He stretched his legs, which gave with an audible crack of breaking ice. His face creased in agony as the circulation returned, but he slowly struggled to a standing position, his body stooped double, as nearly bent and crooked as Alanda's. The old woman tried to help him, but he waved her off.

"I'm all right," he said, grimacing as the blood flowed back into his frozen limbs. "Let's go."

She took Jayal's arm in her hand and helped him to straighten slightly, and they set off, him hopping and stumbling as if he were a hobbled horse, their progress agonisingly slow. As they crested the rise of the hollow, they saw what looked like a fire in the sky above them, coming from the summit of the mountain.

"Someone has lit a beacon: it must be the priest," Jayal said through clenched teeth.

Each step was agony for Jayal, and once more Alanda felt the energy of the staff ebbing away, but after an hour or so, the blaze on the summit of the hill seemed nearer. The path zigzagged crazily up a boulder-littered slope, Alanda's strength ebbed by the second and the light of the staff grew weaker and weaker.

Now they saw the ruins of worked stone set into the surrounding crags, and the remains of a circular wall surrounding the summit above them. The light filled the sky behind the walls. Angular blocks lay on the slopes, and the walls and foundations of buildings could be seen on flat terraces cut into the mountainside. A broad flight of steps led upwards.

Alanda led the way, her steps slow and faltering. Her face was ashen, her hand trembling. Now it was Jayal who helped her, despite the cramping of his limbs. They went past better-preserved ruins, manhigh or more. Then above them, they saw a gap in what must once have been a city wall, and they saw where the light was coming from. A burning globe hung in the sky, brighter than the moon had been before it set. Overhead the stars shone like bright jewels on a satin sky.

"Astragal," the old lady breathed, then sank to her knees, her strength quite given out. Jayal managed to lift her and staggered up the last few yards of the path. He stood there, blinking in the harsh light of the burning globe, his legs wobbling as if they were made of jelly. Then a dark figure came from the shadows on the far side of the orb.

CHAPTER THIRTY-EIGHT

❖

The Witch Queen
of the North

The figure stepped into the light, and Jayal recognised the priest. Urthred saw Alanda lying unconscious in Jayal's arms and came forward to help him. "Is she all right?" he asked anxiously.

Jayal shook his head. "She's very weak. She spent her last energy saving me."

"What happened?"

"The wolf trapped me, was killing me, but then Alanda came with the staff and destroyed it. Now she is near death."

"Let me see." Jayal lowered Alanda to the ground, and Urthred crouched next to him. He saw that though her eyes were closed, she still clutched the staff in her frail hands. "Alanda?" he whispered.

Her eyes fluttered open, but it was mainly the whites that showed and it seemed she could no longer focus. "Priest? Is that you?" she asked.

"Yes, it is I: Thalassa and the girl are safe."

"Reh be thanked. The staff has led us home."

Urthred turned to the tree at the edge of the parapet. "Aye, you are in Astragal now, and there is the Dedication Tree."

The old woman nodded. "Then I ask one last thing. Take me to it; put me under it."

Urthred picked her up and carried her under the branches of the old oak. She sighed as he laid her gently on the ground. "Now I'm at peace," she said. "Fetch Thalassa: I must speak to her before I go."

"Go where?"

"Where we must all go, Urthred, when we die."

"You will recover now; you have come this far."

"The light of the staff is spent. You know it was all that kept me going."

"Then I will cut another from the tree."

She shook her head. "Too late: the magic is gone. My old skin and bones must return to the earth. I feel the roots already, reaching up, drawing me into them. I will be reborn again, another Alanda, another blue-eyed Witch of the North, sometime, somewhere else; they say we cannot die for we come from the earth." He made to speak again, but summoning her last strength, she lifted a trembling hand. "Now, fetch Thalassa, I must see her one last time."

But a voice came from behind them in the shadows. "I am here, Alanda." Thalassa.

"Come into the light, child, I want to see you."

"I cannot: the light hurts my eyes," Thalassa answered.

The old lady screwed up her face, trying to see her in the shadows.

Urthred lifted his right gloved hand and with a scrape of steel talons rubbed his thumb and forefinger together in a snuffing motion. Abruptly the burning ball vanished, leaving them in darkness. The only light was Dragonstooth shining from Jayal's scabbard and, over in the east, a faint grey in the sky: dawn was not far away. Thalassa came forward, into the dark shadows where the old woman lay, only the whites of Alanda's eyes visible. She knelt by her old friend.

"How can I ease you?" she asked.

"You heard me, child. Only the earth and the rocks can ease me now. I have reached Astragal—the place I dreamt of, the place I prayed I would one day see, all those days in Thrull. My magic came from here, through the undercurrents of the earth, flowing all that way, bringing me news of the past and what was to happen in the future. Now it is all at an end."

"Courage, the earth will as soon heal you as take you into it."

"No: they say that seers only once glimpse their own deaths, and that is soon before they die. I have seen it, seen my dust enter the river of time and flow on to another future—I'm beginning the journey soon." She turned to Urthred, raising herself slightly off the ground. "You are a good man. But promise me one last thing, priest."

"Anything," he said, though his voice was hoarse.

"Thalassa knows where my husband, Theodric, is buried. His head is on the pyramid of skulls. One day return to Thrull, or whatever is left of it. Seek out his bones, Reh will show you how, and lay them out for the sacred birds. Then say the sacred prayers over him. He was a creature of fire. Let him be resurrected in fire."

"I will do so."

"Burn my body, and scatter the ashes about this place: let Reh take his part, and the earth that bred me, the rest."

"I will."

Urthred's promise seemed to calm her a bit, and she sank back onto the ground. The first stripes of rosy pink were by now streaking the eastern sky. The old lady was very still. For a moment Urthred wondered if she had not already passed over to the other side, but her chest still rose and fell spasmodically. Her eyes cracked open again. "Give me your hand," she said to Thalassa. Thalassa did so. "With my death, my magic will pass into the one I choose as my successor. I give it to you, Thalassa: use it well, as you did in Goda when you cured the villagers. And when your day has come, give it to another as I have given it to you. Do not ask how it is done, you will just know it, as the priest knows it: for that is the way of magic, whether it be of the fire like his, or of the earth like mine. Use the gifts well, child."

"I promise," Thalassa said, gripping her friend's hand.

"All of you must have hope, despite the loads you carry. Jayal, the Doppelgänger hides in the forest, waiting once more for you to be separated from the others, for when you are weak. Do not let him dominate you. Be strong in your mind. You have a pure heart. A pure heart is stronger than his evil."

"I will," Jayal said.

"Remember, he is powerless to defeat you until your father and the Rod are found. Have courage."

"I will, Alanda. You saved me; you gave your life for mine."

"Use the sword well, Jayal, and that will be reward enough. Urthred; you know what ails you. But think on Manichee's words. Already healing has begun. Pain and triumph lie ahead for you. Let not the first overcome your sense of the last: you will be a great man, will see sights that no other man has seen, command great power, will be a legend. The history books will be full of Urthred of Ravenspur, the Herald." The priest could only hang his head at her words.

"Thalassa," she continued weakly, "visions of gold follow you, child. Though my love is lost, that cup will be filled again, with love as good as mine. A cure for the vampire's curse is all that you need. The Silver Chalice waits for you in Lorn. It is the opposite of the Black Chalice that turns men to death. Filled with a pure man's blood, you will be redeemed for the light. Use the gifts I give you well. You will find happiness before the end." The sky by now was grey overhead, and it was as if the old lady's strength flowed from her like a tide as the light grew.

"Morning is coming: the Doppelgänger has fled; Faran, too, is gone, where I cannot tell, but he is gone. The wolf is defeated forever, but the Master of the Nations still commands the southern sky. His army is coming from the Black Tarn. They will come to Lorn at their appointed time, when the moon is full again." As one they looked to the south, where the southern horizon was still covered by the matt black cloud.

"Why do they wait?"

"The cloud is only the vanguard, filled with lesser spirits. The rest have not emerged from the tarn. Besides, though the Man of Bronze weakens, he still has some power, the warm breeze still blows. But when the warmth dies, then the Nations will come.

"Last," she said, breathing hoarsely now, "though this is Astragal, and the lake lies below, you will need magic to enter Lorn. I had a vision on the mountain. I saw the city of Lorn on that lake yonder, the full moon shining down upon it. The moon is the key, but how I cannot say. But you will find it, I know. Go to the lake."

"The day is getting brighter," Urthred warned Thalassa. Even now, the purple ball of the sun was beginning to heave itself over the eastern horizon. Flat beams of light played in the upper branches of the tree, but, below, there was still shadow. Thalassa would not relinquish her friend's hand, and Alanda smiled.

"It is good to see the light once more, to go out with the dawn," she said, then her eyes closed and her breathing caught in her throat and her chest heaved once and she was still.

Urthred helped Thalassa to her feet. She stared down at her dead friend's face. "The dawn has come," he said gently. "You must go into the shadows." She nodded, not really hearing what he said, not moving though the eastern sky was on fire with rosy light. In the end he had to take her back to the building.

Jayal had remained slumped on the ground watching the dawn, as the landscape slowly revealed itself below their eyrie. The trees basked in the strange pocket of warm air that surrounded the mountain, but further off, where the storm carrying the wolf had passed, they stood bare. The red sparkle of the isinglass of Shandering Plain spread away to the east, and beyond the forest he could see the snowcapped mountains, white gable ends rearing up into the sky.

He rose stiffly and covered Alanda with his cloak. Childhood memories came to him: of those long ago

days in Thrull, his father's hall, now in ruins, Alanda's
husband Theodric, Alanda herself, all the others gathered here. The place ablaze with colour and light. A
time of laughter and plans, his father's great dream of
taking the dark yoke of Iss from the world's shoulders.
Seven years had gone, seven years that seemed an
eternity, in which all certainties had been stripped
away. Now Alanda, their guide, was dead. She had
been his father's guide too, in the dark ways of the
future; she had led him until that day when Illgill had
ignored her warnings about the fall of Thrull and sent
his engineers to open Marizian's tomb. He muttered
a prayer for her, on her journey into the darkness.

They were alone in this alien land, their enemies
not far away. It was safer to think of the past, to will
himself back into that time, a time when there were
certainties, when he had been young . . . Young? He
was only twenty-five now. Half his life or more
stretched ahead, and with it, like a shadow he could
never rid himself of, the Doppelgänger. The creature
was somewhere in the forest below, awaiting his time,
dogging his footsteps, able to come into his mind as
he chose. Nothing could shrug him off: hunger, cold
and pain seemed mere inconveniences to him. He
could not die, unless Jayal died. And every day, Jayal's
mind would be filled with more of these visions, until
evil came to wholly dominate it. He must concentrate
on what Alanda had told him: that good would triumph over evil.

For an hour or more he stared at the rising sun, his
mind full of these thoughts. Urthred remained in the
temple with Thalassa, and he wondered, too, what
would happen to her. Were Alanda's final words true?
Did the Silver Chalice exist?

He got wearily to his feet. He heard low voices from
the temple, but didn't approach. He thought of the
past: what Thalassa had been like in those golden
days, then he shook his head. The contrast with what
she had become was too much.

He reached the edge of the platform. The mountainside dropped away below him, and he could see for the first time how precipitous their path had been the night before. Alanda had given her life so he might live. He owed it to her to rid himself of his black thoughts. Reh would triumph over Iss.

He stared out over the forest. It was then he saw the lake for the first time. The sun now shone a few degrees above the horizon, crimson and lugubrious, its appearance like a red, squashed fruit. But its weak beams were now finding out the hollows between the ridges of the forest, and in them he could see the water stretching away to the horizon.

He hadn't heard Urthred leave the temple. His voice startled him, though the priest spoke quietly.

"The lake, just as I saw it in the Orb."

"Aye, as you saw it." He turned to the priest. "But where is the city?"

"Hidden by magic. You heard what Alanda said: getting here was the easy part. Getting into Lorn is another matter altogether."

"Then the sooner we leave the better. The Nations are coming."

Urthred nodded. "But first let us burn Alanda's body, and pray; we have time enough for that."

They turned their backs to the rising sun and walked to the Dedication Tree, where Alanda lay under Jayal's cloak. Some superstition made them lift the body and place it in the light of the sun. Then they set about cutting wood from the trees that surrounded the platform.

The sound of their work must have woken Imuni, for she came from the temple soon after dawn, her stifled yawn cut off when she saw the body under the cloak. Consciousness returned then, and she remembered: her father was gone. She began to cry. The two men left off their work to comfort her. But soon after they heard calls from below, then footsteps on the path. Garadas and two of the villagers appeared, filthy and scratched from hiding out in the forest all night, but still alive. Of the other villagers who had survived the Plain of Wolves, there was no sign. After hugging his daughter, the headman slumped to the ground, exhausted. Imuni lifted a water bottle to his parched lips, and he and the others began to revive enough to tell them of their flight through the mist the night before. The three men rested a little, but then helped Urthred and Jayal build the pyre.

They worked all morning and early afternoon piling brushwood onto the centre of the platform in front of the Dedication Tree, until they had a pyre twenty feet high. None of them touched any more food or drink the entire day, purging themselves for what was to come. By the evening the pyre cast a long shadow over the summit of Astragal.

They all gathered around it.

Five of them had escaped from Thrull. Furtal had died on the marshes. Now Alanda was gone as well. The three survivors carried Alanda's body to the top of the pyre with due reverence and laid her there in that place from which her ancestors had surveyed the lands of the north in the golden time of the world.

Each of them took in the moonlit view as if they wanted this last scene imprinted on their memories forever. They said their farewells, then descended. They remained in silence for a few seconds then Urthred straightened. Slowly, he began to chant the words of the service that he had said over Furtal's body a few days before—could it only have been a few days before? Then, with a flick of his gloves, he sent a fireball into the heart of the pyre. The dry timber burst into flames. They watched it burn, the smoke drifting towards the clouds hiding the southern horizon.

No one spoke a word: another member of the companionship was gone.

And Lorn had not yet been found.

CHAPTER THIRTY-NINE

❖

The Inland Sea

It took them two days to reach the side of the lake. They travelled at night, avoiding the sun; Thalassa's condition had become worse and worse since the night they reached Astragal. During the passage through the forest she hid her face with the cape of her cloak and didn't utter a single syllable to her companions. Even the light of the waning moon hurt her eyes.

There was no roadway between Astragal and Lorn. They found themselves in dense undergrowth, trees festooned with mosses and creepers; forward progress was slow. Jayal blazed the way with Dragonstooth, the enchanted blade unblunted even by the heavy use it was put to. They headed in the general direction of the lake, though they could no longer see it. The warm breeze blew stronger and stronger the further north they went, keeping the Black Cloud stationary behind them. There was no sign of their other enemies: Faran had not been seen since Ravenspur, and the Doppelgänger had seemingly vanished into the greenwood. For the moment, Jayal was free of the troubling visions that had plagued him ever since they'd come to the Northern Lands.

It might have taken them even longer to find the lake, for once they were in the forest they had only the stars and moon to guide them, and Alanda's staff had been burned with her on the pyre. But at midnight on the second evening of their journey they stumbled upon Marizian's road again. It angled arrow straight through the heart of the wood, overarched by

hanging branches, its surface lopsided and partially overgrown. Marizian's road, heading to the High North.

Jayal paused for a moment, playing Dragonstooth
in front of him like a torch, his brow creased.

"What is it?" Urthred asked.

"The Doppelgänger has been here—I sense him."

Urthred muttered, "He has more lives than any
man." They listened. Nothing.

Jayal gestured at a spot in front. "Look," he said,
"he was here only recently." Urthred helped Thalassa
to sit and approached the place indicated.

In the green-white light of the sword he saw a broken twig hanging from a branch at knee height. The
break was recent, the wood pulp still showing white.
"It could have been an animal, or Faran," Urthred
said.

"No, I'm certain: it is the Doppelgänger," Jayal answered. "He is here, just ahead."

They peered forward into the night. But the woods
gave up none of their secrets. All they could do was
follow the road.

They set off once again. The going was much easier
and Jayal had to use the sword only occasionally to
clear a way. As they continued they saw further signs
that the road had been used sometime in the not-so-
distant past: small saplings growing in the cracks in
the pavement had been cut back. The slash marks
were plain to see, leaves sprouting thickly around their
tops. But the breaks were not a livid white, as the first
had been, but greyed with age. Garadas estimated
them to be a few years old.

Jayal looked back to the south, towards the Palisades. This was the way his father would have come,
seven years before. He inspected the marks again. As
far as he knew, the Doppelgänger had no weapon,
and these had been made by one. "These trees could
have been cut when my father came through here,"
Jayal said.

"Maybe," Urthred answered. "But remember there
were signs that people had been in the tower by the

forest's edge. The path could have been made by them."

"Where would they have come from? No one lives in the forest."

"From Lorn—that is my hope anyway," the priest replied. "If people can leave the place, then surely there must be a way into it, too? The answer will be at the lake."

They pushed on once more. Jayal took the lead. Urthred went back to help Thalassa. She let him take her arm, but kept her hand clutching the hood of the cloak to her face.

"We're nearly at Lorn," he said.

"The moon burns," she said faintly. They were the first words she had uttered in two days.

They continued for an hour, then Jayal halted abruptly. He had come to a thicket of young elm saplings that would have blocked the way ahead had not a path been hacked through its centre, revealing the roadway beneath.

"This is not the work of one man," he said when the others drew up to him. They peered ahead, but whatever waited for them was hidden in the night.

Now they moved forward with even greater caution, afraid almost to breathe. Then through the track cut in the thicket, they saw the silver sparkle of water glinting in the moonlight. The lake!

Suddenly, they all began stumbling forward.

Jayal broke out of the thicket first. Ahead it was as if a million diamonds had been set alight by the setting moon, the lake stretched away over the horizon to an invisible shore, so vast it was more inland sea than a lake. The warm breeze blew strongly from a hidden point far away over its surface. But, just as from Astragal, there was no sign of the islands that Urthred and Thalassa had seen in the Orb.

The roadway plunged into the inky water of the lake and disappeared.

The others joined him, but their eyes were rooted not on the vanishing road, but a cairn of stones some

ten feet high which stood just to the right of the road
over a small creek by the lakeshore.

A rusted helmet was fixed on a pole at its summit:
it glinted dully in the moonlight despite its blemished
surface. Iron, flat-topped, the visor shut, the vision slits
dark, on either side the ventilation around the mouth
stamped out like stylised suns. The helmet of one of
the Hearth Knights! Jayal knew what he was looking
at: a grave. This is how they buried itinerant knights
when they were far from home, far from the sacred
eagles that would take their bones to the sun, far from
a priest who could consecrate the ashes of a funeral
pyre.

Without waiting for the others, Jayal waded into the
creek. The water came to his waist, but it was warm,
the temperature of blood. He scrambled to the other
side and climbed the side of the cairn. One or two of
the stones gave under his feet and fell with a muddy
splatter on the ground below, but he reached the summit. A terrible fear entered his heart then. What if it
was his father who lay beneath the cairn? He grabbed
the helmet with his free hand and held it up in front
of him, into the pool of light cast by the sword.

It was then he heard the hollow laughter in his ears.
He whirled round. The Doppelgänger! He was watching from a distance. He had sensed Jayal's fear, was
mocking him. But there was no sign of his enemy in
the ghostly ash trees that fringed the lake.

Urthred, Thalassa and the others had hurried across
the stream and stood at the base of the cairn, looking
up at him.

Urthred saw at once what he was holding. His eyes
met Jayal's. "One of the Hearth Knights?" he asked.
Jayal nodded. The laughter had died out, but other
images and sounds came to his mind: memories of the
battle flooded in on him once more, just as they had
in Furtal's house in Thrull. The experience was so
vivid that he could smell the smoke, taste his blood
once more.

Then the vision of his father as he had stood behind

the battle lines came swimming into his mind. He had
given his son a final look before the enemy's final
charge, then locked the visor of his helmet down into
position. The vents had been shaped like stylised lightning bolts, not these sun-shaped openings. And it had
been painted red and black, the Illgill colours. Wind
and weather would not have rusted away all the evidence of such paint but, stare as he might, he found
no trace of it on the object in his hand, gleaming in
the supernatural light of the sword and in the light of
the moon.

He slowly descended the cairn, more boulders slipping beneath his feet, and showed the helmet to
Urthred.

"Do you recognise it?" the priest asked.

Jayal shook his head. "No, but it's not my father's."

"Then it must belong to another of the Legion of
Flame."

"How many men were seen on the plain seven years
ago?" Jayal asked Garadas.

"Ten, maybe a dozen," the headman replied.

"A man can't bury himself. The others have gone on."

They looked out over the infinite expanse of the
lake. Apart from the cairn, there was no sign of humanity here, except the road. They recrossed the
creek and stepped onto the last flagstone, where the
road disappeared into the lake. They peered down
into the muddy water. Another flagstone was just visible in the shallows, then nothing further as the water
got darker and darker where the moonlight didn't
penetrate.

They looked at one another. "The road should lead
to the city," Urthred said.

Jayal looked over the lake. The moonlight was quite
strong, but still he could not see the farther shore. The
lake must be several miles wide. The islands might be
hidden over the horizon. Or maybe they were beneath
its surface?

Jayal took a tentative step forward, until he was
knee deep in the water, the sword held so low that

the surface sizzled and bubbled from the blade's heat. Nothing further was visible below. He took another step, and sank waist deep, the sword submerged, glowing eerily in the green depths, the surface bubbling around his sodden cloak. Another step, and he was shoulder deep, floundering to gain his footing. He cursed and struggled back to the shore, his shirt dripping. "Nothing," he said. "There's nothing there."

"Maybe the road continues on the other side?"

"Perhaps, but Lorn is in the lake, not on the other side." Jayal looked back at the cairn. "Maybe there is an answer in that," he said.

"It is a man's grave," Urthred said.

"Yes, it's a grave. But it's something else, too: a sign. Why was it left here on the very edge of the lake, priest? My father came here. He wanted me to find it. Maybe there's a message buried in it." He waded the creek once more and stood expectantly, looking at the priest.

Urthred glanced back towards the forest. Thalassa watched them from the shadows of the trees, keeping out of the moonlight. Even in the shadows he could feel her feverish eyes burning in the darkness. They must find Lorn and the Silver Chalice, and quickly. He nodded, and motioned to Garadas and the two other villagers to help him. Then all five began hauling rocks from the summit of the cairn.

CHAPTER FORTY

Lorn

It was always night in the place that Urthred, Thalassa and Jayal sought, and always a full moon. But Alanda had been right when she had warned them not to look for Lorn on the planes of man. It lay beyond human sight, in the lake, but not part of it. Stare as they might at its surface, they still would never have found it. For it only appeared one night in the month, when the moon shone full upon the Mortal World. Then, and only then was Lorn revealed.

So where was Lorn? Everywhere and nowhere at the same time. A mirror of the Outland, but separate from it, apart from that one day in the lunar cycle. The sun never shone in that land, only a full moon which rested forever in the zenith of the sky. The land remained exactly as it had been left by Reh after he placed the canopy of night over the land ten thousand years before, preserving his people from the doom outside. A huge forest covered the country, stretching away in undulating green waves.

This was the Forest of Lorn that Furtal spoke of before he died. The place where the enchanted lutes of Elder Time had been made. The forest he had sought but failed to find, for he never unearthed the secret of the moon.

The lake, a perfect image of the lake in the Outland, sat in the exact centre of the forest. A pearly mist rose from its surface. Two islands lay in the middle of the lake. The first was whale-shaped in silhouette. Buildings broke the outline curve of its spine, and it rose to a rocky peak on which a palace could be seen.

This was the Isle of Lorn. Once a God lived in its palace. Erewon, God of the Moon, Reh's cousin, who had died in the final battle. Now the servants of Reh lived here, though Reh was long departed from the world.

The other island was some two miles distant from its sister: a tall pinnacle of rock, around which a tempest always seemed to rage. This was the Isle of Winds, where Reh kept his Forge, where the Hammer of the Gods and its Anvil, the Egg of the World, resided. From here came the warm breezes that kept the kingdom of Lorn alive. And here, too, was the Man of Bronze.

Time had no meaning in this place, where it was always night. Around the full moon, the constellations burned fiercely as if they were pinpricks of light in a satin cloth stretched over the firmament. Ringing the shore of Lorn, a thousand lanterns twinkled in dusky groves of trees. The wind played through the groves, and the light blinked on and off as the boughs swayed.

The water washed softly like the gurgle of a child on the pebbled shore of the island. Behind the shoreline, the groves were hung with fruit in season: oranges and lemons and pomegranates glowed in the moonlight like dim beacons. Everything grew in profusion, without the benefit of the sun, in this enchanted place. Houses stood above the orchards, surrounded by wide terraces. The lanes led upwards, the houses growing more numerous, packed closer together.

There were many people abroad in the warm night air. Once they had been the servants of Reh; but, in a land that didn't know time, their duty had been forgotten centuries before. Their chatter and laughter was carried far and wide by the breeze from the Isle of Winds, which ruffled their gay clothing. Their garments were nothing like those worn by the servants of Reh in the Outland, but silver-and-white cloaks edged with brightly coloured braid. They swirled these around them capriciously, in the manner of those going to a carnival.

Though their apparel was brighter than anything to be found in the whole of Old Earth in this age, it was they themselves who caught the eye. Never was there a race more comely than the inhabitants of the ancient city of Lorn. These were children and youths, but no one who hinted at middle age. The rose of life blushed on their cheeks. The oldest seemed but twenty, and there were none any older than that. It was as if all the fathers and mothers of this youthful throng had departed and left their children to revel the eternal night away.

But, despite appearance, generation upon generation was represented here: child, parent, grandparent, great-grandparent and onwards. Close scrutiny destroyed the illusion of youth: that seeming twenty-year-old gallant walked with a stoop; that woman there, who looked no more than a wandlike girl, her tulle dress falling from her naked shoulders, was betrayed by a gaze that had experienced far more than twenty years. Everywhere it was the same: beauty on the surface, age beneath.

Only occasionally, as if through a sudden trick of the light, which revealed an unexpected angle upon the faces of the oldest, did the veneer suddenly peel away and reveal an altogether different face: gnomish, gnarled, ancient. Ready to die.

Higher up in the city there was greater quiet: for here there was only one building, the mighty palace, which occupied a square quarter mile at the top of the island. The former dwelling place of Erewon—the Palace of the Moon.

Raised rampways led up to it through groves of tamarind trees set into the ancient, dusty red soil. It was a flat building, like the humbler ones below it, built around a series of raised walks. Its walls were gypsum blocks rendered with red plaster. The walkways, too, were made of gypsum. Facing the east side of the lake was a shaded piano nobile, its roof held up by more of the downward-tapering columns. A number of porticoed vestibules led off into the darkness behind. Large man-high jars were the only decoration on the terraces. There was a general air of lonely abandonment, of waiting, unlike in the city below. A single tower reached up into the dusk. From it came the melancholy sound of a flute.

A gypsum throne was set back in the shadows of the piano nobile. It was occupied by a man wearing an ornate silver mask: the mask, inlaid with gold highlights around the eyes and cheekbones, glowed like the face of the moon, reflecting back the light of that orb in the sky. Its owner was dressed in a capacious samite robe which hid his frame.

His name was the Watcher. He was the custodian of the palace and the crystal labyrinth below it, where appeared visions of the past and future of the city.

His kingdom, the frozen kingdom under the moon, lay below. A kingdom he enjoyed no benefit from: not for him the wine and music, the women—just the silent wait. He had been married once. But his wife had left him and passed from Lorn into the Outland. She, unlike him, had been a mortal. Her name was Meriel. She had gone with his two boys. Now she was dead, and as for his children . . . The thought of what had happened to them was too much for him to contemplate. It was enough: of all the populace of the island, only he was alone.

Custom dictated that he should remain watching for Reh's return. So he sat, his head turned to the east, waiting for Second Dawn, but knowing that he would never see it in his lifetime. Had he not seen what was revealed in the crystal chambers? What was to come, and come soon, though soon was a relative word in this endless night?

There, beneath the palace, in the frozen white panels that stretched a mile or more, the whole of his people's history lay frozen in an endless wave of alabaster, a wave prompted by an invisible force that crept, year by year, along one wall of the chamber until, as now, it had nearly reached its end. Tableaux of the times of the gods, of the coming of the Man of

Bronze, the battle with the Nations of the Night, the coming of the baron, with his magical Rod, and at its furthest leading edge, which grew with glacial slowness, forms and images of what was to come. And in the crystal wave the Watcher had seen not long ago the features of those who came to save Lorn. To save, and ultimately destroy.

He had called the people to the audience chamber in the palace and told them what he had seen in the crystal. He told them of the end of Lorn. Yet most had not listened, and those who had whispered darkly, thinking he had become crazed in his lonely vigil.

The people feared him, and like all things that are feared, he would be destroyed by the hands of the very people he tried to serve. Soon they would come and kill him. He was the sacrifice that enabled the carnival to go on, endlessly, night after night, without remission.

But perhaps the revels below were more muted now, perhaps the people had already begun plotting, as they had in the past. Generation after generation, the same betrayal, enacted time and time again. The nights when he would die to be reborn again. Then the sleep before he would wake in a new body, the blood ritual satisfied. As long as there was a Watcher, the God would return one day, the people reasoned.

But he knew better. Did they really think they would see the God again? No, he had seen the end of Lorn, and it would not come with Reh's fiery chariot washing the world clean with its flame. The Second Dawn in Lorn would not be brought by the God, but by his emissary, the person he had seen in the crystal: the Lightbringer.

Now, below, they chased false dreams: self-gratification and endless pleasures grown stale in the very first tasting of them. Yet the laughter, though hollow, made the scene on the terrace on which he sat even more melancholy.

Beneath the mask and cloak lay a secret: he didn't have a youthful face and body like all the rest of Lorn.

The moonglow had entered him; his bones had become friable and powdery, ulcers had opened, and the light taken in through the mask now burned like a lantern inside, glowing faintly from his skin.

His people would never see his face while he lived. He would wear a mask until his dying day. And on that day, the day of the blood ritual, when they had killed him, the people would remove it. If the face beneath was young and unlined, they would take it as an augury that Lorn, too, would live long and well. But if the face beneath was old and lined, then the people would lament, knowing disaster and calamity were coming. How many deaths had he suffered? His memories had been washed away by his spilt blood. Yet still he could remember, dimly, a time when it had always been a youthful face they revealed on the day of his death.

Now no longer: this time they would find age and horror. Then they would know Lorn was at an end.

He turned stiffly in his throne, away from his endless contemplation of the east, and to the south, to the lakeshore far away in the moonlight. There stood the bridge to the Forest of Lorn and, beyond it, the road that passed through his kingdom to the Mortal World.

The road was called the Way: it was a mirror image of the one that passed through the forest in the Outland. Yet, here in the magical kingdom, it was endless, leading from the bridge to a place where it curved back on itself, returning to Lorn. Somewhere along its length would be found the Moon Mere, the gateway to the Outland.

In the darkness, only faint traces of it could be seen: a notch in a ridge, a shadowy line through the greenwood. It dated from the time of the gods: trees overhung every yard of it, and weeds and moss grew over it. Leagues and leagues, a once-continuous stretch of flagstones, now broken by roots and buried in marshes, swept away by floods, with only one finite point, where it touched the Mortal World. Once a month at the night of the full moon, when the moon matched exactly that of Lorn's in the sky, the gateway would stand open.

It was as if the Watcher's hidden eyes travelled through the night following the Way, his face beneath the mask furrowed in concentration. He felt each stone beneath his feet, each tiny fraction of the journey as it unfurled, as if by this furious concentration he might be that person that now travelled the lonely road to the mere. The man he had sent into the Mortal World.

How his soul yearned to be the one on that journey! Once before, at the beginning of this life, before he had been called to be the Watcher again, before the silver mask was placed on his face, he had travelled it. He had been one of the few of his people to go into the Outland.

He could still remember the vision that had come before the journey; it seemed Reh had spoken to him. The God had told him to go and find a bride in the world outside. He had gone to the crystal chambers and seen her face emerging from the ice: a dark-haired beauty as comely as any in Lorn. A face he recognised. He knew her name already: Meriel. And he had seen where he would find her: there in the Outland, beneath the mountain known as Ravenspur. The same place he had seen her last.

He had set out immediately. How free the forest had seemed, how musical the wind in the trees, the moonlight shimmering through the green, the birdsong, the exultation of a fugitive glimpse of a deer or fox seen in a glade! Then the Outland: passing through the Moon Mere, the world turning inside out, the sudden cold, the trees turning, the points of the compass spinning, round and round when he reached the edge of this world and the next. Two more days, the autumn trees, first in the edge of the forest, where the tower stood, then onwards over the plain, to Ravenspur.

There he had found her, by a lake under that sinister mountain. He had not asked how she had come to be there. He had known her: the spirit of the wife he had had ten thousand years before lived in her.

He had taken her hand and retraced his steps to the lake, but now there was no city upon it, no islands, the heat only a fugitive memory of that which lay beneath in the Mirror World. Then the long wait for the moon to hang full in the sky, the appearance of the Way, the long journey home. He had held her hand all that time, not daring to believe he had recovered what he had lost those aeons ago.

Now he had sent another on that road he had once taken to find his bride. His name was Nemoc, he had been the last man to see the Watcher's wife and children alive.

Twenty mortal years earlier another dream had come. Again, the voice had spoken to him of things yet to appear in the crystal chamber: of a woman who would banish the darkness from the world. And the voice had told him how he must send his children by Meriel into the Outland, to find her in the name of Reh.

But his sons, the most precious beings he had ever known, were infants, and he, the Watcher, could not now leave Lorn. But Meriel was an Outlander. Already she looked older than the rest of his people. Already his people muttered that she was a curse, that she had brought age to that ageless place. Now, when he told her of his dream, she smiled as if she had always known it would be thus, and together with Nemoc and the children she had gone.

Nemoc told him how she had died at the same place the Watcher had found her, by the lake under Ravenspur. But Nemoc had travelled on, into the Outland, deep into the south. And there he had given the children to the humans he found there.

Nemoc: his only companion in the time since his wife and children had gone. Nemoc, his only hope to find what he had lost, to make amends for these arid years: the unremitting watch of the moon, the inflexible imposition of the law, the judicious use of fear and terror to stir to obedience the people who otherwise would sink completely into their luxury.

Nemoc: the only one left whom he could trust. Now he, too, had gone on that fatal road. How long ago had he left? Again he thought of time, for that was where his heart was, the Outland, where time held sway and Meriel had died—not this barren place. There they felt the kiss of mortality; there, too, he had felt joy, for joy only came with a knowledge of the finite, that pleasures must be plucked while they could be. Here, there was just the ever-present moon shining down, no dawn or dusk save that glimpsed as a far-off glow through the dome of night.

Nemoc had gone for the second time to the Outland because of the new vision in the crystal chambers: a vision of more Outlanders, following the baron. The Watcher had seen the image in the crystal long before Urthred first passed under Superstition Mountain and saw below him the Plain of Thrull: yet though Urthred did not as then know the fate that would see his brother killed, him turned murderer, his flight through the city, his meeting with Thalassa and the succession of events that followed, the Watcher had seen all these things, had felt all the suffering that he and Randel had endured in the Mortal World. For Randel and Urthred were his sons—the sons of Meriel, his wife who had journeyed into the Outland twenty years before.

Now his son brought the Lightbringer, the one who would make Reh's light shine once more upon this kingdom. He had studied her face in the crystal, and seen a beauty singular even in Lorn, where everyone was beautiful. A beauty equal to the dead Meriel. But in those grey eyes he had seen more, he had seen a destiny not human.

The Watcher now heard a sullen undercurrent in the noise coming from the city below, the gaiety more than ever a hollow mockery, showing that the people's hearts were full of fear, which had turned to anger

against him, their protector. For days now the balmy
air that gusted from the Isle of Winds had been weak
and intermittent, the dome of night weakened, each
dawn and dusk of the outside world shone as a ghostly
light in the east and west—shone even though the
darkness.

A chill was in the air. The hundred-year cycle had
passed in the outside world. The Nations were coming.

Darkness had begun to stain the white clarity of the
ice in the chambers below: black ice where purity had
only been before. He saw what came in the Outland:
the mists gathering over the Broken Hines, dark creatures circling eyries of Ravenspur, smoke from camp-
fires sending sooty fingers into the air, tornadoes
raging up and down the borders of the forest, lifting
trees bodily into the skies, dead spirits stealing into
the land and inhabiting the trees so that they wailed,
moaned and dripped blood from their boughs.

The Gaunts who were disembodied shadows seeking for souls, and the bodiless harpies whose screaming heads ducked and weaved like swallows on the
wind, and the basilisks that could turn a man to stone,
the shape changers, and many others. The creatures
that dwelt in the Nations and on Shandering Plain
were coming. Fenris, the ice wolf that would bring
winter to the endless summer, as swift as an arctic
wind. And that would be only the beginning. After,
would come the creatures who wore their bones as
skins and who had the heads and limbs of birds of
prey, the creatures who dwelt in the gas hollows on
the plains joining with the souls of the damned spirits
of decay who already dwelt in the dead, creeper-
fringed trees around the Moon Mere: the Dark Ones.
Those who walked the edges of the forest howling for
the souls of the living.

And then, when the moon was full, once more they
would come through the mere to Lorn. Only the Man
of Bronze could save them then, as he had done for
every hundred years before. The Nations of the Night

had returned, and his son was trapped between them and Lorn.

From the Outland a bitter chill had come into Lorn through the mere. What had happened to Krik and Stikel, the men he had set to watch in the Outland? Where was Nemoc? Was the moon full in the Outland? Had he found Urthred and the Lightbringer?

Now Nemoc and only one or two others were on the other shore. What moved towards them through the invisible night from the Moon Mere? What was left to defend the city? Not the people themselves: dissolute and corrupt in their pleasures. And not the Man of Bronze, whose actions became slower and slower, his arm weary in the Forge. Only the Lightbringer could raise him from the torpor into which he had fallen.

He would go soon, even if she didn't come; go again to the Isle of Winds. Somehow the Man of Bronze must be brought back under the magic that had controlled him these many centuries. Now his eyes turned to the pinnacle of rock two miles across the shimmering surface of the lake to where the Man of Bronze lay in captivity. The Watcher was the only one who had ever travelled there. He had put off the journey for a long time. But now the time had come.

CHAPTER FORTY-ONE

Nemoc

At the moment that the Watcher was thinking of him, Nemoc was standing on the Way through the forest, looking at the moon, the reflection of Reh's glory. How greater was the sun, he thought, than the moon in its mirror?

Unlike the rest of his people, Nemoc had seen the sun and the Outland where it shone. It had been where he had led the Watcher's wife and children out of the enchanted kingdom, through the Moon Mere, into the Mortal World. It had been his first and only time there.

He had seen age and mutability there, in the land beyond the mere. For the first time he had comprehended death, and known fear. And that was when he had betrayed the Watcher—though his master did not know it.

The journey through the Outland had been in autumn. The wild fruit trees hung burdened, bowing their heads to the ground, the hedges full of ripe berries which he guiltily picked, for the fruit of autumn was corrupt, and would bring death to those who ate them. The earth in the early morning light damp from the overnight dew and tiny piles of dirt showing the worms were rising to the surface, gnats filling the air in choking clouds; stinging insects buzzed through the piles of fallen leaves and slowly rotting fruit. Starlings flocked on the trees chattering wildly. The sun, unfamiliar as it was, orange and weak barely warming the earth and his breath a cloud in front of his face. But as they had climbed higher, the dead white hand of the cold fell on them. Winter: that numbness that enveloped his skin, made it blue and puckered, which made his breath visible. The ground as white as his hair. The infants' cries ringing from the frozen peaks.

They had walked out of the forest, up towards Ravenspur. He carried one of the children, Meriel the other. He had been afraid, he knew that this was where their enemies came from. But Meriel led the way fearlessly onto the granite slopes of the mountains and upwards to the summit. They reached the ruins at the top: empty, the dark cloud over the Black Tarn hardly more than a mist on its surface. They began to descend, the Palisades filling the sky to the south. But Meriel's footsteps had got slower and slower. She had been sickening in Lorn. She had begun to look old, for she had lived too long before she came to the immortal kingdom.

They had reached the lake beneath the mountain, the place where the Watcher had first found her. There she held up the child in her arms so the tiny infant's face pointed to the south. "Son, you will come again to this place, after a long journey. Once more we will see each other. Remember my voice." But she said no words to the child Nemoc carried: a chill went up his spine; perhaps this one wouldn't return? Then she turned to the Opener; calmly, she told him that she was going to die and what he must do. She had foreseen everything: she was a prophetess, a Witch Queen of the North. She had seen her resurrection and this second death. And in her previous life she had prepared for herself a tomb deep beneath the mountain.

When she was gone he had carried her body down into the depths and found there a vast iron tomb, its door ajar, light spilling from it. He had carried her into it and laid her on the glowing plinth he found within, then left, sealing the tomb.

And she had foreseen his betrayal, for when he was alone with only the sighing wind and the crying babies for company, and darkness, he could not go on. To the south lay the terrors of the Mortal World, to the North, through the Moon Mere, the disgrace of returning with the children. The night was full of roaming spirits. Meriel's too, perhaps, hovered in the air, watching what he would do. His mind closed down, became a blank. Only dimly did he later remember placing the children beneath a rock on that wolf-haunted mountain. And there he left them, abandoned to their fate.

Long after he had returned to Lorn, and long after he had lied to his master, telling him how he had carried the children to the Southern Lands, Meriel's words had haunted him. How that one child—Urthred—would return. Guilt burned like acid his ever-waking hours; guilt unbearable, until life was an endless torment. He prayed to Reh: a chance to redeem himself, to bring Urthred back to Lorn, or a sleep in which he suffered no more this anguish.

But in Lorn, death didn't exist. Death came when the body grew too old, but the spirit only slept, then was reborn afterwards. Since Reh's departure, Nemoc had slept many times—deep and dreamless sleeps. And when he awoke each time he found he inhabited a new body. He would study his new hands and feet, his face, with a faint incredulity, as if they were a stranger's. And in his many lives, each time he had been called to the office he fulfilled now, the Opener of the Way. The same office he had fulfilled since Reh created this land. Only his memories remained, and with each new incarnation his recollection of his past lives grew weaker.

He knew his current body well: it was the body with which he had betrayed his lord. Now his hair was white, his skin pale, the face of a youth's despite the color of his hair, his eyes startling blue. He stood six feet tall. So he would remain until he reached the Outland. Then the transformation would come.

How many Outland years had it been since he'd last travelled the Way? All was lost in the undifferentiated and endless night of Lorn. That endless time of guilt.

But now he was on the Way again. Now he had a chance to redeem the sins of the past. Now he would bring Urthred home.

Around him the moonlit forest slept its eternal sleep. The air was warm. Lorn was far away from him. The paving stones of the road stretched in front; somewhere in the forest they would turn back into themselves in an endless loop. After a million steps or a thousand million, he would return to that place from which he had set out. The sensation was strange but familiar: how many of his incarnations had trod these flagstones, how many lungs breathed the balmy forest air where it was always summer, how many hands had carried the ceremonial staff, how many heads had worn the mitred cap of office? One sensation he remembered above all others: an iciness had settled on his spine the moment he had left the island. It took him a while to recognise it for what it was: fear. The same emotion he had felt the last time he had passed into the Outland. The same that had made him betray his master.

He was travelling to that point where the gateway to the Mortal World stood: The Moon Mere. Where in his journey he would find it, he didn't know. After many miles of pacing the Way, or only a few yards? That in itself was reason enough for fear, not knowing when it would come, not knowing how the moon shone on the other side, not knowing when, if ever, he would return.

But greater still was the terror of what lay ahead of him in the forest: the Nations of the Night were abroad in the Outland. But just as everything had its shadow in that world, so they, too, would be here, in spirit form, the ones his people called the Dark Ones. Slowly they slipped through the mere at each full moon, and their dark wraiths inhabited the trunks of the trees, turning their leaves to autumn colors, causing them to fall to the earth, the spirit of ice and cold. Winter: in his many lives he had seen it only once, but he had never forgotten it.

Now the Nations would bring winter to Lorn. Once the moon was full over the mere they would come, not only the Dark Ones, but all that had been created in the Black Tarn at Ravenspur.

The Dark Ones would be waiting for him now. Time had come to Lorn: even here on the sacred Way the warm breeze was weak: he had smelt Autumn in the air and a cold wind came from the direction of the Mere, the first that had ever been in this land. Never before had the concept "to hurry" entered his head, but now his stride lengthened and his cape billowed out in the cold breeze. His hat was blown from his head, and he turned and fetched it—that must remain: it was the symbol of his office. Once it was gone, so was his integrity, his identity.

As he hurried on, the sky in the direction he travelled grew even darker, the colour of fire-blackened iron: then he saw the clouds reaching up in ragged claws towards the moon, threatening to black out its light. As he had gone forward all the animals and birds had grown quieter and quieter. Now he heard the weird undulating trill of the nightjar, disturbed by something ahead, and the Way was suddenly lost in shadow. He stopped and listened: the cold wind sighed through the trees. It grew darker and darker. No one had come this way since the last men who had gone to the tower. But they had never returned.

Cobwebs, stretched from one side of the path to the other, brushed his face and he flinched: the creatures he feared were made of them: the feathery touch of the Dark Ones would be like a drawing of cobwebs and decay on his face.

He ran, pleased at least with the strong legs that this most recent life had given him. The sky darkened even further: he had never seen a sky so ugly, a cloud that painted the forest floor an utter black.

He thought of Lorn: the eternal night in which nothing changed. The sound of music and the smell of woodsmoke filling the air and his wife Aphala: she would come and he would feel the soft touch of her fingers on his shoulder and he'd clasp her hand and all the world would be at peace. But thinking was no good; his steps slowed and he recognised the madness of what he did, hurrying towards danger rather than away from it. He'd planted a rose in the Midnight Garden, a white rose that glowed in the dark and opened to the moon—that was their love, let it not wither while he was away, he prayed. But nothing had ever withered in Lorn—nothing would, until the Nations came.

He sensed he was very near the Moon Mere. Some of his brethren lived here, close to the Mundane World. But they were mystics who could see where the boundary was, gleaming there like a curtain between this world and the next. They lived as Outlanders did—eating the flesh of animals, though they were immortals and should never consume mortal flesh. He thought of Krik and Stikel, exiled into the Outland for the same crime these seers committed. No words from them. He knew they were dead.

The sullen threat in the air was like a living thing. The cloud which had stood over the fringes of the forest seemed to rise up like a gigantic wave, its edges curling and probing downwards in dark vapours. Where the mist fell the Dark Ones would take shape. First a small wisp of mists that would slowly coalesce into a thing that was human-shaped, but was made of all things insubstantial: fog, cobwebs and darkness. Creatures that sought to steal the living souls of men, for only the immortal soul of one of Reh's chosen would give them animation. And in the forest edges, where the darkness had set in, they would creep into the trees, their skin indistinguishable from the rotting bark that they infected with their plaguey hands, whose breath spread rot and fungus into any animate thing.

He slowed even further, and just then a cold wind, colder even than the breath of winter, ripped through the forest. His hat blew off again and he stooped to recover it. He thought then how alone he was, how he would give anything to hear a human voice.

It was as if the God had heard his silent wish, for that instant there *did* come a voice. It came from the shadows of the trees. Nemoc froze as he bent over his hat. It was a voice he'd heard on only a few occasions before, yet he recognised it almost immediately: Whitearth the Hunter, deep and bass like the thunder of a waterfall. Whitearth, one who lived in the Midnight Forest away from the God's sanctuary. The man kept to the heart of the greenwood most of the time, far from his fellow countrymen, whom he shunned. As he was shunned for, unlike those who lived in Lorn, Whitearth was a flesh eater, who ate what he trapped. One who would have been sent into exile like Krik and Stikel if he had ever returned to the city.

Nemoc's heart had already been chilled by the prospect of the dark night ahead. The sepulchral voice penetrated his very marrow. Even if it had been the whispering voice of one of the Dark Ones himself, he doubted whether he could have found the willpower to flee. He straightened slowly, the hat crushed in his white-knuckled fist, and stared hard into the dark line of bushes and overhanging branches.

"Whitearth?" he called out tremulously.

"Aye, it is me, Opener," the voice called back.

"Come out of the trees," Nemoc said. "Let me see you."

His words were met with a mirthless chuckle. "Oh, do not wish too lightly, Opener . . . you may get what you wish for."

"What do you mean?" Nemoc answered, his heart if anything beating even faster.

But Whitearth didn't answer him directly. "I heard you coming a long way off; you townsfolk fill the woods with your noise. I thought of leaving you—none in the city have been friends to Whitearth—but then I thought you must see me, see what will come to all the people of Lorn."

"See what?" Nemoc asked. Some feeling had returned to his frozen limbs, and he suddenly remembered that he could flee, run as fast as his legs could take him from the eerie voice. There only came a faint rustling of leaves from where he guessed Whitearth was hiding by the side of the road.

He found that he had unconsciously taken a few precautionary steps up the Way.

"Wait," came the voice. Immediately Nemoc stopped, the chill returning tenfold. "I will come out—but prepare yourself."

Prepare himself? Nemoc didn't have time to guess what Whitearth's warning meant before he saw the face of the hunter, white as if covered with lime emerging from the undergrowth. It glowed in the green depths like a ghost's.

Then he stepped into the light of the moon glancing across the clearing.

Nemoc stepped back in horror, nearly tripping on the old paving stones of the path, his face ashen, his heart beating madly. Whitearth had changed: his face was revealed—not Reh's face, the face of the fair folk of Lorn. No, Nemoc now saw Whitearth's mortal face: hair grey and lank, his face a chalky grey, like a February sky, his jowls hanging heavy like a bloodhound's, his eyes red-rimmed and their whites yellow as if his whole body was racked with a liverish fever. His high-crowned hat was missing; the fallen collar around his neck was stained and ripped. His back was bowed under a weight of traps and snares, dead woodcocks were slung on his belt and a hare over his shoulder.

Nemoc had only seen such an old face before on those who had died, when the mask of their faces slipped and the accumulated years beneath stood revealed before they woke again, young and new. But the hunter was now very close to him, so close that Nemoc could smell the faint smell of rotten leaf mould on his clothes, and see the deep lines that gouged his face beneath the white lime. The feverish eyes sought Nemoc's, but he looked away, towards the moonlight falling across the Way. But Whitearth's voice could not be denied.

"Aye—as I expected—my face is ruined and old: though Whitearth has no mirror, I can guess."

"It is your true face," Nemoc said, though his lips wrinkled involuntarily into a sneer of distaste.

Whitearth cut in. "True it is—all that ever lived in Lorn will come to this, no matter what magic keeps our faces young."

"I can't speak to you," Nemoc managed, stepping further away, knowing he would be cursed for the words that had already been exchanged. He had already contravened the holy laws. He caught Whitearth's stare once more. He knew what the expression on his face betrayed: he couldn't prevent his lips curling again at what he saw there; age and misery and despair.

"Now I see," Whitearth said. "I see one who thinks I abandoned the God. Isn't that what you're thinking?" His creased face sagged like a bloodhound's. "I did not abandon Reh, but he me: you have felt the cold wind—already the trees by the mere have turned sere and yellow. I heard them last night, the Dark Ones, spying out the land—the animals have gone, all save these," he said, nodding at the trophies at his belt and on his shoulder. "The wind blew more and more bitter yesternight—it blew down my hut and the branches all about it. It howled until I thought I'd go mad and deaf together, and in it I heard the voices of the Dark Ones calling each to each." He paused, as if gauging his next remark for maximum effect. "And I heard the howl of the wolf coming from the Outland, through the mere."

"Fenris?" Nemoc said with a shudder.

"Like a shard of ice that cut my soul. Am I mad?" he asked, advancing another step and plucking at the hem of Nemoc's cloak.

Nemoc shrank back. The hunter's haunted eyes would not leave his face. Whitearth nodded slowly as he saw Nemoc's fear. "Aye, I am mad, but not as mad as you who will live after me. This morning the wind was gone, but the trees were dead, blasted with ice. I called for my dogs, but the Dark Ones had taken them. Their skins hung from the trees. I picked up my traps and yesterday's game. Then I felt he cold wind on my face. Then I knew: my face was gone."

Nemoc merely stared in horror commingled with pity.

"Don't worry," Whitearth said. "I know death is coming. But I don't fear it—I will go to the city now, let them see what has happened to old Whitearth. Let them who have slept in their luxury all these years see what will become of all of us."

"You'll never be able to cross the lake," Nemoc said.

A grim determination showed on Whitearth's face. "They won't deny me."

"Then what will happen?" Nemoc asked, despite his failing courage, eyeing the old man's still-strong frame.

He laughed then, the dry, mirthless chuckle that Nemoc had heard from the bushes. "They will see that their God, your God, will not save them from what comes. Who knows? I may help my people though my day has come. Finally they must arm themselves against the Nations."

"There is the Man of Bronze."

Whitearth tilted his head back at where the warm breeze from the interior played with the boughs of the trees in the moonlight. "The wind is growing weaker, the bellows in the Forge are dying: the Man of Bronze is old, old as the moon: He will die with it." He closed his old eyes momentarily.

In the respite from the mesmerism of his eyes, Nemoc shrugged free of the horror. "I must go now."

The old man's eyes snapped open again. "Where to?"

"The Outland."

"Then you are as mad as I. If the Dark Ones are already here, the Nations will not be far behind."

Nemoc nodded. "I have no choice."

"Give me your cap then. It will hide my head when I enter Lorn." Whitearth's gnarled hands reached out and plucked at the cap in Nemoc's hand, but the Opener whipped it away from his groping fingers.

"I cannot: it is the symbol of my office."

Whitearth's old face was suddenly filled with anger and bitterness, his eyes took on an evil, hooded appearance. "Go then—go like all your kind that still wear the Face. Think yourself better than me for now. I'll laugh when Fenris has you in its icy claws."

But Nemoc had already backed away from him, then turned quickly and headed up the Way, his gait a strange one, half-stumbling as his eyes darted behind him where the hunter stood rock solid in the middle of the path. What did he see in those melancholy yet angry eyes? His own mortality? Something so shocking that he could not stay for a moment longer. He ran off into the slanting beams of the moon. He heard Whitearth calling behind, but the words were now indistinct. Then the old man's voice was silenced by the thudding of his feet and the rustle of the fitful breeze through the trees.

He ran, not only to keep the fear of the Dark Ones and their familiars from his mind, but to stave off a strange lassitude that came over him. He must never sleep. Couldn't sleep. Whitearth would sleep soon, the endless sleep, the sleep from which he would never awaken. He would never be reborn into a new body. That sleep that was the bride of death, a death that would last forever. Ten thousand years ago, Reh had banished it from his kingdom. But now it had returned.

But though sleep whispered to him, telling him to rest his limbs, to close his eyes and let the dreams come, the voice was barely heard beneath the hammering of his heart and the drumming of his feet on the ancient way. But despite the danger ahead, his heart was strong. He would bring the Outlanders back. He would fetch the Watcher's son back to Lorn: he would redeem himself. It was the nature of the Way: all things were circular. He had a chance to put right the past, for the past had returned. The Moon Mere was just ahead.

CHAPTER FORTY-TWO

Shandering Plain

Urthred had been right. It was only a grave. They'd pulled the rocks from the cairn for two hours or more. Dawn had come, but the men had barely noticed it, so intent were they on their backbreaking labour. The smell had wafted slowly up from the rocks the lower they had dug. The smell of decay, of living matter long steeped in the slow ooze of the marsh. As the smell got worse, their activity slackened, until it was with a huge mental effort they lifted the stones and tumbled them down the sides of the half-demolished cairn. Finally, they'd worked with rags tied over their faces, their heads half-turned away, fearing what they would find.

Then they saw it, a glimpse of rusty vambrace. They'd slowly lifted away the last of the stones, and the body was revealed: mail armour, the hauberk a field of bright red rust, the naked head a horror of green slime and yellow bones and matted hair, rotted away by the wet, the gauntleted hands folded on the chest as if in prayer, a rotten roll of parchment clutched in them. Jayal had reached forward with trembling hands, plucked the rotten parchment away from the iron fingers, and stumbled down the remaining slope of the cairn, followed by Urthred.

Jayal's eyes had been pricking with tears; he realised he'd been choking on the foul stench. Calming himself, he carefully pulled the sodden sheet of the parchment open. There was his father's spidery writing.

He read the text: a prayer to Reh, given for the dead man Andul Whiteblaze, begging Andul's forgive-

ness for not following the mortuary rituals of Reh;
they had had no fire to burn him, nor had they seen
any of Reh's sacred birds in the forest. So, since there
were none to take his bones to Reh's fiery paradise,
they had buried him here under the cairn. The scroll
ended: "Now we go into the land beyond. The gateway stands open, and Lorn will be ours, though there
are only nine of us remaining. We go to glory or to
death. If we return, brother, we will send your bones
to the Hall of the White Rose." It was signed by the
baron, and the dead man's brother, Gorven. The
baron seemed to have to guess at the date, written
under his and Gorven's name, but it was a date in
spring, seven years earlier.

Jayal's eyes lifted up, over the lake, as if expecting
to find the gateway that his father had written of,
standing there in the misty morning light. But there
was nothing, save the drifting wraiths of fog and the
rippled surface of the lake stretching away out of sight.

The gateway must be in the water. He went back
into the woods and found a tall sapling, which he cut
down and trimmed of its branches. When he returned,
Urthred was gathering tinder to pile over Andul's
body. The priest looked at him wordlessly as he went
by: Jayal waded into the shallows once more and
began to probe the lake bottom with the bough. The
muddy depths were stirred up, and decayed fragments
of leaf mould whirled to the surface, but labour as he
might, going up and down the bank, he found nothing
more than sucking ooze at the bottom of the lake.

So the morning went by, both men at their own
tasks, Thalassa back in the shadows of the woods, her
cape thrust down over her face against the sun.

At midday, the priest climbed down from the remnants of the cairn and, spreading his arms, uttered the
same prayer he had used for Alanda two days before.
Then staring for a while longer at the sun, he cast his
hands forward at the pyre, which burst into light and
burned with an oily stench for the rest of the afternoon, the priest keeping watch over it all the time.

By now Jayal accepted that there was no gateway hidden beneath the surface of the mere, and his eyes went up, to the horizon over which the lake disappeared. Perhaps his father had meant the road continued on the other side?

"I'm going to the north," he said.

Urthred looked up at him. "The road won't lead you to Lorn: remember Alanda's words," he said. "It is a magical gateway."

Jayal nodded his head. "I remember." It was late afternoon, and a pale sickle moon could just be made out low down on the horizon. "But there are many days before the moon is full again. I have to do something."

"Then Reh go with you. Watch for the Doppelgänger. I will tend Thalassa," Urthred replied.

Without another word, Jayal had set off, circling the lake. For two days and nights he travelled, the low reed-covered shoreline always to his right, nothing visible at its center, shrouded in a heat haze from the warm breeze that seemed to blow from its surface. At last, one evening he stood in what he judged, from the position of the sun, to be the opposite shore to the one where he had left Urthred. There was nothing visible to the south save the unrelieved monotony of the grey waves and the grey cloud hugging the horizon.

Gnats swarmed in the dying light, and the deciduous trees looked sere and brown as if Autumn had finally arrived. Trackless expanses of forest stretched away as far as he could see to either side. A sense of futility came: the purpose of his quest slipping away with the light. Suddenly a double vision came to him: a scarecrow figure, Dragonstooth in its hand, standing by the shore looking south. A vision of himself.

The Doppelgänger was here. Watching him. Why didn't he come out of the woods, confront him as he had in the mists? But the creature didn't have to, he realised. He had another purpose now: to send him mad. Drive him further and further from his senses until the evil entered in and took complete possession of his mind.

He must continue: the longer he stayed in one place, the more hold the Doppelgänger had on him. He pressed on, towards the north, for another day. Iskiard lay that way, but how far? The forest stretched on and on. An air of ancient mystery hung here, of secrets long hidden from human eye. Yet no one stirred in the forest heart, no animals even: his innards began to gnaw with hunger, there were only stale crumbs left in his backpack. There was no relief from the endless green, only the passage of night and day told of the passing of time. But slowly, in the three days he travelled, he sensed the heat from the lake grow less, the trees begin to change colour the further from its shores he went.

Each day his double was with him; unbidden, his voice came into Jayal's mind: undeniable, all-conquering. Telling him to give way to his despair, to give up hope. Where was he? Near or far? He turned again and again, expecting to find the Doppelgänger right on his heels, but each time there were only the dark trunks and the green boughs.

The third morning the sun, purple and etiolated, rose above the forest; the early beams broke in a red prismatic haze through the dying vegetation, painting orange and light green patches on the forest floor carpeted by moss and the fall of leaves. There came a gust of wind revealing the white underside of the leaves on those trees that were still green, lifting them in a wave. Then he saw the birds, a flash of emerald-and-red plumage: woodpeckers. They flew in the strange, tail-down hovering flight, disappearing into the heart of the forest. Life at last! Would they guide him to Lorn? Or even to Iskiard? He followed, careless of the path.

He had circled wider and wider into the forest, certain that the birds were a sign that would lead him to his father's gateway. Another night passed, the only protection from the cold, his ragged cloak. His food was long gone. He followed the birdsong, ever eastwards.

Finally he'd reached the eastern edge of the forest: he'd looked out onto Shandering Plain, and saw the snows of winter drifting over the mica fields. Shandering Plain, where the gods had once lived, now a wasteland of isinglass, blasted stone and snow. The north winds had piled the snow into ridges and valleys, icy dunes running away to the far horizon. The earth groaned and heaved beneath his feet, and he felt the ground tremble, as if a giant of the Elder Times lay pinned beneath the earth, struggling to escape. Steam hissed from fissures in the snow, creating wide crevasses fifty feet across. No one could have passed this way. This was not the route his father had taken. In the distance, where he thought he could see the world curving away, vast columns of smoke rose into the air: the final battlefield of the gods. Alanda had been right: it was as desolate a place as anywhere in this dying world.

Now he was far from the lake. The full moon was coming, and he was alone with the visions that ate his mind.

CHAPTER FORTY-THREE

The Fever

Urthred had built two crude wooden huts: one for him and one for Thalassa. Neither Garadas nor the other two villagers had offered to help him, nor would they come near him or Thalassa. They had seen what she was becoming without having to be told. They saw how she kept to the shadows, avoiding the light of the sun and even the moon.

Garadas and the others kept their distance, making a camp a hundred yards away down the lakeshore. The sound of their voices came to him sometimes during the days that Jayal was gone. Thalassa remained in the ramshackle hut. He spent his time on the shore trying to puzzle the mystery of the lake. What had Alanda meant: the moon was the key? What was the magical formula? But he was unfamiliar with the magical study of opening the hidden ways between this plane and the next. He had no conjury, no prayer that could reveal what he needed to know. And time was running out. The Nations would come soon.

Once, when Garadas and the others slept, Imuni had stolen through the night to their huts. He was woken by her voice softly calling for Thalassa. He listened in the dark, wondering if she would reply. But no sound came, and after a little while he heard the girl sobbing. How he longed to go and comfort her. But what good was he? The scarred priest. His appearance would have sent her screaming back to her father. They were joined in this one thing at least, he and Thalassa: now both of them were outcasts.

Evening came on the seventh day, as the new moon

began to appear in the violet sky. Urthred left his hut and went to Thalassa's. She must have blood or she would go mad. A few days before he had placed a stout wooden bar over the door, hating himself for doing it, hating her for what she was becoming.

He pulled the bar down cautiously. Inside, the hut was cool and smelled of the damp earth of the lakeshore. He creased his eyes, blinded by the sudden darkness. Gradually they adjusted, and he saw a white glow at the far side of the hut. Thalassa's face: it seemed suspended, remote from the crude cot upon which she lay.

He approached and stood over her. She lay upon her back, her hands crossed on her chest, her ankles together, her matted hair spread like a fan under her head, her eyes closed. He was like a lover who came and watched his loved one asleep. Yet though desire was now almost a memory, still it stirred faintly, despite himself, as his eyes took in her face, the lines of her body. How could he desire something that had the animation of a stone effigy on a tomb? But she wasn't stone: would that she were, then he could worship her cold beauty forever.

The silence had been a long one. So long, that his mind had even forgotten his present danger: how hungry she would have become with the full moon approaching. With a start he realised that her eyes had opened, and she was looking at him. Vampires could mesmerise, but it needed no such magic to be drawn into those grey depths. . . . He snapped his head away and looked back to the faint outline of the door in the afterglow.

"Has Jayal returned yet?" she asked weakly, stirring so the crude wooden cot creaked slightly.

He shook his head. "He wanders still. The forest is limitless, it's cursed: its boundaries move as one moves, forever and forever further away: there is no centre; only the lake and the moon. It is as Alanda told us—the moon is the key."

"Will he ever return?"

He turned and looked at her once more. "He is half-mad with the voice. He alone can fight the Doppelgänger. But I feel he's coming back: he knows the full moon is close."

"Aye, the moon: our hope and my enemy."

There came another rustle from the darkness as she sat upright. "It was all only a dream, Urthred: everything that we wanted is a dream—out of our reach. There is no Silver Chalice; Lorn doesn't exist. I am what I am now, no medicine can change that. Alanda is dead, Jayal is cursed. There is no way to escape the Nations."

"It was no dream—Alanda made us promise . . ." He heard a hiss of breath, as if she stirred in pain.

"Thalassa?"

"It has been a long time, priest: the moon waxes. My blood is on fire."

"We will find the Silver Chalice."

"You forget, priest: that is in Lorn, that place that cannot be found."

"As you say, the moon waxes: soon it will be full; the Master of Ravenspur told me that is when he would strike at Lorn. If he can pass through, we can as well."

"But then it will be too late for me."

He lowered his head. "I have brought the leeches."

"Yes, the leeches—Faran's feast: now mine. One lesson we learned in Thrull: how to keep the undead alive," she said bitterly. She seemed to get control of herself after a moment. "Put them on the stone. Don't get too close."

Urthred stepped forward. There had been a large flat stone on the fringe of the forest over which he had built the hut. Thalassa used it as a table. He felt for the edge of it, then knelt and unloosened the wriggling life from his cloak. He had collected the leeches from the lake shallows and the creek during that first morning, realising that this was the only way. How he hated the creatures that for the last few days he had allowed to suck on his skin! Was he no better than

one of Iss' servants now? Unburdened, he stepped
back quickly. He heard Thalassa stirring in the dark,
then her strangled voice telling him to go. She couldn't
allow him to see her need, her craving.

He felt behind him for the door of the hut and
pulled it open. It was already quite dark outside, there
was merely the barest afterglow of sunset in the west,
but as he looked back into the interior, he caught a
glimpse of her white face in the dark, dark circles
under her eyes, her hair matted over her face. Yet
despite the transformation, she still lived for a second
in that face, the young girl he had briefly loved.

But then she leaned forward, with a look of hungry
anticipation, and suddenly the face was transformed
into a mask of greed and hunger.

He stumbled out of the hut, throwing the bar over
the door. He walked back down the shore to his own
hut. As he did so, his eyes went up. There, just above
the tree line, he saw the mountains where the ruins of
Astragal stood. Somewhere up there were the burned
remains of Alanda's bier. Had she been their last
hope? Why hadn't she told him the secret of the gateway? Perhaps she too had not known, but only sensed
that this was the way.

Beyond Astragal, the sky was black: the cloud under
which the Nations advanced had grown nearer and
nearer by the day. Yet paradoxically that was their
hope. Why did they come if there wasn't actually a
gateway to Lorn here? He felt the presence of the
Master, coming on the wings of that cloud. Soon he
would arrive and they would have their final reckoning. Would Urthred's magic save them then?

He sat by the entrance to the hut on the springy
turf and slowly stripped off a glove, revealing tapering
fingers. He was still healing. Like a flower that opens,
he had seen the fingers growing day by day, joints like
roots sprouting miraculous life, then the nails. The
same was happening to his face: his cheeks, the nubs
of his ears, the nose, the lids that now covered half his
eyes. He was healed just when Thalassa was damned.

But once born, the habit of hope was difficult to abandon. How long had it taken him to learn this lesson? That humankind was sustained by it, and it alone. Through hunger, starvation, disease, the ingrained belief like a burr stuck to the soul, the belief that life would get better, a belief that could not be shaken off, not even in the mouth of death. He remembered his master's words, and still he had the belief that Manichee would not have brought them to this place if there wasn't some hope somewhere out there. The Silver Chalice would be found. Thalassa would be cured.

CHAPTER FORTY-FOUR

The Moon Mere
and Beyond

Finally, after many days of wandering, Jayal turned his back on Shandering Plain and went back into the forest. He saw that the moon was approaching the full. He knew his quest had been a false one right from the start: was it to flee the struggle in his mind he had gone on it? He had no answers, disoriented with hunger and the recurring visions. The voice was never silent. Didn't the Doppelgänger sleep? He set his face back towards the dark cloud hanging over the mountains in the south, knowing that whatever route he took through the tangled glades would lead him inevitably back towards the centre and the enigma of the lake.

He reached it after a few days. He saw three rough shelters in front of him, two nearby, and one further along the shore. As he watched, the priest appeared in the doorway of one of the nearer ones. He went forward and greeted him. He felt Urthred assessing him from behind the mask, wondering, no doubt, whether he had been possessed by his shadow. Eventually he seemed to be satisfied that he was still the man who left the camp two weeks before. He had offered him the remaining scraps of food. Jayal ate them ravenously.

He rested for one day: the priest and he sitting together by the lakeside. They conversed in a rambling way, of their childhood, the years in between. Of his six-year quest, the priest's ten years in the tower. The death of Urthred's brother. Of Thalassa. Garadas and the two villagers never came near them. From where Jayal and Urthred sat, they saw that the villagers had fashioned crude rods and were fishing in the lake. Like the southerners, they could not return through the Black Cloud to their village, nor go on, for there was nowhere to go to.

Hunger was gnawing both of them as well. Jayal fashioned a rudimentary net of creepers as he talked through the afternoon, hoping that there might be something to catch in it soon.

The moon rose over the lake. One day until it was full.

They went to bed still hungry. Jayal woke at dawn. In the grey light outside the hut he saw the mist hanging on the lake and a new sound, the song of a pair of thrushes from a nearby stand of trees. But it was not their song that entranced him, but the thought of food. He took up the homemade net of creepers, his head cocked to one side, praying for the birds to stay close. Urthred had raised himself on his elbows and listened, too.

"There will be meat for our table tonight, priest," Jayal said. And with that he was gone, moving stealthily out of the hut and through the early-morning mists that hung like a veil on the surface of the lake. Soon he was very near where the thrushes chattered in the fringes of the forest. But the birds fluttered away at his approach, alighting a little further down the lakeside. Again he stalked them, and again they fluttered off a tantalising distance. He followed again, and again the pattern was repeated, until he found himself being drawn deeper and deeper into the forest again. The birds flew ahead, enticing him onwards into the dark stands of oak and beech, where it was always twilight. His hunger was acute, their song a goad to his appetite: he could almost taste the sweetness of their flesh in the sweetness of their song.

All morning he followed into a part of the woods

where he'd never been. Here and there he saw that the trees had been carved: leering faces, boles for eyes, totems of a forgotten time, perhaps even from the time of Alanda's people. But he barely noticed—his hunger was everything. It was only when one of the birds had alighted in the branches of an ancient oak, and he set up the net and beaten it into it, that he realised how far gone he was, how near madness. Once more visions flooded into his mind, of his dead friends from the battlefield, of Alanda, of the Doppelgänger. A cacophony of voices filled his head, in tune with the remaining thrush's song that echoed amongst the trees, calling to its companion. The whole of the wood seemed full of the noise, the dead calling to the dead, his dark half pulling him into insanity.

He had entered the dark heart of the forest, and darkness had entered him. He should let the bird go: it was hardly more than a mouthful. By releasing it, his own spirit would be released from this world. He would lie down and die here. But darkness was in his blood, a black gall that must be drunk. With a quick movement, he wrung the creature's neck and then plucked, gutted and cooked it with indecent haste, the carved faces of the trees staring through the carved boles of their eyes like silent avatars of another time.

The bird's flesh nearly choked him. He suddenly felt ill, possessed by a strange fever, as if its unquiet fluttering spirit had entered his mind. He put the uneaten portion of his kill in his bag.

Then he had wandered all afternoon, not knowing where he went, until somehow he had found himself back at the side of the lake as evening fell. The moon rode the clouds like a ship above its waters. Suddenly he remembered it was the night of the full moon. He looked up and saw the dark cloud, riding over Astragal towards the burning orb, dark fingers of it falling into the forest only a few miles away. He could see the trees at the lakeside were turning brown. A cold wind began to contend with the warmth. A thin sheen of ice had already begun to fringe the edges of the

lake. He heard a strange noise, like the twittering of
the birds in his ears. Movement: shadows like ghosts
in the trees.

He went to the lake and knelt and drank, trying to
drown the fever in his veins. The water brought him
some relief. He stood and contemplated his reflection.
By now the fur cloak that he had been given in Goda
was torn and dirty, through its many encounters with
the dense forest vegetation. In many places his leather
cuirass showed through its rents. His boots were held
together by rags and bindweed. His face, covered by
a thick blond beard, was lit up in the gathering gloom
by the eerie light of Dragonstooth shining through the
stitch holes in the growing dark. As he was on the
outside, so he was on the inside—a tattered scarecrow
of his former self.

The moon rode higher and higher until it stood over
the dead centre of the lake, each pockmark on its
sallow face exactly mirroring its reflection in the water.

Like the moon, he hung between two worlds: one
real, the other its shadow. He knew, even this evening,
his double watched him from a distance. In the corner
of his vision, he saw an image of himself, standing
here, by the lakeshore.

He saw too the ruin of the cairn—it had been his
last hope. But there had been no message for him
there, merely an enigma which would never now be
solved. His father had commanded him to live, to
fetch the sword, and he had done so. But now the
quest had foundered, on this lakeshore, the very
threshold of the hidden land beyond. He felt anger
then, a malicious doubt seeded by the Doppelgänger.
A bleak self-recognition: since the exorcism he had
always been his father's instrument, never his own person. Always his father had ordered him and he had
obeyed. Maybe the Doppelgänger was the only one
who was truly free.

He shook his head. Once he began believing that,
it would all be over.

He realised that Urthred had come out of the hut.

He now sat down on the last flagstone of the road staring at the water, and the moon, rising over the trees. Jayal slumped down next to him, too exhausted to speak. Then he remembered: he had brought food. He laughed out loud, and the priest swung his mask round at him. "What is it?" he asked. But instead of answering Jayal proffered the charred remnants of the thrush, and, as he did so, tears, inexplicably, began running down his cheeks. The priest merely looked at him, before turning his face once more to the rising moon.

"It is too late for food," he said bleakly. "The moon is full. Tonight Thalassa will join the Dead in Life."

Jayal calmed himself. "And tonight the Master promised that the Nations would come."

A low keening came from Thalassa's hut. Jayal wondered what mental struggle was going on in Urthred's mind. But his expression as always was hidden beneath the mask.

Urthred spoke again. "I spoke with Thalassa last night. I told her the moon was nearly full. She told me not to come again. . . ." His voice trailed off.

Jayal nodded. He looked at the lakeshore. No fire burned near Garadas's hut as it had the night before. "Where have they gone?" he asked.

"They saw the cloud coming. They came earlier in the afternoon and called to us, saying they were going further north."

"Nobody can outrun the Nations," Jayal said, then fell into another silence, watching the clouds flowing over the lake. Yet as he watched them, a new feeling came—gone was the hopelessness of a moment before. It was as if his mind had suddenly unfrozen. He stood, the priest looking up at him, startled by the sudden movement.

Alanda had spoken of Lorn as a place where natural law held no sway, where there were no seasons, no age, no change, where a full moon always shone upon the land.

But this forest was not that place: mutability could

be seen all around him in the fallen, rotten trees, with
their thick polyps, the ooze of the marsh with its vege-
tal stink, the charred remains of the creature he had
been forced to kill to remain alive.

But now the moon was full.

It was almost at its zenith. Jayal stood rigidly staring
up at its great immensity that seemed to fill the sky
and his mind. Now it corresponded to the one in that
other land, and Alanda had said it was the key. The
moon, the God Erewon to his ancestors—oldest of all
of them—God of wisdom and knowledge, for did not
the moon teach man that all was mutable? The God
who was buried in Lorn and hung forever in the skies.
He looked down, fearful that his mind would be wiped
clean in that constant silver glare. . . .

He looked down, and the moon blindness passed
and the source of the mere swam back into focus. . . .

His spine froze.

He still stood on the last flagstone on the edge of
the lake, but it was as if a veil had been stripped from
the surface of the water, and a whole universe was
revealed beneath it. The waters were suddenly limpid,
like a giant looking glass bringing faraway details ach-
ingly clear to his eyes. He saw the road plunge beneath the surface of the water, but now there was a
series of glowing stones leading away to a distant vanishing point. Golden lamps burned on either side of
the road, marking its immeasurable length as it
stretched away into the world that had opened up before him. It was as if his pilgrim eyes would never
stop, but continue on and on, down the road . . . then
he saw where the lights gave out, and the shore of a
lake, and beyond it the lights of a city . . . Lorn.

He would have shouted out to the priest, but his
voice wouldn't come. His body had been left behind,
for now it seemed as if he had passed down the road
and stood by that lakeshore, and looked across its vast
expanse. A mist hung over the surface of the visionary
lake. At its far distance he could just see an island.
The island rose to a low eminence, on top of which

he could see what looked to be a palace gleaming whitely in the moonlight. Further away he saw another island some miles distant from its sister: a tall pinnacle of rock, around which a tempest was raging: the lake seethed with whitecapped waves. A full moon, an exact replica of the one that burned in the sky over the lake in the Outland, hung over the vision of the islands.

Now sensation followed and he felt a balmy air playing on his skin. Ringing the shore of Lorn, a thousand lanterns twinkled in dusky groves of trees. He heard the wind playing in the groves and saw the light blinking on and off as the boughs swayed. Now he heard the strains of music, a lute, perhaps one of the lutes that Furtal had spoken of, wafted to him by the wind.

He shook his head, trying to rid himself of the vision. But when he looked again, he was still by the lakeside. He turned. Behind him the road stretched away down the avenue in the diminishing row of lamps, stretched, it seemed, an infinity, but still he could see the lake in the mortal world and the lonely figures at its end. Urthred and he both standing by the edge of the lake. He had travelled so far! He stood simultaneously on the border of the two worlds: the real one and the place of shadows. He willed his body to step forward into the mere, so it could join his spirit in Lorn.

Suddenly his spirit was back in his body. Urthred stood next to him; he, too, stared at the roadway plunging into the depths of the water. "The lake: just as I saw it in the Orb!" he whispered.

"The road is open," Jayal said, stepping towards it.

"Careful," Urthred cautioned, but Jayal had already drawn Dragonstooth: the blade blazed, sending a stab of light across the surface of the lake. His foot splashed into the shallows. Instantly the vision shattered as if it were made of glass. The ripples ran out from his foot over the lake, further and further, into the distance, sweeping away the image of the far-

distant lanterns one by one. He plunged after them.
Suddenly he was floundering up to his chest in the
water, just as he had the first day. He sank, taking in
a mouthful of brackish water. He thrashed back to the
surface, spluttering for breath.

He struggled back to the shore, then twisted around;
the broad ripples marching across the placid face of
the lake were all that was visible. The vision had
disappeared.

He held his breath; Urthred, too. Both had the same
thought: would the vision come back when calm returned? The two of them watched intently. Slowly the
ripples flattened out and, waveringly, the reflection of
the full moon was restored to the surface, but nothing
now could be seen beneath its surface, however hard
they stared. Jayal had had it in his grasp—the vision
had been his, and he had torn it to pieces—destroyed
it just as if it had never been.

Then he cursed, and stepped into the shallows
again, kicking the water until it churned whitely and
he lost his balance and fell once more. The cold lake
water seeped through his rags, the heat of Dragonstooth's blade making the water boil and bubble
around him. He leaned his head back and howled. He
would go mad, he was sure, and he tilted his head
back and laughed at the uncaring moon.

The priest had to drag him from the water. Jayal
heard Urthred muttering soothing words to him, but
the keening in his head had returned, and for a while
he heard nothing. Then his mind cleared once more.
He turned and looked into the priest's mask.

"This is why Furtal never found Lorn," he said. "It
doesn't exist upon this plane; it is in the Shadow
World."

"There must be a way," Urthred said. "How did
your father get there?"

"He had the rod. Think, priest, what are its powers?
To open this world to Shades. I have seen it, when I
lay dying on Thrull field, when my double came on a

bridge of light. How can we follow, where only moon-beams travel?"

"There must be another way," Urthred repeated, though with less certainty. He paced up and down the flagstone. A low moan came from Thalassa's hut. Both men stared at one another. "It is nearly time," Urthred said in a strained voice. Jayal thought he heard his teeth grind together. Suddenly he, too, felt panic. They had been so near! He stared once more at the surface of the water.

The moon was now nearly at its apogee. Now he knew Thalassa's thirst would be raging, burning her veins, her poisoned blood transforming into the black ichor of the damned.

He stared back into the forest: the dark clouds were very close. A terrible storm was brewing there. But as yet its winds had not reached the edge of the lake. There was no retreat. The only way was forward, into the lake. Then he heard a sharp intake of breath from Urthred, and he turned.

And there for the second time was the vision: it was as if all the time he had been looking into the forest, he knew it would be there, but some superstitious fear had prevented him from acknowledging it lest it disappear again. Just as when a lamp is set behind white alabaster, so he saw now a luminescence deep beneath the lake, a muted light but one that grew slowly, as if something were rising from its depths, or if indeed another moon, fresher and brighter than the one in the sky, was rising from the waters. He stood absolutely still as the light grew and grew, approaching along the line of the road he had seen in the vision.

Both of them instinctively stepped back into the shadows of the trees, Jayal drawing Dragonstooth, Urthred readying his gloves.

They didn't have long to wait. The waters of the lake, liquid a moment before, suddenly became opaque and splintered like ice; shards flew upwards and rained down on either side. There emerged at the center of the disturbance, in the shallows by the edge

of the lake, what looked to be a creature of light. Fair
and tall it stood, clad all in a white samite robe, its
features fine and chiseled with a lock of white hair
and a high forehead, and piercing blue eyes. It held a
white staff in its right hand. It stood for a moment,
the water falling slowly like a crystal cascade from its
cloak, then it breathed deeply through its fine-boned
nostrils. . . .

And then the image began to dissolve. The figure
shrank; no longer lean, it became squat and hunched,
and only some five feet tall. Where its high forehead
once had been was a bald gnomic head, hung with
loose folds of flesh which hung lugubriously from its
misshapen skull. Folds of flesh were bunched around
its chin like a bloodhound's. Its eyes were red and
deeply recessed into the sockets, and its dress was
revealed as a crude woolen tunic which floated on the
surface of the water like a brown lily pad. The blazing
staff of a moment before had shriveled into a
gnarled root.

Now the creature turned and looked at the moon,
which at that moment fell behind the cloud, casting
the scene into deep shade. It sighed, and it muttered
something in a language that neither men understood.
Then, shifting its gaze from the moon, it lumbered
clumsily onto the shore, its legs hidden by the trailing,
sodden cloak which fell from its hunched back like a
snail's carapace. It stopped when it saw the glow of
Dragonstooth in the darkness. It peered forward and
saw the two men.

Jayal and Urthred stepped forward from their hiding place. The knight advanced until he towered over
the squat creature and thrust the sword point just beneath its chin.

"Speak," he said. "If you have a tongue and can
understand me." The thing seemed unperturbed,
blinking slowly as it took in Jayal's features, then
Urthred's mask.

"Yes, I speak the tongue of the Outland." Though

the accent was heavy, they recognised their language in the thick guttural growl.

"Where have you come from?" Urthred said urgently, for the moon was struggling with the cloud, and the vision in the lake seemed to be fading.

"From Lorn," he replied. "I have come to fetch you."

"To fetch us?" The creature merely nodded its misshapen head. "You don't know who we are!"

"Oh, I know you," he answered, his eyes never leaving his mask. "You are Urthred, Urthred of Ravenspur and this," he said, turning to Jayal, who still held the sword point to his chin, "is the baron's son."

Now finally the sword wavered. Both men were momentarily speechless. "How do you know us?" Urthred asked.

"All things will be revealed once we are in Lorn. But now time is short. The Nations are nearly here," he replied.

"The road is open?"

"The moon is full," he said. "When the moon is full and stands at its height, the Way to your world is opened."

"Yet the people of Lorn are beautiful, and you are . . ."

"Ugly?" he supplied. "Aye, but you saw how I looked when I came through the mere. The mortal air corrupts the immortal body given me by Reh."

The two men looked at one another, then at the Black Cloud arching overhead.

"Then let's hurry," Urthred said. "I'll get Thalassa." He ran back towards the huts, leaving Jayal with the creature. He lowered his sword. The wind by now had begun to howl through the trees.

"Is my father still alive?" Jayal asked.

"He lives, but he has gone from our land. He went with his men to the far north, to a place called Iskiard."

"He left? Why? He should have waited for me. I have brought the sword."

"He discovered something in our country, something that would not suffer any delay."

They saw Urthred was leading Thalassa from the hut. She was gripping the priest's arm, very weak. Another blast of icy air howled through the trees behind them.

Urthred looked up at the cloud obscuring the moon, then back at the creature. "Do you have a name?" he asked.

"I am Nemoc, the Opener of the Way."

"Then, Nemoc, use your magic—take us to Lorn."

"Quickly then," he said, glancing nervously at the forest. "They're coming."

"Who?" Jayal asked. A sudden silence fell, and the wind died to a whisper. There it was, from far off, a sinister rustling sound which at first he couldn't identify. But then he understood: it was the sound of a thousand bodies breaking through the vegetation, far off, but coming closer by the second.

"The Nations," he whispered, not waiting for Nemoc's reply.

"Come," Urthred said to Thalassa, who slumped against him, barely conscious, a tin dribble of spittle at the corner of her mouth. "It is time to go."

"Go where?" she mumbled.

"To Lorn; the place Alanda told us of."

"You have found it?"

"You will see, we will find the Silver Chalice tonight," he said, taking her hand.

Now the sound from the south was deafening. The approaching army was hurtling through the trees towards them, and they heard the moaning of a thousand lost souls. Nemoc delayed no further but lifted the gnarled root in his hand and the surface of the mere calmed slightly. Then he stepped forward and sank down into the water. Urthred turned to Jayal. The young Illgill took Thalassa's other arm, and the three of them stepped into the water.

And from this world into the next.

CHAPTER FORTY-FIVE

✤

A Revelation at the Palace of the Moon

Urthred placed a foot in the water, right onto the glowing vision of the road, instinctively shutting his eyes as he did so. He felt his foot sink beneath the surface, his body with it, and he suffered a sudden feeling of weightlessness as if he had stepped not into water but into an empty shaft down which he now fell. The water didn't touch him but roared by his ears with the sound of passing thunder. Then, suddenly, his feet met broad paving stones and his eyes snapped open.

It was as if he had walked through a mirror, for now, instead of descending into the water, he was rising up out of it. Ahead, Nemoc emerged from the lake surface, the water falling from him like glass. Once more, the creature was transformed: erect and straight, a young man's face, his white hair glowing in the moonlight.

He followed, wading to the shore in front, his clothes strangely dry, untouched by the water. He turned, expecting to find the endless lake stretching away, but instead, there was only a mere about a mile across, surrounded by ash trees, the moon hanging over its exact centre. But he could still see reflected the image of the shore in the Outland: the forest, their huts and the dark cloud which now covered half the sky. Even as he watched the trees bent inwards as if sucked in by a tremendous pressure. Then the edge of the forest erupted, trees flew up into the air, branches whirled forward like so many dismembered limbs, and from it burst what appeared a dark tide, but was in fact one solid line of heaving life. Dark forms, skulls and fangs and leathery wings, clad in dark carapaces and with horned heads; a collage of body parts mixed with the black mist: the legions and legions of the damned, their mouths agape, mad for slaughter, their horned bodies twitching. The huts disintegrated as they swept through them and onto the lakeshore, where they halted, their ranks pressing close to the water, staring into it, red eyes glowing as if waiting for a command.

"Come on," Nemoc shouted, but even as he did so the first rank plunged into the water and suddenly the vision was gone and the calm surface of the mere turned into a maelstrom, then erupted upwards in a geyser of water and dark vapour. The first horned head appeared, its eyes like coals, followed by another and then a hundred more. All of them were struggling towards the shore, only their numbers hampering them as they tried to clamber from the mere. One of the creatures pulled back its hand and made a throwing gesture—twisting black mist flew from it, arching over their heads into the forest. It landed with a sinister, sibilant hiss, and fog began pouring out of the trees, snaking towards the humans, twisting around their ankles.

The four of them ran, leaping over the tendrils of mist. Behind them they saw that the first line of the creatures were coming onto the shore. The water had almost disappeared, such was the number emerging from its surface. Then the seething surface of the mere fell away entirely, its centre like a whirlpool sucking back the Nations still struggling to get out of it or as if a plug had been opened at its bottom and the water was beginning to drain from it. A dark mist began forming over the draining surfaces of the mere. A heavy, corrosive smell filled the air, prickling their

noses, a damp chemical vapour that seemed to cling
to every bough and shred of vegetation.

"Quickly," Nemoc screamed from in front. "The
magic barrier has been destroyed." He pointed ahead
of them: the gnarled bough was once more a shining
staff. Just as in the vision, the Way ran arrow straight
in front of them. Unlike the vision, there were no
lamps to either side—nor was there any sight of the
city at its end.

The two men dragged Thalassa along between them.
There was froth on her chin, and she threw her head
from side to side like a frenzied dog. The wind howled
past them again, warm wind, being sucked from the
land. Looking back, they saw the Black Cloud rising
out of the mere like a tornado, soaring up into the
moonlit sky, its dark tendrils rushing across the
moon's face. Black hail came suddenly, ripping
through the thick green foliage of the trees, sending
frost radiating out like ripples in a pool. Behind, their
pursuers came with a curious gait, throwing their arms
out to each side like sowers in a field, and where they
threw, dark mist sprang up from the ground, and the
very trees stirred and shuddered, shed their leaves,
then tore up their roots and followed.

"Arm yourselves," Nemoc said urgently. He thrust
the staff into the air, so it blazed with the light of a
shining star, casting long shadows into the undergrowth. The woods were full of shuffling forms, their
figures naked and grey, hidden partially by a white
vapour that billowed and undulated as they crept forward, skull faces glowing in the dark. They hesitated
for a moment upon seeing the light of the staff. Jayal
brandished Dragonstooth, and the moon played upon
its blade. It was as it had been a month before in
Thrull, a dull coppery red, the blade pulsed as if laden
with magic, the magic of the full moon.

Then one of the creatures broke forward from out
of the ranks of those following behind. It held up its
hand and threw it forward. It was as if its body had
been made only of empty air, for it shriveled to a husk

with a faint whining noise. But where its hand had
been pointing at them, a tendril of mist shot towards
them rolling along the ground at a terrific speed, bil-
lowing up to head height. Instantly, they were enveloped in a choking gas vapour, each of them gasping
for breath, then the creature's skull suddenly materialised in front of them with an earsplitting shriek. It
flew at Urthred, its jaws agape, its teeth snapping.

But just before it reached him, Nemoc swung his
staff, and the wood hit the skull with a brittle snap.
The head exploded, spattering them with shards of
bone. He shouted to them to hurry again and set off
once more in a loping run. The humans followed as
more black hail hammered into the trees. More of the
creatures dematerialised, their skulls appearing in the
air with more screams. The humans ducked and
weaved, the skulls flying after them, rapidly catching
them. They stopped and hit out at them with the staff,
sword and gloves. More of them exploded.

Urthred batted another skull away with a balled
glove. It flew away into the forest, but more vapour
trails flew at them as he watched.

"We'll never make it," Jayal said, Dragonstooth
glowing redly in his hand, the skulls dodging inside
the arc of the great two-handed sword. One almost
grazed his face.

They were now surrounded, with no possibility of
both defending themselves and running. The creatures
circled in from all sides. The air chilled as the skulls
spewed frost onto them.

Thalassa was in the middle of them; kneeling on the
road where Urthred and Jayal had lowered her so they
could fight. Her cloak was thrown over her head
against the pitiless light of the moon. But now its light
was suddenly extinguished as the tornado roaring out
of the mere reached up and covered it, leaving them
in a pitch-darkness illuminated only by the staff and
sword. As the darkness fell, she suddenly flung back
the cloak from her head as if she had just woken from
a dream and stood, heedless of the flying skulls and

weapons arcing through the air. Her gaze was fixed to the east, down the road towards Lorn. She raised her arms high into the air. On the instant she did so, they heard, even over the shrieking of the skulls, a rumble like thunder echoing over the forest. Then there was a white flash in the sky ahead, its source masked by the trees. Instantly the chaos of the whirling skulls was stilled.

"It is coming," she said in the sudden silence, her eyes closed as if she saw something there. Her companions still looked to the north, from where there were more lightning flashes in the sky.

Then a typhoon seemed to explode in the forest to either side of them, flying boughs scythed overhead on the wings of a furnacelike heat. Though they were at its epicentre, in a place of relative calm, the wind nevertheless threw them all to the ground and rolled them over as if they were bits of straw. All of them, that was, except Thalassa, who stood erect and proud in the teeth of the tempest, her hands held high over her head.

Then the wind was gone, towards the mere. Urthred lay on his back. He could see the sinister tornado above them shredding away from the face of the moon. Then there was silence. He stood shakily, loose twigs and leaves raining from his cloak. The others stood as well and retrieved their weapons.

They stared at Thalassa, who stood at the centre of the Way, her arms still stretched upwards. "What did you do?" Jayal whispered, finding his tongue. Thalassa shook her head, lowering her hands to protect her eyes from the moon, which once more shone brightly. Her brow was creased as if she heard a distant sound that she was trying to make out. Urthred noticed that her skin glowed faintly, a greater white than the moonglow would create, as if once more a light burned from within her as it had done at the Lightbringer's Shrine.

"It was as if I heard a voice; the voice of the Man of Bronze," she said, her eyes still clenched against the light. "I called on him to help us, and then the wind came."

Nemoc gazed silently at her. "It is true what the prophecies said: the Man of Bronze obeys you."

"Do you hear his voice still?" Urthred asked.

"I hear him. He is there, down the road," she answered.

"Then hurry, the moon is still full. The Dark Ones will return soon," Nemoc said.

Urthred went to Thalassa, who wavered unsteadily on her feet. She sank against his chest when he drew level with her, drawing the cloak over her face. "How do you feel?" he asked.

"The moon burns me, Urthred," she murmured.

"How far is it to Lorn?" Urthred asked Nemoc.

"The edge of the forest moves, and the mere does, too; it may be many miles, or it may be close."

"We must get there soon," he said urgently. They set off down the Way again, Urthred carrying her.

The warm breeze was now blowing constantly from Lorn, holding back the Black Cloud and whatever advanced in its shadow. For the moment they were safe. They were all tired, and their pace slowed slightly. What might have been an hour in the Mortal World passed, yet the southerners noticed that the moon still beamed down from the zenith of the sky, not changing its position at all. Everything glowed luminously in its light.

They had now mounted to the top of a ridge and the land dropped away precipitously below them. In the far distance they could see a wide expanse of water glinting in the moonlight. There were dark smudges that might have been islands on its surface. "Lorn," Nemoc said, his voice rising with excitement.

Below, the forest fell in serried waves a thousand feet or more to a flat, forested plain. Far away the lake shimmered like sapphire. The mountains stood revealed in the moonlight, the clarity of the air and the brightness of the moon such that every small crevice in their sides could be seen even at this vast distance. A river to their left vaulted out from the sheer cliff and fell in a thundering cascade three hundred feet to a mighty pool, and from that pool to another two hundred or so feet below and, from that, to yet another pool. The road went down from the platform in a series of switchbacks close by the side of the falls.

Now the warm breeze began to falter again, and Nemoc gestured for them to hurry. Looking back, they saw that the Black Cloud over the forest had reformed and was growing darker and darker by the moment.

The going was more difficult as they started down the zigzag path. Soon Urthred became conscious of the ache of his muscles in his legs as he braced himself for the next steep step. The dark cloud was once more reaching overhead, covering the moon. Speech was impossible because of the roar of the falls. By the time they got to the bottom, the sky was dark overhead. They passed an old ruin of what must have once been a large building with a ring wall and many outbuildings all now overgrown by lush vegetation so that only one or two lonely spires of rocks stuck up from the trees. A green lawn stretched back from the swiftly rushing river that hopped over one or two more minor tributaries before plummeting down a deep gorge to their left.

Urthred looked back at the forest hanging above them. The face of the moon darkened again as the roiling edge of the northern clouds passed over its face. Instantly the warmth blowing from the interior was replaced by a dank chill, and a cold rain began to weep down from the overcast sky. A mist started to roll over the edge of the cliffs and down towards them.

They hurried past the ruins, following the side of the gorge for a time, then the ground leveled out in front of them and the river flowed broad and wide over water meadows sprinkled with meadow flowers glowing silver in the moonlight. Strange tortured shapes, like giant termites' nests, could be seen clustered thickly about the field.

"What are those shapes?" Urthred asked, gasping for breath.

"All the remains of the last army the Nations sent," Nemoc said over his shoulder. "Here the Man of Bronze stood before their might and withered the Nations with his molten breath so they turned to stone or fled back to their lands. The city is close now," he said.

Now the trees began to thin, and thick stands of bulrushes could be seen ahead. Beyond were the waters of the lake, throwing up brilliant sparkles of moonlight from the top of the small waves that played on its surface. They saw again the dark shape of an island right in the middle of the lake. Ahead, the road rose gently onto a stone causeway which crossed the space between the edge of the woods and the shore and the lake in a series of ever-higher arches leading up to the beginning of a bridge. It curved gracefully over the lake for fifty yards, then disappeared into thin air.

Nemoc led them towards the bridge. Jayal and Urthred exchanged glances: there was no way across. But Nemoc strode on undeterred, the staff held high over his head, catching the light of the moon. He reached the end of the bridge, the dark waters of the lake now a hundred feet beneath him, but without hesitation he walked forward into the air. He didn't fall, but went on as if he trod still on stone. Jayal and Urthred followed, then stopped at the edge, staring down in fear at the dark waters below. Thalassa's head was swathed in the hood of the cloak so she was unaware of what lay before them. In front, Nemoc was getting smaller and smaller as he strode forward on the night air, towards the distant island.

"We must go on," Urthred said, still clutching Thalassa's sleeve.

"What is it, priest?" she whispered.

"We are at the end of a bridge: there is only a drop in front of us, then the waters of the lake."

"Nemoc has gone on, has he not?"

"Yes," Urthred replied.

"Then follow him. Reh's magic will protect us."

Urthred closed his eyes and, taking a stronger grip on her arm, stepped off the end of the bridge, expecting to plummet to the waters below. But it was as if his feet still met the solid pavement of the bridge. He opened his eyes again. He strode on air. He fixed his eyes on Nemoc's blazing staff and went on.

The grey mass of the island loomed larger as they continued, and he saw white buildings, clinging to its cliffsides, glowing in the moonlight. Stone jetties stood to one side of the opposite bridge end, which he could see protruding from the shore. Behind it was a long, colonnaded terrace planted with cultivated trees. Burning lamps swung to and fro erratically in the wind. A steep stairway rose up from the colonnade towards the large palace on the summit of the island. Even at this distance, he could see it was made of layer upon layer of tiered granite, supported by vast flying buttresses, the whole surmounted by a large building.

Both the bridge and the quay ahead were deserted. Nemoc was fifty yards ahead. He passed onto the solid ground again, and turned, gesturing for them to hurry and join him.

They travelled the short distance. Nemoc was waiting, his back turned to them, his head cocked to one side as if he was listening for something.

"What's the matter?" Urthred asked.

The creature turned his blue eyes on Urthred. "It's too quiet. Normally the people are in the streets."

"What are they doing?"

Nemoc looked grim. "They're plotting."

"Plotting? Why? Can't they see the danger?" Urthred asked, gesturing to the south.

"They see it well enough. They plot against my master, the Watcher. There is a custom here that when the Watcher's powers weaken, the people kill him."

"But you have brought the Lightbringer. She will drive the Nations away."

Nemoc shook his white locks sadly. "It is too late. I was on the road too long."

"Come, we might still be in time to save your master."

They hurried up the broad flight of marble steps towards the top of the island. Here the cold wind that had blustered around the jetties had died out, and the heat was almost oppressive. Wildflowers and climbing plants clung to the walls on either side of the alley. The streets were still and empty all around them.

They followed the ceremonial way, climbing between large stone town houses, their doors and windows barred, like empty eyes fronting the street. In the shadow of the storm cloud, they could see eerie blue lights passing up and down the far shore of the lake. The Nations had arrived.

It took half an hour to reach the palace, the air cooling all the while. The light of the moon was suddenly cut off by the looming presence of the vast structure above them. They passed up a broad avenue lined with poplars, and onto a flagstoned path in the shadow of the buttresses holding up the upper tiers of the palace. It reared up into the sky above them. Each tier housed line upon line of statues, staring like an army towards the lake. The features of the lower ones were just visible, depicting fiery gods and goddesses from the distant time when they had inhabited the earth. To their left was a huge arcade formed by the vaulting stone piers. More statues stood in the shadows. Huge entranceways blocked with vast walls of granite stood at the rear of the arcade. They walked for several minutes under the echoing buttresses and walls before they saw at the end of the arcade a glimpse of the night sky again. They had still seen no one.

The arcade opened out onto a terrace. Below them the hillside fell away. There was another startling view to the east. They could see miles over the forest, to where a vast plain glimmered in the moonlight far away. Above them a wide swath of marble steps doubled back on their route, climbing to a gloomy entranceway.

They climbed slowly to the top of the steps. A fountain trickled water into a grey granite basin. They were now on the same level as the upper tier of the palace. Its grey walls loomed before them. Three arched entranceways were set into the wall. Nemoc held the staff up to the light of the moon, and, instantly, fire blazed up and down its length, casting a gentle glow that illuminated a twenty-foot radius. He led them through the courtyard and under the middle arch and beyond. Instantly they were swallowed by the shadows.

Jayal held up Dragonstooth, its coppery red light adding to the light of the staff. They were in a vast chamber. It was completely empty, its pillared hallways fading into the darkness.

Here they halted and drew breath. Thalassa was barely able to stand, her breathing was strangled.

"Which way?" Urthred asked.

"The council chamber is in front."

"Are there any of your people here?"

Nemoc shook his head. "They have gone: only my Master is left."

"Keep your sword ready, anyway," Urthred said to Jayal. The young knight nodded grimly. They crossed the hall, and now they could see a faint white glow coming from its far end. An unpleasant odour grew as they approached. Nemoc stopped abruptly, and Jayal was hard-pressed not to run into his back.

"Why have you stopped?" he growled.

He looked at him. "Can't you smell it?"

Jayal breathed in deeply, the odour of death and decay, one he knew all too well from Thrull. "There is a dead body near," he said. "What of it?"

"No one dies in Lorn. Mortality has come to the land."

"A dead body does not scare me," Jayal said, gesturing for him to go on again. Nemoc swallowed nervously, but did so. In front a domed circular room opened up, paved with white marble. A body lay at its exact centre, on a mosaic of a sickle moon. Now they could see a white radiance in the distance, through another archway. Nemoc entered the room, holding his cloak over his mouth and nose, and peered down at the corpse.

"Who is it?" Jayal asked, pointing at the body.

Nemoc stared at it for a moment. "Whitearth," he breathed. "One of those who lived outside Lorn. I met him on the path before the Moon Mere. He was old and dying. He told me he was going to Lorn to warn the people that the Nations were coming."

"He got here all right."

Nemoc nodded sadly. "The townfolk must have fled in terror when they saw him."

"Let us find your master."

But meanwhile Urthred had led Thalassa towards the glowing chamber where a cold white light blazed from within. The walls of the farther chamber seemed to be made of ice stretching away in a great wave down one wall, the leading edge closest to where they had entered. But then they saw that it wasn't ice at all but a plastic substance that slowly twisted and writhed at the end nearest them. Darker images smudged the whiteness, and, looking closer, they saw the dark areas were forms slowly emerging out of the white light.

Thalassa had rallied slightly and was staring at one particular part of the wall. In it, just as one might view someone long-frozen in a glacier, three faces had emerged from the ice. Her face and Urthred's and Jayal's. It was like looking into a mirror. Farther back, one entire area was black. Purple forms were fixed in the dark, full of malevolent life. The Nations.

"Come," Nemoc said. "My master waits in the upper reaches of the palace. It's not far." He gestured towards a flight of steps leading upwards just beyond the entrance to the crystal chamber.

They climbed them, feeling again a fresh breeze on their faces. At the head of the stairs was a shadowy antechamber. Beyond, moonlight fell through colonnades which gave onto a wide balcony overlooking the lake. A figure sat hunched on a chair on a stone throne, raised on a dais in the middle of the terrace, its face tilted up to the moon. The face glowed eerily and they saw it wore a silver mask.

"Master?" Nemoc called out, and the figure stirred, and turned its face, so the moon glinted off the mask, revealing its delicate craft: the diamond-shaped face, the high cheekbones. Only the eyepieces, dark and threatening, betrayed the merest flicker of life.

They stood thus in silence for a few seconds, the Watcher staring at them, but particularly, as it seemed to him, at Urthred, as if his mask had an affinity to the one the priest wore.

"You are Urthred: Urthred of Ravenspur. You have brought the Lightbringer," the man said eventually.

"You know my name. How?" Urthred asked. A premonitory shiver went up his spine as the figure rose, and approached slowly.

"How? Because I gave it to you," the Watcher said, the eyepieces of his mask locked on Urthred's.

CHAPTER FORTY-SIX

The Silver Chalice

A stunned silence greeted the Watcher's words. After a few seconds he spoke again. "I am your father, Urthred. You have arrived from where you set out, twenty mortal years ago. You've come home."

"But my name is Ravenspur, not Lorn."

"Ravenspur was where I lived in the Mortal World."

Urthred shook his head, his mind whirling. "But I had a vision on Ravenspur: a woman by a lake. She gestured at me, warning me not to go to the summit," he murmured.

"The ghost of your mother, Meriel, warning you to keep away from that place."

"The tale is so strange . . ." Urthred began.

But the Watcher held up his hand, motioning him to silence. "Strange to a mortal, but not one who has lived ten thousand years and who has suffered two hundred different bodies. It is a long story, one that should take a day of your time to tell, but you have seen what evil comes. Once there was no time in Lorn, but now even I, who have lived so long, know how short it is before the end."

The silver mask sank to his chest as he gathered himself, then he looked again at Urthred and told him everything of his origins; how Reh had come and showed him how Urthred would lead the Lightbringer to Lorn in its time of danger, how Meriel had lived and begun to die in Lorn; and how she and Nemoc had gone back into the Outland with the two boys.

How after her death, Nemoc had taken the children over the mountains to Forgeholm.

But at that point his tale was interrupted by a curious choking noise from Nemoc. They all turned to stare at the white-haired man. They saw tears glistening in his eyes.

"Forgive me, master. I have hidden the secret too long." He took a faltering step towards the Watcher, and sank to his knees. "It was not I who went to Forgeholm. I abandoned the children on the mountain and fled."

The Watcher stared at him. "Then if you didn't take the children, who did?"

It was Urthred who spoke. "A creature of darkness—the monks at Forgeholm used to tell the tale to fright my brother and me. They spoke of its eyes like coals and the dark charger he rode, like the one of the mounts of the apocalypse."

The Watcher's gaze had never left Nemoc's tear-stained face. "You gave my sons over to my enemy?"

Nemoc was incapable of saying anything. The Watcher nodded slowly, as if finally understanding something. "So that is how the Master knew you were coming. You were given over to his power, he marked you as his own; all these years his spirit has watched you from Shades, watched for your return to the Northern Lands and drew you up to Ravenspur."

"Yes, he saw my coming," Urthred replied, "and he tempted me, yet I resisted him. The vision of my mother saved me, I knew what I was looking for was here in Lorn."

The Watcher nodded slowly. "You saw your destiny—you did well." He reached out a hand hesitantly towards Urthred, but, before it made contact, he wavered, and the hand fell. He turned away, his voice strained and hoarse. "Now listen to the rest of my tale. We are fated to meet only now, when the kingdom of Lorn is nearly finished.

"I have lived and died many times, and each time I have been reborn. Ten thousand years ago I was the

king of that land called Ravenspur. Even then, my
queen was called Meriel, the woman who was your
mother: she was a sorceress, one of the Witch Queens
of the North. She could make flowers grow from
naked rock and tears turn to honey, could bring the
dead back to life: such was her power. Yet she was
not of Reh, but of that people who worshipped the
God of the Moon.

"But the gods brought strife to the world. They de-
vised tournaments for their idle gratification, and these
events became bloodier and bloodier. Thousands of their
servants died, and their great machines sent tremors
through the earth. Then that day arrived when the strife
boiled over. Bitter that day, Urthred, when the dawn
sky was like marching flame coming from Shandering
Plain, and the air was rent with the dying anguish of
the gods.

"As I wept that day a vision came to me: it was the
God, Reh. He told me that Erewon, the God of the
Moon, was dead and his kingdom empty. That was
where we would have to go, for neither the sun nor
the moon would shine for a thousand years. There he
would draw a canopy over the firmament and there
we must live away from the sun, awaiting its rebirth.
But those who did not follow Reh could not enter.
And I knew what this meant: Meriel my queen could
not come with me.

"Without my telling her, she knew. Beneath that
fiery sky she turned to me, and I saw a sad light in
her face, for she saw that we would be separated, until
the circle of prophecy returned again. She told me that
she would return one day from the lake under the summit, where her garden stood. She would come in the
Dark Ages of the world, to save man from the darkness and the dying sun. Then she kissed me once and
went down from the summit. I saw her a long way
below, her white robe glowing in the twilight that had
settled on the world. Then she was gone. I called my
people and led them away from that place and into
Lorn and never once looked behind.

"A hundred, hundred times I have lived and died only to wake again. And each time I have been the Watcher, waiting for the rebirth of the sun. Always on this terrace, the moon, and not the sun, our only light. All other memories fled away in that interminable time, yet Meriel's face never died. Each time I woke again in a new body, there it was burned forever in my mind.

"Many incarnations later, another vision, a voice calling me to travel into the Outland. I went through the Moon Mere. Saw the Mortal World for the first time in ten thousand years. My body withered, and I became hunchbacked and deformed. How would Meriel accept me now, I wondered? But yet I travelled on, under the mortal sun until I came to Ravenspur and found her there, where I had last seen her, by the edge of the lake. I thought she would spurn me, ugly creature that I was, no better than those of the Nations. But she took me by the hand and we returned to the borders of Lorn. Reh's curse, which had forbidden her to enter ten thousand years before, was finally lifted, and we passed through the mere. We came to the city and for a little while lived in bliss.

"Two children were born, you and Randel, but the curse came upon her, the curse of age, and she left me, left me alone, waiting for you to return with the Lightbringer."

Urthred knelt, tears rolling down his ravaged cheeks behind the mask. "It is as Manichee promised. Now I know the mysteries of my origins. Yet one thing I don't understand."

"Speak it."

"Why did the Master of Ravenspur let me go?"

The Watcher was silent for a little while. "The time is coming when you will hear his tale from his own lips. But know this: the Master is my brother. He remained in Ravenspur and died, swearing revenge on me and my people. And so, as it now appears, when Randel and you were left in his power, he thought to draw you back there one day, and turn you against the Lightbringer and so destroy the one hope of Lorn. But now he knows that though he, too, will be destroyed, so, too, will Lorn, for the Man of Bronze will follow Thalassa to the north, and the firmament that Reh set in the sky will be destroyed and Lorn returned to the Mortal World."

Thalassa now spoke, her voice very weak. "I will not take the Man of Bronze from you," she whispered.

The Watcher shook his head. "Lorn is finished. But you have work to do. You must follow the baron to the north, to Iskiard."

"Why did my father go?" Jayal asked.

"It is not easy for a mortal to live in Lorn," the Watcher answered. "The absence of time would bring anyone to the brink of madness. And the absence of time corrupts. Look at my people. They have lost all purpose, cannot now defend themselves even when great danger arrives. He knew time passed in the outside world—that he had to hurry on to Iskiard."

"But he needed the sword!" Jayal protested.

The Watcher lowered his head. "The Rod of the Shadows, too, is a weapon of the gods. No mortal should wield it. All the time your father was here he would not relinquish it though his face and hands were badly burned. It was as if his sole purpose in living were contained in that thing. He never gave up his faith in you. He watched the crystal chambers, seeking your image, praying that it would appear. Then one day an image did appear: you with my son and the Lightbringer. He left soon after."

"Why didn't he wait?"

"Though time stands still in Lorn, the Rod was killing him. But he left a message for you. I will fetch it now." He hobbled into the darkness, followed by the others. The room was lined with writing desks and high bookcases, filled to overflowing with ancient scrolls. "The records of my people," he said, gesturing at the disorder. He approached an ornately carved desk sitting alone at the end of the scriptorium. On it, as if in readiness for their arrival, was an ancient battered scroll case. In the light of the staff and sword they saw it still carried the Illgill crest of the salamander on its side. "Here," he said, picking it up and offering it to Jayal. The young knight's hands trembled slightly as he took it.

Jayal hesitatingly pulled open the leather thongs holding down the lid of the scroll case and drew out a yellowed roll of vellum. He strode out to the terrace, where the moon gave him enough light to read the message.

After a few minutes he let it furl back on itself. He held it out to Urthred. "Read it, priest: it concerns us all." The priest took it, and gingerly parted it again with the pincers of his gloves. The writing was barely legible, as if penned by someone in the height of a consuming fever. Ink spots splashed the page, and the letters were scratchy and nearly indecipherable. This is what he read:

"My son: I do not know what day I write this, nor how long I have been here. There is no time in Lorn. We passed through the mere on the night of the full moon. The Rod allowed our passage, for this is how Marizian must have travelled many years before. The Watcher welcomed us, tended our wounds.

"Now I have seen your image in the Crystal Chamber. You are coming to Lorn, but I will have left before you come. I have seen the great dangers you have endured, I have seen the Shadow that stalks you. Manichee was right. The Rod is a curse, has cursed us both. But whatever the curse, you must follow me, to the north. I have seen the secrets in the crystals, why the sun dies and what must be done to rectify things. Whether I can do this alone is in doubt. Bring the Man of Bronze and the sword: when they are reunited with the Rod, our enemies will perish by them.

"I go tomorrow through a portal like the one through the lake. Whether it leads to our world or another I do not know, nor care as long as it leads me to Iskiard. There is little time." There the message ended.

"You have heard the words of the baron, humans," the Watcher said, his voice sad.

At that moment they heard a sinister drumbeat coming from the lower town. "I'd almost forgotten," he murmured, "the people. Now my hour has come. . . ."

Nemoc knelt before him. "Master, can you forgive me for what I did?"

The Watcher nodded slowly. "Perhaps I had known it all this time, though I never saw it in the crystals—I forgive you. Go now, see how near the townsfolk are."

Nemoc hastily scrambled to his feet and went to the edge of the terrace. "There are lights in the lower reaches of the palace," he said.

"You were gone too long," the Watcher said sadly. "Since Whiteearth came they know my powers have gone. They are determined I will die. They didn't believe me when I told them the Lightbringer would come. They don't realise that tonight Lorn will end, its ten thousand years over."

"But the Second Dawn has not come, master," Nemoc said.

The Watcher pointed at Thalassa. "She is the Second Dawn that we have waited for: now the circle is full. We must hurry: soon the cloud will cover the moon. The lake will freeze over, the Dark Ones will cross it and the Lightbringer will be lost." He turned to Thalassa. "You will not save this kingdom, but you may save the world. But just like Reh, who suffered his serpent's bite in the battle of the gods, you have been wounded by Iss. But there is a cure. There is a cup here which Reh drank from as the Worm's venom burned his blood. It cured him as it will cure you."

The Silver Chalice?"

"The same. Come, I will take you to it." He led off into the darkness, towards the gloomy heart of the palace. The others followed. They passed through a series of halls the size of cathedrals, where the merest spattering of moonlight fell from the ceilings to the marble floors. Their footsteps echoed loudly in the vast spaces.

They entered a large room, its roof upheld by a thousand pillars. At its centre stood a deep well in the floor. A silver light filtered up from below. They peered down and saw a steep drop and, a hundred feet below, a silver well, glowing like a newborn sun.

Thalassa flinched away from its radiance. "The light!" she breathed, "it will blind me."

Urthred peered down into the depths. Beyond the glow, he saw a low stone altar at its bottom some six feet wide and eight feet long. The light was streaming from a silver bowl, which stood on the altar.

"The Chalice," he muttered.

The Watcher nodded. "As I said, Reh himself drank from it. It will bring he who drinks from it a second life. It is said the God toasted Iss with it before the final battle of Shandering Plain. And after the battle, as he lay wounded from the serpent's sting, he sipped from it and lived."

Urthred steadied Thalassa and turned to the Watcher. "How do we get down?"

"By faith, and faith alone: you must step out into the well: that is all I know, for no one has ever gone down into it as long as Lorn has existed."

"Very well," Urthred said. He turned up the sleeves of his cloak, revealing the harnessing of his gloves. "Now you will see what creature I am," he said to his father. "No better than one of the Nations."

"No, you are not like them. You are burned only on the outside."

Urthred looked at him for a second or two, then stripped off the gloves, revealing his mutilated arms and fingers. He turned to Thalassa. "Take my hand," he said quietly.

"I cannot go. The light is too strong."

"You are a creature of the light. Would Reh harm you? Close your eyes and trust me," he said. Falteringly, she held out her hand, and he took it gently in his fingers, marveling at the softness against the cal-

luses of his scars. He turned to the others and inclined
his head, then took a step forward into thin air, still
holding Thalassa's hand.

Instead of plummeting like a stone, they fell gently,
as if the light buoyed them up. They sank down and
down until their feet touched the ground and they
stood before the gleaming bowl.

The light was otherworldly: its silver was not quite
silver, but an ethereal translucence, as if light had
been captured underwater and imprisoned in its shape.
He reached forward his free hand and touched its
edge. It seemed to melt before his touch, his hand
distorting as it entered the bowl as if it was submerged
in silver liquid. He felt a delicious coolness caress his
fingers and run up his arm. He immediately felt refreshed, the fatigue of their flight washing away.

He let go of Thalassa's hand and stripped off his
mask. He drew the light to his face and felt the liquid
wash over him. Then, cupping his hands, he held some
of the liquid up to her.

"Wash yourself," he said, touching her skin with
some of the water. Her eyes were still clenched shut
against the light.

She shivered as she felt it touch her skin. Her eyes
opened, and she stared unflinching at the horror of
his face. Then she lowered her head over the basin
and brought up some liquid in her cupped hands to
her face. It was not wet to the touch, but felt like a
thousand jewels passing through her fingers and over
her skin. And where it touched her, she felt the taint
wash away and the fever die. She brought some of the
liquid to her lips and drank. It was like pure liquid
fire, burning away the infection inside her.

And as the liquid coursed through her, she had another vision of Reh, of the land before the final battle.
It seemed the gleaming face of the God smiled and
he raised his hand, saluting her, then vanished. And
in that moment she knew she was cured.

Now Urthred leaned towards the bowl: his true face
loomed in the refracted light of the surface. It was the

mouth he saw first, a shattered hole, with shreds of skin puckering and twisting around exposed rows of teeth, then the black and red of the cheeks, the cavity where the nose should have been and the badger patches of unburned skin around the eyes.

He uttered a prayer to Reh, then cupped his hands and, dipping them into the bowl, brought them to his face. The chamber was bathed with more of the underwater light refracted from the bowl.

As he washed, the reflected ripples grew ever stronger as the translucent waves bounced around its edges, casting striations and patterns around the well, chasing the shadows in the pillared hall above. He washed and washed compulsively, as if he were washing all the sins of the world away. As he washed he muttered to himself and, there came a sound, a moan, a terrible sound even to his own ears, as the tight scar tissue on his face burned with fire, a hundred times greater than the agony of the Burning itself. Then the motions of his mutilated hands stopped, and he straightened and relatched the mask.

He turned to Thalassa, who stood to one side. He expected her to flinch away, but she looked at him directly, a small smile on her face. She was transformed, a thing of pure radiance. "Now you have seen my true face," he said.

"Soon you won't need any more masks, priest," she said, and took his hand. "As the Chalice has cured me, so it will cure you. Now let us go."

She lifted her head and looked up. A cone of light fell from the distant ceiling above, bathing them. Then their feet lifted from the ground and they rose, as gently as they had descended. Jayal, the Watcher and Nemoc stood at the lip of the well, covering their eyes against the glare of the light as they appeared.

The three remained silent as Urthred handed Thalassa back onto solid ground.

Thalassa turned to the Watcher. "I am cured by Reh's will. Let us go—go to the Man of Bronze and bring the sun once more to Lorn."

The Watcher inclined his head. "He waits for you, as he has waited these last thousand years." He motioned to them, and they passed back through the vast halls and out onto the balcony where they had first met him.

The moonlight glittered outside. It would not shine for much longer. Groping tendrils of cloud stretched from the south, enveloping its glowing face. A broad swath of the lake was already frozen. Even at this distance, they could see a rank of spectral figures leaning over its surface, breathing frost upon the waters, sending out spider's webs of frost further and further towards the island. Sulphurous flames burned in the fringes of the woods and in the reeds, and purple smoke floated across the water. The Watcher and the others stood, huddled together against the cold blasts of wind coming from that direction. They listened for the sound of the drum they had heard earlier, but for the moment the palace was eerily silent.

The Watcher turned to them. "Go now, to the Isle of Winds. There is a barge down by the lakeside, Nemoc will show you the way. Though a tempest rages in its waters, do not be afraid. The Lightbringer will protect you."

"Aren't you coming with us?" Urthred asked.

The Watcher turned to him. "You have heard what fate awaits me. I cannot escape it: the people will have their sacrifice."

"The people don't deserve your death: the sun will return soon—save yourself."

"Nevertheless, they are my people. I must be with them when Lorn is lost."

"Lorn may be saved yet."

He shook his masked head. "Not even the Man of Bronze can save us now. Go to the island, follow Baron Illgill, take the Man of Bronze through the portal to Iskiard."

Thalassa interrupted him. "No! I will command the Man of Bronze to fight your enemies. Lorn will be saved, you will live to rule it again."

As she said this they all heard a noise drifting up from the lower stretches of the palace. The drum again, beating a funeral dirge, but now growing louder as it passed along the path under the buttresses below them. They hurried to the edge of the terrace and peered down. They saw a thousand torches passing below them, heading towards the entrance to the palace.

"Go quickly, they are coming now to finish me," the Watcher said urgently. "It is tradition: the Watcher will die so his people may live."

"We still have time," Thalassa said. "Come with us to the Isle of Winds."

Another blast of freezing wind blew over the terrace, making them all huddle in their cloaks. The air was heavy with the sudden scent of autumn. Even as they watched, the first few snowflakes whirled in the air.

"How long before the lake freezes?" Urthred asked.

"Ah, Urthred, you should know by now: there is no time in Lorn: the only time will be when the moon goes out. But it will be soon."

"Come with us, master," Nemoc pleaded. Already his face had begun to sag like a bloodhound's: the darkening of the moon had begun the aging process, returning him into the shape of the creature they had first seen at the lake.

The Watcher nodded, relenting. "Suddenly I hold time precious, just when I had given up hope. I will be with you a little while longer, Urthred. Lead on, but promise me one thing: if we meet with my people, let them have me. Only make sure she is safe," he said, looking at Thalassa.

The Watcher wrapped his cloak tightly around his body, indicating to Nemoc he should lead off. He wondered if he would have the strength to make the crossing. Only he knew how weak he was becoming. Only three times before had he gone to the Isle of Winds: the last time with the baron: not long ago, by these humans' reckoning. In front of the mask, his breath,

unfamiliarly, clouded the cold air. The trembling of
his limbs told him what he already knew: an old man
lived under this mask, his body was as moon-ravaged
as his face and mind. His son must never see it. He
shuffled across the deserted expanse of the piano nobile after Nemoc. The others followed close by him.

The shadows were empty in front, but the noise of
the dirgelike drum was closer now, near the end of
the ceremonial stairs. And that was the way they
would have to go down. He urged the others forward,
forcing quickness into his own step. Down the flight
of broad marble steps, the shadows sinister in the
moonlight. In each he imagined an assassin with a
knife waiting to plunge the instrument into his heart.
A strange calm entered him. He would meet whatever
fate unflinchingly.

They passed the antechamber to the crystal rooms.
Here was that cloying scent of death again. Why had
Whitearth come? There would have been peace in
Lorn for a little while longer if he hadn't. Peace at
least until the Moon Mere had opened and the Black
Cloud appeared in the south. Whitearth had brought
death with him. Through the open doorway he could
see the hunter's body, surrounded by his kills, laid out
in a fan around his corpse. Now Whitearth was as
dead as the animals he'd lived off. Justice? There was
no justice, nowhere in the land; the God would never
return. He paused, gasping for breath, looking at
Whitearth's corpse: would he soon be like this? The
body seemed to writhe slowly as the maggots devoured him. Twice already he had passed that body
in his trips to study the crystal vats: each time the
sight of the corpse had sent a silent shudder wracking
his limbs. The sound of the drums echoing through
the arcades below grew ever louder.

He nodded, showing that he was ready to go on.
Another broad flight of stairs. They descended, the air
getting fresher the lower they got until they faced a
wrought-iron gate. There the Watcher took a key from
his pocket: he had used it only three times in his many

lives, tonight would be the fourth and last. It slipped into the lock but it was as if the mechanism had been oiled and greased every day, for the bolt clicked open silently and easily, and he passed through into a covered walkway overhung with orange blossoms and vines that dropped, blasted by a white hoarfrost that hung tenaciously to all the plants. He motioned for the others to follow.

His trailing cloak disturbed fallen leaves, sending them skidding along in front of him in the breeze. He reached another gate set in the garden wall of the palace. The key did its silent office again, and now they were in the town itself, the houses quiet to either side, unlike the three previous occasions on which he had left the palace: how the laughter and song from the town had tugged at his lonely heart then. But now he had contentment—his son had returned, then, in a little while, he would be with Meriel again. Destiny was fulfilled.

Down and down they went until he heard the lapping of the water on the lakeside and saw the fishing boats bobbing up and down at the wooden quays. Already the water looked like it was covered with a sheen of oil, so sluggishly did it move under the swell. The ice was slowly forming. Beyond, the far lakeshore was lit with hellish fires.

They paused in the shadow, looking at the frozen edge of the lake and the legions waiting there to swarm over into Lorn. In front the quayside was deserted. There were no townspeople in sight. To their left stood a dark stone building with crenellated machicolations. No windows were visible, just a solitary iron door facing them. He gestured for the others to ready themselves, and they hurried forth from the shadows. Behind them he heard a shout, and looking back, they saw a knot of figures that had just rounded the line of buildings there.

"Quickly!" he cried, and set off at a run. His feet took him over the intervening distance with him barely noticing their movement. All he was focused

on was the iron key in his hand, the lock of the door
acting like a magnet that tugged him towards it. He
thrust the key into the mechanism as the others
formed a protective semicircle around him. Once more
the lock gave easily, and he desperately pushed open
the door. The others tumbled in and thrust their
shoulders against the gate as the footsteps behind got
louder. It shut with a hollow clang. He turned the key
and heard the lock slide heavily back into position.

Darkness within, lit only by the young Illgill's sword
and the strange glow from Thalassa's skin that had
not left her since the room of the Silver Chalice. The
heavy silence was broken by the sound of muffled
footfalls outside, and then a hammering of fists on the
door, but the sound barely penetrated here. They were
safe for the moment.

The Watcher turned to the others. "Now, I must
take off my mask. Then you will see what no one else
has ever seen in Lorn. It will not be pretty." Nemoc
made as if to speak, but the Watcher gestured with
his hand, silencing him. He reached up and removed
his mask, which peeled away as easily as a second skin
from his face. He heard the others gasp, and knew
too well what they saw. Not a man fair like all the
others the God had created in Lorn, but something
else altogether.

His eyes were cold-white spheres—opaque and
blind, through which the moonglow, like a sepulchral
light, poured, deep into the heart of the old building.
His skin had a deathly pallor, and, like the craters of
the moon itself, was a mottled grey, sunken into
hollows.

"You see, I have watched the moon for an eternity,
and it has entered me, just as the fire has entered you,
my son," he said to Urthred. "Both of us were cursed
to wear masks, both were cursed by what lay underneath. But you," he said fervently, "you will be
healed."

Urthred made as if to speak, but no words came. All
he could do was look with pity into his father's eyes.

The Watcher turned to the back of the building. There was a basin of oily black water thirty feet away. Beyond it, massive iron gates led directly onto the waters of the lake. A barge, covered in a film of grey dust, bobbed up and down in the gently undulating waters of the shallow harbour. It was some thirty feet long, its masts laid over its thwart, ready for raising once the vessel had cleared the doors that gave onto the lake. Four grey figures, wrapped like mummies in an ancient cloth, yellowed and frayed, stood as still as statues in various attitudes about the vessel: one appeared to have just finished furling a sail, another stood over one of the mooring ropes, his hand securing a knot. One was halfway out of the barge, hauling himself onto the side of the quay, another stooped about some unidentifiable task at the bottom of the boat.

The Watcher turned his gaze on the others, and they cringed back from the dazzling light of his moon-ravaged face. "Now I must wake the servants. They will take us to the Isle of Winds."

"What are they?" Jayal asked, fearfully glancing at the statues.

"They are revenants—ones that fell asleep and never woke again: now only magic will stir them."

The Watcher approached and stepped onto the thwart of the vessel. There came a sudden groaning sound, and the figures moved slowly to life, turning towards him. Now their faces were revealed: white and leached of colour, they appeared animated corpses. He had no idea how old they were, what knowledge was preserved behind the blank eyes, what crime apart from sleep they had committed to deserve this eternity of punishment, only broken after an abyss of time by visits like these.

Now the four revenants set about the tasks they had been pursuing before they had been frozen in time. Their atrophied bones creaked audibly, yet they moved purposefully, casting off the ropes from the quayside. As they did so, the humans and Nemoc

scrambled aboard. The hammering on the iron door
of the building was now louder.

The Watcher took station at the prow of the vessel,
and with an expansive motion of his right hand, the
iron gates over the lake groaned open. The waters of
the lake stood revealed in the moonlight. The revenants poled the barge out through the narrow opening,
and set to work stepping the twin masts and unfurling
the sails as the Watcher walked back to the stern. One
of the ghostly figures joined him and grasped hold of
the large steering oar, turning the prow of the boat
into the wind. The brown sails caught and filled with
an explosive retort, and the barge keeled over slightly
as it came round at a sure touch from the helmsman.
Suddenly the prow of the barge was cutting through
the waves, flying out into the lake. For the moment,
the Isle of Winds was hidden by a promontory, but the
harbour side was in plain view.

The Watcher looked back at the receding shore.
The townsfolk stood on the quay, their white robes
glowing in the subdued moonlight. They stared after
the barge, making no attempt to man the fishing boats
moored to the quay, as if accepting that for the moment they had missed their opportunity. He wondered
if they could see his face; what thoughts would they
have if they could see the cold light and the white,
moon-cratered blankness of it. Then he waved the
mask slowly above his head; there was a sudden vacuum in the air, then a squall of wind hurried over the
water from the island and came roaring down on the
town and the harbour, and the barge keeled right over
and sped away around the headland, its prow biting
into the waves.

They were in open water, the waves in the darkness
like hurtling black bulls that lifted the prow of the
barge violently, then threw it down again. Spray flew
backwards down its length. Two miles away, the spire
of rock known as the Isle of Winds rose out of the
churning waters, its two-thousand-foot cliffs and summit shrouded by swirling clouds. Even at this distance,

ferocious, combing whitecaps were visible, breaking
high up its granite cliffs. But as the boat sped towards
it, he held up the mask again, and the wind subsided in
an instant to a light breeze, leaving the barge crashing
through the rocky swell.

The vessel plunged and soared like a dolphin in the
uneasy motion of the waves. The Watcher cast another
anxious glance at the moon lost behind the clouds.
The light was almost gone, the chill deepening; he felt
it now on his back, like a frozen bar of iron—cold so
intense that it would eventually freeze even this turbulent expanse of water.

The others were in the waist of the vessel, crouching
low to avoid the spray. The Watcher stared at the girl,
so slim, so waiflike—yet the saviour of the world, the
Lightbringer. Urthred sat next to her, his eyes fixed
on the stern. He was staring at him, his father. Suddenly, the Watcher was filled with sorrow. Something
was exchanged between them in that look because,
heedless of the violent motions of the barge, Urthred
stood and, riding the swaying motion of the vessel,
approached him. He took a position next to him, gripping one of the aft halyards. They stood together in
silence for a moment.

"Come with us to Iskiard," Urthred said. "You
don't have to die."

"I have told you already," the Watcher replied.
"The people of Lorn cannot live in the Mortal World.
We only know this world with its endless moon—you
saw what Nemoc became in the Outland—there we
wither. But you will go on, you will be my spirit in
the outer world. Your enemies will bow before you.
Look after the Lightbringer. I have seen what she will
become. I saw her birth under a full moon like this,
when the planets conjoined: I felt Reh stir at her coming, for the divine spark was born in her, a spark that
Reh follows through the Dark Labyrinth of the night,
seeking the dawn, a spark that will inspirit him, will
make the sun shine constantly again, will make the

moon glow brighter in the sky, in answer to Reh's
golden light."

"Father, you have known many things—once looked
upon the face of the God. Answer one question."

The Watcher shook his head. "My memory has
gone. I have lived through too many lifetimes. But
ask: maybe I will know the answer."

"One mystery remains: the sun's dying."

The Watcher looked away. "Some say that the pallor over the sun was set there by Marizian. He dabbled
with magic in the lost city of Iskiard. But all those
who dabble in the God's secrets fall into temptation.
So one day long ago, Iss, having been banished forever
to the darkness of the nether regions of the skies,
projected himself through time and space and appeared before Marizian, flattering him to do what no
mere mortal ought. And so the God, who was otherwise powerless to influence the world of men from his
place of banishment, tricked him. Marizian had found
the portal to Shades. Iss told him that all the magic
of the gods was hidden within. He unlocked the door
to that place with the Rod of the Shadows. Therein
he saw what it was: how the souls of the damned flock
like autumn birds. They poured from that place, like
swallows in the sky, climbing higher and higher until
they hid the face of the sun. That is the cloud that
casts a shadow on the Outland: that is the doom of
the world, and the secret of the dying sun."

"Then that is why the baron took the Rod to the
north," Urthred said excitedly, "to seal the door
again."

"Yes, but he is only a mortal. Only the Lightbringer
can succeed in that task. Iskiard was destroyed by the
Shadows in a day," the Watcher continued. "And
Marizian fled south, fearing that the damned would
follow him and harrow his soul from this earth. The
rest you know: there in Thrull he wrote the Books of
Light and *Worms,* but corrupt priests changed their
words over the millennia until Iss was held up as a

god as great as Reh, and his false promises spread throughout the world."

"And the *Book of Light*?"

"It, too, was changed, and corrupted. But buried in all the falsehoods there is wisdom. And the words concerning the Lightbringer are true."

"What will she do?" Urthred asked, looking at Thalassa.

"She will go to Iskiard, where the portal still stands open to the Mortal World. The baron already battles with the creature set to guard the place, but only Thalassa can succeed in driving the damned back into Shades. Then the sun will be reborn again." He followed the direction of Urthred's gaze down the length of the barge. "You are fond of her, are you not?"

Urthred turned and faced his father. "You knew a love that did not die, though ten thousand years came between. Still you never forgot Meriel. So I feel for Thalassa, though I have known her a bare month."

"In another life, no doubt my child, you knew her," the Watcher said. He drew closer to Urthred. The pale orbs of his eyes suddenly dull, the blaze dying. Behind, Urthred saw the sad eyes of an old man, a man who had lived too long. "You see: I must rest now. Ten thousand years is too long to live. The Hall of the White Rose awaits. I will die the final death tonight. You are my successor. Live well and do not be bitter. You will lose more that you cherish, for it is said that the sun will only be rekindled by a sacrifice."

A sudden chill fell on Urthred. Involuntarily, he glanced at Thalassa, then back at his father, but the Watcher had turned away, and Urthred was too afraid to pursue the question. A heavy silence followed.

CHAPTER FORTY-SEVEN

✦

The Isle of Winds

The only sound was the wind humming in the rigging. They tacked again and again into the wind, the sails luffing at the end of each reach. Each tack bringing them closer to the Isle of Winds. The shores of Lorn behind them were so distant it was as if they were alone in a great sea, save the towering cliff face in front of them nearly blocking off the light of the moon.

At the base of the island, between two rocky outcroppings, they could see a cave mouth protected by a massive iron grille some fifty feet high, rusty red even in the moonlight. Above it, the cliff face shone like polished marble in the light: sheer and jagged schist two thousand feet high. The only marks on the shining slopes were jagged fault lines and dark oblong openings through which the winds moaned and howled like the voices of the dying.

"Easy now," the Watcher called to the pale-faced servants. They tugged on the halyards, and the barge came about again as they hauled in the sails. They drifted slowly towards the gaping cave mouth, bobbing up and down gently on the waves. The Watcher picked his way slowly forward through the tangle of ropes and canvas to the prow of the vessel, the mask still held high above his head.

"Open now, ye gates that have stood since Reh departed the land," he shouted, his voice nearly lost in the low moaning of the wind through the holes in the cliff face. There came a distant roaring and the metal grille began in a series of juddering stops and starts to winch up into the dark ceiling of the cave. Showers of flaking metal fell from it, staining the churning waters red. As if controlled by an invisible hand, for the steerage from the sails had long dissipated, the vessel glided into the darkness. Yet even here the moon pursued them, slanting down on the oily waters within and illuminating a wide set of stone stairs that rose up above a mossy wharf. The barge kissed the stone of the wharf and came to a gentle stop.

The Watcher turned to the revenants. "Sleep again, for a little time," he said, and immediately they froze in mid-motion.

"Come, Lightbringer," he said to Thalassa. "The Man of Bronze is waiting."

He stepped onto the wharf, and the others followed, looking warily around them into the sepulchral gloom. The Watcher, too, looked up into the darkness, the moonglow pale on his face, showing every aged line, each dark crater. His heart beat painfully in his chest. He listened to the wind whistling down the great spire of rock. The Man of Bronze was high above.

He strained his ears for any sound, for any creak of the creature's mighty harness. The ratcheting of his metal hands as they rose, ready once more to beat the Hammer on the Forge, to send the wind that would dash them all to atoms. But there was only silence: the thing waited, sensing the Lightbringer. They were safe for the moment. But they had little time: every moment the warm air ceased to breathe over Lorn, the cold, the cold of an ice cap's heart, would settle like a vice upon the land and freeze the lake. And in that cold, the Nations would grow stronger, massing on the far shore of the lake, ready to cross over and destroy them.

He started to climb upwards, the mask held like a doffed cap in front of him, followed by the others. His nostrils were assailed by the tang of rotting iron, and he saw the great serrated columns of metal soaring up on either side of the circular stairwell, which, like a coiled python, rose and rose into the dark heights of the Isle of Winds, rusty red, exuding a corrosive stench that prickled his nose. The Forge of Reh: the lungs, the bellows that had once spread their warmth over this imperishable land. Every moment that the Man of Bronze laboured, this chamber would be a roaring inferno of supercharged air. None could hope to live near this place then. But, for the moment, all was quiet.

How long did they climb? An hour or more in mortal time, until they were halfway up the island. The metal columns with the shuttered mouths were silent save every few minutes when an errant whistling from somewhere in the huge labyrinth of metal pipes like a far-off moan would arrest them in mid-step. The sound echoed away, and they let out their breaths and continued upwards.

At last, they reached a huge bronze door at the head of the stairs. Fifty feet high, it had bevelled surrounds, the centre was a field of beaten embossed metal, hammered into an abstract pattern. The Watcher craned his neck up. No human hand could open it, but he waved the mask in an arc and there came another rumble and the doors started opening inwards, revealing a chamber beyond.

Three times before he had stilled the wind and come here, and each time the sight within had amazed him.

Here was the magic of another time: a single beam of light—was it the light of the moon?—fell straight down onto the floor from a tiny pinprick in the vaulted ceiling a hundred feet above their heads. Reh had commanded metal, had bent and forged it to his will. And here his work was preserved.

Huge cranes, levers and harnesses beaten from what looked like gold, hung from the metal gantries on the black granite walls. The looped ends of the four cranes would have held the torso of any creature that had ever lived, but here each was looped around one mere limb of the thing which stood in their midst.

It stood thirty feet tall at the very centre of the

chamber where the moonlight cast its form into sparkling radiance so that it looked more gold than bronze. Bronze greaves and vambraces covered the mighty arms and legs, over a hauberk of beaten metal that glittered a thousand suns in the light. A massive bronze coif weighing ten hundredweights hung around the neck, and a beaten-metal cuirass, shaped to its titanic musculature, was fitted over the glittering coat of mail. Each fist was the size of a cart, each foot was clad in iron sabatons, the size of a boat.

It held the Hammer upraised in one hand, a glinting silver metal mass which shone like the moon in contrast to the bronze metal of which it was made. The light fell onto the plinth in front of it, on which was mounted a glowing oyster-white dome: it swam with a blue-and-white energy, and dim shapes could be seen in its pearly depths. It was said Reh had taken it from the Heart of the World at the beginning of time when his touch had sparked the world into being in a fiery explosion. The Egg of the World.

Tingling energy warped the air in front of the Egg, so that nothing seemed still in that most still of all places. All of them felt a buzzing in their minds. Slowly, very slowly with shaking hands, the Watcher put the mask back onto his face. Only then did he dare look up above the coif of the towering creature in front of him, and contemplate the actual face of the Man of Bronze.

If the hands and feet had been huge, the face was as if carved from a great bronze monolith a story high. Each feature was chiseled, a square jaw, a straight nose, ruby eyes that glowed piercingly, throwing twin beams of light onto the far wall of the chamber. Its face was framed by a huge basinet, the open visor overshadowing the piercing eyes, further accentuating their glittering light.

The Watcher raised his hand slowly, and the huge head turned in their direction, the beams of light painting them in a violet light that seemed to burn on their cloaks. What had shown as dark wool and fur now shone mauve, every speck and weave glowing

whitely in the luminance. Each of them averted his
eyes except Thalassa, who lifted her head and met the
burning light of its gaze evenly. The glow upon her
skin was now even more golden, as bright as it had
been in the Lightbringer's shrine in Thrull. The
Watcher, his eyes clenched against the light, spoke the
words that he had learned so long before, in a time
he now barely recalled.

"Guardian of the Land, do you hear?"

"I hear." The voice boomed and echoed around the
metal and granite, like a crashing cymbal, like a thousand kettledrums; it rolled on and on, reverberating
through the metal vents and pipes till they took up its
bass echo, returning it to them again and again.

"I have come with the one you wait for."

There was momentary silence. They heard the grating of gears and a strange mastication from the thing's
metal jaws, as if it hovered on the edge of speech.
Then it spoke again. "Many things I see, Watcher. I
see the sword that Marizian once carried in another
time. I see another"—and it raised its free fist until it
hung there like a meteorite in the flashing light—
"whose hands are modeled on mine. They are welcome, they will be brothers in arms. There," it said,
gesturing again with one of its mighty hands, "in the
world outside, Reh's steeds have flown Harken's Lair.
Aye, things begin again—the tide has turned, Iss' kingdom comes to a close. The darkness will turn to light,
through her, the Lightbringer."

At this, Thalassa stepped forward. The creature regarded her through the burning cones of light that
were its eyes.

"I have come in faith, though I am only mortal,"
she said, bowing her head.

"No mere mortal have I waited for these long years,
Lightbringer. I who knew Reh and the other gods that
ruled here, before your seed was a seed in the seed
of your furthest ancestor—I knew them all. I fought
upon the plains in their jousts, was carried through
the air on the backs of their dragons. Then the dark-

ness came, Marizian's time, when the shadows entered the world in Iskiard. Many dark hours, hours that I have counted, though you cannot. Now the shadows have returned, and the dragons have wing once again.

"Reh saw you in the first spark of time when the fires gushed like fiery water from his hands, the stars bowed their heads to you at their birth. I will obey you, and together we will go to Iskiard. Though the gods be long departed, I was set upon this world to save your race."

Thalassa turned to the Watcher. "Release him." The Watcher inclined his head, and once more removed the mask. The thigh-thick steel cords that bound the Talos's arms fell with a thunderous clang to the floor, sending up a cloud of dust.

"My power over you is gone," he said to the Talos.

The creature flexed its titanic arms, feeling their sudden freedom. "I will obey you," it said, its eyes on Thalassa.

"The Nations of the Night have come to Lorn again," she said.

"Aye, I have seen them, just as I saw the dragons in the sky. When I came first to this land, through the Moon Mere, the Dark Ones were here, those cursed by Reh. I halted them with fire and the Hammer, with the furnace blast of my eyes. They perished in droves, fossilised to a one."

The Man of Bronze bowed its head to Thalassa with a mighty creaking of the rivets in the circular discs of its metal neck. "Though you are a creature of light, you must leave this place. There are two ways: one lies across the lake, where your enemies lie. But there is an easier way, one taken by the baron."

"The gateway?" Jayal asked, speaking for the first time. He looked around the chamber.

"It is here, in the shadows yonder, a hole in time through which you may pass. But soon you must decide to go through it or not. For I will strike the Anvil once more and make a mighty wind, greater even than the one the Lightbringer called for earlier. It will destroy this spire of rock, and the gateway forever. It will roll before me against my enemies: the lake will be divided, and a mighty wave will swamp them. I will march across the lake bed, which will be as dry as the dust of Shandering Plain, I will drive the Dark Ones back to Ravenspur."

"You will destroy Ravenspur as well?" Urthred asked, shielding his eyes against the blinding light with his gloved hands.

"Yes, that, too. I will seal the way from Shades through which his kind have come. They will never enter this world again. But I will spare Meriel's tomb. If you remain here, when the evening is gone, and Ravenspur destroyed, go there again, to its ruins, and you will find what you have sought all this time."

The others were staring at the priest in the white light of the chamber.

Again there was a pregnant silence, punctuated only by the whistling of the wind in the pipes like an organ tune, whispering far off, barely heard. Then Urthred spoke. "Thalassa, Jayal, you must go on without me, through the gateway, to Iskiard. I will return to Ravenspur once more."

"If you go back to Ravenspur, we will all go," Thalassa said.

"But what of the gateway? My father is waiting on the other side," Jayal protested.

Now the Man of Bronze turned to him. "We all wait, some for a day, some for a year or more. Some for an eternity. But if you would go, here is the way," it said, raising the Hammer high so it glinted in the darkness of the chamber. "This instrument, this Hammer: it is the door to the unseen world. A gateway through which all energies flow. Approach it if you dare, stare into its mysteries, choose the path you will take on the river of fire that is all around us."

"I cannot," Jayal said, squinting up at it. "The light blinds me, its heat will kill."

"Then you have not the faith of your father. But he had the Rod to guide him on his journey, the Rod that shows the paths beyond, paths that man has never seen. You have only the sword, but perhaps it will take you to him. But if you err from your path, beware; you will wander in that darkness forever, never being able to find your way home again. Choose, knight, do you dare this passage?" It lowered the Hammer so it glowed nearly at floor height. In its surface they could see winnowing lights, much as they had seen in Marizian's tomb.

For a moment it seemed that Jayal would go forward and touch it, but he wavered. His hands fell to his sides, and his shoulders slumped. "I have travelled here for nothing," he said. "I cannot pass through. Only the Rod could guide me to Iskiard."

The Man of Bronze turned to Thalassa and Urthred. "Will you go through the gateway?" it asked.

Thalassa spoke for them both. "No, we will follow you to Ravenspur."

"Then, go now," the Man of Bronze said, "before all of you are destroyed. And after the destruction, when Lorn is drowned, follow me to Ravenspur. There we will do battle, the four of us beneath the mountain; let the Nations come in battalions, they will not defeat our power."

It now turned to the Watcher. "Go to your palace, speak to your people. Tell them their immortality is at an end, Lorn will be destroyed, and they must flee to save themselves."

"I will do so," the Watcher said, inclining his head.

The Man of Bronze continued. "Tell them to go to where the Moon God is buried on the far shore of the lake. You and they will be safe there."

"What place is that?" Urthred asked.

"Erewon's Tomb: it is where Reh carried the Moon God after he was slain. Erewon, too, will live again when the firmament is destroyed. Once more the land will see the rise and fall of the moon and its many cycles.

"The people of Lorn must live henceforward in the Outland, and live under the sun as all men live." Its head swiveled towards Thalassa. "Lightbringer: send the signal from the top of Erewon's Mount, and I will strike. Now go!" And with this final interjection, it raised the Hammer threateningly above its head so that it reflected the furious light of the shining Anvil in front of him. The Watcher was the first to back away, then Nemoc, then the humans.

The Man of Bronze turned its great helm away from them and the cones of light from its eyes once more seemed to burn holes into the far wall of the chamber. The four of them hesitated only for a moment, then hurried away from the curving staircase up which they had come.

As they went they heard the metal vents and pipes of the island like a mighty organ humming with the sound of a mounting energy.

CHAPTER FORTY-EIGHT

❖

A Second Dawn
in Lorn

The Watcher's barge sailed across the lake. The wind thringed in the rigging, blowing from behind them, filling their sails, driving them back towards Lorn through the dark night. The moon was now nearly totally obscured by the cloud, and snow fell in blizzards from the slate grey sky. It was bitterly cold. Despite the Talos's promise to wait until they were in safety, each second they feared the striking of that last blow and the apocalypse to come.

But as each minute went by, no sky-splitting crack of thunder came from the Isle of Winds. They were approaching Lorn. Urthred stared at his father, wondering what he intended. As they rounded the headland, they saw, even in the deep darkness, what seemed like white glowworms moving on the shore by the jetties, and as they drew closer they saw what they were. The white cloaks of the islanders waiting for them.

The Watcher looked at them for a moment as the shore grew closer, then held up his hand, and the revenants pulled in the sails so they merely drifted slowly onwards.

"What will you do?" Urthred asked.

"I have promised the Man of Bronze: I must land and tell them that it is the end of Lorn."

"They will kill you."

The Watcher turned to Urthred. "The king of Lorn

must die, my son. You have seen that the moon has eaten my face and my bones, just as the fire once ate yours. Did you not feel in your days of suffering that death was preferential to an existence of such pain? I have felt that way for longer than I can remember. I will land. They will do what they must do."

"This is madness!" Urthred cried. "Call to them from here. Tell them the city is finished. Come with us to Erewon's Tomb."

"We are creatures of the moon: we cannot live under the sun. The contrast between our current state and what we became would be too much to bear. Did you not see what Nemoc became? A creature that not even the Nations would have called their own. Reh ordained that we should be fair and straight, not misshapen creatures, crawling under the sun."

"You cannot deny your nature, Father."

"As you cannot deny yours: my nature is to be the sacrifice as my people demand. Yours is to follow the Man of Bronze to the lands in the north. I will land. Go with Nemoc: he will show you to the tomb."

"But master, I cannot leave you. . . ." Nemoc began, but the Watcher cut him off with a wave of his hand.

"You betrayed me once—now help my son and the Lightbringer. By doing so, you will find peace and my forgiveness." Then he turned to the humans. "You will have to fight through the Nations at the Lakeside, but you have your powers: your magic, Urthred, Jayal, the sword of the moon, Dragonstooth. And you have her, the Lightbringer. When you reach the top of the mountain, call upon the Man of Bronze." Then he turned once more to Nemoc. "You and I were once friends. Redeem yourself: your punishment is enough: you alone of Lorn will have to live in the Mortal World again. Tell our history to those who will listen once the sun is cured; tell them of us, how we lived in glory after the gods departed the world. The world of men should know there was a race like ours."

Tears sprang to Nemoc's eyes. "Surely the people

will go with you if you tell them what is about to happen?"

"You know them as well as I. They think my death will cure all things. It is for the best: They cannot live disfigured in the world to come. Now take the barge after I land, to that spot beneath Erewon's Mount. Command it as you would have commanded it if you had been the Watcher, as you will be, for a little while."

"I shall, master."

"In the world outside, give reverence to the moon. Remember me when it is full."

"I will, master," Nemoc answered, hanging his head.

Now the Watcher turned, and held his hand up to the revenants who hauled the sails back onto the mainmast. Once more the prow cut through the lapping waves, and the tiered hill of Lorn came nearer, rising above them. But now its terraces were dark and barely a light flickered. The driving tendrils of cloud had enveloped the moon, the feeble light struggled in its choking hold, slowly dying. The silent figures on the quayside were still, as if in hushed expectancy of their arrival. They stood in a semicircle looking out on the boat flying towards them on the wings of the blizzard howling in from the south.

They were only a stone's throw from the quay when, at an unspoken command from the Watcher, the revenant at the tiller hauled it over with a subtle twist of his hand and the others lowered the sails. The boat glided gently to the side of the quay.

The Watcher was over the side of the boat onto the quay before the others could move. He stood for a moment, glancing back at Urthred, then once at the dying moon hanging over the city, then walked rapidly forward. The ranks closed around him silently. Not a sound was heard, only a slight commotion, an eddy at the crowd's centre as he was sucked into their middle.

Urthred cried out and turned to the others. Nemoc had not moved all this time, his eyes fixed on the place where his master had disappeared, one hand slightly

outstretched as if begging him to return. Then one or
two of the townspeople at the edge of the crowd
turned and stared at the barge. Nemoc looked like he
was about to call out something, but then his shoulders
slumped and he held up his hand, and the revenants
pushed the barge away from the quay, the sails once
more rattling up on their blocks.

More of those at the fringes of the crowd stirred
when they saw the sails unloosened, but by the time
they had begun to move forward the barge was making way, and the wind filled the sails and it heeled
over, its prow kicking up in the sharp swell that
howled in from the southern shores. Behind them the
people of Lorn stood by the water's edge, staring
after them.

The barge beat into the wind, fighting into the teeth
of the gale. Soon the city of Lorn had diminished to
a speck behind it, and with it, its doomed inhabitants.
The dark and sinister shore lay two miles in front of
them; the trees, the lake surface, the sky were all coal
black, so no distinction could be made when one
began and another ended.

None of them spoke, Urthred and Nemoc stood
next to one another shivering in the bitter air, too
stunned even for tears. Hoarfrost settled on the sails,
stiffening them so they didn't draw the wind properly.
Patches of ice floated by them on the surface of the
lake, and ahead, they saw that the choppy surface of
the water suddenly became calm, freezing over, assuming the appearance of glue. A white glow came
from deep beneath: ice was forming not only on the
surface but to the absolute depths. The next second
the keel drove fiercely into the shelf of ice, and the
masts broke off at their mountings, sending the rigging
and sails crashing into the well of the boat. One of
the revenants was knocked overboard. It sank like a
stone towards the bottom of the lake.

The humans and Nemoc scrambled back to their
feet. All around them the ice was thickening. The

thwarts of the boat splintered and cracked under its pressure; icy water burst in, soaking their feet.

Thalassa was the first to act. "Come," she said. "The ice is thick enough, we can walk to the shore." She held her hand out to Nemoc, who all this time had been staring numbly at the wreck of the boat, unable to move. Jayal and Urthred joined her at the prow, looking at the ice. It looked thick enough to take their weight. Thalassa stepped over the thwart, leading Nemoc. There was a faint cracking, but the ice held. Urthred and Jayal followed. The revenants remained in the barge, doomed to be crushed in the iron claw of the frozen water.

Apart from the glow of the ice, it was absolutely black ahead. Thalassa snapped her fingers. A small imp of whiteness suddenly appeared: the thing sparkled like a small star in her fingers before she released it, sending it hurtling forward into the driving gale coming from the south. All around it, a circle of light disproportionate to its size fell on the ice field and the farthest shore. They were still a long bowshot away.

They started off, picking their way between monstrous hummocks and shards of frozen water pushed up by the unrelenting pressure from the south. "Which way?" Thalassa asked Nemoc.

"There," he said, pointing at a high cliff rising from the shoreline. "That is where the Watcher told us to go."

The outlines of the ruins could be seen from its top, silhouetted in the moonlight.

They picked their way towards it through the arctic landscape, their breath frosting the air. Urthred and Jayal were now in front, their eyes searching the dark shoreline for danger. Yet even the ghostly lights that they had seen earlier had disappeared as if they had been doused, ready for their arrival. All was sinisterly quiet. They reached the shore: the frozen sand was like concrete underfoot and the reeds by the lakeside as hard as iron bars.

"Where are they?" Jayal asked, his sword quarter-

ing the ground in front of them. But nothing stirred;
it was as if whatever force waited for them hung back,
assessing their strength. But what strength did they
have? There were only four of them.

The only sound for the moment was the groaning
ice behind them and a strange tinkling sound like wind
chimes from in front. Jayal thrust forward the sword,
and in its light they saw that the sound was made by
the frozen forest leaves falling onto the rock-hard
ground.

"He is here, I can feel him," Urthred said.

"Who?" Jayal asked.

"The Master. He is in the air, in the ice, every
breath we breathe."

"Come," Nemoc said, "the Man of Bronze must
strike soon."

He led them off to the left, and presently they saw
a gap in the solid line of the trees and a pathway
heading towards the dim outline of the mountain.

They approached the gap in the tree line cautiously.
They could sense safety in the air, like a smell. They
were so close. But just then, there came the rattling
of what sounded like bones from the darkness. It
drowned even the strange tinkling of the frozen leaves
falling to the ground.

They stopped dead in their tracks. The rattling came
again. Then out of the darkness came a thin creature.
Its emaciated face was green, sunken eyes shadowed
by a pointed hood, its body wrapped in the folds of
its cloak, dragging behind it an articulated skeleton
held to its wrist by a rusty chain. Its eyes glowed in
the moonlight as it stared at them. "Will no one take
this burden from me?" it said plaintively, nodding towards the skeleton it dragged behind. It gave it another tug, sending another bony rattle into the silence.

"One of the damned," Nemoc said.

"Just take this burden from me, and I will be free,"
it said again, beseechingly.

"The Master is weak—his creatures cannot approach the Lightbringer. That is why they try to snare us with these tricks," Nemoc said.

"Enough talk," Jayal said. He strode forward, the sword in front of him. But as he drew level with it, there came a tremendous blast of icy wind, and a thick wall of snow obscured the scene. When it had passed over them they saw the cloak had emptied and fluttered to the ground; the bones of the skeleton lay scattered around it.

"Where has it gone?" Jayal asked, looking in all directions.

"Cover your faces," Nemoc shouted. "It has become a spirit again—it will enter your ears and mouth; it will take your soul. And once it has eaten away your soul, you will become another like him, dragging your skeleton behind you, moaning for release." They flung their cloaks about their faces and hurried past, giving the skeleton a wide berth.

But that was only the first test. To begin with the forces they sensed lurking on either side of the dark avenue of trees kept at bay, though they felt a thousand eyes upon them, but presently they saw the way blocked by winged forms, their spans some ten feet across, their eyes dark red in the pitch-darkness. They halted, confronting the new foe who flew forward.

As the red lights of their eyes fell upon them, they, too, felt the skin stretch over their skins and a stony hardness enter every artery and limb. Basilisks! Their blood began to turn to a liquid stone, and they found their limbs would not obey them. But the transformation seemed to take no hold on Thalassa: she strode forward alone and with a flick of her fingers the light in front of her exploded in a sudden flash of white over the creatures, with a dull retort. Superheated air rushed past them, and fragments of matter. Suddenly the rest of them could move again. Their eyes adjusted to the near darkness: the air was full of particles of what looked like ash floating down from the air. The way ahead was clear.

"He is only playing with us," Urthred said. "He

wants us to suffer before the end." Sure enough, at
that instant, a hail of black rain thundered down on
them from the sky. More creatures began emerging
from the woods. Disembodied purple shadows seeking
for their souls, and the screaming skulls they had seen
before came swooping upon them like swallows on the
wind. With them came fly-headed creatures with the
bodies of men, which spat a pestilent cloud towards
them. This surely was death, but Thalassa once more
advanced fearlessly towards them.

"They cannot harm me," she shouted. "I am the
Lightbringer." Sure enough a gap began to slowly
emerge in the ranks in front as if there was an aura
several feet ahead of her which pushed them back,
however hard they strove to approach her. Then
Urthred understood: that is why the Master had tried
to set him against her, had sent Faran into the underworld. He knew, once Thalassa was cured, her powers
would be too great; he couldn't defeat her now. He
had needed others to do that for him, human creatures
like Faran and he, if he had fallen to the Master's
temptation.

Now they passed down a narrow tunnel surrounded
on all sides with the spirits of the damned screaming
and wailing but unable to get any closer to them. They
reached the beginning of the pathway climbing up to
the ruins. As Thalassa's foot touched the first step,
many of the creatures melted away into the darkness
behind. Now only one or two of the ethereal shapes
followed, hovering in the air, shrieking and howling.

It took them the better part of two hours to make
their way up the winding track to the summit of the
mountain. Now only one silent spirit followed, hovering to one side, like a malignant firefly.

Their ascent was silent; each was locked in their
separate thoughts. As they ascended the view unfolded more and more below them: a deathly hush
presided over the near shoreline. The cold blasts of
wind rippled the surface of the lake below them into
a corrugated ice mirror. No warm breeze had come

from the Isle of Winds for many hours. Sinister lights still moved up and down the shore, waiting for the ice to reach Lorn. Far in the distance, like distant whales on the horizon, were the dim shape of islands, awaiting their fate; to the north the land was obscured by the choking mist. Harsh screeches filled the air, but save for the one hovering spirit, they remained below: nothing dared follow the Lightbringer.

Above them the jumbled rocks of the mountainside fell away in chaotic scree slopes to the surface of the lake below. Some hundred feet ahead they could see the pediment of a building poking up over the shoulder of the mountain. The slopes and the path ahead were surrounded by ruined walls and fallen arches. They started climbing the remaining steps. They could see that the roof of the place had fallen in, leaving only two mighty rows of pillars and the black sky above.

As they approached the top of the steps, a figure appeared above them. The moon had been obscured a long time before, but the barest silhouette of the man was still visible. He was clothed in a white robe which fluttered in the freezing wind. At the man's sudden appearance the spirit that had followed them fled back down the slope with a shriek.

"Who comes to Erewon's Tomb?" the figure asked, its face not pointed to them, but to the hidden moon. The voice was gentle and ethereal, a thing of the breeze itself, so much so that they could hardly hear it.

"We come for refuge," Thalassa said.

"Who are you?"

"People from the Southern Lands beyond the Moon Mere."

"Ah! No, you are more than that. You who glow with the moonglow, you who have imprisoned its light which is the reflection of my brother Reh. I know you," it said, still not looking at her. "You are the Lightbringer. The end of Lorn is come."

"Who are you?"

"I am Erewon, God of the Moon, the moon that

changes, is a sign of mutability. My bones have sat
singing to that full moon for an eternity. My brother
Reh, whose mirror I am, brought me here after I was
slain in the final battle on Shandering Plain. Here he
entombed me and froze forever the moon in the sky.
Now the time of Lorn is over: the Lightbringer will
restore Reh's light to the land and the moon once
more resume its cycle. The land will be healed."

He turned to Jayal. "Lift your sword, warrior," the
apparition said. Unconsciously, Jayal did so. "It is
Dragonstooth, my sword," he said, laying his hands
directly onto the blade where the moon symbol was
engraved. "There is old magic in the sword, magic
from when these bones still bore flesh and I carried it
in the last battle. Use it well, in the name of the light,"
Erewon commanded. Now the coppery red blazed
with swimming light, energies shimmered around it in
the air, bright forms that writhed and twisted in the
air. "Use the power well, for you will have need of it
when you reach Iskiard," he said.

Jayal stared at the blade, but at that moment there
came a shrieking in the air much like the sound of a
whistle but a thousand times louder, and the dark air
began to turn violet around them. Then they saw, in
all directions in the sky around, in the dark forest and
on the frozen surface of the lake below, the armies of
the Nations appear as if they had been there all the
time, waiting to materialise.

They turned back to where the old man had stood,
but he was gone, vanished into thin air.

"Where is he?" Jayal asked. No one answered—the
others were staring down the mountain, where they
could see the lights all begin to move through the
frozen wasteland and over the ice towards the city.

"Come," Thalassa said, "before the Nations reach
Lorn."

They hurried up the last steps to the base, where
the columns soared up into the sky. An altar stood at
the centre of the platform, its sides decorated by an
elaborate frieze depicting the successive phases of the

moon. Behind it the temple had been built into the mountainside, and there was a dark opening: a cave.

"Make the signal," Urthred said, turning to Thalassa.

Thalassa hesitated, looking out at the islands, and Urthred could guess why she did so. At a gesture, Lorn and all its inhabitants would be destroyed: and it would be she who brought their doom upon them. But they had been given their chance—his father had tried to warn them and been killed for his pains. He had known that a thousand years of custom could not be changed at one stroke. Nothing could save them.

"Hurry," he said urgently, and Thalassa came out of her reverie. She raised her hands to the Isle of Winds, and with a cry brought them down. "It is coming, soon," she said, dreamlike, as if from a long distance away. Then the dark world turned to midday, a bright dazzling midday in which there was only light and shade, no gradation of colour. It was as if the skies opened above the lake, a shaft of lightning, a hundred yards wide, soared upwards from the Isle of Winds and back again. There was an eruption of red-and-orange flame, as if the air had been transformed to molten lava. For an instant the Island of Lorn stood starkly illuminated and also the far shores and mountains, previously hidden by the night. And in the light they saw the roiling mass of figures moving like a dark tide across the frozen lake.

Then the light was gone, leaving only an afterimage stamped on the retina. In that darkness, which was even greater than the darkness that had preceded it, they heard the howling of a mighty wind, coming from afar. A fierce gust of hot air ripped through the blackness.

They flung themselves into the cave mouth behind the altar of the God. The air was suddenly full of debris. Rocks and pieces of timber smashed into the face of the altar, then an even greater wind hit the side of the hill with a thunderous roar. They saw the mighty columns of the temple begin to lean over drunkenly, then fall,

shredding in their descent into their constituent rings
of masonry. They fell with an earth-trembling impact.

Above them, the Black Cloud had shredded from
where the full moon had stood. But now the moon,
too, had vanished. The violent colours had drained
from the sky, and darkness began slowly to return,
and, with it, silence. A wan light shone lower down in
the firmament: the real moon, in its rightful position
in the sky. The magical dome that Reh had thrown
over Lorn had been ripped apart as if it were nothing
more than a flimsy tent. The real world stood revealed.

Nemoc groaned, and they turned and saw that his
transformation was complete: he had once again re-
verted to the shape he had had when he emerged into
the Outland: he had shrunken to about five feet in
height, the cloak falling to his ankles, the blazing staff
now once more nothing more than a gnarled root.

But they didn't stare at him for long. From in front
came a muted roar. They saw in the light of the moon
that there was something wrong with the surface of
the lake: the face of the waters had tilted up about
thirty degrees, and the Island of Lorn was sinking into
it. The island disappeared completely beneath its
surface.

Then they realised what they were seeing: a massive
tidal wave, which, as they watched, surged towards the
shoreline, as high it seemed as they were. They
watched it come towards them, paralysed by the
wave's immensity. The horizon was now filled with the
sheet of curling black water, not a fleck of spume to
be seen on its surface, nor any noise, yet it stood
above the level of their eyes. The mountain began to
shake, and then came more sound, a noise like thunder, growing and growing.

There were steps behind them in the cave, and they
flung themselves down them. Below was an even
deeper cave, with another altar scattered with human
bones. Even over the roaring of the tidal wave they
heard a strange noise: the wind sighing over the bones

and a sound like a distant moaning. The bones were singing. They strained their ears, but could make out no words: it was a doleful threnody, a dirge. Then the moon was finally obscured by the rising wave, and the bones fell silent.

A small area of the night sky was still visible though they had climbed so deep. After the moon, the stars disappeared as the wave mounted up and up until it was pitch-dark outside. They cowered together, the four of them holding each other: Urthred and Thalassa, Jayal and Nemoc.

Then it was as if all sound was sucked from the air except the roaring of the wave as it bore down upon the shore. It fell with a noise not of water but of the sky falling; the mountain juddered as if struck a mortal blow. Urthred and Thalassa looked into one another's eyes, expecting the end, holding each other as if that would somehow save them from the titanic force outside.

Then the water was gone, but its noise was still there, the noise of a mighty waterfall intermingled with the sound of a huge rockslide as half the mountain fell away with a sullen roar. They heard the wall of water receding in the distance. Then all was silent save for the sound of the torrents rushing off the crest of the shattered mountain.

Thalassa was the first to move. She found she had been gripping the priest's arm very tightly, but he didn't seem to have noticed. She patted the leather harness and got up slowly and went to the cave mouth, followed by Urthred. They stepped through the water that fell from the top of the entranceway and looked at the scene below. The moon was still there, just over the horizon, just beyond its fullness, showing them that real time had passed in the outside world. The Isle of Winds had disappeared, but Lorn was still visible. Buildings had stood all the way to its summit, but now all was wiped bare, as if a giant hand had passed over them: not even foundations were left. The lake surface chopped backwards and forwards unevenly, water poured back into it from the ruined interior of the forest, but its level had fallen some twenty feet.

To the left, a jagged knife edge marked the point where half the mountainside on which they stood had been carried away. Below, pointing away from the direction of the wave, were row upon row of felled trees, floating on a vast sheet of water, as if a hand had meticulously arranged each separate trunk towards the fractured peaks of the Broken Hines, which now appeared very close, the magical barriers that had separated this world from the Outland having been destroyed.

There was no sign of the far cliff line, or of the Moon Mere. They could see Astragal, still intact above the black chaos of swirling waters, thrashing and contending at the base of its mountain. Far in the distance were the Broken Hines and beyond, a mere glimpse of snowcapped mountains, the Palisades.

The Outland. They were back: the magical kingdom of Lorn was gone, the Nations were destroyed. They searched the darkness, looking for the titanic form of the Man of Bronze, the cones of light that would mark its progress through the wilderness of water and smashed trees, but there was nothing visible. Had it destroyed itself? Had the explosion blown it to a million parts, as it had the Isle of Winds?

Urthred turned and saw that Thalassa must have had the same thought.

"I don't feel his presence: he has been destroyed."

"No, he was a creature of the God: he survived the fires of Shandering Plain." Urthred had taken off his right glove and gripped her hand.

"Perhaps he has destroyed all our enemies. Perhaps Faran is dead, too, and the Doppelgänger."

Jayal stood next to them. His eyes scoured the drowned wasteland. "No, the Doppelgänger at least is alive; for I am alive," he said grimly. "Somehow, he lives even through that. Nothing can destroy him save the Rod."

"Then we must find your father before he does. We

have a long journey in front of us," Urthred said, "all the way to Iskiard. Unlike the baron, we will have to walk it."

Nemoc still kept to the shadows, staring at his transformed withered limbs. "And what of him?" Jayal asked.

"He will come with us. He is the last of Lorn. My father wanted the world to know what had happened here, and he will tell them, tell them of Reh's kingdom on earth."

They stood for an hour or more, watching the moon sinking over the drowned world that once had been the paradise known as Lorn.

CHAPTER FORTY-NINE

✦

Meriel's Tomb

They remained by the ruined temple through the night, waiting for the floodwaters to subside below. Strangely, they all slept except Nemoc, who they found the next morning on the edge of the cliff muttering a prayer for his dead people.

They buried the dead Moon God's bones and Thalassa and Urthred offered prayers: to Erewon, to Lorn, to the Watcher and to the Man of Bronze. They were sure of only one thing: that nothing could have survived the destruction they saw below, not even the Talos, Reh's champion. Nothing remained of the Isle of Winds save a small jagged stump of rock around which the waves crashed; a solitary memorial to the creature that had preserved this kingdom for so long. It looked like a stump of tooth above the waters.

They descended the mountain slowly: the path had been destroyed, and the only handholds were the roots of fallen trees. All around there was the sound of water still running downhill from the deluge of the night before. As they descended they got a closer look at the forest of Lorn: only one or two trees remained standing, the rest had been ploughed down by the tidal wave; and a faint haze hung over the tangle of shattered branches and roots and boughs. Here and there dark shreds of leathery tissue hung from the splintered boles of the trees, and they saw fragments of bone. Astragal and the summit of Ravenspur lay directly to the south. They made their way through the wasteland and found the Way. There was the first surprise of the morning. The fallen tree trunks had been cleared from the road surface, thrown to either side by some titanic force.

"Who has done this?" Jayal asked.

"Perhaps the Man of Bronze," Urthred answered. "Maybe he is alive after all."

He must have struggled from the heaving surface of the lake sometime in the night and gone onto the south, towards Ravenspur. He might be there already, destroying all that he could find.

Urthred stared intently at the mountains. A dark cloud still hung on the peaks, but it had been pushed back, was no bigger than the one he had noticed when he had first come to Goda. Far off he fancied he could see halfway up one of the tortured spires of the Broken Hines a bronze gleam in the early-morning light, and then there came dull retorts of explosions carrying over the still air. The Man of Bronze! But, even with the road cleared, it would take them all day or more to reach the mountains. They hurried on.

They passed one or two of the creatures that had somehow survived the tidal wave: they were trapped under the limbs of trees, their own limbs slowly dissolving back into the mist from which they came. They cried out piteously in a strange language, but the four of them hurried on, leaving them where they lay. They passed under the lee of Astragal.

All afternoon they walked, following the Way, making good time, moving past the muddy wasteland of broken tree trunks and onto the plain beyond. Ahead, the ground rose.

They looked up to the peak beyond with its dark cloud. All was silent: the air was heavy with a metallic tang and prickled with a hidden energy but there was no sound of battle from the mountains now. They paused on the foot slopes where the path came down to the edge of Iken's Dike. The four of them eyed the ascent. Each of them wondered whether the Master still lived, or whether he had been destroyed by the Man of Bronze.

"We must go on," Urthred said, but just as he said

the words, they heard the distant baying of hounds coming from the south. They looked at each other questioningly. How could anyone have survived the deluge?

But then they saw a group of thirty or forty of the villagers of Goda coming down from the summit of Ravenspur. It seemed every able-bodied man left behind after they and Garadas had left three weeks before was in the party. They were armed with bows and hunting spears; the entire pack of village dogs preceded them, a torrent of black, and brown and white. They were still a long way off, but the group spotted them and quickened their pace.

The dogs came first, their baying dying to a whimper as they sensed Nemoc's alien presence. The villagers stopped behind them: each of them looked exhausted and filthy, showing the privations they had suffered to get here. Presently Garadas's deputy, a man called Samlack, stepped from their ranks and approached them, the mongrels stepping uneasily from his path as he made his way through them.

He bowed low before Thalassa.

She smiled at him. "You are welcome, but why have you followed us?" she asked. "I thought the way down to the plains was impassable."

"It is normally," Samlack replied, "but two nights ago there came a hot blast of wind from the north; so strong it was, that even at midnight the air seemed warm as summer and the banked snow began to melt. I got together some of the menfolk and we set off, hoping to find you still on the Plain of Ghosts, or in the Broken Hines." The men behind nodded their agreement.

"We carried the dogs down with us. It took all day. We halted when we were a thousand feet from the end of the climb. From there we could see the mist and the shapes moving in the mountains opposite and the cloud driving over the face of the moon. The Nations were abroad: the dogs fell quiet.

"Then we saw it: it was as if a new mountain range

had appeared in the sky, higher even than Ravenspur. There was a dark band there, the moonlight glinting off its peaks. But this was no mountain range, for it was moving towards us, rolling ever closer. It was as if the surface of the earth had peeled away from its core, and everything was lifted up towards us. Then we saw it was a wave. It broke there, over the Broken Hines, falling over them into the Plain of Ghosts, filling the dike to the brim. The roar brought avalanches falling upon us from the heights, and the mountain shook. After we got free of the snow we looked down and the whole Plain of Ghosts was a sea, waves lapped at the base of the mountains. There was a terrible silence. Then we knew all had perished: the Nations, the ghosts and you.

"We climbed down in the night and when morning came we made our way over the plain. The mud was thick, holding us back, but the going got better when we started climbing into the Broken Hines. Then the hounds fell silent, their ears pinned back, listening to something. Then we felt it rather than heard it, the ground trembling and we saw a giant in the mountains ahead, some thirty feet high, his armor glinting. It was the Man of Bronze, returned as Marizian said he would!

"At first we were too afraid to cross the Broken Hines: the summits were still cloaked with the mist and we could hear loud explosions and the cloud was lit up with flame. But we climbed up: the slopes were covered with smoke and fire. We hurried down the northern side, and that is when we saw you." He paused, trying to regain his breath.

Thalassa looked away to the north "I'm sorry, Samlack. I have no news of Garadas or the others. The last we saw they were by the edge of the lake, but that was before the wave came and destroyed everything."

"Then they are dead," Samlack said sadly.

Thalassa was about to utter some words of comfort when there came a call from the wasteland behind them, and they saw through the wisps of mist that

curled up from the drying earth four figures picking
their way through the wreckage; Garadas, Imuni and the
two surviving villagers. A hubbub went up among the
group in the middle of the plain.

Garadas approached, holding his daughter's hand.
Their clothes were filthy and wet through. He stared
hard at the southerners, clearly finding it hard to believe they had survived as well. He halted a few steps
away. Then, curiously, he smiled.

"So," he said, "you found Lorn?"

"Yes, Garadas. We got to Lorn. It was very close
all the time, just beyond the lake."

"And now?"

"It was destroyed, by the wave."

"Then we will never see that paradise," he said.
"Perhaps it's as well."

"How did you survive?" she asked.

"After we left the camp, we hurried to the north,
trying to escape the cloud. We saw its shadow fall on
the lake and it seemed as if it were sucked right into
the surface like a tornado. Then it was gone. An hour
or two later we saw the lake explode upwards in a
great wave and thought we must die, but the waters
flowed to the south, away from us, and we were saved.
It was then we returned."

Urthred now stirred. "The day is getting on. We
made a pledge to the Man of Bronze to follow him
to Ravenspur. I, at least, will go."

"There will only be the spirits of the dead there
now," Garadas answered.

"No," Urthred said grimly. "The Master lives, I feel
it. And while the Master lives, his servants will return
every hundred years, and every hundred years Goda
will suffer as it has before."

"Then we must go and end this thing once and for
all," the headman replied. He turned to his men.
"Come with us as far as the saddle under Ravenspur.
There our paths will split. I will go with the southerners into the mountains, and then, if Reh allows, will

guide them to the north, to Iskiard. The rest of you return home."

"I will come with you," Samlack said. Then there came a chorus of other volunteers, until all the villagers agreed to come.

But Garadas shook his head. "Some of us must return to the village, before the snow comes again and we're all trapped down here. You," he said, squeezing his daughter's shoulder, "will go with them."

"Father!" she cried. "I want to be with the Lightbringer."

"You have seen and done enough for one lifetime, Imuni," he said. "In years to come, when you are an old woman, the villagers will gather round and hear how you travelled to the Plain of Ghosts and through Iken's Dike to the Haunted Forest. But that is enough, enough for anyone. Now promise me; go with those I send back to the village, comfort your mother, for the rest of us will not be back before spring, if then."

The girl's shoulders slumped, but she nodded. "I will, Father," she said reluctantly.

"Good," Garadas said. "Let's go before night falls."

"What of him?" Samlack asked, nodding at Nemoc.

The gnarled creature looked up when he felt them staring at him. There was despair there, in the lugubrious eyes that once when the moon of Lorn had shone, had burned so brightly. "My work is over," he said. "I am exiled to live in the Mortal World. I will remain in the forest to tell any who wander here of Lorn and how the immortals once lived there. It is as the Watcher wished. At least finally, I will keep my word to him."

"So be it," Urthred answered. "The day passes. Let the rest of us follow the Man of Bronze."

They left Nemoc standing on the Plain of Wolves, a lonely and incongruous figure. The creature that had felt he would live forever in a world without time, now had more time than he could ever have imagined. How long he would live no one could guess.

As they approached the foot of Ravenspur they saw

that a lake now occupied the base of the mountain, and Iken's Dike was completely submerged. The road too had disappeared. The lake was a mile or so across and it looked like they could not pass, but Samlack unleashed one of the dogs. It began snuffling at the edge of the lake, then took a tentative step into it and another, and then, only its paws covered by the water, bounded away, stopping a hundred yards out and looking back, its tail wagging expectantly.

"It's found the road!" Thalassa cried, stepping forward herself and finding that there was a solid surface beneath her feet. They passed over, the illusion of walking on the surface of the water, which mirrored the dying flecks of red sunlight, almost complete.

They began to climb above the plains as the moon rose. Below them the land opened out; they had a good view of the shattered forest, the Plain of Ghosts, Astragal, the submerged line of Iken's Dike running like an arrow to the north. And, beyond, the Lake of Lorn. If any of them thought of resting, they didn't say so, and they climbed up over the tree line and towards the summit.

Darkness fell. Then the sky ahead was illuminated by bright explosions which shot through the blanket of cloud hiding the peak. More dull retorts carried to them on the cold night air.

They reached the first ice fields and found a line of gigantic footsteps two or three feet deep in the solid ice. They continued towards the ruin sitting on the summit of Ravenspur. There they took their leave of the other villagers and Imuni. Thalassa said a sad farewell to the girl. The villagers clasped their friends' hands fervently: many of the first party had died, and many who returned to Goda had fears that this was the last time they would see the lonely group of southerners and villagers who remained behind. Then the others faded away down the reverse slope towards the Plain of Ghosts. They disappeared into the darkness below.

Urthred told the remaining villagers to remain where

they were with the dogs. Then he, Thalassa, Jayal and
Garadas continued their climb, the silence even more
terrifying, each of them secretly longing to return to
the saddle below and leave this cursed place forever.
Instead they followed the line of the giant footprints
round the mountain up to the building where Urthred
had first encountered the Master.

The summit was deserted. Urthred took a deep
breath and entered the building, but it was cold and
empty. Gone was the dark brooding presence he had
felt the first time he had been there. They passed
through its dark interior, their footsteps echoing.
Below they found the path he had come up three
weeks before. They descended it until they stood on
the cliff overlooking the Black Tarn. The bowl of the
amphitheatre was filled with thick smoke in which
nothing was visible. There was an intense smell of
burning metal and flesh hanging in the air. In front of
them a precipitous path had been cut into the side
of the amphitheatre. Gigantic steps had left footholds
leading down into the smoke-filled hollow. They climbed
down, tentatively feeling their way. As they descended, the sulphurous smoke was so thick they had
to wrap rags over their mouths and noses to keep
themselves from choking. Shattered rock and leathery
scraps of skin, shattered armor, and weapons littered
the slope. Huge scorched blast holes had been scoured
out of the solid cliff faces.

Now they were on level ground again: their feet
sinking into swampy dirt. Ahead a grey building
loomed through the yellow fog, built into a strange
beehive of mountain rocks some fifty feet high, its
pediment canted slightly into the bog. The Talos's
footsteps led directly to it. They could see smoke
belching from the entrance as they came close. Inside
there was a dark throne, upon which sat a mummified
figure burned to a cinder, rows upon rows of charred
corpses lying at its feet.

Urthred stopped. Was this the corpse of the Master?
He thought not: the Master had not been a physical

entity like this burning corpse on its throne, but a creature of Shades. This, then, must have been one of his lieutenants only. One or two of the burned creatures still squirmed on the floor, as if the power that had created them was still not extinguished.

They paused, their eyes streaming in the prickling smoke. The others looked at Urthred expectantly, but he shook his head, waving them on, farther into the choking mists. Now he saw the surface of the Black Tarn to his right. It was still, like liquid midnight. They skirted around it, their way momentarily blocked by a creek feeding into the tarn. Ahead they saw a bridge: two winged creatures, gorgons, wings outspread and mouths agape, loomed out of the mist, perched on either parapet. But the creatures didn't move as they approached, and they saw that they, too, had been burned to a crisp on the spot, their wings no more than gossamer sails of charred metal grey ash.

One of them toppled slowly onto its side as a stray gust of wind blew it down. There were two towers, one on either side of the track, just where the path began to mount up the cliff face again. A line of petrified creatures of stone had guarded them, but a path had been blasted through their centre. All that remained of them were the being's feet; the rest of their bodies lay in scattered fragments. Still not a single enemy challenged them.

They started to climb upwards again, following the path from the tarn. The mist, if anything, crowding them in even more. A little while later they reached a ridge. The moon shone through the mist like a grotesquely distorted face. The ridge led directly into a huge natural opening in the cliff face.

Here they paused, staring at the darkness ahead of them. It was Urthred who spoke first, turning to Thalassa in the half-light.

"Do you still hear the Man of Bronze?"

She stood very still, her eyes clenched shut, her head tilted back. "I hear him, but only faintly," she said. "As if from deep in the mountain."

"Then let's go and find him," Urthred said.

"I would sooner enter the mouth of Hel," Jayal muttered, hefting Dragonstooth. "Come, old friend," he said addressing the blade, "one last time."

Urthred turned to Garadas. "You don't have to come with us, headman."

"What, and remain here with these ghosts all night long?" Garadas replied, his teeth shining in the gloom as he smiled. "I'll take my chance with you."

"Then let's go," Urthred said, staring ahead. There came a glowing in the darkness beside him, and he turned. Thalassa nursed the same magical light as she had created at the lake the night before.

"Alanda's magic is with you," Urthred said.

She turned to look at him, her face bathed in the mellow white light. "It is as she promised," she answered, releasing the ball of light and casting it gently forward in front of her so it entered the cave.

"Come," Urthred said, stepping forward after it. The others followed close by his side, the floating orb drifting ahead of them. They came into a wide hallway carved from the mountain rock. Scorch marks twenty feet high or more soared up the walls, and there were charred bundles lying scattered on the floor. A stench of burned flesh filled the air. Ahead they saw wide rock steps cut into the mountainside.

They began to climb, following the trail of destruction, the darkness ever more oppressive. Now Thalassa could no longer hear the Talos's voice. All ahead was silent except their footsteps echoing off the ancient stone. All of them were ever more conscious that they might be advancing into a trap.

At the top of the stairs a corridor led away in the darkness. Bare poles flanked the corridor as far as they could see into the gloom. Bone littered the floor, the remnants of crushed skulls. Their feet crunched on the fragments as they passed down it. Each of them heard a low humming in the air, as if they heard the spirits of the dead.

There were many side corridors, but the ball of light

moved on as if it was being drawn towards something.
As for the four companions, they kept a breathless
hush in the sepulchral silence. Another broad staircase
rose up before them, chiseled from the solid rock of
the mountain's core. Above them they saw enormous
rock doors barring their way. Thalassa stopped with a
small cry. The others whirled around. Her eyes were
closed tightly shut, as if she were concentrating on
something beyond human sight. "What is it?" Urthred
asked.

"He is very near; I feel it."

"Where?"

"Ahead, through those doors." As they watched
there was a grinding noise, and the portals began to
roll slowly open with a titanic grating of stone. A
squat toadlike creature stood revealed in the doorway.
It lacked a lower jaw, and there was a wide gap that
might have been a mouth at the base of its throat.
The creature that Thalassa and Jayal had seen in Faran's ambush in the underworld beneath the mountain.
Its head had been smashed to a bloody red-and-green
pulp, but it still lived: wounds and poison had not
killed it.

All of them stiffened, Jayal raising the sword,
Urthred his fists. But the creature just regarded them
impassively, the hideous wound at its neck slightly
open. Then it spoke, the words exiting the slit in its
neck in a throaty wet rattle.

"Welcome to Ravenspur," it said. "I have seen
some of you before, in less happy circumstances. My
name is Smiler. Put up your weapons; my master will
not harm you."

Urthred advanced. "Tell me, devil spawn, where
your master is, since you command our language."

"Hah, strong words: I would expect better from
Urthred of Ravenspur."

"You know who I am?"

"Twice before you have been here: once when you
were an infant, then two weeks ago before Lorn was
destroyed. The second time you went away without

answers. Now my master will give you all the ones you require before you die."

Urthred took two steps more towards the creature. "I listened to his threats: heard how the wolf would rend us limb from limb, how the armies of the Nations would crush all in their path. But what do I see now? The wolf destroyed, the army returned to Shadows. Tell that to your master: tell him that I live."

"Ah, there is no need to tell me this. He will hear the words from your mouth. Come, he waits with an old friend of yours." Smiler's mouth opened into what might have been a grin in any other creature had not the mouth permanently suggested one. It gestured behind it as Urthred reached the top of the stairs. "See, the Man of Bronze," it said, stepping to one side, revealing the long nave of the chamber behind, the same that Faran Gaton had come to days before. As then, the wind howled in from the two huge entries to either side. But it was not the wind or the dizzying drops to either side that dominated the scene. The Talos stood in the center of the chamber, its head hung, the ruby light no longer glowing in its eye sockets, its arms hanging uselessly to either side.

"See, my master does not need your foolish swords or your gloves or," it said pointing at the ball of light glowing above their heads, "that." It clicked its fingers, and immediately the light was extinguished, replaced only by the glow of the sword. Urthred pounced forward, but his balled fist met only empty air. The creature had vanished, though its laughter echoed around the hall. The sound gradually died away and was replaced by the sighing of the wind coming through the openings to either side. The moon could be seen rising through the one to their left.

"Gone!" Jayal exclaimed hard by Urthred's side, the sword quartering the vast echoing chamber.

"But there is something else here," Thalassa said slowly. Jayal lifted up the sword. In its light, at the furthest extreme of the hall, they saw a figure enfolded

in a cloak, sitting on a throne. "Is it alive?" Jayal
whispered.

"Yes." It was Urthred's voice, very quiet. They
turned to him, and realised that he had been staring
past the massive bulk of the Man of Bronze all the
time they had been searching the chamber for signs
of Smiler. As if mesmerised, Urthred took a step towards the far end of the chamber. "Wait," Jayal said,
but Urthred was already walking forward, past the
towering limbs of the Man of Bronze. As he approached, the figure rose in one fluid motion from the
throne, its face still hidden by the cowl of the cloak.
Urthred stopped a few feet in front of it.

"Urthred," the voice came from the cloak, but as if
from far away. "Once more you have come. Will you
join me now? Your struggle has achieved nothing. The
Man of Bronze has been defeated."

"You already had my answer: it is still no. But now
I will have the answers I sought the first time I came."

"Then ask: but be warned. Though your powers
have saved you up till now, I will be avenged."

"So be it," Urthred replied. "One of us will die."

There came a long-drawn-out sigh from the flickering of flames, and they all dimly saw a human face
fleetingly limned in the dark glowing shadows, a face
that wore a look of inexpressible sadness before it
disappeared again like the glow of a coal in a fire.
"Then ask on, Urthred of Ravenspur, for the night
grows old, and by dawn one of us will be dead."

"What are you?" Urthred responded.

"Ah, I am many things. This morning I was Master
of a mighty army, and a kingdom drawn from the
damned regions of Shades, but she, the one you call
the Lightbringer, has changed all that." It was as if he
pointed out Thalassa. But what should have been a
finger was not a finger, but a burning mass of flames
that shot from its cloak sleeve, and now its face finally
stood revealed as its cloak fell back with the motion,
the semblance of a skull glowing behind the red embers of its face, a mummified skull, cast in glowing

flame. "Now you see me, see that I am a thing of flame, a flame that burns forever, like the fire in your body, Urthred: a flame that will never be at rest. Only the pain has kept my spirit alive these centuries, since the last day I was a human. I stood upon a balcony in a fair white palace in these mountains and saw the white fire of the gods' last battle irradiate the earth, so shadows ceased to exist and the mountains melted and flowed away like a river. Since then, this is what I have been.

"But now my army is destroyed by the Man of Bronze—I and Smiler, and my hostage over yonder," it said, indicating the Talos with another flicker of its fiery fingers, "are all that remain. But though the day has brought defeat, it has brought something far more precious."

"What is that?" Urthred asked.

"That belongs to the remainder of my tale. They call these lands the Nations of the Night. Why? At the gods' departure, coal dust and sulphur was the air, a man could not see his nose in front of his face. The sky was on fire, and the sun hid its face for a hundred years or more. Those blessed with magic went to Lorn, where Reh had made a paradise for his servants. You have seen the place, have seen how fair it was. How its people were fair, fairer than the gods. But I and my armies were never to conquer it, I see it now: fate and coincidence saw that we would never get beyond its peripheries.

"Many died, but those that didn't change became the essence of the fire, grew into their disfigurements. There was once a king of this land. My brother. He followed the ways of Reh, I of dark magic and prophecy. He had a wife called Meriel, one of the Witch Queens from Astragal. I loved her, courted her, but she chose my brother. Yet when the end of time came, he did not take her into Lorn, but left her with the damned, for she too worshipped another god and only Reh's servants could pass through to that magical kingdom.

"My last days on earth, I was becoming more and more the essence of fire. And the queen? She was not one of those who could live in the fiery air: she sickened and her limbs withered, and she coughed blood. I still loved her. Surely now my brother would take her to that land where death was unknown. I went there, through the ravaged land, carrying the queen, and stood as you have done on the edge of the lake as the full moon shone through the clouds of poisonous gas. Presently a messenger came from Lorn: the Opener of the Way, the ancestor of the one who brought you to Ravenspur. He told me she could not be brought to Lorn, for she was a mortal. I importuned the creature, telling him that even if all others died in the outside world, to at least take her. But the Opener said that death could never be let into Lorn, that the dying queen was an affront against his god. And holding his staff high in the air, he returned into the waters, closing the Way behind him, so the vision of Lorn faded with him.

"I returned to the blasted mountain that had once been their home, where now I was king of the souls of the damned crying in the air. Down I went, down into the heart of the mountain, and laid her to eternal rest in an iron vault where her pure flesh would never corrupt. Two things I promised then. First, that one day I would bring death into that Land of Lorn and be revenged. The queen was a seeress. She had a book of prophecy in which she wrote, and everything that she had ever written had come to pass. But as I have said, I, too, dabbled with prophecy: now I would have my turn. I seized the book and, with burning fingers, wrote that once more, ten thousand years hence, she would rise a final time." His burning face seemed to bore into Urthred's, who had started at the mention of the book.

"Yes, you know of this book. The world is full of spirits, but none more powerful than your teacher Manichee. He saw as he trod the fiery clouds and sent lightning to the earth, this book, buried though it was deep beneath Ravenspur. And when he came in a vision he told you of it. Told you to come to Ravenspur and find it. Why else would you have left the comfort of your friends and come here where no other human has dared to tread? Or was it for another reason that you weren't afraid? Didn't you know that whatever lay here for you, whatever dangers, you would be spared, because you were of the essence of this place?"

Urthred kept his silence, so the Master continued. "Now, for the prophecy concealed in this book, a prophecy which I could not tell you of during your first visit, for I knew its knowledge would assist your friends in going about the destruction of all that I have hoped and dreamed. Too late for that now, too late for anything but sorrow. I scorched into those yellowing pages a prophecy that once more Meriel's line would take human form. Not immediately, for the earth was sick and dying. But in a better time, in ten thousand years. Then at last there would be issue from the ashes of my kingdom: a child would go into the world and take my revenge where I could not. I gave that child a name: I called him the Herald. But, as I wrote, the dying queen reached up and grasped these burning digits, and her fair flesh blistered and cracked, turned my hand, so it was not I but she who wrote.

"And this is what she wrote: how this Herald would bring forth one called the Lightbringer in a time when the world sank into darkness again and midnight came at noon. I wept molten tears that burned the pages, but she would not let me relinquish that fiery pen till every word was written. She still loved the king my brother, not I, I who had nursed her in the final days. Then she fell back upon the iron tomb beneath the mountains and died. The damned spirits moaned and cursed, telling me to destroy the book. But I was deaf to them, and left the book in her ever-sleeping hand and threw shut the door on her tomb.

"I could no longer live upon the mountain. Instead I called the invisible armies of the Night and opened

a gateway between this world and the next. I took the
Nations into Shades, all those that could go, leaving
only a few behind, like Smiler, who still kept the semblance of one who lived. There they have dwelt all
these aeons, every hundred years to issue forth again
into the world and attempt once more to batter down
the gates of Lorn. For one hundred of every thousand
years they were cursed to dwell there, allowed only a
little time in the Mortal World.

"So, some twenty-five years ago in human time,
those that dwelt here on the mountain saw a miracle.
The iron vault that held the queen's corpse opened
and she walked from it up to the lakeside where she
used to have her pavilion. And there she waited until
the moon was full and one who was my brother,
though he had been reincarnated many, many times
since I last saw him, came from Lorn and took her
back through the Moon Mere. Five years later she
returned, old and withered, led by that creature that
took you into Lorn: Nemoc, the Opener of the Way.
He led her to the mountain, to the tomb, and there
she lay down to rest one final time. Then Smiler and
the others came, and the creature fled in terror. . . .

"Smiler and the others called my spirit from
Shades," the Master continued, "and I saw the prophecy had come about: two human infants lay there, by
the corpse of the queen. I ordered the servants to
take the children away and threw shut the iron doors
of the vault.

"The queen's words written in that fiery hand had
come to pass; prophecies of hope and not my own of
hate. The children were perfect, not the blasted creatures of anger and revenge that I had hoped for. No
perfect human thing could be left in this benighted
place. So it was I sent the children away with one who
had descended into the Black Tarn and taken physical
shape once more. Far over the mountains did he go
to a place called Forgeholm, where he gave the children over to the monks. Yet though the children were
far away, I heard them from the spirit world, felt their

tribulations, felt the fire that changed the perfect child into one who could have passed as one of my own, saw his face become a mirror of my own. Saw hope that he would become like me and take his revenge upon his father. Saw the blow that killed the other, felt you come here. The rest you know."

The Master finished. The priest's mask was unmoving, staring at the fiery apparition in front of him.

"And Manichee knew all this?" he said, finally.

"Knew it, and understood it: does he not dwell now in Shades with me?"

"Then the prophecy is fulfilled. I have done as my mother wished, though I have been a pariah in the human lands, more of your kind than my own. Fate has made us strange bedfellows.

"So," Urthred continued, bracing himself. "The night draws on. Now comes the end as you said when we entered here. Randel is dead. I, too, will follow where he has gone. I ask you only to spare my friends."

"Aye, one of us and one alone can live. Is that not what I promised when you left the Chamber of Winds? You threw in your fate with humankind. You are everything I have lost, save by the curse of the God you have my face. But where can I go now? Lorn is destroyed; it was a dream that my people would never have. I see that now. How can the damned live in Paradise? I have had revenge of sorts. Live, in the name of your mother, the woman I loved. I will wait out the end of time in Shades, never to return. At least there I will have peace at last."

"You will let me live though I brought destruction to the Nations?"

"My people are not dead: their souls have merely gone to Shades, where they will dwell forever. Let us never meet there, Urthred. Go on, go until your death, meet your mother and brother in the Hall of the White Rose, a place I will never see. Embrace them for me. You will surely find them there, spirits of the blessed air.

"Now take the Man of Bronze: he only sleeps. Go to the north, to Iskiard: fulfill the prophecy that Meriel ordained for you. But beware." He turned to Jayal. "Your double still lives. He returned from the forest after Lorn was destroyed. Badly injured and half-drowned by the wave, yet still alive. He passed through the remnants of my army and came to the chamber where the portal lay open to Shades. He went through, going to Iskiard, I would guess, for a great path leads from Shades to that place. He is probably already there."

"But my father is there," Jayal said.

"Then let the God you follow have mercy on his soul, for your double will do anything to get the Rod of the Shadows.

"Yet there is more danger," he continued. "I sent Faran after you. Yet like all his kind, he betrayed me. He went to Iskiard, travelling the road in Iken's Dike. Perhaps he has drowned, but I suspect not. What else lies in front of you? Terrible creatures, more terrible than my poor servants. And the journey itself: these are dangers enough to bequeath you.

"Go now, to the north and to your destiny. But one last word before you go. You said you were once of the damned, but look at your face, Urthred; you are not one of us anymore."

And with that the cloak suddenly emptied of the flame and floated to the ground and a great sigh of wind swept through the chamber as if carrying the ghost of the Master of Ravenspur away. The four companions were left standing looking at one another in wonder, not knowing what to say. Behind them they heard a stirring of metal, and the Talos lifted its head, its eyes once more beaming red.

"All is fulfilled." Its stentorian voice filled the empty chamber. "The Nations have been defeated." But even its words didn't register with the four humans, whose gaze remained fixed upon the empty cloak.

Eventually, Urthred stirred from his reverie. "I must

go and find this tomb where my mother has lain all these years."

"Come then," Thalassa said. "We will go together. For her prophecies brought me to this place. She it was who drew the lines of fate we have followed all these years."

And so, hand in hand, they left the chamber: the Man of Bronze, Jayal and Garadas standing unmoving against the panoply of driving cloud through the huge openings. Outside there was no sign of Smiler: it was as if it had indeed vanished into Shades with its master. The staircase wound down into the darkness of the mountain.

They turned and looked at one another and silently embraced, then, still hand in hand, descended into the depths of the mountain.

They followed the wide circular staircase down and down, in seemingly endless circles, the spiral below seeming to suck them into it, like a dark whirlpool. The fortress was deadly silent, and it would have been easy to imagine it had been deserted for the ten thousand years since the gods departed.

All the remainder of the night they went down. Eventually they stood at the very base of the mountain. A high arch lay open in front of them, and there a solid rectangle of iron lay in the very centre of the chamber. A screen of worked iron lay between them completely surrounding it, but the gate hung open, and they passed through. Urthred lifted up one of his iron gloves and rapped it softly on the metal of the tomb. The noise of metal on metal seemed to resonate in the still air. He shook his head. "Where will these mysteries end?"

"In Iskiard," Thalassa answered. "Come: there is a long journey ahead of us; let us find the book and say farewell to your mother and this place."

Urthred screwed up his face in an expression of intense pain and concentration. Then he gently touched the sarcophagus once more. Instantly there came a rumble as of thunder, and the tomb cracked open like an egg. White light streamed from it, and they stood blinking in its splendor. Inside they saw a metal bier and on it a white form: a beautiful woman so perfectly preserved it seemed she must live. The same he had seen in the vision by the edge of the lake. Raven hair, high cheekbones, very pale of skin, her hands crossed on her chest where she held an ironbound volume. Urthred knelt and Thalassa, too, before her. Slowly he uttered a silent prayer that her soul had now joined that of her other son, Randel: that they now had peace together.

Then he stood, looking into the shimmering radiance.

"Will you take the book?" Thalassa asked.

He shook his head. "It has rested here for ten thousand years. What secrets lie in it that we don't already know? Let it rest here another ten thousand, or until the end of time has come. She has given me and the world everything she owed it." He took Thalassa's hand and stepped back. Unprompted, the iron of the tomb closed like a fist around the body of his mother.

"Farewell," Urthred said. "I will honor your legacy."

He turned: a hitherto invisible line opened in the rock side of the chamber, widening to reveal the night air outside. They passed out of it, and found themselves at the base of the mountain, in the amphitheatre around the lake where he had first seen the apparition of his mother. Above them, the sky was flecked with the first pink streaks of dawn. They could see the pathway which led to the summit of Ravenspur clearly in the first light. Somewhere up there Garadas, Jayal and the Man of Bronze were waiting for them.

"Let us go to Iskiard," Thalassa said. Her skin was glowing in the sunlight, so she seemed once more, exactly as she had been called in the prophecies, the Lightbringer.